And **Carter** grew up in Ballyfin, Co. Laois. She graduated in La from Trinity College, Dublin, qualified as a solicitor and move to the Inishowen peninsula where she lived for eleven year In 2006 she transferred to the Bar. Having practised as a barr er for a number of years, she now writes full time. Her first three books have been optioned for television. She was shortlisted for e Irish Book Awards in 2019. She lives in Dublin with her husb nd.

By Andrea Carter

Death at Whitewater Church
Treacherous Strand
The Well of Ice
Murder at Greysbridge

The Body Falls

An Inishowen Mystery

Andrea Carter

CONSTABLE

CONSTABLE

First published in Great Britain in 2020 by Constable

1 3 5 7 9 10 8 6 4 2

Copyright © Andrea Carter, 2020

The moral right of the author has been asserted.

All characters and events in this publication, other than those clearly in the public domain, are fictitious and any resemblance to real persons, living or dead, is purely coincidental.

All rights reserved.
No part of this publication may be reproduced, stored in a retrieval system, or transmitted, in any form or by any means, without the prior permission in writing of the publisher, nor be otherwise circulated in any form of binding or cover other than that in which it is published and without a similar condition including this condition being imposed on the subsequent purchaser.

A CIP catalogue record for this book is available from the British Library.

ISBN 978-1-47213-114-0

Typeset in Bembo MT by Initial Typesetting Services, Edinburgh
Printed and bound in Great Britain by Clays Ltd, Elcograf S.p.A.

Papers used by Constable are from well-managed forests and other responsible sources.

Constable
An imprint of
Little, Brown Book Group
Carmelite House
50 Victoria Embankment
London EC4Y 0DZ

An Hachette UK Company
www.hachette.co.uk

www.littlebrown.co.uk

For Christopher

Chapter One

I stretched my arms above my head, stood up, and taking my coffee with me walked from my desk to the window, if you could call floor-to-ceiling glass a window. It was still early, pink and grey streaks the only traces of a sunrise that had been spectacular earlier on. I gazed out over the city, my eyes moving from downtown on the left, with its mix of high- and low-rise buildings: Morgan Stanley Chase, Bank of America and the Art Ovation Hotel, to the right where I caught a glimpse of the marina with its perfect white yachts moored in gentle rows. The seafront was the pink and blue palette from *Miami Vice*, below, it was white and green, the green contributed by the ubiquitous Sarasota palm trees, lining the roads, nestling around buildings, lush in car parks.

Palm trees as ubiquitous as Starbucks. I took a sip from my coffee, a huge cardboard cup of the stuff from the café on the ground floor. I was getting a worrying taste for it. Tony from the Oak would be appalled.

I rested my forehead briefly on the glass. Eight o'clock and I'd been here an hour already. My ninth-floor office was in a prime spot. Blown away at first by the view, I couldn't stop staring at the city and the water when I'd first arrived, but I'd soon become accustomed to it. Accustomed, also, to the early mornings.

Traffic was heavy, the morning rush hour kicking in properly now, although the triple glazing blocked out all sounds: the huge saloon cars and SUVs, the open-backed trucks with their monster wheels. Everything was super-size in America, not just the coffee. The temperature would be rising too, now that the sun was up – I could see traces of blue in the distance – although the air conditioning created enough of a chill for a suit jacket, blocking out the humidity.

Was that what I'd been doing for the past six months: blocking everything out? Running away to Florida? I'd worked hard, giving me little time to brood. If there was one thing this grudging Irishwoman admired about the Americans, it was that they put the hours in. Ten days holidays a year; the Irish would never stand for it! Nor would any of the other Europeans for that matter. But they got things done, the Americans, and they made money. This trip had been lucrative for me and I'd go home with a nice little nest egg.

When I'd been here ten years ago, I'd taken the Bar Exams, making it easy enough to return, and this time around I'd found the work absorbing. I'd been practising Elder Law, something that had always interested me but I'd never been able to specialise in. It was quiet work, meetings with clients were rare and regulated – unlike in Glendara where people called into the office 'on spec' – and many of the clients had Irish roots, happy to hear an Irish accent to remind them of 'home'. Plus, I had three support staff, unlike in Glendara, although Leah had often seemed like three people in one.

I rubbed the window with my sleeve, force of habit from Glendara where the central heating was usually on full blast, cold from outside fogging up the inside. Although we'd had an exceptional summer last year in more ways than one, with a heatwave bringing the highest temperatures for many years, two murders and a wedding. And a proposal.

I forced myself not to think about the last one. I wondered instead what the weather was like at home now, tried to remember how cold it usually was in April. But I dismissed the thought. I'd find out soon enough. I returned to my desk, threw the empty coffee cup in the bin and started to look through some papers. No time for daydreaming, I had work to finish.

I heard a knock and looked up. 'Come in.'

A face appeared around the door. 'Got a minute?'

I put down the Power of Attorney I'd been reading. 'Of course.'

Mitch Stevens, tall, greying and handsome with a tanned face from sailing every weekend, strode into the room with a mock sad expression on his face. 'Are you sure you need to go back? Can't you just advertise your job, so you can stay here with us?'

I laughed. 'It's not a job, Mitch. It's my practice. I own it and I'm responsible for it. I'm not an employee like I am here.'

He perched on the edge of my desk and crossed his arms. 'Don't you like being an employee?'

I couldn't deny it had been nice for a while to not have to shoulder all the responsibility as I did in Glendara. The firm here had a mentoring system. You met with your mentor every couple of weeks: Mitch was mine. The same three questions were asked each time, cleverly formulated to weed out worries and ensure that employees weren't carrying too much stress: *Tell me something good, something bad and something really bad?* It had certainly made a nice change to be able to share my work worries, but . . .

'It's not me.' I smiled. 'I like to control things too much.'

Over the past few months, I'd realised that might be my problem, needing to be in control. I'd always had difficulty sharing worries, until the day when I found someone I could do that

3

with, a person I trusted completely: Molloy. Then he'd left. He'd had his reasons and eventually he had come back, but the vacuum he'd left behind had left me feeling vulnerable, as if I'd been leaning on a gate that collapsed under my weight. It made me unsure about leaning on that gate again when he'd asked me to marry him, out of the blue, with no warning whatsoever. Six months later that proposal still seemed like a crazy thing for him to have done. We hadn't even been together at the time.

Mitch looked across at me and sighed theatrically. 'Okay then. If you have to.'

'I have to.' I thought how amusing a city lawyer like Mitch Stevens would find my gate imagery. I may have grown up in Dublin, but it seemed I was a country girl at heart.

'What time is your flight in the morning?' he asked.

'It's not till the evening but it's from Orlando so . . .'

'You want to leave in the morning?'

I nodded.

He raised his eyebrows. 'Lunch? A last supper so to speak?'

'Sure. That would be lovely.'

'The Greek place?'

Mitch was already at the table when I arrived even though I was early, and he wasn't alone. Ten other people from the office were seated at a big round table in the middle of the restaurant, and they all cheered when I walked in. Mortified, I mouthed an apology to one of the waitresses who just smiled in amusement. It was no skin off her nose.

If I'd given it any thought, I should have anticipated some type of a send-off, but Mitch had such an ability to dissemble I hadn't noticed anything other than a casual invitation to lunch. I suppose that was what made him such a good trial lawyer. You'd be forgiven for thinking that lawyers were incapable of subtlety in a place where billboards along highways and on taxis bellowed *Get Aggressive Attorneys – Timberlake and Yonkers* or *Auto Accident dial 1800 – ask Gary!*, but that would be a mistake. I'd grown hugely fond of Mitch, but he had the capacity to be as sneaky and manipulative as hell when required.

And he'd gone all out for my send-off. There were balloons and streamers, even a bottle of champagne in the centre of the table, which I eyed as I took the seat beside him.

'I hope you don't expect me to do any work this afternoon!'

'It's only a glass. One bottle isn't going to go too far with this lot.'

He was right. In fact, during the lunch, the one bottle remained in its ice bucket, and I suspected it wouldn't be opened, its presence only for show. Instead I sipped my iced tea, another beverage I'd acquired a taste for, and tucked into a very good veggie moussaka.

While the conversation was busy elsewhere, Mitch leaned in, fork raised. 'There was something I wanted to ask you.'

I narrowed my eyes, my own fork halfway to my mouth. 'Yes?'

'I don't want us to cut our ties entirely.'

Thankfully there had never been anything romantic between myself and Mitch, not even a hint of it, so I had no fear that he meant anything like that.

He grinned as if he knew what I'd been thinking. 'I'm talking about professionally. Sometimes we need a contact on the other side of the Atlantic. Any interest in being that contact?'

I frowned. 'For what kind of work?'

He took a bite of his food, chewed and swallowed, taking his time to respond. 'Outstanding warrants, that kind of thing, I guess.'

'Do you get many of those in Ireland?' I was surprised. I hadn't come across a single outstanding warrant for Ireland in the six months I'd been in the US. But then I hadn't been working in crime.

'A few.' He took a sip of his Diet Coke. 'Maybe the odd tax issue?'

I shook my head. 'I'm no tax expert, Mitch. And you know my practice is a small operation – nothing like here. There's only me and my legal assistant.'

He shrugged, not quite meeting my eye. 'Well, whatever comes up that you *might* be able to help us with? What do you think?'

I smiled, taking a sip of my iced tea. 'Can I decide on a case-by-case basis?'

'Sure,' he clinked his glass against mine. 'I'm glad it's not goodbye, completely.'

We walked back to the office together, just the two of us, down Main St with its pretty shops and restaurants, then across Pineapple, and towards the water. My attention was taken by a wooden wind-mill in the window of a café, and a blue ghost bike leaning against a telephone pole with a bird on its handlebars. I liked Sarasota. It was arty and creative, with a significant retirement community of readers and painters. Bookstore1, a bright independent bookshop with regular events, had been my refuge since I'd arrived. It was a place Phyllis Kettle would have appreciated.

We reached the traffic lights at the seafront and crossed the road, walking out towards the sea and back along the marina, returning to the office the long way around.

The sea glistened in the sunshine beyond the boats. When I'd decided to come back to Florida for a while, I'd asked to be put in the Sarasota office because I wanted to be close to the sea.

I'd thought it would remind me of Inishowen, but I couldn't have imagined how different it would be, a marina full of yachts instead of fishing trawlers. The sea today was mirror-still like a lake; it looked as if you could walk across it without any divine power. I'd never seen the sea in Inishowen look like that.

I put my hands in the pockets of my trousers as we walked. I'd lost weight while I'd been here. I wasn't sure why. Maybe it was the heat. We tried to stick to the shade as we walked, from palm tree to palm tree, but my shirt still felt damp; a trickle of sweat worked its way down my back. I'd never mastered the art of looking cool in this weather and I suspected I never would. In the air conditioning I wanted a jumper and each time I left a building I was shocked anew by the heat. I ran my fingers through my damp hair.

Mitch looked at me curiously. 'You all right?'

I smiled at him. 'Just hot.'

Mitch had been there for me when I'd worked for the firm more than a decade ago, just after my sister had died. I'd told him everything then and he'd been a huge support. This time around, things had remained strictly professional between us, but I was sure he suspected I had my reasons for coming back even for a short while, that there was something I hadn't shared with him.

We walked past the statue at the marina, a rather kitsch sculpture of a sailor kissing a nurse based on the famous photograph taken in New York at the announcement of the Japanese surrender at the end of the Second World War. The picture was called *V-J Day in Times Square*, the statue *Unconditional Surrender*. Every time I passed it, I thought of Molloy.

I'd been in Florida for six months. It had been just what I needed but the respite was about to come to an end. Reality was about to seep in.

Chapter Two

A sweaty fug enveloped the cabin, and a loud snore came my way when I pulled the earplugs from my ears. I rubbed my neck and slid the window shade all the way up allowing light to flood in, into my little section of the plane at least. Morning had broken without my being aware of it, curled up under the tiny blue blanket which hadn't quite reached my feet. I'd had almost two hours' sleep, not bad for the red eye from Orlando. I'd been lucky – the flight was only 70 per cent full (according to the man with the startlingly white teeth who'd checked me in), which meant I'd had an entire row of three seats to myself. But now I was awake, headachy and dry-eyed.

I gazed out the window. No land yet. I had a seat over the wing and the sky below was nothing but white cloud. I tapped the screen on the back of the seat in front of me and brought up the map with the little aeroplane and the arrows – an hour and thirty-five minutes to go.

I tried to remember where I'd put my plastic bag of toiletries and wondered if I could be bothered to go to the bathroom and brush my teeth, when the squeak of a trolley brought a smiling air steward with a beard, a bun and a broad Scottish accent. He handed me a bottle of water and a warm cardboard box. The water went down in one, but I struggled to swallow the gloopy cheese croissant even with the later addition of coffee and orange juice. Still, it took up some time and once I'd finished there was only an hour and twenty-one minutes to go. So I drank the last of my juice and turned on a film.

I wasn't yet ready to think about what lay ahead, to re-programme my brain to my Irish life.

By the time we got to Dublin my head was pounding and there was a red hue around everything I could see. Two hours sleep in twenty-four hours will do that to you. The sky outside was grey and rain blistered down the windows of the plane when we landed. Irish spring weather.

As I trotted down the marathon corridors of Dublin Airport with the rest of the herd, it was hard not to recall my return from the States nearly ten years earlier and how different things had been then. How raw I'd felt after the death of my sister Fay, who had been killed by my ex-boyfriend. How I'd dreaded facing my parents and their grief. In retrospect, how selfish I'd been.

But then, I'd found a home in Donegal on the Inishowen peninsula, which was where my life was now, a life I'd made for myself. I'd realised in America how much I valued that life, how much an anchor Inishowen was for me. I wouldn't be leaving again in a hurry.

At the carousel I collected my bags, stumbled through passport control and grabbed a taxi. Thankfully, given the sleepless fog I was in, I didn't have to drive back to Glendara till the morning. I'd left the Mini with my parents in Dublin and I was spending the night with them. I had some concerns as to whether the engine would turn over; she was an old car, but I suspected my dad would have started the engine periodically while I'd been away. It was the kind of thing he would do. It would be good to see them both; we'd all come a long way in the past couple of years.

The journey took longer than I expected; I'd hit Dublin at rush hour and rain bucketed down the whole way into town. But eventually we pulled into my parents' road and rounded the corner to their house, a 1940s semi-detached in a row of identical terraces with neat front gardens, although my parents' house was easy to spot today because there was my old Mini parked out front. I smiled when I saw her.

They'd told me they might not be here when I arrived, but I'd had a text from my mother saying that they wouldn't be long and to use my key and let myself in. So, I hauled my case out of the taxi and stood on the steps trying to balance it while I turned the key in the lock.

Once inside, I left my luggage in the hall and made my way towards the kitchen, thinking suddenly of tea, something I realised I'd missed. Americans don't understand tea, not in the way the Irish do anyway.

I pushed open the door, then stopped dead. There was a man poking about in the fridge, a man who certainly wasn't my father, a man I didn't recognise. I must have yelped in surprise because he turned around quickly, a carton of milk in his hand. Then his face broke into a smile and he put down the milk and came over to me hand outstretched, welcoming me as if he were the host.

'Hello, you must be Benedicta.'

His hand was clammy and his handshake limp. It didn't help to warm me up. I saw now that he was conservatively dressed in chinos and a shirt and tie, not the attire of your average house breaker, but who the hell was he?

'It's Ben,' I said. 'And you are?'

He studied my face. 'Stuart. Stuart Chambers. I'm a good friend of your parents. '

'Right.'

He went back to the fridge and closed the door. 'You must be tired. I'm making some tea – would you like some?'

The fridge was the same one my sister and I used to make a beeline for when we came home from school and college. My parents had never changed it and I could still see traces of cartoon stickers we'd stuck across it over the years. Ridiculously it made me resent this man's hand on it, even more, and his apparent familiarity with what was inside. Who was this Stuart Chambers and why was he treating my parents' kitchen as if it were his own?

Begrudgingly I accepted his offer of tea and sat redundantly at the table while he made it, answering his questions about Florida without enthusiasm. I was aware I was being rude, but as time passed, I became more and more uneasy as I wondered where exactly my parents were. When I asked, all I managed to extract was what my mother had put in the text – that they'd be back soon.

Then I heard the front door and seconds later the two of them walked into the kitchen laden down with grocery bags. Relieved, I stood up to take one from each of them, giving them both hugs.

My mother lifted her remaining bag onto the counter by the sink with a groan. 'So, you've met Stuart then?'

'I have.'

It seemed rude to ask who the hell he was while he was sitting there. So, I helped my mother unpack the groceries and put them away while Stuart made another pot of tea, which the four of us sat down to drink with a ginger cake my mother produced from a tin in the cupboard. It was like some weird double date.

'Would you like me to take your bags up to your room?' Stuart asked while pouring the tea.

This was the final straw. There was something about the ease with which he offered to go upstairs that made me realise he knew his way around up there too. Was he staying here?

So I asked the question directly.

'Yes,' my mother replied, taking a piece of cake. 'Stuart's been helping us around the house. He needed somewhere to stay, and we needed someone to help with certain things. So, it seemed to make sense.' She smiled over at him.

'What kind of things?' I asked, trying and failing to keep my tone light.

'Oh, just some house maintenance, that sort of thing. Nothing you could have done,' my father added hurriedly as if to assuage my guilt, making me feel even worse. 'Guttering, some electrical stuff, things I can't do since I had my fall.'

'Right,' I said, still baffled as to how a handyman doing odd jobs had managed to get his feet under the table. Literally. His shoe brushed off mine and he looked up at me with a rather creepy smile.

'And how did you meet?' I asked, taking a sip of tea.

There was a pause during which all three of them looked at each other, leaving me feeling even more excluded than I did already.

'We met through the group,' my dad said finally. 'Remember the counselling group I mentioned – the one we went to Iceland with the Christmas before last?'

I nodded.

'Well, Stuart is part of that. Stuart lost his wife and daughter in an accident a few years ago. She was twenty-seven and his daughter was only a baby.'

I looked at Stuart. His eyes were moist, and I felt guilty as hell. 'I'm sorry. That must have been awful.'

Stuart didn't reply. He just closed his eyes as if the mention of it was still too painful.

'Anyway,' my father added brightly. 'We've been a good support to each other, I think.'

Stuart placed his hand on my father's shoulder and then reached out and took my mother's hand in a gesture that reminded me of a séance. I shivered. God, what was wrong with me? Maybe I just needed some sleep. I could feel myself getting light-headed.

I stood up. 'I think I need a nap.'

I shook my head in response to Stuart's renewed offer to take my bags upstairs. The idea of him walking into my childhood bedroom was one step too far, although something told me that it was a bit late for that, that he'd already explored every inch of this house.

I woke up three hours later, feeling marginally more clear-headed than I had earlier, deciding I needed to get up or I wouldn't sleep tonight. Also, I was hungry. I pulled on jeans and a shirt and made my way downstairs to find my parents watching a wildlife documentary in the sitting room while Stuart cooked in the kitchen. Uncomfortable as I was to see another example of his installation, I had to admit it smelled great.

Dinner was a repeat of the earlier tea party with different food, this time a lasagne and salad. Stuart didn't drink 'any more' so there was no wine. I was happy enough with that since I'd had gin and red wine on the plane, but it was unusual for my parents who liked their Shiraz. But I kept my opinions to myself.

After dinner, I tried my best to stay up, but it became increasingly clear that Stuart was a night owl and I wasn't going to out-sit him, especially with my repeated yawning. So eventually I turned in and left them all watching a crime drama, determined to get a chance to talk to my parents on their own before I left for Donegal the next day.

Which thankfully I did. The morning was bright, allowing us to go for a walk in the park. I half-expected Stuart to join us, but I was relieved when my dad asked him to clip the hedges, I suspected to get him out of the way. I was pleased they wanted a chat, with just the three of us, as much as I did.

It was only when we walked through the turnstile into the Phoenix Park that I realised why. One question followed another until it became clear that they'd been worried I would decide to stay permanently in Florida. The relief on their faces when I explained my time there had been temporary pricked again at my conscience.

My mother looked up at a particularly majestic tree with green leafy shoots. 'We'll have a good summer. The Oak is coming out before the Ash.'

I remembered the rhyme from school. *If the Ash comes out before the Oak, then the summer will be a soak, if the Oak comes out before the Ash then the summer will be a splash.* When we were kids, we'd joked it meant the summer would be wet no matter what happened with the trees.

We walked towards the papal cross and watched a small herd of red deer jaunt past. The ground was wet underfoot but the park felt fresh and cool, with sweet spring scents. We stood for a while to watch the deer and on our way back to the house, I asked some questions of my own.

'So, this Stuart. How long has he been here?' I gazed at my feet as I kicked away some dried beech nuts. Why did I feel so odd about asking them what was going on?

My mum glanced at my dad to check. 'A few weeks?'

He nodded, striding along, hands clasped behind his back, cap shading his eyes.

'Yes,' she said. 'A few weeks.'

I was amazed. My parents usually disliked house guests. My uncle had always said that house guests were like fish, nice for the first day and not too bad the next, but after a few days they start to smell, and they'd always agreed with that.

'Does he work?' I asked. 'Have a job?' Surely doing odd jobs for my parents couldn't take up all his time, I thought.

'Oh yes,' my mother said. 'He works for the civil service – he has a good job.'

My father looked at my expression and smiled. 'It's only temporary. There's no need to worry. He'll move out as soon as he finds somewhere to live. He sold his house after his wife and baby died. He couldn't bear to live there any more.'

'Understandably,' my mother added, and I felt another twinge of guilt.

Until my dad said, 'But he *is* looking to buy somewhere new.'

This revelation made me feel worse instead of better. If Stuart Chambers was intending to buy somewhere new rather than renting, then he'd be living with my parents for months rather than weeks. I told them this as gently as I could, but it didn't seem to faze them. They insisted they were happy to have him.

Dad looked up at the sky as we left the park. 'You'd better get on the road soon if you want to get there in daylight.'

'I know. I'll go shortly.' I grinned. 'I hope the Mini starts.'

'Oh. I'm sure it will,' he said, pushing his cap back. 'Stuart's been driving it and he says it's been going fine.'

I stopped. 'What?'

My father shrugged. 'It seemed to make sense when you weren't here. It's good for it to be driven. And it was simple enough to insure – he's on ours anyway and we just transferred it over.'

15

Chapter Three

The drive back to Inishowen was a bit of a struggle, not helped by an ache behind my eyes from too little sleep. Despite my yawning in the sitting room the night before, when I'd gone to bed, I'd fallen asleep for only half an hour before waking again, then lying there, mind racing, staring at the ceiling until nearly half three. I realised in retrospect that sleeping for a few hours in the afternoon hadn't been the wisest move.

Not only had I had a lousy night's sleep, but I wasn't as comfortable driving the Mini as I used to be. It felt strange. Maybe it was the stiff steering, or the gears (I'd been driving an automatic in the States) or how low it felt to the ground, but there was also a strange smell in it; eucalyptus or something else medicinal. It was possible, of course, that I was imagining the smell since I knew the Usurper had been driving it, which was how I'd come to think of Stuart.

I'd been reluctant to leave Dublin. It felt weird seeing Stuart and my parents waving me off from the doorstep like a family of three. I was aware I was being a dog-in-the-manger about this; I wasn't around for my mother and father and couldn't be for the foreseeable future since my life was a four-hour drive away in Inishowen. They were perfectly entitled to have some company if they wanted it. But I kept asking myself what his game was? Why would a man like that want to spend so much time with a couple who were so much older than he was and whom he'd only just met? Yes, there was their common grief, but did that explain it entirely?

I felt uncomfortable even thinking this, but I wondered if he was paying them rent? It seemed intrusive to ask; it was none of my business and it wasn't really the reason I was concerned. So, what was it then? My parents had told me they were fine, and they'd seemed happy enough, but it was just so bloody odd. That was it: it was odd. *He* was odd. I resolved to visit them more often, if only to check in.

When I reached the journey's halfway point at Monaghan my concern about what I was leaving behind began to fade and what lay ahead seeped in. I started to think about all I had left behind in Donegal.

My practice, I hoped, had been left in relatively capable hands. Mitch had suggested a solicitor from Castleblaney to take over while I was gone but I'd found my own locum surprisingly easily, someone who'd had kids, taken ten years out of work and was now anxious to return: a solicitor named Marina Connor from Sligo, a town a good 170 kilometres from Glendara. From what I could gather, Marina had been through a rough time; her parents had recently died, her kids were in their teens and her marriage had broken up, which was, I suspected, the real trigger for her return to work. I was happy to give her a chance. She'd done a few stints covering maternity leave before stepping into my shoes for six months, so she hadn't been starting afresh and, in any event, Leah was there as a rudder. Also, I'd said that I'd be on the other end of the phone if either of them wished to talk to me at any stage.

Which neither of them had, strangely. I hoped that was a good sign. When I'd rung every week just to check, I always got the same response from Leah. *Everything's fine. Everyone misses you, looking forward to getting you back.* When I tried to press her for detail, she found some reason to get off the phone, as if she was afraid that she'd let something slip if she stayed on too long. Which left me wondering if there was something she wasn't telling me. But that was probably just my usual paranoia. Today was Thursday which meant that Marina would work a full day, and then hand the reins over to me tomorrow so I could start back properly on Monday. At the weekend she could leave and go back to her life in Sligo. I wondered if she would heave a sigh of relief or of sadness.

As I turned left onto the wide main street of Aughnacloy, I recalled the manned border which had been there when I first visited Inishowen, the barriers, the soldiers with their guns. There was no trace of it now, although I'd just crossed into Northern Ireland, a separate jurisdiction, and I hoped it would never return. I would cross another seamless border after Derry to enter Donegal, that odd contradiction of driving north but leaving the North behind jurisdictionally. I'd had some interesting chats in the States trying to explain it, usually resorting to a map on my phone to dispel the confusion.

I left Aughnacloy and drove on towards Omagh.

After work, my next concern was my home, not just my cottage in Malin but Glendara, the town where my practice was, where my friends lived and where I spent most of my time. I hoped people would be glad to see me back. I'd missed them. As I'd missed my cat Guinness who Marina was supposed to be keeping an eye on, since she was staying in my house. Cats are independent creatures, and Guinness was a particularly cantankerous feline, so he'd probably barely noticed my absence once there was someone to feed him.

But then, and I felt a pinch at finally letting him in, there was Molloy, who might not be quite so straightforward. After a stint in Cork and overseas, Tom Molloy had returned as Glendara's sergeant once the Garda Station had reopened, though he wasn't expected to be there long – rumours abounded about an inspectorship. And though I'd missed him more than I'd thought possible these past six months, Molloy was the dilemma I still hadn't figured out, the smudge on the glass I wasn't quite tall enough to reach.

The sun shone low in the sky most of the way up the road, making me regret packing my sunglasses away with my Florida clothes, but by the time I reached Derry the weather had changed. The day darkened, clouds were purple and full over the Foyle and the light was a strange grey and yellow, casting an eerie hue over the houses on the Waterside. The rainclouds stayed above and ahead of me as I drove through the city, past the restaurants on the quay, through the Strand roundabout and out past Sainsbury's and the big DIY shops. At Pennyburn the sky looked like a Turner painting, turbulent and angry.

At the big roundabout at Culmore I passed the signpost for the airport at Eglinton. There was a time when I'd used the Derry–Dublin flight regularly and I was sad to hear that the service was no longer operating. I hoped it would be reinstated. It had been an important communication link – the drive to Dublin took nearly four hours, the flight was about forty minutes.

Once I'd passed through Culmore and was on my way to Muff, where the second border checkpoint used to be, I turned on the radio, just managing to catch the weather forecast on Highland Radio.

Heavy rain is expected all over Ireland tonight and tomorrow, particularly in the north-west where there may also be heavy winds. Possibly storm to gale force. Met Éireann have issued a red weather warning for counties Donegal, Sligo, Leitrim, Cavan and Monaghan. A yellow weather warning is in place for the rest of the country. People are advised not to undertake any unnecessary travel.

The second I crossed into Inishowen at Muff it began to rain, as if to corroborate the forecaster's words. Heavy drops splattered against the windscreen and the lightweight Mini struggled on the Muff strait; it was an effort to keep her on the right side of the road. The water in the Foyle was grey-green and rough, although oddly I was glad to see it like that. Constant sunshine and blue skies were all very well, but this felt more like home.

I turned left at Quigley's Point and headed up and inland, past the old Riverside Bar, across the bridge and along the winding mountain roads of Glentogher, lined now with dandelions. Blazing yellow gorse covered the hills on both sides and the river flowed through the glen below, first on my right and then on my left. Eventually the rain began to ease off and I could see the purple mound of Sliabh Sneacht in the distance, and by the time I'd passed the small housing estates and the Beacon Hall on the outskirts of Glendara at about five o'clock, it had stopped completely. Although glancing at the sky, it was clear the hiatus was only temporary.

An undertow of anxiety tugged at my thoughts. What was ahead of me? I wondered.

In contrast to the grey rain, the town, at first glance, looked to be a blaze of colour, yellows and reds, blues and pinks, like an aviary full of exotic birds. My first thought was the carnival. But no, the carnival was at Halloween. This was only April.

It was only when I drove fully onto the square that I realised that it was full of bikes and the colour was Lycra. The town was packed with cyclists: checking gears, adding oil, checking tyre pressure, changing wheels, wheeling their bikes around the square and cycling out the sideroads. They didn't appear to be locals, at least none I recognised, though some were wearing helmets, so it was hard to tell. There were bikes upended in the square, being lifted from bike racks, being assembled and disassembled.

Searching for somewhere to park, I noticed that there were extra cars taking up the usual parking spaces, along with two minibuses and a large truck. Negotiating my way around the square for a second time I spotted a car pulling out and nabbed a space in front of the bank, alongside a huge motorbike. The bank's doors were shut, and I reminded myself to call in to change my dollars in the morning.

I climbed out of the car and crossed the road to the square, my shoulders stiff from the drive. I intended to call briefly into the office to let Leah and Marina know I was back, then buy some food and wine and head back to my cottage in Malin. But once in the square, I found myself in a bit of a daze, mesmerised as I watched the bikes and cyclists in my orbit, calling out to each other and chatting as they worked. There must have been about fifty of them.

'Anyone got a spare spider?' a young blonde woman called; her bike upended.

I stepped back suddenly as the item was flung in her direction, right across my path. I didn't know what a spider was, but it had the look of a lethal weapon, an elastic boomerang with hooks.

'Oh shit, sorry. Are you okay?' another voice said. I looked over to see an older man in full length cycling trousers and a red top smiling at me sheepishly.

Before I could respond properly another figure entered my eyeline and gave me more of a jolt than the spider had done, a man in a navy Garda uniform asking some cyclists to move a van that was blocking the square. My stomach flipped. Molloy.

But the shape was wrong, and a closer look revealed ginger hair beneath the hat. It was Garda Andy McFadden, Molloy's second when Glendara station had last been open. He was red-faced and hassled, trying to explain something to the cyclists while waving his hands about in an attempt to create some kind of order out of the traffic chaos that had erupted in our usually quiet town.

I made my way over to him and tapped him on the shoulder. 'You're back.'

He spun around, allowing the cyclists to escape. But he beamed when he saw me, which was gratifying at least. 'Aye. And so are you by the looks of things.'

'Just this second as a matter of fact. When did *you* come back?'

He lifted his hat and scratched his forehead, which was looking a little pink. 'They moved me back from Letterkenny about a month after they reopened the station.'

'That's great. It's good to see you.' It *was* genuinely good to see McFadden's smiling face about town. I hadn't seen him in Glendara since he'd left to go to rehab for a gambling addiction over a year ago, although I had run into him in court in Letterkenny once when he'd been re-stationed there. 'I'm sure you're glad to be back.'

'Aye, I am.' He narrowed his eyes curiously. 'I heard you went off to America.'

'I did. Just a six-month stint. Back now though.' I looked at the ground. 'So, the old team are back together then?' I hadn't told anyone about Molloy's proposal, not even my friend Maeve, so I didn't know why I felt so uncomfortable mentioning him. Only a few people had even known that we'd been together.

McFadden frowned before he realised what I meant, confirming that my embarrassment was all in my head. 'Oh, you mean Molloy.' He smiled. 'Aye, I suppose you could say that.'

Before I could ask anything else, I was forced to hop to one side as a cyclist wheeled her bike past. McFadden's eyes followed her with ill-disguised irritation.

'What's going on with all the bikes?' I asked.

'Ach, it's one of them Malin to Mizen charity cycles,' he said. 'In aid of Alzheimer's or dementia or some such. Some class of a nursing home down the country, I think.'

Malin Head to Mizen Head was a popular route for charity drives and cycles, being the most northerly and southerly points in Ireland. McFadden pointed to a large banner which I'd somehow missed, attached to two telephone poles and stretched across the main street.

The Amazing Grace Malin to Mizen Charity Cycle. 23rd–27th April. 5 days – 120 km per day! In aid of the Jameson Grace Homes and the Jameson Grace Charity for Alzheimer's and Dementia.

He followed my gaze. '"Amazing Grace" is a bit of a stretch. They're not even going by Lough Swilly. They're going down to Quigley's Point, Muff and Derry.' He shook his head mournfully. 'Decided not to point that out to them.'

I grinned. The story was well known locally. It was said that John Newton, a sailor in the slave trade, had a Road-to-Damascus moment when his ship was tossed about on rocks during a violent storm on the shores of Lough Swilly about ten miles from Glendara. He'd pleaded for God's help and when he came ashore safely, believed his prayers had been answered, after which he resolved to live a better life. The ship was repaired, and they were able to continue their journey. Newton had become a clergyman and written the hymn 'Amazing Grace'.

McFadden grimaced. 'I'm sure it's a good cause but you wouldn't catch me doing it. I hired a bike on the Aran Islands for a day and I couldn't sit down for a week.'

I laughed. McFadden had put on a fair bit of weight since I'd seen him last – a stint on a bike would do him no harm. Maybe he'd replaced his gambling addiction with something more calorific.

'They're supposed to be leaving from Malin Head in the morning, so they're taking the bikes up there tonight.' He nodded towards a couple of men wheeling bikes up a ramp onto a large truck. One stood out rather oddly, a large man with a beard dressed in motorcycle leathers who must have been about six foot four. 'Thank God that thing will be gone from the square anyway.'

I saw what he meant. The truck was taking up three full spaces in front of the courthouse. I frowned suddenly. Despite the regularity of these cycles, I'd never seen such a gathering of cyclists in the town before, and I'd just realised why – because Glendara was about ten miles from Malin Head.

'Why *are* they here?' I asked. 'Why aren't they in Malin Head?'

'A group of them are staying in Glendara tonight. I think they decided to do a last check on the bikes here, together, so they're all set for the morning.'

I was still confused. 'But why aren't they all staying in Malin Head? Wouldn't they be better off there? Or Malin Town even?'

McFadden gave a small shrug. 'Most are, I think. But Mary from the guesthouse knows someone involved apparently, so she got in on the act.' He grinned. 'Her place is full to the rafters.'

'Ah,' I said. Now it made sense. Mary McCauley ran a large B & B guesthouse with about ten bedrooms just on the outskirts of the town and a cannier businesswoman you wouldn't find, except for Phyllis the bookseller, who coincidentally was a buddy of hers.

McFadden spoke out of the corner of his mouth. 'To be honest, I think they must have thought Glendara was closer to Malin Head than it is. Typical Dubliners – didn't bother to check the map. Anyway, there's a minibus taking the Glendara contingent up to join their bikes in the morning.'

I looked at the crowd and frowned. 'How many are there?'

'About seventy cyclists altogether. Seventy-five? Plus hangers-on. Twenty of them staying in the town.'

'Bloody hell.'

He nodded. 'I know – there's a right number of them. It's good for the town but I'll be glad to see them sail on through tomorrow.' He checked his watch. 'Anyway, the fish factory's about to let out so it'll be complete chaos if I don't get this lot shifted before then.'

'Fair enough.' I checked my watch too. It was a quarter past five. 'I'd better get going too. I need to try and catch the office before it closes.'

McFadden waved me off as a loudspeaker made an announcement that the truck with the bikes was about to leave. I walked across the square, stretching my arms. My back was aching after the long flight and drive, and I was looking forward to lighting the fire in my cottage and curling up with a glass of wine, but I knew I should call into the office first – we opened till half past five, so I should just about catch them.

I reached the bottom of the square, turned the corner and suddenly I was there, standing in front of the small terraced house that accommodated O'Keeffe & Co. Solicitors. My practice. I was back. I took a breath, pressed down the handle and pushed open the door, expecting it to give way since we kept it unlatched, but it didn't move. I tried again, wondering if it was stuck – it did that sometimes but no, it was locked.

I checked my watch again. It was still only twenty past five and the sign in the window gave the same opening hours, but the office was closed. I stood for a few seconds wondering what to do. I looked in the windows but could see no sign of life. I had no key since I'd left mine at the cottage; there had been no point in bringing one to the States. I could ring Leah on her mobile, I thought, but I decided against it; they probably hadn't been expecting me till the morning. Maybe it was just as well; I'd have a good night's sleep tonight and call in first thing tomorrow.

Although it was a bloody strange sensation being locked out of your own office.

Chapter Four

I turned to make my way back up the street. In the short time since I'd left, the square had cleared considerably. I assumed most of the visitors had decamped to Malin Head. The bikes were gone, along with many of the cars, and there were three free spaces in front of the courthouse where the large truck had been. McFadden would be happy, I thought, although there was no sign of him now either.

There was a brisk wind as I walked along the lower end of the square. Ahead of me, one of the remaining cyclists was on the footpath looking into a shop window. As I watched, he pulled off his cycling gloves and squatted down on his hunkers to get a closer look at whatever it was he was examining. When I got closer, I realised he was outside Phyllis Kettle's bookshop and when I reached him, I stopped and followed his gaze.

Phyllis's window was entirely taken up with cycling books: David Walsh's *Seven Deadly Sins*, *The Secret Race: Inside the Hidden World of the Tour de France* by Daniel Coyle and Tyler Hamilton, and Bradley Wiggins's autobiography among others. She'd even added a cycling helmet and gloves, although both looked as though they'd seen better days. And a vintage bicycle horn with a rubber bulb! I suppressed a smile, wondering where she had come across all that paraphernalia. It was hard to imagine the bookseller on a bike. Maybe her grandfather (who'd sold pots and pans in the square and was the source of her nickname) had used a High Nelly to get around? However she'd done it, I was impressed. She'd anticipated things well.

The man noticed my presence and twisted around, hand on one knee. It was the man who'd thrown the spider tie earlier on. 'Quite a selection, for a small-town bookshop,' he remarked.

He'd pulled on a blue waterproof jacket since I'd seen him earlier, with the words *Trans-Pyrenees Challenge 2015* across the back and front. He was tanned and lean, a grey goatee giving him a rather distinguished look, and his eyebrows were bushy, threaded with silver and black.

I grinned. 'It's quite a bookshop.'

'So, I see.' He stood up using the wall to steady himself and stretched his legs.

'You should have a look inside,' I said. 'Phyllis can get you any book you want – new or second-hand. People buy books from her and when they've finished reading them, she buys them back and sells them some more.'

He flashed a smile and creases formed around his eyes. 'What a great idea. A bit like a library, but if you like the books you can keep them. Someone in Galway should catch on to that.'

I shrugged with a half-smile. 'Maybe it only works in a small town.'

The man was very thin; an indent appeared in his cheeks when he smiled, showing the outline of his skull. He was in his fifties, I guessed, but I could see from his legs, muscles bulging at the thighs, that he was strong. He put his hands into the pockets of his jacket. 'Sorry for almost braining you earlier, by the way. I should be more careful. I could take someone's eye out.'

28

I laughed. 'You sound like my mother. Is Galway where you're from?' I remembered McFadden's assumption that all the new-comers were from Dublin.

He nodded.

'And you're doing the race, I assume?'

'I am. Although it's not supposed to be a race – it's a charity cycle.' He gave me a wry look. 'Not that you can tell some people that.'

'I can imagine. Seems like a good thing to do though.' I looked up at the banner, which was directly above where we stood.

His gaze followed mine and then he lowered it. 'My wife has early onset dementia. She's fifty-seven. She was diagnosed five years ago.'

My face fell. 'Oh, I'm sorry.'

He bowed his head. 'Thanks. Although oddly it gets easier. It was hard at the beginning when she was very depressed and anxious.' He closed his eyes briefly. 'It's harder for the people who love her now, but I hope it's easier for her.'

The man's phone beeped, and he took it from his pocket. He read what I assumed was a text, then looked up, squinting. 'Do you know where the bank is?' His eyes flickered to somewhere over my shoulder.

I nodded. 'I'm parked there myself. I'll show you.'

We walked together up the street. He had an odd gait, his left leg seeming a little stiff, but it didn't inhibit his progress. I had to work to keep up with him.

'Your wife,' I said tentatively. 'It must be hard.'

'Ah sure, we all have our burdens to bear, don't we?' he said brightly, although his eyes showed a pain he wasn't expressing. 'Meg has profound memory loss now, so little awareness of her surroundings, I think. We have no kids and she hasn't recognised me for some time.' He took a deep breath. 'But she's in a great residential place now and she's not distressed, which is the important thing as far as I'm concerned.'

We'd reached the corner. 'The bank is just over there,' I said, pointing.

'Thank you.'

'I hope the cycle goes well. You certainly brought a bit of colour to the town this afternoon.'

His mouth curled up into a smile. 'The scourge of middle-aged men in Lycra.'

A woman in cycling shorts and a bright pink top crossed the square, the same woman who'd asked him for the spider tie. She waved and he waved back.

'And women,' I added. 'You seem to have good numbers.'

He nodded. 'We have. The charity is called the Jameson Grace Charity, so when someone spotted the "Amazing Grace" connection to this area and had the idea of doing something here, a cycle seemed to make sense. And it's proved surprisingly popular.'

'Are you staying with Mary then, in the guesthouse?' I asked.

'We are. Just one night unfortunately. We're due to leave early in the morning – about eight I think.' He glanced around him. 'Seems like a nice place to spend some time.'

The square *was* looking well, with tulips and daffodils in pots and hanging baskets above some of the shop fronts.

I smiled. 'You should try and get up for a visit sometime, when you don't have to ship out so quickly.'

'Believe me, I'd love to.' The sound of a car horn interrupted him, blaring aggressively from the other side of the square. 'I'd better get a move on, that sounds like my lift.'

I looked across to where the noise was coming from. A massive black Lexus was parked in the space beside the Mini that had previously been occupied by the motorbike and was also taking up half the space next to it.

'Not mine,' my companion said with a laugh, holding his hands up in protest on seeing my expression. 'It's my brother's'.

There were two people in the car, a man and a woman. The man in the car tapped his watch.

'He seems in a hurry,' I said.

'He's always in a hurry. He can wait a few extra minutes. My name's Derek by the way. Derek Jameson.'

'Like the whiskey?'

He smiled. 'Like the whiskey. No connection unfortunately. If it was, this charity cycle wouldn't be necessary. I'd just donate a big bucket of cash!'

'I'm Ben. Benedicta. Is it your charity then? The Jameson Grace Charity?'

He shook his head. 'My brother's.'

He waved and said goodbye and I watched him cross the square before heading back to Phyllis's bookshop.

The old bell tinkled as I pushed open the door and I walked in, happy to see that, opportunistic window displays aside, Phyllis's bookshop never changed. And neither did Phyllis. The bookseller was perched at the counter, drinking a mug of tea and reading a book while feeding biscuits to her border collie Fred, who lay in his usual spot at her feet. She looked up as I walked in, struggled to her feet and threw her arms open to envelop me in a huge hug. She was dressed rather startlingly in various shades of yellow.

When she released me, I indicated her outfit. 'In honour of the yellow jersey?' Phyllis is a large woman; she was quite the sight.

She grinned, nodding towards the bookshop window. 'What do you think of my display?'

'Timely.'

She went to get a second stool for me, but I stopped her. The bookseller was clearly ready for a good chat, but I was tired and anxious to get home.

'Sorry Phyllis. I can't stay. I've just arrived back, and I'm absolutely wrecked. I haven't been back to Malin yet.'

She put her hand to her face. 'So, you haven't even seen your poor cat.'

Her tragic expression made me laugh. 'I'm not sure "poor cat" applies to Guinness but no, I haven't. I need to pick up some groceries and head back to unpack. I just called in to say hello.'

She seemed disappointed, but very quickly brightened again. 'Fancy a welcome home drink in the Oak tomorrow night?' she suggested. 'We can have a proper catch up and I'll give Liam and a few other people a nudge. We could even have finger food. I'll do some of my dips, some guacamole, tzatziki . . .'

Knowing that any food conversation with Phyllis could go on for a while, I cut her off. 'That sounds lovely, but don't go to any trouble. Really. A quiet drink would be great.'

She rubbed her hands together enthusiastically. 'Leave it with me.'

After a quick visit to the supermarket I drove home along the coast, glancing across at Trawbreaga Bay and the Isle of Doagh, rolling down the window so I could hear the sea. The waves were a balm I'd found calming even at the most difficult times. I didn't think I'd ever be able to live away from the coast again, and hoped I'd never have to. Seagulls soared and swooped low over the greeny-blue water. I could hear their squeal.

The clouds had cleared a little, allowing a glimpse of blue with a wash of lilac and orange, but the sky ahead of me over Malin didn't look so good; an ominous black cloud had settled just above the village. I hoped the forecasters were wrong and the cyclists would get a good start to their cycle in the morning, but it didn't seem likely. The supermarket had been full of people in tracksuits buying energy bars and sun cream. I had a feeling they might not be needing the latter so much.

I drove across the old bridge and onto the village green, pulling up in front of my cottage. I was home. This was where I'd found refuge, it was somewhere I could be myself, alone when I wanted to be, with company when I didn't. The problem was, where did Molloy fit into that? Did I feel ready to share my space with someone else full time? Had he even meant it when he'd come out with that strange proposal? Would I lose him if I said no? One thing for sure – we needed to talk. For the moment though, I was home, and that was enough.

I walked up the path and turned the key in the lock. Marina had been living here while I was away, so I fully expected to encounter a stranger looking into my fridge just as I had in my parents' house. But no, the house was silent, deserted. There was a note on the kitchen table.

Welcome Back! I'll be gone for the night so I'm sure you'll be glad to have the place to yourself. Hope you had a great trip and I'll see you in the office in the morning! Marina

I was relieved – the prospect of another house guest hadn't been particularly appealing, even for one night. I crumpled the note up and threw it in the bin, happy to be able to unpack and gather my thoughts, alone.

Now where was that cat?

No sooner had I asked the question than there was a scratching at the window over the sink and I looked up to see a black tom with a white patch on his head sitting on the outside sill. Guinness! Delighted, I opened the latch to let him in, but he hesitated, looking up at me, his eyes narrowed. Hesitation was unusual. Usually the cat was in like a shot when I opened the window, like a rat up a drainpipe before I changed my mind. Now he sat there, tail wrapped around himself, eyeing me suspiciously.

'Ah, Guinness. Don't be like that. You were taken care of while I was away, weren't you?'

The rain and wind were building again, cold air was coming in and I was anxious to close the window. So I reached out to lift him in, but he yelped at me as I did it, spat and hissed. And when I put him on the floor, he circled around me, tail swishing angrily. The cat wasn't at all happy with me.

Despite his temper I fed him. I'd bought his favourite cat food, and reluctantly he ate it, looking up at me reproachfully as if every bite was choking him, but he was hungry so had no choice.

I knew the cat's moods, so I left him to it, poured myself a glass of wine and went upstairs to unpack. He'd forgive me eventually. At the top of the stairs, I was glad to see that Marina had slept in the spare room – my own was untouched. Her door was closed, and I resisted the impulse to open it.

In my bedroom I unpacked, but I was distracted. I picked up my phone, put it down, then picked it up again any number of times. Until eventually I sat down on the bed and did what I had been putting off since I'd landed at Dublin Airport. I texted Molloy.

I'm back. Bit jetlagged. Ran into McFadden in the square. Good to see him back! Are you around tomorrow to catch up?

Faux casual. I put the phone down on my bedside locker, not really expecting a response, for a while anyway. But still I glanced at it. I jumped when it pinged immediately.

I am. Looking forward to seeing you. You were missed.

I smiled and lay back on the bed, phone in hand. In the past I'd have overanalysed that text. I'd have wondered why he had said *you were missed* rather than that *he had missed me*. Now that I knew Molloy better, that message seemed positively amorous.

Chapter Five

Guinness demanded to be let out again when I came back down the stairs and he didn't come back. He was a tomcat, so it wasn't unusual for him to stay out all night, but it was a rotten night and I woke a couple of times to the sound of rain battering off the windows and the roof, imagining him sodden.

It still hadn't stopped the next morning, and after a shower with the rain drumming on the eaves, in accompaniment, I made it down to the kitchen relieved to find Guinness back in his position at the window looking much sorrier for himself than he had last night. I opened the latch and he stepped in without hesitation, flopping wetly onto the floor. Amazingly he consented to let me towel him dry and after I'd fed him, he curled up on an old blanket in a box in the back kitchen.

I left early for the office. Despite my ministrations the cat looked reproachfully at me as I closed the back door: it appeared I wasn't quite forgiven yet. But I had no intention of doing a full day in the office, so I'd be back to let him out. Marina was still on duty today – this morning was just for the handover of files.

Though it had stopped raining, the drive was difficult, to put it mildly. The roads were saturated, large pools of rainwater had gathered at regular intervals the whole way in, something the

Mini didn't cope with too well. Despite my best efforts to take it slowly, the old car cut out twice, meaning I had to wait for a minute each time to start it again. Quite the contrast to Florida.

In Glendara I parked in the square, noticing the same motorbike I'd seen the day before in the space beside me again. I was early for the office, so I decided to call in to Stoop's newsagent to buy the papers and save Leah from doing it. But before I even took the key from the ignition, the heavens opened and it started to rain again, hammering down on the roof of the car. I sat for a bit waiting for it to ease off, watching people scurrying between doorways.

A crowd of people trooped into the Oak pub across the way, unusual for this early on a Friday since Tony would only just have opened up. There were about ten of them, all wearing waterproof jackets and hoods. I rubbed the condensation from the windscreen for a clearer look. By his gait, and his blue jacket, I thought one of them was Derek, the cyclist I'd met the day before outside Phyllis's. He was with another much larger man and a very thin woman, possibly the couple who'd been waiting for him in the Lexus. Behind them were two younger women in leggings and brightly coloured jackets in purple and red; one had a toddler in her arms.

I assumed they were all part of the charity cycle, although the couple with Derek didn't look fit enough. I wondered why you would bother coming along if you weren't participating? But also, I checked my watch and it was a quarter to nine. Weren't they due to leave Malin Head at eight o'clock?

Frustrated, since the rain showed no signs of abating, I caught sight of something in the mirror, something red on the floor behind the passenger seat. I reached back to get it, pleased to find it was an umbrella. It must have slid out from under the back seat.

It wasn't mine so I supposed it must belong to the Usurper, but I was grateful to have it in the circumstances.

I climbed out of the car and put the umbrella up, glad to have something to shield me from the driving rain but taken aback by the force of it. I'd become used to heavy rain in Florida, but this was unusual for Inishowen. Our rain was generally soft and constant; a drizzle; *down for the day*. This was almost tropical, falling straight like stair rods, making it difficult to keep the umbrella upright. The rain bounced off the footpath – my feet were wet just from standing on the street for a few seconds. I needed to get a move on.

The umbrella's discovery turned out to be not as serendipitous as I thought; it was a cheap specimen given away by some business or other and within seconds I realised that it was in danger of blowing inside out. A sudden blast nearly blew me off my feet, outside the newsagent's, the rain sharp and stinging on my face. It was a real struggle to stay standing and avoid embarking on a Mary Poppins style flight above town.

Finally, I regained control of the umbrella, and ducked into the newsagent's doorway, closing it up and shaking it out on the step. Breathing heavily, I turned towards the counter.

Stoop was grinning at me over the chocolate bars he was restocking. 'I thought I'd have to come out and pull you in out of that.'

'That's some weather,' I said, brushing the wet from my face.

'Aye, it's cat.' He leaned on the counter. 'I heard you were back. How was Florida? Wee bit drier than this, I suppose.'

I shivered. I needed to dry out my feet. 'A damn sight warmer anyway. It's good to be back though.' I picked up two papers, the national *Irish Times* and the local *Inish Times*, one letter difference in the title, considerable difference in the coverage. 'What's the story with the charity cycle?' I asked. 'Have they postponed it? I've just seen a load of them going into the Oak.'

Stoop nodded, ringing up the papers on the cash register. 'Aye. They're leaving it till this afternoon to set off. A few of them were in here buying papers.' He shook his head. 'I can see them having to abandon it altogether, the forecast is so bad. But you couldn't be saying it to them, people always think they know best. Some of them thought they should get going this morning as planned; there was a bit of a spat about it in the shop.'

I looked at the open doorway, rain hammering off the step. 'Really?'

'Aye.' He clicked his teeth. 'Not wise. They don't know the roads around there. They could get rightly stranded.'

The rain had stopped again by the time I paid for the papers and braved the street, stuffing them beneath my jacket just in case. The footpath was sodden, water running down the street in rivulets. I saw that the bank was open and remembered I needed to call in, but as I crossed the square, a couple standing outside the doctor's surgery caught my eye, umbrellas at their sides. It took me a second to recognise her, but it was Marina, my locum, saying goodbye to someone with a kiss. And, I was surprised to see, the someone she was kissing was the doctor himself: Dr Harry. Leah's cousin, newish man about town and a man I'd been seeing myself very casually the previous summer, until Molloy had returned and complicated matters.

Dr Harry had found himself in hot water when he'd concealed his past in the context of a murder investigation, and he'd been lucky not to be charged with anything. Which was just as well for Marina, I thought, because from where I was standing, they looked pretty close. I tested how I felt about Harry having a new love interest but there was nothing. I had no feelings for him any more. I wondered if I ever had. Despite sometimes wishing otherwise, it had always been Molloy. The realisation hit me like a bolt. But I decided to put that thought away for later.

In the meantime, I turned my head away so they wouldn't catch me staring and took the long way to the bank, ducking in quickly when I reached it.

The bank teller gave me a friendly smile. 'Morning.' With her glossy brown hair and freckles Connie always managed to look as if she'd had about ten hours sleep. As she counted out my cash, she nodded towards the door. 'Has it stopped?'

'For a while, I think.'

She shook her head. 'The road from Buncrana was dire this morning. Massive wee puddles the whole way in. I was sure the car was going to give out and I'd have to get out and swim.'

When I sloshed my way back to the office, Marina and Harry were still outside the surgery deep in conversation, so I avoided them a second time.

I was relieved the lights of the office were on and the door opened easily this time when I pushed it. The smell was instantly familiar as I made my way down the narrow hall; an office smell, I supposed, but so different to the American office. This was the scent of paper, of cardboard files, old title deeds, dusty wills, and slightly inefficient heating. It was stale and musty, and some might say not that pleasant, but it brought a lump to my throat. I was telling myself not to be so ridiculous, that I'd only been away for six months after all, when I emerged into the reception area to an excited shout.

'Ben!' Leah was up out of her seat to give me a hug just as Phyllis had done the day before.

The bookseller was a much bulkier woman than Leah, but when I put my arms around my legal assistant, I quickly realised that there was more to her now too. I stood back, holding her at arms-length and saw what I had suspected. She was pregnant. This was what she hadn't told me.

My face broke into a smile. 'Why didn't you let me know?'

She beamed. 'I wanted to tell you face-to-face. I was afraid I'd blurt it out on the phone – that's why I kept trying to get away.'

I laughed. 'I thought I was pestering you. How far along are you?'

She smoothed her top over her neat bump. 'About four months – it's showing sooner than I thought.'

'That's only because you usually don't have a pick on you.'

'Not the case any more! I'll be a whale soon.'

'Don't be silly. You look great. It's lovely news.' I hugged her again. 'Congratulations. How is Kevin? Is he thrilled?'

Her face creased into a gentle smile. 'He is. It's helped him get over all the family stuff.'

Kevin's islander family had found themselves in trouble the year before when an illegal diesel-laundering plant they'd been running had caused his cousin to make some desperate choices, criminal choices. Kevin had known nothing about it but was still trying to help his family as much as possible while his cousin, who had been badly hurt, started his life sentence in hospital.

Leah looked down at her bump. 'Now he can concentrate on the family he's creating with me rather than the one that brought him up.'

'How are you feeling?'

'Great now that I've passed the first three months. I've stopped throwing up at least. And wanting to sleep all the time.'

'And how has Marina been?' I asked quietly.

'Good . . .' Leah said slowly, before the door opened and there was the sound of someone coming along the hall. I'd missed the 'but' part, but I'd get it out of her later.

In the meantime, Marina herself walked into reception, all smiles. I'd met her only twice before I'd left for the States, once to interview her and once to show her the ropes over an afternoon at the office, but she was prettier than I remembered. Dark hair with pale skin and ice blue eyes, she looked a lot younger than the years her CV claimed she'd clocked up. She shook off her umbrella and left it carelessly against the wall, allowing it to slip and fall onto the carpet. I noticed Leah give it a sideways look, but she said nothing. It reminded me that I'd left mine behind me somewhere, in Stoop's or the bank, I couldn't recall which.

Marina kissed me on the cheek. 'Welcome back!' She dropped her bag onto the floor too, causing a lipstick and tissue to spill out. 'Sorry I wasn't there to greet you last night, but I thought you might prefer the place to yourself.'

'No, you were right, thank you. I've had a great old sleep and I'm ready to face the world and my practice again,' I said brightly, choosing not to mention that I'd seen her with Harry. I wasn't sure why.

'No jet lag?' She bent down to shove the lipstick and tissue back in.

'Either it hasn't set in yet or I'm going to be lucky enough to escape it.'

'Coffee?' Leah said, looking at both of us.

'Great,' I replied. 'Thank you.' I smiled. 'Decaffeinated for you?'

She raised her eyes to heaven. 'That's one of the disadvantages all right.'

Marina turned to me and clapped her hands. 'So, are you ready to start? Do you want to have a look at the files and see what's been happening?'

I inhaled deeply and pushed back my shoulders. 'Sure. Might as well get it over with.'

'I'll bring these up,' Leah shouted from the kitchen from where I could hear the kettle starting to hum.

I followed Marina up the narrow stairs and into my office at the top, with slight trepidation, but even I couldn't have imagined what awaited me. I stopped in the doorway in shock.

I was the type of solicitor who filed things away so I didn't lose them, who prioritised her work carefully, leaving a neat desk every night and a to-do list ready for the morning. Marina, from the evidence laid out in front of me, was very different. My office looked as if a bomb had hit it. The desk was buried in correspondence and documents, files littered the floor and there were heaps of papers on every surface (not neat stacks which I could have forgiven, but chaotic-looking piles). I was appalled to see an Oak takeaway coffee carton on the desk and, Jesus, was that a chocolate wrapper between two title deeds? My skin prickled and my face flushed. Was I the one who was going to have to disentangle this mess?

I don't know what my expression revealed but it was clearly not what I was thinking. Marina beamed at me as if the chaos showed what a good job she'd been doing, how hard she'd been working. I sighed. There was nothing for it but to dive in. I took a notepad and pen from the stationery shelf in the office next door and braved my office again, stepping over the debris on the floor and plonking myself down on one of the client chairs. Marina took my usual one at the desk, brushing the old coffee cup into the bin with her elbow.

'Okay,' I said through gritted teeth. 'Bring me up to speed on where everything is on each file and I'll ask questions if I have them.'

Two hours and three coffees later, my head was spinning. Not as badly as I'd expected it to be, but spinning, nonetheless. Thankfully, despite the bombsite of an office, Marina appeared to be getting the work done, but by God did she have a different way of working to mine. To Leah's too, I suspected. Leah was like me in that she ran a very organised office; it was one of the reasons we worked well together. I wondered if Marina had driven her demented while I was away. Her glance at the floor as Marina had abandoned her umbrella made sense to me now.

I sat back in my chair as Marina upended the final file in a way that made me wince. Naturally all its contents fell out, tumbling onto the floor beneath the desk. Oblivious to my pain, she bent down, gathered the documents up in an untidy sheaf and shoved them back onto the file.

Then she tossed it to one side and checked her watch. 'Are you coming for lunch or are you heading off?'

'I'll come for a sandwich and then I'll leave you to it if that's okay. I'd like to get back to the house for the afternoon. I still have a load of laundry to get through.'

'Okey doke.' She stood up and straightened her perfectly ironed skirt. Her untidiness didn't extend to her personal grooming apparently.

I stood up too, closing my attendance pad. 'Thanks for all your hard work. I should be able to pick things up easily enough on Monday.'

'It was fun. I'll be sorry to leave.' She came out from behind the desk with a smile.

At the top of the stairs, I almost mentioned Harry, but the sound of the front door opening below interrupted my train of thought. And by the time we reached the bottom Mary from the B & B was in the hallway, having just closed the door behind her.

She was deep in thought, gazing anxiously at the floor, but her face broke into a half smile when she looked up. 'Ah, Phyllis said you were back.' Her brow furrowed again. 'Have you a minute?'

I stalled, glancing at Marina for permission. Strictly speaking she was the solicitor who was insured until the end of business today; mine didn't kick in until half past five. But she held her hands up in a 'be my guest' gesture.

Mary saw the exchange and I explained the problem. 'Please?' she said, clasping her hands together. 'I'm not asking you to do anything. I just want a chat.'

I sighed. If this wasn't true, I'd have to palm her back onto Marina in the afternoon, but if it was anything serious, I'd have to deal with it anyway the following week, in which case I'd also have to decipher Marina's attendance notes. Having seen what they were like, it was easier in the long run to see Mary myself.

'Just a quick chat,' I cautioned, checking my watch, remembering that I also needed to get back to my cottage to let Guinness out. 'I don't have a lot of time.'

Relief flooded her face and I brought her into the front room, unable to face going back upstairs to my messy office. I'd deal with that on Monday once Marina had left. I turned on the light, seeing that the room had suddenly darkened, and Mary took a seat. I noticed her hair was damp.

'Sorry about the state of me.' Her cheeks glowed as she pushed a tendril behind her ear. 'I've just been for a swim.'

I took an attendance sheet from a drawer. 'I thought you'd got caught in one of the showers.'

She smiled. 'Thought I'd do it while I got the chance. It helps me sleep.'

I'd seen Mary in Culdaff slicing powerfully through the waves, heading so far out she became nothing but a tiny speck. I was more of a teabag swimmer, a quick dip in and out. And I hadn't felt that shuddering icy shock in six months; the sea in Florida was a warm bath in comparison.

I dated the attendance sheet and looked up. 'But you must have been swimming in the rain. Was it cold?'

She breathed out and closed her eyes. 'It was absolute heaven.'

Mary McCauley was one of life's natural beauties. She never wore make-up, dressed in the simplest of clothes – today she was wearing a simple shirt and jeans with a sprig of sea pinks in the buttonhole – and she had allowed herself to put on a little weight as she'd grown older, achieving what could best be described as a sort of a voluptuous elegance. I'd heard she was a fabulous cook, which was part of the success of her guesthouse.

'What was it you wanted to speak to me about?' I asked.

Mary leaned in; hands tucked between her thighs. 'I don't know if you know about this charity cycle that's happening. Or supposed to be happening, if it ever stops raining.' She glanced towards the window where, sure enough, drops began to race each other down the glass.

'I do. They were pretty hard to miss in the square yesterday.'

She nodded. 'Well, I have some of them staying with me up at the guesthouse. And something happened last night that I'm not very happy about.'

'What was that?'

'Noises.' Mary looked at my attendance pad, patiently waiting for me to write it down. 'Late at night.'

I obliged. 'What kind of noises?'

She tilted her head. 'Like a row. Shouting. It was coming from one of my double rooms; there was a couple staying there.'

'And?' I'd spent so much time with Americans who were only

too willing to 'share' that I'd forgotten how hard it was to get Irish people to talk about personal matters, or even give instructions. Even someone like Mary.

'I knocked on their door and when they didn't answer, I opened it with my key. She was throwing things at him. His wife.'

I studied her face. 'What kind of things?'

Her eyes widened; she had green eyes, almost turquoise. 'Whatever she could get her hands on. Things from his bag, aftershave, facecloths, a toothbrush. And he was just juking about. As if it was a game.'

'And was it?'

Mary gave a tight shake of her head. 'No. She was angry, really angry. He's a big man but he was just standing there while she screamed and threw things at him. I'm sure he could have stopped her, but he was just taking it, like he didn't care.'

'And what did you do?'

'I asked them to stop, that they were disturbing the other guests. But it didn't make any difference. They just ignored me.' She looked down at her hands and I was surprised to see the nails were bitten right down. She covered them quickly and looked up. 'The man's brother is staying with me too, so I called him. He told me he'd sort it out and I left. It was quiet in a few minutes.'

A couple travelling with the man's brother. Could this be the cyclist I'd met the day before? I wondered. 'Did you see them this morning?' I asked.

Mary nodded. 'The brother apologised this morning, but the other two just behaved as if nothing had happened. All sweetness and light to each other like that couple from the shop in *Father Ted*.' She gave me a wry look.

I knew what she was referring to, a couple in a comedy series who were loved up in public but foul-mouthed and vicious when they were on their own. I suspected the situation wouldn't be quite so funny in real life.

Although I was a little stumped. I couldn't see any legal problem unless there had been damage to the room, but Mary hadn't mentioned any. 'That all sounds very unpleasant, but at least it was resolved.'

Mary took a deep breath as if finally coming to the crux of the matter. 'The problem is, they were supposed to be leaving this morning but now they want to stay tonight too.'

I put the pen down. 'I thought the cycle was happening this afternoon?'

She began to play with a silver chain around her neck. 'It's not safe, there's too much water on the road. They're hoping it will have cleared tomorrow and they'll be able to set off.' She glanced doubtfully at the streaming window.

'I see.'

'So, what should I do?' she asked anxiously. 'Can I ask them to leave? I don't want them staying with me tonight but they've nowhere else to go. With the cycle, the town is booked up.'

I rested my chin on my hands. 'They only booked for one night, so you don't have to keep them for any longer than that if you don't want to. And even if they had booked for two nights, it's probably reasonable for you to ask them to leave, if they were disturbing other guests.' But Mary would have known all of that, I thought. 'Haven't you encountered this kind of thing before? I mean, you've been running the guesthouse for what?'

Her eyes drifted towards the wall as if trying to work it out. 'Twenty years this June?'

'What would you usually do if something like this happened?'

She shook her head. 'It's never happened. I mean there have been rows, people coming in late after a load of drink, but this was different.' She dropped her voice to a whisper. 'The truth is, I wondered if I should report it to the guards. I mean, it's domestic abuse, isn't it? There are all those ads on the television now, aren't there? About not ignoring it if you see it.'

I sat back, realising that she might very well be right. Just because it was a woman attacking a man rather than the other way around didn't make it any more acceptable. 'Would it help to speak to the brother?' I asked.

Mary massaged her temples. I was surprised by how distressed she was about this. 'Maybe.' She sounded unconvinced.

'It might be somewhere to start. See what he thinks and, if it happens again, then definitely report it. And make it clear that that's what you will be doing.'

She nodded. 'Okay, I'll do that.'

But when I showed her out, I noticed her hands were balled into fists.

Chapter Six

I closed the front door and returned to reception where Leah was alone, typing furiously. When she saw me, she looked up, took off her headphones and rested her elbows on the desk.

'So, was Mary as good as her word? Was it really only a chat?'

'You heard?'

'Marina told me.'

I nodded. 'Ah yeah. Although I'm pretty sure I didn't give her what she was looking for.' I glanced towards the hall door, still feeling a little concerned. 'I can't help thinking there was something she wasn't saying.'

'Really? I hope she's okay.' Leah sighed. 'I like Mary. She's such a child of nature. I want to be like her when I'm her age.'

I knew what she meant. There was an earthy quality about Mary that I wished I had, but knew I probably never would.

Leah's eyes narrowed in amusement. 'You know she has a tattoo of a mermaid?'

'You're kidding. How do you know that?'

She grinned. 'I met her coming out of Derry Ink a while back and she showed me. It's on her back, so you wouldn't see it unless she did. She said she just took a notion and did it.'

'She's a smart businesswoman,' I said. 'That B & B has been a great success. Hard work though.'

'I know, but she seems to be able to just go with the flow. She says she really likes the company it brings. She's got such an open, giving kind of a nature,' Leah said dreamily.

I raised my eyebrows. Not my trusty legal assistant's usual turn of phrase. Had pregnancy turned her all New Age? Her eyes drifted and her smile faded suddenly.

'What's wrong?' I asked, concerned.

'Oh, I don't know.' She rested her chin on her hands. 'I've always thought there was something a little sad about her. She's so gorgeous, Mary. You know she's supposed to have had her heart broken when she was young, and she never got over it?'

'No, I didn't.'

'She's had loads of offers over the years apparently, but she could never fall in love with anyone else.' Leah's eyes glittered.

I smiled. 'Are you crying?'

'Oh, for God's sake.' She widened her eyes and slapped herself on the cheek. 'It's these blooming hormones. I'd cry at the Angelus at the moment.'

I placed my hands on the counter. 'Tell you what, pregnant lady. I'll make you some chamomile tea.'

It turned out that Mary wasn't the only client who insisted on seeing me that day. I supposed it was good to be missed. Leah brought me back a sandwich and takeaway soup from the Oak to keep me going but being trapped in the office all day meant I couldn't get back to Malin to let Guinness out.

So, at a quarter to three when I emerged from the front room to find yet two more clients waiting for me, I rang Maeve, local vet and my good friend, who clocked up quite a few miles around the peninsula. Maeve had a key to my cottage, and I hoped she might be passing through Malin at some stage during the afternoon. She picked up on the second ring.

'Hey, you're back!' She was driving and had me on speaker. I could hear the jeep's windscreen wipers battling the same rain shower I was looking out at on the street.

'In more ways than one,' I sighed. When I explained my problem, Maeve said she was about two miles from Malin, on her way back from a calving, and would let the cat out on her way through.

'So, you're back at work?' she asked, raising her voice above the torrent.

'Trying not to be and failing,' I said. 'Catch up at the weekend?'

She started to reply, but her voice began to cut in and out and eventually the connection went completely. I tried to ring her back without success, assuming she was passing through one of the many black spots in Inishowen.

Before my next clients, I ducked into the bathroom. But, on closing the door behind me, my hand flew to my collar: something wet and icy was creeping down my neck. When I looked up, my heart sank. A steady drip was coming from a tiny crack in the ceiling and the carpet where I was standing was sodden. Our bathroom was a one-storey extension that had been built onto the back of the building, so it was perfectly possible the water was coming from a gutter either next door or above, but with clients waiting, I didn't have time to check.

So, I opted for a more temporary measure and fetched a basin.

At four o'clock, while Marina was finally seeing a client about some conveyancing case she needed to finish up, I was standing at reception telling Leah about the drip when the front door opened again. The first item to appear was an enormous purple umbrella with yellow and orange flowers, and the second was Phyllis.

Dressed in a red trench coat that reached her ankles and a green bucket hat, she shook the brolly out, took the hat off and ran a hand over her brow, flicking drops of rain onto the carpet. 'Jesus, it's biblical out there.'

Leah grinned. 'Need a towel, Phyllis?'

She shook her head. 'Nah, I'll only get drenched again on the way back, thanks anyway pet. Those brollies aren't worth a curse. That's rare weather.' She leaned her considerable bosom on the counter. 'I just called in to say that it's all arranged. The Oak from six o'clock onwards.'

I frowned. 'What's all arranged?'

She clicked her teeth impatiently. 'Your welcome home "do" of course. Don't tell me you've forgotten.'

I had. I'd forgotten completely. I was all set to head back to Malin once I'd seen off the last client. 'Ah, Phyllis. I don't need anything arranged. I've only been gone six months. It's hardly worthy of a "do".'

'Aye, you might have been gone only six months, but you were missed,' she said firmly, casting a glance at Marina who had emerged from the downstairs office and was making her way upstairs with a file. I presumed the client was still in there. 'Liam will be there and so will Hal and, well, a wile lot of other people. They all want to welcome you home.'

I think it was the word 'home' that got to me. I realised I'd sounded ungrateful and so I gave in. 'Okay, then. Thanks, Phyllis. It's kind of you to go to so much trouble.'

The bookseller grinned in smug satisfaction. I'd long since learned that Phyllis generally got her own way, managing to push her own agenda with such gentle stealth that it was only afterwards you realised she'd been the one in charge all along.

After she left, I sent a text to Maeve to tell her about the gathering in the Oak. She responded by saying that Phyllis had already been in touch and she'd see me there, that she'd been trying to tell me that when she'd been cut off. She sent me a second text to say that she'd called to my house, that Guinness had darted out and back in again very quickly and so he was back in the warm and dry. After a brief hesitation, I sent Molloy a similar text and he responded to say he knew about the drinks too and he'd see me there. It seemed Phyllis had covered all bases.

At half past five we closed the office and Leah went home. She looked tired and pale and a crowded pub on a damp evening held considerably less appeal for her now that she was pregnant. Marina, on the other hand, was happy to come for a drink. It was her last night in Glendara – she planned to drive home in the morning.

It was dry when we left the office, but the aftermath of the earlier rain was impossible to miss and, worryingly, it was beginning to look as if the gutters and drains were struggling to cope. More puddles had formed in the street and water was flowing downhill rather than draining away, pooling at the lower end of town. Glendara was built on a slope; my office was on one side of that slope, which might explain why I had a leak in the bathroom. I made a mental note to call someone to have a look at it in the morning. I hadn't had a chance all afternoon.

Corpses of umbrellas lay on the footpath and in bins and the walk through the square was an obstacle course to be navigated carefully to avoid wet feet. I was glad to have despatched Leah safely in her car, and when we pushed open the door of the Oak, I knew she'd made the right decision.

It was only a quarter to six, but the place was hopping, having clearly become a refuge for the cyclists stranded in town overnight. McFadden had said there were twenty-odd people staying in town and I reckoned most of them were here, on top of the usual Friday evening crowd. The two booths at the rear of the pub were full.

A smell of wet wool and smoke pervaded the room and it didn't take long to see why. A row of chairs had been placed in front of the fire with coats hanging on them, steam rising like the sulphur from a great volcano. The smell reminded me of Glendara's courthouse in winter and it would have turned Leah's already delicate stomach if she'd been here. Tony wouldn't put up with it for long either, I thought – the chairs were blocking the heat.

But seating wasn't a problem since Phyllis had commandeered a large table at the front of the pub. I was pleased to see that Liam McLaughlin, estate agent, auctioneer and all-round decent stick, was with her, minding the seats. When he spotted me, he stood up and shook my hand, pumping it up and down like a saw.

'Wile good to have you back. Hope you haven't gone all Yank on us!'

'Hardly, Liam, in six months.'

'I don't know.' He grinned. 'I know people who've picked up an accent on the bus to Dublin. Pint?'

I nodded. For the first time in months, I felt like a beer. Liam headed up to the bar to get drinks for Marina and myself, and I was glad to see that Stan was serving. Stan, the local hairdresser, and Tony, the Oak's proprietor, were half-brothers who'd only recently found each other so it was good to see them working together. It looked as if Stan was in his element, tossing glasses around the place like Tom Cruise in *Cocktail*.

55

I joined Phyllis and Marina at the table, taken aback to see Marina suddenly stony-faced, with no trace of the beaming smile of earlier. Did I imagine it or were things a little frosty between herself and Phyllis? I'd thought it odd that she hadn't joined us for a chat at reception earlier and now they just nodded to each other, without smiling. Feeling slightly uncomfortable, I mentioned the extra clientele in the pub.

Phyllis shrugged as she took a sip of her gin. 'Nothing else to do I suppose, since they're stuck here for an extra night. Although I don't see them getting out on the road tomorrow either – the forecast is cat.'

'Not sure I can take much more of it anyway!' I looked up to see Maeve, peeling off her waterproofs and stuffing them into a bag. She leaned in to give me a hug and I offered her a drink since Liam still hadn't reappeared.

'Thanks. I'm on call so just get me a 7Up or something.' She plonked her phone on the table. 'That yoke is likely to ring before I even sit down.'

I made my way through the pub, meeting Liam halfway. Despite his laden hands he offered to get Maeve's drink, but I wanted to say hello to Tony and Stan, so I kept going. When I got to the bar, I squeezed myself in beside a huge bearded man in motorcycle leathers, with his elbows on the counter, hands wrapped around a pint. I waved hello to Stan and gave my order to Tony, who welcomed me back before moving off to get my drink.

The man at the bar shifted aside to give me more room and I recognised him as one of the men I'd seen wheeling bikes onto the truck the day before.

'You not with the rest of your gang?' I asked, glancing towards the back of the pub. Derek, the man I'd met outside Phyllis's shop the day before, was in the company of about a dozen other people. He spotted me and gave me a wave.

The man in the leathers shook his head without looking over. 'Needed a bit of headspace.'

Tony reappeared with Maeve's 7Up and he nodded at my new acquaintance. 'This man's an accountant. Did he tell you? I wouldn't have guessed in a million years.' I paid him and he winked. 'Mind you, this one's a solicitor and you wouldn't guess that either.'

'I'm not sure either of those are compliments,' I laughed as he headed off with my tenner.

The man in the leathers looked at me with amusement. 'He's right though – you don't look like a solicitor.'

I glanced down, realising I was still wearing the jeans and boots I'd put on this morning, when I'd no intention of spending the day at my desk. 'No, I suppose I don't. I do sometimes, I suspect.'

The man proffered a huge paw-like hand, on which he wore several interesting-looking silver rings. 'I'm Jude, by the way. Jude Burns.' He also wore a single stud earring in the shape of a book.

'Good to meet you. I'm Ben – Benedicta.' I picked up Maeve's drink. 'So, you're involved in the charity cycle?'

'Peripherally.' Jude took a slug of his Guinness, giving his beard a white trim, then placed the glass back on the counter, tapping it four times as he did so, tap-tap-tap-tap. 'I'm sort of a marshal, bringing up the rear in case anyone has any trouble. There's another motorbike at the front. I'm a trained paramedic as well as an accountant.'

'I think I've been parking beside your bike.'

He looked up. 'The Harley?'

I shrugged with a smile. I had no idea. A bike was a bike as far as I was concerned. 'Not too many motorbikes in town usually. Do you think the cycle will go ahead?'

'I hope so. Although it has to actually stop raining first.' He brushed foam off his moustache. 'It's okay if it starts somewhere along the route, but they won't set off in heavy rain. If they do, they're in wet gear for the day. My daughter is supposed to be doing it; my two daughters are here, as a matter of fact.'

I mentioned the two women with the toddler I'd seen heading into the pub that morning and immediately his face lit up. 'Yes, that's them. Lissa and Sue. They're both back at the guesthouse with the chiseller.'

A loud guffaw drew my attention back to the tables at the rear. A large man had appeared beside Derek, appearing to dwarf him, and dominating the conversation across both tables with expansive hand gestures, making everyone laugh. There was a slim, blonde woman with him. I wondered if this was Derek's brother and his wife.

'It must feel good, doing a cycle like this, doing something useful,' I remarked.

'Maybe.' Jude took another drink from his pint and placed it back on the bar with the four-tap routine. 'My mother had Alzheimer's. She died a few years back and the girls have raised money ever since. It did seem to help them get over her death.'

My first thought was, what a coincidence: first Derek and now Jude with family members suffering from dementia. Then it hit me: most people involved in the cycle had probably been affected in some way by the illness they were raising money for.

'I'm sorry,' I said.

Jude gave me a wry look. 'We've moved past that, on to the next crisis. Lissa's little boy is sick too – he has childhood leukaemia. It's Sue who's doing the cycle. Lissa wouldn't be able to.'

'God, it sounds like you've had a rough time of it.'

Jude rubbed his eyes. 'Ah, the young fella is doing well. We think he'll be okay.' He had dark circles as if he didn't sleep well. 'But Lissa's bastard of a husband has just left her. As soon as there was any talk of bone marrow donation, he couldn't handle it.' He shook his head and looked down into his glass. 'People always can disappoint you, can't they? You think you have the measure of them, and they go even lower.'

I said nothing, feeling a little awkward, standing there holding Maeve's drink, ice gradually melting in the glass. I glanced down at my own table and saw that Maeve was on her feet. I realised that she might have left by the time I got back.

Jude cleared his throat, noticing my discomfort. 'Don't mind me.' He closed one eye and nodded at his glass with a half-smile. 'Too much of this. Oversharing with a stranger. Not a good look.'

Before I could respond someone clapped him loudly on the back. 'Not going to join us, Julian?' It was the large man from the back table.

The sweaty sheen on the man's brow showed that Jude wasn't the only one who'd had a bit to drink. But he had surprisingly clear blue eyes, his polo shirt almost the same shade, the effect only slightly marred by the stomach straining over his belt. Overweight but handsome, a touch of the playboy gone to seed.

But Jude's face had hardened. He didn't meet the man's eye. 'I'm fine here, thank you.'

'Ah go on. You're here, aren't you? Don't be standing all on your own. Come and have a bit of craic.' The man noticed me for the first time and held out his hand. 'Hello. I'm Bob Jameson.'

I introduced myself and was rewarded with another firm handshake. So, this was Derek's brother. At a push I could see that their features weren't dissimilar.

'You've a grand town here,' he said with a twinkle. 'Lovely part of the world, Donegal.'

His accent was different to his brother's, with an infusion of upper-class English, making me recall Liam's bus comment. I glanced down at the man's red trousers, brown boat shoes and striped socks and pictured him having the contents of his wash-bag thrown at him the night before.

'Plus, they serve an excellent pint,' he added, raising his voice and his hand at Tony who responded with a thumbs up.

'You've made a friend there,' I said.

'Good sign of a town, a decent pint.'

Jude had turned away and was morosely calling another drink. Bob glanced briefly at his back before returning his attention to me. 'So what do you do?'

'I'm a solicitor.'

His eyes narrowed in amusement. 'Are you really?'

Derek appeared, beside his brother. 'Two more Cokes needed.' He shot me a smile.

Bob turned to include him and do the introductions. 'Derek, this is Ben, the local Perry Mason. Ben, this is my brother Derek, the runt of the family.'

I was impressed that he remembered my name, even more so that he got it right first time. Most people had to ask twice.

'We've met,' Derek said. 'As a matter of fact, it was Ben I was trying to have a conversation with yesterday while you were sounding your horn at me.'

Bob raised his eyebrows and bowed an apology. 'I am most sorry for my rudeness.'

While Bob ordered a round and Derek waited to help him carry it, I took the opportunity to leave and go back to our table. I was glad to see that Maeve was still there, although Marina had left without saying goodbye, which seemed a little odd. Maeve must have been standing up to let her out. Maybe she had gone to meet Harry, since it was her last night.

I slipped back into my seat and Phyllis nodded towards Jude, on his own again at the bar, the two brothers having returned to their seats. 'Did you get much chat out of him?'

'A bit.' I passed Maeve her drink. 'Why?'

'He seems like a nice man. He's been in the shop twice, bought at least six books but I can't get two words out of him.'

Liam's amused voice cut across us. 'Jesus, that man must be steaming!'

The estate agent raised his eyebrows and we followed his gaze towards the back of the pub where Bob Jameson was giving his wife a kiss, at least I assumed the blonde was his wife. It seemed to go on forever and when they finally came up for air, he began rubbing her hair while he chatted to the others at the table.

Maeve smirked. 'Looks as if he's grooming a horse.'

Phyllis nudged me. 'Speaking of love's young dream . . .'

Molloy was standing at the edge of our table with a soft smile etched on his face.

My stomach turned over. In a good way, a very good way. I stood up and he reached for me and gave me a hug. I was stunned. Normal affectionate behaviour from Molloy! Had someone been giving him lessons?

He offered me a drink, which I turned down since I was starting to line them up; I'd been left two by clients while I'd been fetching Maeve's 7Up. And when he returned from the bar with a beer, Phyllis shunted over to make space for him beside me in a way which wasn't obvious in the slightest.

He clinked my glass. 'I'm glad you're back. I was afraid you wouldn't be,' he said in a low voice.

'Really?' I took a sip from my drink. 'It was only ever for six months.'

But I didn't meet his eye. I was being disingenuous; the truth was that when I'd left, I hadn't been sure. And while Molloy and I had stayed in touch with texts and phone calls, we hadn't discussed anything directly. Nothing was resolved. His proposal hung there like a bare lightbulb between us, demanding an answer.

But this wasn't the time for questions or answers. I was back with my friends and it felt good. With a surge of unexpected contentment, I realised that's what the people around the table had become, almost without my noticing, friends. Although Maeve, as predicted, had to get up and go to a calving about half an hour later, the evening was fun. Phyllis provided the food she'd promised, hugely welcome when it arrived. And when the party broke up, Liam stayed for a last pint while Phyllis departed discreetly, leaving Molloy and I standing alone on the doorstep of the pub.

I brushed some non-existent lint from my jeans. 'I need to get a taxi.'

Molloy looked at me, hands in the pockets of his coat. 'I could give you a lift. I haven't been drinking.'

'I thought you had a beer?'

'Non-alcoholic. Tony's got a new range in.' He smiled. 'They're not bad.'

'Okay.' I hesitated. Maybe it was the fact that I *had* been drinking, but I asked, 'Will you stay?'

He arched an eyebrow. 'If you want me to.'

I nodded. At that moment I couldn't imagine anything I wanted more. To hell with it, I thought – let's not overthink it. For tonight anyway.

Chapter Seven

A phone rang, slicing through my consciousness. My eyes opened and blearily I looked at the luminous figures on the clock on my bedside table. It was 4.27 a.m. I reached my hand out of bed and felt about for my phone until I registered that what I was hearing wasn't my ringtone. Seconds later I realised that I wasn't in my bed in Sarasota either and I wasn't alone. Molloy was beside me and it was his phone that was ringing.

By the time I'd figured all of this out he'd already picked up. 'Yes? What is it?' His voice was sleepy.

I switched on the light to watch him run his hand through his hair, propping himself up on the pillow, and felt a wave of happiness on seeing him there. We'd fallen asleep with our arms around one another, no conversation, just a weird contentment.

But now, there was a pause and he frowned. I heard a voice on the other end, shouting, I thought. Outside probably, in the rain. I was blearily aware that it was raining again, drops splattering against the bedroom window.

'Where exactly are you?' he said. Another pause. Then, 'I'll be there as soon as I can.'

Molloy put the phone back on the locker and lifted the duvet to climb out of bed. I looked at him quizzically.

'McFadden,' was all he said as he dressed rapidly in the gloom of the bedside lamp.

I sat up. 'McFadden what?'

But he shook his head. 'I'll give you a call when I can. Get some sleep.'

And then he was gone. I heard his footsteps on the stairs and the door slam, leaving me wide awake, alone and uneasy. I turned on my phone. It beeped immediately with a text from Maeve, sent two minutes ago. I read it in disbelief.

I know you're probably asleep, but I've just had a body fall onto the jeep. A body! I'm at Mamore Gap. McFadden's here and he's just called Molloy. WTF??

I sat jerk upright in the bed and rang her back straight away, but she didn't answer. So I got out of bed, pulled on some clothes and a waterproof jacket and ran outside, grabbing, as I left the house, a newspaper that Marina had left in the hall.

I just about managed to catch Molloy. He was on his phone again and starting his car. He must have made some extra calls between my bed and the footpath or he'd have been well gone. I knocked on the window in the rain, the newspaper on my head, and he looked up, worried and exasperated. Expressions I'd seen more than once when he looked at me.

He rolled down the window. 'Go back inside. You'll get soaked.'

I screwed up my face. He was right. 'Can I come with you? I know what's happened and I know it's Maeve – she's just texted me.'

He looked at me doubtfully, hand on the key in the ignition.

'I might be able to help. She's going to be upset and I'll be able to calm her down.'

A moment passed.

'Come on,' I pleaded. 'She's my friend.' Rain streamed down my face. The newspaper was disintegrating. Why hadn't I put my bloody hood up? I was still half-asleep, that's why.

'Okay,' he said finally. 'Get in then.'

I ran over to the passenger side before he changed his mind, and climbed in, just before he pulled away. We circled the green and crossed the old ten-arched bridge, through the pelting rain, windscreen wipers going constantly.

'Bloody hell. Is it ever going to stop?' Molloy said. 'It's like Noah's ark.'

I chucked the sopping newspaper into the back seat. 'That's what Phyllis said. Biblical.'

We drove towards Glendara along the coast, past McSheffrey's Bridge, the mudflats and the ruined thatched cottage, then over another bridge where we turned right, crossing a fourth almost immediately. For the first time it struck me how many bridges there were in Inishowen – usually it was the sea that dominated.

Visibility was lousy and the roads were a quagmire; the head-lights illuminated branches, weeds and other debris being swept along in the swollen rainwater. Twice we stopped at a huge body of water, unsure if we could make it to the other side, but with no option but to try. Some routes were barely passable and if it kept raining the way it had been, I suspected they wouldn't be for long.

When we hit the main Ballyliffin road, we turned right, driving out past the golf links, then on towards Clonmany where the square was almost entirely under water. After the village, Molloy indicated to turn left before Urris GAA Club.

'I always go right to Mamore,' I remarked.

He glanced over at me briefly, the windscreen wipers reflecting on his face. 'I think the higher road is a better option tonight, don't you?'

He had a point. The 24-kilometre journey from Malin to Mamore Gap had already taken us half an hour. I wanted to ask him more about what McFadden had said, but I suspected he knew little more than I did at this stage, and his expression didn't invite chat.

Fields fell away on either side as we drove through the valley. I was glad we were in Molloy's car rather than the Mini and I was glad he was driving; keeping the car on the road can't have been easy in the pitch black. At some point it stopped raining, but silence remained between us as he focused on the road ahead.

Eventually we passed lights and a couple of houses and we turned left, heading again into blackness. I knew the route snaked ahead before cutting through the hill but could see only as far as the headlights permitted. We passed the sign saying *Fáilte go fod duchais an amhráin Grásta Iontach. You are welcome to Amazing Grace country*, and I recalled the story of John Newton. Tonight it was easy to imagine the storm he'd experienced. Molloy's grip was tight on the wheel.

Eventually, the road climbed with rocky outcrops high on either side. We emerged from a particularly severe hairpin bend and suddenly I saw flashing blue lights. The shrine and St Columcille's holy well appeared to one side, like a hologram, eerie in the headlights. A crunch of stones beneath the car and we were here: Mamore Gap.

I squinted, trying to see shapes and figures as we pulled into the little parking area. Molloy glanced across at me. I knew that look – it was his 'stay put' look – like the glare you'd give a pet before crossing the road. But I ignored it and we climbed out of the car at the same time.

Banks loomed high above us on either side. As we approached, I saw that the squad car was parked at an odd angle across the narrow road. Its headlights were on full and immediately ahead of it was Maeve's jeep with a cordon around it and a tarpaulin thrown across the front. Jesus, was Maeve's jeep a crime scene? Beside the jeep's right front wheel, lying in between the two vehicles and illuminated by the squad car's lights, was some more plastic sheeting, another tarp, covering something. McFadden was alongside in his waterproofs as if standing guard. He was on the phone.

Molloy made straight for McFadden, who looked relieved to see him. He waved at me and indicated the squad car where Maeve was sitting in the passenger seat. When I opened the door, she had her head in her hands.

'Are you all right?' I asked softly.

She jumped as if I'd given her a fright. She was paler than I'd ever seen her, her lips almost blue. Wordlessly she indicated the back seat and so I opened the rear door and got in.

'Did you call Charlie?'

She nodded. 'He wanted to come but I didn't want him to wake the boys.'

'What on earth happened?' I asked.

She twisted around to look at me. 'Just what I said in my text. I was on my way back to Clonmany and I heard a loud thump. I was blinded for a second, but I knew something had hit the windscreen.' She took a deep shuddering breath. 'I thought at first it was a large bird, an eagle or something. I knew it couldn't have been an animal – it seemed to come from above.'

'From above the road?' I rubbed the window of the car and tried to peer out. There were high rocky banks on this side where the road had been cut through, but I couldn't see clearly enough in the dark.

'I think so. But it was just so shocking. It was like I'd been attacked. I swerved and pulled in straight away. As soon as I stopped shaking, I got out of the jeep to have a look, in case something was hurt.' Her voice quivered.

'Go on,' I said gently.

'It was a man, a middle-aged man. Dead.' Her voice went up a notch and her eyes welled. 'And then I thought, fuck, did I run him over? Was it my fault he was dead?' But no, I'm certain it was a body that landed on the car, not a person.' Her voice lowered to a whisper as her eyes widened in renewed horror. 'The windscreen cracked.'

I reached out to touch her arm between the two front seats. 'What did McFadden say?'

'He says he's no expert, but he thinks the man's been dead for a while. That I wasn't the one that killed him. Thank Christ. I mean, I knew that; I didn't think I had, but it was good to have it confirmed.'

'So what happened to him then? Did he just . . .'

She shook her head in disbelief. 'I think he rolled down the hill. I know that sounds crazy, but I think it must have been the rain. There's rain coming down the hills and dislodging all sorts. Landslides. Rocks and everything. I was hit by a flying fertiliser bag yesterday, scared the bejaysus out of me.' She gave a wry look. 'I thought I was scared then.'

I looked out the window again, but I still couldn't see anything, just Molloy and McFadden talking to one another with the tarpaulin at their feet. McFadden began taking pictures on his phone. And as I watched, Molloy took out his own phone and made a call.

Maeve was still speaking, almost as if she was talking to herself. 'He must have been lying up there and the rain washed him down. That's all I can think. I mean, there's no one else about. I hadn't met another car for an hour. No one's out in this weather that doesn't have to be.'

'So he just fell on your jeep as you were passing?'

She gave a weak smile. 'Lucky me, eh?'

'At least he was found. If he was lying dead up there, he might have been there for a while before anyone came across him. Nothing but sheep.'

Maeve hugged herself with a shiver. 'I wonder how long he was there.'

The passenger door opened, and Molloy's face appeared, looking worried. 'We have a problem. We're trying to get a pathologist up here. The State Pathologist's Office never want us to move a body before they get here but the road from Strabane to Derry is flooded . . .'

'Uh oh,' I said. 'That's not good.'

'We're hoping to get some extra backup from Letterkenny too, but we have the same problem there. The roads are impassable. So we'll have to stay put until someone can get here.' He looked at Maeve. 'Are you okay to stay?'

She nodded silently.

'Do you know who it is?' I asked.

Molloy nodded. 'He had ID on him. A wallet in his pocket with cash, a driver's licence and credit cards. His name is Bob Jameson.'

I looked up, my eyes wide. 'I met him last night in the Oak. He's part of that Malin to Mizen charity cycle. I think he might be the head honcho.'

'Right. Well that's something at least.' Molloy narrowed his eyes as if trying to recollect if he'd seen the man himself. 'Large man? Blue shirt?'

'Yes. That's him.'

'I think someone pointed him out to me. Do you know anything else about him? Family?'

'His brother and wife are here too. They're all staying in Mary's guesthouse in Glendara.'

'Okay, good. We'll need to get a medic of some sort out here as soon as possible. Because we're going to have to move the body soon. We can't leave it out here in this. It could rain again any second.'

'What about Harry?' I suggested.

'Already done,' Molloy said. 'He's on his way.'

Chapter Eight

Harry arrived within about twenty minutes. I half-expected Marina to be with him – she hadn't returned to my cottage in Malin so I assumed she'd stayed with him – but he arrived alone. He parked behind Molloy's car, then exchanged a few words with Molloy and McFadden before approaching the body. He glanced briefly in the direction of the squad car, brow furrowed, but if he saw me, he gave no indication. We hadn't spoken since our little interlude last summer. He'd kept his distance before I left, and the only time I'd clapped eyes on him since my return was the morning before with Marina.

I knew enough about Molloy to stay out of the way, so I watched from the squad car with Maeve. Harry stood for a few seconds, hands on his hips, looking around him as if taking in the scene, then he knelt, gently removing the tarpaulin. There was a sharp intake of breath from Maeve when the man's face came partially into view, though it was just for a second. Though difficult to tell in the harsh glow of the squad car's lights, it looked as if it was smeared with mud. We watched silently as Harry lifted the man's wrist to check for a pulse and then moved to his chest, pushing aside the collar of what looked like a red waterproof golfing jacket and placing his finger and thumb on the man's neck. Necessary formalities, though it was obvious the man was dead if he'd fallen on Maeve's windscreen.

Then something unexpected: Harry lifted the man's wrist again, but this time it was the hand he examined, turning it carefully to the left and right. He touched the skin with his gloved fingers, peering curiously.

'What's he doing?' Maeve said, echoing my thoughts.

'I don't know. Is there something on his hand?'

Maeve was beginning to look decidedly queasy. 'I wonder how he died.'

I shrugged. 'Heart attack? With no one here to help him, he'd have probably died very quickly.'

I was trying to make her feel better, but the truth was I hadn't a clue, and there was no fooling the vet. She shot me a sceptical look. 'He was hardly out for a stroll in this kind of weather. It's barely stopped raining since yesterday.'

'True.'

'And he was in the pub last night so he must have ended up here after that. I don't know about you but a midnight stroll along Mamore Gap in the bucketing rain wouldn't be my idea of a post-prandial constitutional.'

'No, fair enough.' Of course, she was right. 'So how did he get up here then?' I asked. 'You said you hadn't met another car for an hour. There's nothing parked here, is there?'

She shook her head. 'Not on the road anyway. And the banks are too high and rocky to drive up so he couldn't have gone off road.'

'So, he was dumped here?' I said. 'Someone drove him out here and left him?'

'That seems the only possibility to me,' Maeve said darkly. 'Before or after he died, I wonder?'

I shivered. Dead or alive, to be left on this bleak hill in this relentless rain seemed brutal and personal.

Half an hour later I was back at my cottage, having been despatched there by McFadden on Molloy's orders. McFadden had needed to return to Glendara anyway to collect evidence bags and a tent from the Garda Station, so he'd dropped me on his way.

I closed my front door with a sigh of relief, made a pot of tea and sat at my kitchen table with Guinness curled up on my lap, grateful for his company. It was 5.30 a.m. but I was wide awake, nerves jangling. I couldn't tell if it was jet lag or shock. What an ending to the charity cycle, I thought. Postponed twice because of the weather and then the organiser is, what? Killed? Murdered?

A post-mortem was obviously needed, but it had to be delayed until the pathologist could get here, so Hal McKinney, the undertaker, was to collect the body and take it to the morgue at Glendara Community Hospital. McFadden was to accompany it back into town after he'd left me home while Molloy stayed to take photographs and carry out a cursory search of the area. He was anxious to do it before it started to rain again, and evidence was lost.

As Maeve's jeep was evidence, it had to be impounded for examination whenever the Garda tech bureau managed to get here, so a tow truck was coming to move it. In the meantime, she'd have to use her husband's car to do calls, though she was relieved to be allowed to take essential drugs and equipment out of the jeep. I'd offered her a bed, but Harry wanted to speak to her so McFadden said he'd drop her home too. Poor Andy would be on the road for the rest of the night.

As I poured myself a second cup of tea, the memory of Harry

paying such close attention to the dead man's hand refused to shift and I wondered if it would come up in his conversation with Maeve. I checked my phone but there was nothing. There had been nothing from Molloy since I'd got home. I presumed I wouldn't see him again tonight.

I rubbed the top of Guinness's head and he purred, showing I was finally forgiven, which was something, I supposed. He stretched luxuriously on my lap and I finally felt a wave of tiredness wash over me. Maybe I'd be able to sleep now. I put the cat into his bed in the back kitchen and wearily climbed the stairs to my unmade bed. The last thing I registered before I drifted off was the rain pelting off the roof.

The following morning it was pouring again, the gutters dripping loudly outside my window. Guinness stretched again when I opened the door to the back kitchen, wrapping himself repeatedly around my legs as I tried to make some breakfast. All was back to normal in one area of my life, at least.

Still reeling from the events of the night before, it took me a while to work out that it was Saturday morning, the day I'd normally head into Glendara to pick up the newspapers. But looking out at the streaming rain, it seemed more appealing to stay put. Plus, I had no car – the Mini was in town where I'd left it the night before. So, I lit the fire and made a pot of coffee instead.

I'd just finished my first mug and was back in the kitchen seeking a second when I heard a key turn in the front door. It gave me a jolt, until I remembered it must be Marina. She was due to leave today and go back to Sligo.

She appeared in the doorway of the kitchen pulling off her waterproof jacket, her face tense. 'Morning.'

'Morning,' I replied. 'Another beautiful day in Inishowen.'

She smiled tightly. 'It's a bit damp all right.'

'Coffee?' I offered, indicating the pot.

She looked relieved. 'Yes please.'

I poured her a cup and she took a seat at the table while I stood at the sink to make another pot. In my peripheral vision I saw Guinness make his way over to her and she leaned down to rub his head. The silence between us seemed strained. Was she expecting me to be upset with her for staying out overnight?

I put the kettle on to boil and turned. 'I presume if you stayed at Harry's, you know what happened last night?'

She looked up, surprised and then sheepish. 'Yes, yes I do. I'm sorry. I should have told you I was seeing him. He said you wouldn't care but I felt a bit strange about it, when you used to go out with him. I mean there I was, working in your office, staying in your house and . . .'

'And making friends with my cat.' I smiled. Guinness was rubbing himself enthusiastically against her shins. 'Honestly, don't worry about it. There was never anything serious between me and Harry – it was only ever a bit of fun. If you like each other I'm pleased, for both of you.'

She breathed out, tension leaching out of her face. 'I do like him, a lot.' She frowned again. 'He was very shaken up when he came back earlier.'

'I'll bet – it was pretty shocking. Poor Maeve got the brunt of it, of course. You heard the poor man fell on her jeep?'

Marina nodded. 'Harry said he thought there was something strange about it, but he wouldn't tell me what it was.'

'About how he died?' I asked.

'I think so.' She shrugged. 'Although when I asked, he said that was a matter for the post-mortem and that it was up to the guards to release information when they're ready.'

'I saw him look very closely at the man's hand. I wonder if it was anything to do with that?'

'His hand?' Marina's eyes narrowed. 'Were you there?'

'Sorry, yes. Maeve texted me.' I turned to spoon coffee into the pot. I chose not to mention Molloy for some reason, though if Marina had come back the night before, there was a good chance she'd have seen him at breakfast. I poured boiling water into the pot and stirred it up.

I realised Marina had been silent for a few seconds. When I turned around, she was pale, hand over her mouth.

'Did you see anything else?' she asked.

I shook my head. 'Only what I've said. The body was covered. Why?'

Marina frowned. 'Harry seemed very disturbed. He made a beeline for some medical books when he came in, started looking at pictures on the internet on his phone.'

'But he didn't say why or what it was that was bothering him?' I joined her at the table.

'I think he was being very careful not to say too much, kept saying he was a GP not a pathologist.'

I sighed. Harry was right. I guessed I'd have to wait with everyone else to find out. Marina's reaction to Harry's upset showed that she cared about him. I poured her a top-up. 'Are you heading back to Sligo today?'

She made a face. 'If I can. I don't know what state the roads are in.' She glanced at the window. 'It's only drizzling now, but I think what fell yesterday is the problem.'

I nodded. 'The pathologist couldn't get here last night. I don't know if she's managed it today.'

The rain did seem to have eased off and I was beginning to come around to the idea of heading into Glendara after all, if only to see what was happening. Curiosity was getting the better of me. But then it always did.

Marina stood up, mug in hand. 'Anyway, I'd better go up and pack, on the off chance I actually get to travel. Do you mind if I take this up with me?'

'Of course not.' I tried not to think about how many half-drunk mugs of coffee might be in my spare bedroom. I hadn't been able to find my favourite *Trust me, I'm a lawyer* mug since I'd got back. 'I think I might brave it into Glendara to get a newspaper, considering I haven't seen an Irish weekend paper for six months.'

'Be careful of the road at the turn off to Culdaff,' she said in the doorway. 'There's quite a lake there. You don't want to flood the Mini.'

'Noted.' I didn't bother to tell her my car was in town, but I was surprised she hadn't noticed its absence from outside the house. I called Glendara Taxis.

As the taxi circled the village, I could see what darkness had cloaked the night before: the green was saturated, park benches and trees emerging from it as if from a swamp. And on the way into town I saw that Marina was right, the entire route was awash, rain running off the roads in streams and rivulets, the fields below waterlogged, sheep standing mournfully on any patches of higher ground.

At McSheffrey's Bridge, the turn off for Culdaff, there was a wide junction with a slight dip where a huge amount of water had gathered. Without the wall it would have been hard to distinguish between rainwater and sea.

Jack, the taxi driver, drove through it at a snail's pace, clicking his teeth as he did so. 'We're going to have trouble. This water isn't going anywhere.'

I looked at his concerned face from the passenger seat. 'Surely it'll clear eventually?'

He shook his head. 'There's nowhere for it to go. There's been too much of it. All night it's been raining in those heavy blasts. It's wile dangerous to drive in, so it is.'

We emerged from the flood and he changed gear, causing a cigarette lighter he'd left on the dashboard to skitter across when he speeded up. 'I hear one of the visitors died last night.'

I nodded. 'So I gather.'

'Heart attack, was it?'

So, the full story wasn't out yet, I thought. I responded, 'No idea.'

Jack drummed his yellowed fingers on the steering wheel. 'I drove that man back to Mary's last night. He looked like a heart attack waiting to happen, to be honest . . .'

I leaned forward with interest. 'Why do you say that?'

He shrugged. 'Ach, carrying a fierce pile of weight so he was . . . big pink face on him.'

'Was he on his own?'

'No. His wife was with him and another man. Thinner fella with a limp.'

I made a mental note to pass this information on to Molloy. As I did, Jack frowned as if something had just occurred to him.

'What the hell was he doing out by Mamore Gap?'

Glendara hadn't fared any better than Malin. It was sodden. The footpaths were slick; water dripped heavily from the drainpipes and guttering and ran in gullies down the street. Unusually for a Saturday morning, the square was deserted. People had obviously decided to prop their sopping feet in front of their warm fires, those with sense at any rate. I, on the other hand, picked my way, slipping and sliding along the footpath, and into Stoop's newsagent.

Stoop himself was leaning with his elbows on the counter staring glumly at the door, his expression unchanged when he saw me. And before I even had a chance to say good morning, he said, 'No papers. No delivery this morning.'

'Which papers?' I asked.

'All of them. Any of them. Local or national. The delivery van couldn't get through – or didn't bother. One or the other. Anyway, I have no papers to sell. On a Saturday morning.'

'Oh.' I was genuinely disappointed. I'd been looking forward to the Saturday supplements, my first helping in a while, of the Irish ones at any rate.

Stoop shook his head, reading my expression. 'You're not the only one. Mary was in first thing. I thought she was going to cry – never misses her *Indo*, that woman. Mind you,' the newsagent brightened somewhat, 'she has enough drama going on up at the guesthouse. You heard what happened out at Mamore last night?'

I nodded. 'I did. Awful.'

'Snakebite,' Stoop said with satisfaction.

'What did you say?' I couldn't have heard him right.

'That's how the man died. He was bitten by a poisonous snake.' Stoop repeated each word as if I was deaf or dim or both, straightening himself to his full height, which legend indicated was about six foot four. 'We're all to be vigilant because there's a snake on the loose.'

I was stunned. 'Where did you hear that?'

He gestured towards an old transistor radio humming away on a shelf above the ice-cream machine. 'Highland Radio had it, just five minutes gone. The guards released a statement to warn people to look out.' He scowled. 'Someone must have been keeping the feckin' wee thing as a pet. All sorts of lunatics out there.'

I kicked myself for not turning on the radio or asking the taxi driver to do it. Trust Stoop to be first with the news, even if he didn't have any newspapers to sell.

He lowered his voice. 'Isn't that rare? A snake on the loose in Inishowen? So much for St Patrick driving them all out of Ireland.'

I made my way back to the Mini, still parked in the square where I'd left it the night before, remembering again Harry's close examination of the dead man's hand. Was that where he'd been bitten? Relieved when the car started first time, after a bit of shudder, I decided to call into the Garda Station.

McFadden looked up from his computer, tired and red-eyed, when I pushed open the door. He couldn't have had much sleep: the last time I'd seen him was at 5 a.m. and he still had several trips to make. It was now ten and he was back (or still) on duty.

I dispensed with all preliminaries. 'Bob Jameson was killed by a snake?'

McFadden frowned. 'Where did you hear that?'

'Stoop told me he heard it on Highland Radio.'

'Stoop's making a bit of a leap,' McFadden said. 'What we actually said was that a man's body was found last night at Mamore Gap, and that we wanted people to be vigilant, and contact us if there were any sightings of a snake.'

I gave him a wry look. 'I suppose you can't blame people for adding two and two together and getting five.' I paused. 'So was Bob Jameson bitten then?'

McFadden nodded. 'Aye, he was. On his hand.' His brow was

furrowed. 'So Dr Harry tells us. He's seen snakebites over in Canada, so he recognised it.'

I knew Harry had worked in both Canada and the States. His mother was from Inishowen but he'd grown up in Canada. 'But you don't know if that was what killed him?' I asked.

McFadden took a deep breath, choosing his words carefully. 'What Harry said was that from what Maeve told him, it looked as if the man was dead when he hit her jeep, that he couldn't find any broken bones and that it appears as if the man *was* bitten by a snake at some point. But we don't know if it was a poisonous snake that bit him, or if it was the bite that killed him. We can't tell anything without blood tests, which can't be done until the pathologist gets here.'

'Right.'

McFadden rested his head on his hands; he looked as if he could easily drift off if he was allowed to. 'The doctor's being very careful to say that we have to wait for the post-mortem. But we can't afford to take any risks if there's a poisonous snake out there. We have to let people know.'

'So, we don't know what kind of snake it was?'

The guard shook his head wearily. 'Not a clue.'

Questions tumbled through my mind one after the other. Where had the snake come from? And why would it bite? I'd thought snakes were generally not aggressive. In Florida I'd been told that they were usually as scared of us as we were of them, or more so.

Before I had a chance to ask any of this, McFadden spun his computer around. He was looking at a website with images of poisonous snakes.

'I'm to do up some posters with pictures so people will know to be careful and call us if they see anything.' He tutted to himself. 'Seems a bit pointless to me. It's not as if we're so used to having non-poisonous snakes about the place that we'd be able to tell by the marking if it was harmful or not. A snake's a snake as far as an Irish person is concerned.'

McFadden was right. We have no native snakes in Ireland at all. Not even a harmless grass snake. He pointed at the screen, to a photograph of a two-foot-long snake with red, yellow and black stripes. 'Look at this one.'

'He's colourful,' I said.

'It's a coral snake. *Red to yellow, kill a fellow, red to black, venom lack,*' he rhymed.

'What?'

McFadden gave me a half smile. 'It's a saying apparently, to determine whether he's poisonous or not.'

I looked again at the picture. The red and yellow stripes were next to one another. 'Hopefully he's not in the vicinity.'

'Or this boy.' He pointed to another snake, an olive-coloured creature with dark brown scales. 'This one is the Inland Taipan, poisonous enough to kill 100 people or 250,000 mice.'

'Yikes.'

McFadden was getting a taste for this.

I crossed my arms, still trying to take it in; a snakebite, in Inishowen. It did suggest a new possibility, though, as far as the death was concerned. 'So could the death have been accidental, then? Bob Jameson was just unlucky enough to come across a snake that had escaped from somewhere?'

McFadden shook his head. 'The sergeant doesn't think so. It's not as if he would have been out for a stroll on a night like last night. Plus his car wasn't there, so someone else drove him. And didn't bring him back.'

I leaned on the counter. 'That's what Maeve and I thought, last night. So what was he doing up there, then?'

McFadden gave a little shrug.

I looked around me. 'Where is Molloy, by the way?' It couldn't have escaped McFadden's notice that Molloy and I had arrived together last night, in the early hours, but he made no comment. I supposed he had more pressing things on his mind than gossip.

'He's back at the Gap. Mountain Rescue were helping him do a search of the area, though they've had to call it off for health-and-safety reasons. It's started lashing up there again.' He returned his gaze to the screen.

'Right.'

He looked up from his snake images, as if something had just occurred to him. 'Of course, we should be asking the vet about this, shouldn't we? She'd know about snakes, wouldn't she? What species it might be, where it might have got to, how far it could travel, that kind of thing.'

'Well,' I said slowly. 'She's more of a sheep, cows and horses type of a vet but she might know something. Or know how to find out, at least.'

At that point the door opened, and Molloy came in shaking the rain off his coat.

Chapter Nine

Molloy looked every bit as tired as McFadden. His forehead was creased with lines and he looked more worried than I'd ever seen him, as he dumped his sodden hat on the counter. He was carrying some plastic evidence bags, which he handed to McFadden who logged them and took them to a locked room behind the counter.

'Two bridges are down.' Molloy ran his hand through his damp hair.

'What? Which bridges?' I said.

'Two bridges on either side of Quigley's Point. The bridge past Glentogher at the Riverside Bar and the one on the Muff–Derry road.'

'There's a bridge on the Muff strait?' I asked.

He nodded. 'You wouldn't have known it was there, but now it's broken in two. The bridge at the Riverside Bar has come apart. The road just opened up.' He shook his head, as if he could barely believe it himself.

McFadden emerged from the room behind, looking shocked. 'Is everyone okay?'

Molloy replied wearily, 'Thankfully no one was hurt. But they've closed the Cockhill Bridge on the way into Buncrana

84

too. The river is so swollen, they're afraid it'll engulf the bridge so they've evacuated the houses close by.'

'God, that's awful,' I said.

McFadden locked the door of the back room and returned to his seat. 'So how are people to get home? What about the people that work here in Glendara who live in Buncrana or Derry?'

'Anyone starting work this morning won't have been able to get here,' Molloy said. 'But the night workers, people who work in the hospital, for instance, they won't be going home tonight. We're just going to have to find accommodation for them here. All four major roads into Glendara are impassable. There are trees down, up to a metre of water in some places, and some other bridges are in danger of collapse.' He took a deep breath. 'We are officially cut off.'

'You're kidding?' I said.

'I wish I was.' He counted off the routes on his fingers. 'The road between Glendara and Quigley's Point is inaccessible, between Quigley's Point and Muff, from Muff to Moville is especially dangerous. Road from North Pole Pub to Clonmany is closed . . .'

'So, we're cut off from Derry too?' I asked.

He raised his palms in a gesture of surrender. 'We are completely cut off from everywhere. Farm animals have been washed away, there are abandoned cars all over the place. Burnfoot is filling up, the Coast Guard are there with boats. The Fire Service are doing their best to pump floodwater away, but it's an impossible job. They've been out rescuing people from cars and houses all night.'

I was appalled. This had all been happening while I'd been tucked up in bed.

Molloy dragged a stool over and sank onto it. 'I'm told that we've had a month's worth of rain in the past twenty-four hours.'

'What about the council?' I asked.

'The county council are out trying to fix things as best they can, and we'll have defence force crews to put up temporary bridges as soon as possible. But there's only so much they can do until the rain actually stops.'

I looked towards the door. 'It's stopped now, hasn't it?'

'For the moment, but there's more to come, according to the weather forecast.'

'Jesus Christ,' McFadden said. 'It's apocalyptic.'

Molloy nodded wordlessly as if he'd run out of the energy to speak.

'So where are the extra beds going to come from?' McFadden asked. 'All the B & Bs are booked up with the charity cycle.'

Molloy said exhaustedly, 'We're just going to have to work something out. They've opened up the Foyle Arena in Derry as a rest centre for motorists who can't get home from there, so we'll have to do something similar. The hospital must keep a few beds free in case anyone is injured. So we may have to open up the county council offices or the Beacon Hall and work out something there.' He pressed his hand to his forehead. 'It looks as if we're in trouble.'

McFadden and I were silent. It seemed unnecessary to add that we were already in trouble with an unsolved death and a possible poisonous snake on the loose. There was something that I thought I should share with Molloy about Bob Jameson's death, so I asked if I could have a word with him. He handed McFadden a list of calls to make, and we headed towards the back office.

Molloy closed the door behind him, took off his heavy Garda coat and hung it sopping on the coat rack. I didn't see how it was going to dry before he had to put it back on again. There was a chill in the room, though the heat was on, but the old storage heaters had never been particularly efficient.

He rested his backside on the desk while I stood against the wall, giving me a flashback to the way things had been when we had just been colleagues and friends of a sort. One way or another we'd been part of each other's lives for a long time.

He folded his arms. 'What's up?' he asked.

'Bob Jameson was bitten by a snake?' I said.

He nodded solemnly. 'I know, it sounds incredible. But Dr Harry saw the puncture marks on the hand when he was checking the man's pulse and recognised them as a snakebite. Obviously, there's been no post-mortem yet, so we don't know the cause of death and it may not be the bite. But we have to alert people to the possibility of a poisonous snake in the area, especially with the town being cut off. We can't have kids approaching it.'

'No, I can see that.' I asked Molloy the same question as I'd asked McFadden. 'Is there any possibility that the death was an accident?'

He shook his head. 'Someone drove him out to Mamore Gap and left him there. There was no car there when we arrived, so he didn't drive himself. We know where he died or at least where his body lay at some point.'

I raised my eyebrows.

'We found his other shoe. He was only wearing the one when we found him.'

I gave an involuntary shudder – a sudden image of the body under the tarp came into my head. Was that what was in one of the bags he'd given McFadden? I wondered. 'Where did you find it?'

'On the ridge. The rocky outcrop just above the road,' he said, rubbing his jaw. 'The flood must have washed his body down the hill.'

'And onto Maeve's windscreen.'

'Yes. There seems to have been a bit of a slide. We found mud and stones around the jeep. The floods are causing landslides and earth falls on any steep slopes.'

'How long was he there, do you think?' I asked.

'We're not sure. Another matter for the post-mortem, unfortunately.'

'I suppose it couldn't have been too long if he was in the pub last night.'

'True.'

'A matter of hours.'

Molloy nodded. 'In the meantime, we need to find the bloody snake, just in case it's venomous. Harry told us his suspicions last night, so we did as thorough a search as we could in the conditions, and we could find no sign of it.'

'How far can they travel?'

He shook his head. 'I'm not sure. But I'm not taking any chances. Even if it's completely harmless, we need the creature found. Most snakes aren't normally aggressive, so this one lashed out for some reason.'

'Did you talk to Bob Jameson's family yet?'

Molloy rubbed his eyes, wearily. 'I've just been up at the B & B. His poor wife was in a state already because he hadn't come to bed. She said she went to bed after they came back from the pub, fell asleep, then woke up at the crack of dawn to find that he wasn't there. She wears earplugs apparently. Her husband snored.'

I said, 'Jack from Glendara Taxis drove them all back to the B & B from the pub. Bob and his wife and brother.'

Molloy stared at me.

'He gave me a lift in from Malin this morning to pick up my car,' I explained.

'Good. I'll have a chat with him.' Molloy paused. 'I wondered if maybe they'd had a row, Bob and his wife.'

And with that he'd hit on exactly what I'd wanted to talk to him about. 'Did you speak to Mary?'

Molloy nodded, looking at me curiously. 'Yes, but only briefly. Why?'

I braced myself. 'I probably shouldn't be telling you this but, according to Mary, there was a big row between Bob Jameson and his wife, the night before last, in the B & B.'

Molloy crossed his arms. 'Go on.'

'What's the wife's name?' I asked.

'Amanda.'

'Amanda. Well, there was a row between Bob and Amanda. Mary had to get Bob's brother to intervene.'

Molloy narrowed his eyes. 'What kind of a row?'

'Loud enough to disturb Mary and possibly the other guests. Amanda was throwing things at him apparently, things from their suitcase and washbag. According to Mary he was just taking it.'

Molloy absorbed this for a second. 'So not the love's young dream they were in the pub?'

'You saw them?'

He gave a wry smile. Public displays of affection weren't really Molloy's thing. 'They were hard to miss.'

'Presumably they'd made up by last night.'

'Presumably,' he said. 'But if they were that volatile a couple, maybe I was right about them having a row when they came back? Maybe they're the kind of couple who fight when they drink?' Molloy straightened himself. 'Okay. Thanks for letting me know. It might mean nothing, but we could do with all the help we can get, now.'

89

'That's what I thought. Mary might not be too thrilled with me for telling you, but in the circumstances . . .'

'No, I'm glad you did.' He reached for his coat. He looked set to go. 'She was being very kind to the wife when I left. Amanda wanted to go up to the church, but Mary said she'd call the priest to come down. I'll have a longer chat with her when I get the chance, see what she knows.'

He took his coat from the hook and started to put it on, grimacing as he did so. It must have been still wet.

'And the brother, Derek?' I asked. 'Did you see him?'

'He was there too, comforting Amanda. Distraught too, of course. Can't understand what happened. Has no idea what his brother could have been doing out at Mamore Gap.' Molloy took his phone from the pocket of his coat and wiped it with his sleeve. 'Unhelpfully it's already made the national news.'

He tapped at the screen and handed it to me. Molloy stood at my shoulder while I looked at the front page of the online *Irish Independent*.

I read the headline. *Charities boss Bob Jameson dies in mysterious circumstances in Donegal on eve of charity cycle* . . . I looked up. 'Uh oh.'

'I know,' Molloy said with a sigh. 'We could do without the eyes of the country on us when we don't have the proper personnel to deal with it. He was quite the big wig in the charities sector apparently.'

I scanned the article. 'Chief executive of the charity he founded, for ageing and dementia, with care home in Sligo and Galway. They're raising money for a third in Dublin. That must have been what the cycle was for.'

Molloy added, 'He also headed up a Nigerian charity at one point and he's been on the board of a number of Irish hospitals.'

90

'Yikes. Lots of friends in high places.' I handed the phone back to him. I could read the full article on my own phone or laptop later.

'Exactly,' he said, putting the phone back into his pocket. 'Right. Now I definitely need to get going.'

'Thanks for talking to me about this, I know you didn't have to.'

He took a deep breath. 'I suppose I could do with an extra brain, with us being completely cut off.' I smiled, flattered, until he shot me a half smile. 'Plus, I know you won't be able to resist sticking your nose in anyway so you might as well have the full facts.'

There wasn't much I could say to that. The man had a point.

'We'll do our best to find out what happened to him, look at his background, family and friends, emails, financial transactions, anything that could tell us what occurred in the days leading up to his death. But our priority must be to keep people safe, from the floods and any other threats.'

'Of course.'

'We know he died sometime between quarter to twelve last night when he arrived back at Mary's B & B and four a.m. this morning when he fell on Maeve's jeep. I'll put an appeal out to see if anyone saw anything, but I'm willing to bet that Maeve was one of the few people driving on Mamore Gap on such a dirty night.'

'Apart from the killer. Or killers.'

He nodded wearily as he reached for the door handle. 'Anyway, I'd better get back out here. McFadden's going to need my help.'

He was right. During the ten minutes or so that we'd been talking, I'd heard the station phone ring at least six times.

★★★

I left the Garda Station wondering if I should go to see Mary, to let her know what I'd told Molloy. My intention had been to head back to Malin and spend the day by the fire with the papers, but I had no newspapers, and this was no ordinary Saturday morning.

I drove back up town and parked in the square. It was hard to imagine that we were so completely cut off, though the effects of the past twenty-four hours' rain were impossible to miss. Wherever you looked the surface water levels just kept rising and rising. Suddenly I remembered the leak in the office. Whatever I decided to do, I'd better go there first. God knows what state it was in with all the rain that had fallen since.

Crossing the square, I saw Phyllis standing outside her book-shop, gazing into the distance as if looking for someone. Her face was pinched and anxious.

I called over to her. 'Are you all right?'

She looked up in alarm. 'Oh, Ben, perfect timing – can you give me a hand here?'

I crossed the road and when I reached her, she gestured towards her feet. She'd shoved sandbags against the bookshop door and I immediately saw why; water was lapping about twenty feet away. 'Cripes, Phyllis.'

'I know. The Fire Service gave me those. But that's not going to last too long, not with what's coming.' She was breathless, almost wheezing with panic.

And she was right. The floods were going to reach her sooner rather than later. Like my office, Phyllis's shop was on a slope but at the lower end of the town. Plus, the bookshop itself was on an incline; the floor of her shop dipped at the back. One thing was sure, she didn't have long.

She pushed open the shop door and I followed her in, standing for a second on the threshold to take in the Aladdin's cave that was her bookshop, imagining the devastation if the flood reached the door and water came pouring in.

She looked around her and breathed in. 'I'm going to have to move the books.'

'All of them?' I asked incredulously. There were books everywhere, not just on the shelves but on stray chairs, on stools, piled up on the floor too. Stacks and stacks and stacks of them.

She placed her hands on her hips. 'Aye, as many as I can. I'll move them upstairs to the flat. The flat should be safe enough.' She looked at me quizzically. 'Can you help or are you in the middle of something?'

I shook my head. 'No. Of course I'll help. But it's going to take more than two of us. Shall I call Liam?'

Phyllis nodded, arms already full of books, and making for the winding staircase that led to her flat. 'I have some boxes upstairs. I'll bring them down and we can fill them. That way we can move more at a time.'

There was a knock on the glass of the shop door, and a bearded face appeared. It was Jude, the motorcycle guy from the night before. He pointed to the sandbags. 'Are you closed?'

'Flood danger,' I called back.

'Everything all right? Need any help?'

Phyllis shouted from halfway up the stairs. 'Oh, yes please! Let him in.'

I opened the door and with a tinkle of the bell he was inside.

'You're a life saver,' Phyllis said from the stairs. 'Grab an armful of books, there's a good wee man.' I had to laugh, the man was about six foot four, and broad with it.

It turned out we didn't need to call Liam after all. With the only route upstairs being the narrow winding staircase from bookshop to flat, any more than three people moving books would have been chaos. It took the three of us about two hours to move everything.

By the time we'd finished, Phyllis's flat was almost impossible to navigate with books on every surface, every inch of floor and every stick of furniture, but at least we had saved them all. Every last volume. And the flood was unlikely to reach the first floor, with a bit of luck.

My arms ached as I sat with Jude in Phyllis's sitting room, surrounded by walls of books, having tea and ginger cake, Phyllis's reward for helping out. Fred, Phyllis's dog, was sitting with his head on one of Jude's Doc Martens-clad feet, enjoying the attention and the ear rubs on offer.

Phyllis smiled as she set a second pot of tea on the table. 'Do you have a dog?' she asked.

Jude shook his head. There was a film of sweat on his brow. Like us, he looked done in. 'I used to. A border collie just like this handsome fella. But he died last year.'

'Ach, I'm sorry.' Phyllis managed to convey sympathy as well as amusement at the notion of Fred as handsome. Loveable though he was, having transferred his affection to Phyllis after his previous owner died, Fred had always been a bit of a scruff.

'Ah, he was a good age,' Jude said. 'And it was becoming difficult after the girls moved out. I wanted to travel on the bike, and I couldn't take him with me.'

'You could have got a sidecar.' Phyllis grinned, and I imagined her doing just that with Fred if she ever took up biking. She sat back down on the sofa with a groan. 'So, what about this poor man who died last night? Did you know him well then?'

Jude's smile faded. The hardening of his expression was such a contrast to when he was talking about his dog that it gave me a jolt, and I remembered his frosty exchange with Bob Jameson the night before.

'Not really.' His voice was flat as he returned his cup to its saucer. It looked surprisingly delicate in his large hands. I noticed he tapped it four times just as he'd done with his pint the night before.

'But he was the head of the charity you're raising money for, wasn't he?' Phyllis persisted.

I wondered where she had found this out. I wouldn't have put it past her to be googling like mad as soon as she heard the news. Jude seemed surprised too. But he just nodded.

'There's a piece about his death in the *Independent* this morning,' I said. 'He seems to have been pretty well known.'

'You didn't like him,' Phyllis said, eyeing Jude over her own teacup.

'No, I didn't,' he said finally.

'Why not?'

His tone was cold. 'Let's just say Bob Jameson believed very much in the principle that charity begins at home.'

Phyllis's eyes widened. 'You mean corruption? Embezzlement?'

Jude shook his head. He didn't want to say anything more. Phyllis sat quietly for a few seconds and I wondered if she'd pursue it. But she didn't.

'Still, his wife and brother must be very shocked,' I said eventually. 'It seems likely that his death wasn't an accident.'

Jude bowed his head. 'I'm sure they are, and I'm sorry for them. But I think if they're looking for someone to blame, they're going to have quite a list of people who would have been more than happy to see Bob Jameson dead.'

There was an uneasy pause, broken suddenly by a noise from downstairs, a kind of cracking, creaking noise, followed by the sound of something breaking, and running, gushing water. The three of us stood up simultaneously and made our way to the top of the stairs.

We stood there in shocked silence as dirty rainwater flooded into the shop. I felt Phyllis shudder at my shoulder, and I reached out to touch her hand. We'd been just in time. Fifteen minutes later and all her stock would have been destroyed. Everything from Jackie Collins paperbacks to P. G. Wodehouse first editions.

Chapter Ten

Phyllis loaned me some wellies which were both pink and huge, but they got me across her bookshop floor and the waterlogged square, and back to my car while I left Jude to finish his tea. He and Phyllis had moved on to an enthusiastic travel chat by the time I left. It turned out that Jude had toured quite a bit on his bike, and they'd visited many of the same places.

I turned the key in the ignition – it was time to go and see Mary. I knew I shouldn't have shared what she'd told me with Molloy, but with the town completely cut off I couldn't just sit back and rely on client confidentiality if people were in danger. Whoever had killed Bob Jameson was still in the vicinity. I hoped there was something in the *Guide to Good Professional Conduct for Solicitors* on which I could rely, but I might well have been stretching it. So some damage limitation might be needed.

Mary's guesthouse was half a mile away, on a hill above town, so in little danger of flooding. I drove slowly up the long straight road, hawthorn hedges dripping on either side, with a clear view of the house. It was large, ugly and modern, with chimneys on either side, like rabbit's ears. Built for purpose as a B & B or in anticipation of a much larger family than Mary had ever had, it must have had at least ten bedrooms. Mary had been single for as long as I'd known her; the first hint of a relationship I'd heard was Leah's mention of a broken heart, long in the past.

A garden in front of the house was bounded by a concrete wall and a gate. A sign swinging from a post bore the words *Mary's B & B*. She needed to come up with a better arrangement for her car parking, I thought, it was a little chaotic. There were cars parked all along the front together with Jude's motorbike, which was blocking the entrance to a shed containing another car. He must have walked to the town, I thought, taking advantage of the brief break in the weather. The dead man's black Lexus was there too, the car Derek had been looking for on Thursday afternoon.

I parked beside Jude's bike, which was becoming a bit of a habit, climbed out of the car and pushed open the gate to make my way up the path. A sad row of daffodils and narcissi lay flattened along the front, beaten and battered by the rain. The house may not have been a thing of beauty, but a valiant effort had been made to soften its edges. There were rose bushes on either side of the front door, luckily not yet in bloom or they'd have gone the same way as the daffs.

I rang the bell and, when there was no answer, I knocked on the heavy door knocker. After a few minutes Mary herself came to the door. She was wearing a simple olive-coloured dress, which with her green eyes would have been stunning, were it not for the fact that they were red-rimmed. She had been crying.

'Mary, I'm so sorry,' I said. 'What an awful thing to happen to one of your guests.'

'Shh,' she said quietly. She inclined her head towards a door leading to what I assumed was a guest sitting room. It was shut, but I could hear the hum of voices beyond.

'Sorry,' I said again, hurriedly. Then lower, 'Can I have a quick word?'

She nodded silently, and I followed her down a long hall to the right of the stairs, past a huge, ticking grandfather clock.

The door swung open into an industrial-style kitchen, full of gleaming chrome, spotlessly clean with a scent of lemon. There was a toaster with ten slots, a commercial dishwasher of the kind I remembered from student summer jobs, and various other commercially sized appliances designed to cater for big numbers of breakfasts. I wondered if Mary had a smaller kitchen somewhere for herself, that she could use when it was off season and she was on her own, somewhere she could just sit, have a cup of tea and read the *Irish Independent* she liked so much.

There was a workstation with two stools, and we took them; they were the only seats in the room. A red tea towel neatly folded was moved to one side and Mary looked at me expectantly. I had the sense that she really wanted to be alone.

But I needed to confess. 'I thought I should tell you that I told Sergeant Molloy about the row the other night. I wouldn't normally share something a client told me, but with the town cut off like this and the difficulty of investigating a death like this with no back-up, well, I thought he should have as much information as possible. I'm sorry . . .'

I trailed off when I realised she wasn't listening to me. Her gaze was fixed somewhere on the far wall.

'Mary, did you hear what I said?' I prompted. 'He'll probably ask you about it.'

'That's fine,' she said dully, with a nod. She looked down and slid the tea towel back across in front of her.

I was relieved. She could have been threatening to report me to the Law Society before I'd even managed to get the words out, although that probably wasn't Mary's style.

'Are you okay?' I asked, putting my hand on her arm.

She shook her head and I was shocked to see that her eyes were full.

'He was my first love,' she said quietly.

'Who was?'

'Bob. I thought he'd be my only. I thought we'd get married and have a big family.'

I was lost for words. Was Bob Jameson the man Leah had been talking about? The man who'd broken Mary's heart. The man she'd never got over?

She looked down again, playing with the tea towel, folding one of the corners. 'But then you're stupid when you're young, aren't you?'

'You're not stupid,' I said, 'just a little naive sometimes. We all are.'

As I said it, I was painfully aware that my own experience of first love had been with the man who killed my sister. I *had* been stupid.

'What happened between the two of you?' I asked softly. 'Why didn't it work out?'

She moved her head as if trying to shake some memory loose. 'We met in Dublin when I was doing my nursing training. Bob was in college. We were very young, but we were happy. Had lots of plans to travel, like you do when you're young.' She smiled. 'We were together for five years. Then my mother got sick and I had to come back, my dad couldn't cope. I had to give up the nursing.'

'And Bob?'

She gave a wry smile. 'I had to give up Bob too.' She folded the tea towel again. 'Ach, I probably wasn't good enough for him. He wanted something else, something better . . . I was too rural. Too Donegal.'

'But he must have known you were from Donegal when you met?'

'He did, but I think he didn't anticipate having to live here, and I couldn't leave my parents. I was an only child.' She straightened herself and her tone became more determined. 'Also, I wanted to travel but I wanted to *live* here. I love Inishowen.'

'But you were still in contact?' I asked. 'After all these years?' I remembered McFadden saying that Mary knew someone involved in the cycle, which was why she'd got the gig. Had that someone been Bob Jameson?

'We met again a few years later, after he married Amanda. Since then we've never really broken off contact. Not properly. I was just glad to have him in my life in some way.' She looked up. 'It sounds weak, doesn't it?'

'No. But if he hurt you . . . if he broke your heart?'

She sighed. 'He was young when he made that decision and I think he always regretted it. But by then it was too late. The course was set for both our lives.'

'Regretted getting married, do you mean?'

A tear ran down the side of her mouth and landed on the chrome surface. She rubbed at it with the tea towel. 'Maybe. He married a year after we split up.'

'And what about . . .?'

'Me?' She smiled sadly. 'My parents lived on for ten years, then died within three months of each other. I bought this place and I've been running it ever since.'

She looked around her huge empty kitchen and suddenly I saw her in a new light. I'd always seen Mary as someone who was completely content in her own skin but now I caught a glimpse of her loneliness, a loneliness that she tried to fill with guests. I wondered if her determination to have her guesthouse always full had more to do with not being alone than the money her guests brought in.

I looked at her face, her beautiful ageing face. 'And there's been no one else?'

She smiled through her tears. 'Oh, I've had offers. But I always compared them to Bob, and they came out wanting. So I stayed here, hoping . . .' She trailed off. 'Oh, I don't know what I was hoping.'

She lifted the tea towel and shook it out. She'd made such a mess of it with her fidgeting that it needed refolding. On it was an image of Joseph Stalin and his quote, *When we hang the Capitalists, they will sell us the rope.*

Mary followed my gaze. 'A present from Phyllis, from Georgia. Not America. Caucasus, near Russia,' she added with a half-smile. 'She wanted me to go with her that time, but I was happy here.' The smile became a full one, if still sad. 'I've always been happy here.'

'Did Bob's wife know about your relationship?' I asked hesitantly. It was hard not to think of the row and wonder if they were connected.

Mary shook her head. 'No, she didn't. Doesn't. Bob didn't want her to know. It wasn't as if there was anything . . .' she flushed. 'I mean most of the time it was only a friendship. But it meant a lot to me.'

I considered this. *Most of the time?* Bob and Mary were in their fifties and they'd known each other since college. What did 'most of the time' mean, over a period of thirty years? Whatever their relationship, it seemed certain that Mary's continued contact with the dead man had stopped her moving on and meeting someone else.

I paused. 'Can I tell Molloy this, Mary? Or will you?'

She nodded. 'Go ahead. I want to help find out what happened to him.' She mustered a weak smile. 'But ask him to be discreet, will you?'

I saw myself out, leaving her to pull herself together for her guests. She still had the cycling group staying with her, including Bob's grieving family, plus she was managing on her own since the Buncrana girl who worked for her hadn't been able to get in because of the floods.

As I walked back up the hallway, the door to the sitting room opened, giving me a bit of a shock. Derek Jameson stood on the threshold, with his back to me, finishing up whatever he was saying to whoever remained in the room. I stopped and stood there uneasily, feeling that I couldn't just walk out and close the front door while he was there. Eventually he turned, saw me, came the rest of the way out into the hall and closed the door behind him with a soft click.

I offered my condolences. He looked grey and shaken, his mouth set, with none of the spark and humour I'd seen outside Phyllis's bookshop two days before.

He thanked me and looked down. 'I've just been helping Amanda ring their kids.'

'That can't have been easy.' It hadn't occurred to me that Bob and his wife would have kids, but of course it was more likely than not. I noticed Mary had chosen not to mention them.

'It wasn't.'

'How old are they?'

'Twenty-one and nineteen – two boys. The younger one's hysterical. The awful thing is that they can't be with their mother because the roads are impassable.'

I looked at his face. 'Are there any other aunts or uncles who can take them in? Grandparents?'

He shook his head. 'They have no relatives to speak of. I'm their father's only sibling and Amanda was an only child. Both sets of grandparents are dead.'

'That's hard. For all of you.'

He smiled weakly. 'We're twins, did I tell you that? Bob and I. I know we don't look alike but we've had very different lifestyles.' Like most people recently bereaved, he used the present tense, and I didn't correct him. 'We started out looking quite similar.'

'No, I didn't know that.'

There was silence between us for a few seconds, then he raised his head and looked at the ceiling. His eyes were wet. 'I feel so bloody guilty. This blasted cycle was my idea and it's been a disaster since the beginning. First the weather and then this. And now we're stuck here, in this wretched place, in the middle of nowhere and Bob's kids can't even get to him.'

I decided not to mention that he'd previously expressed a desire to return to Inishowen. I guess a place takes on a different feel if your brother is murdered there. Instead I delivered the usual 'if there's anything I can do' line and left him to head up the stairs on whatever errand he was on, quietly shutting the front door and taking myself back down the path.

I glanced up at a sky that was grey and threatening again before climbing into the car – it seemed the weather hadn't finished with us yet either – and I started the ignition. I was amazed the Mini was still going. I was starting to feeling affection for my little car again.

I had just begun to reverse when I heard a shout and I looked up to see Derek Jameson emerge from the house dressed in a waterproof jacket and hiking boots. I stopped the car and wound down the window.

He came over and leaned in. 'I want to see where Bob died,

and I've just realised that I don't know where it is. I thought that you would. Can you show me? We can go in the Lexus.'

Suddenly I felt very uncomfortable. I had no idea if he knew I'd seen his brother's body and I'd probably have to tell him now. 'I'm not sure that's a very good idea . . .'

But he was gone, striding off to his brother's car, keys outstretched to zap the alarm, assuming I'd follow him. I noticed his limp was quite pronounced this morning. I sighed and got out of the Mini. It appeared I had no option.

We drove back down the hill towards Glendara. A few cars were stranded in a large body of water at the bottom of the road, appearing to have stalled, with people clustered around trying to help. I was grateful anew to my Mini and its stubborn refusal to be beaten by the weather.

'I suppose that's one advantage to driving an old car,' I joked feebly. 'No electrics.'

But Derek didn't even look. Instead he turned on the radio, where the news was just ending. I hoped there would be nothing about his brother's death, but if there was, we missed it. Instead the weather dominated.

Donegal is experiencing very heavy rainfall resulting in extensive flooding on roads and damage to property. Inishowen remains the worst affected. Reports are coming in of a number of bridge collapses, trees down and road closures. Road users are advised to take extreme care and not to undertake any unnecessary journeys. In the meantime, updates are available on the RTÉ website.

I glanced across at Derek. 'Are you sure this is a good idea?'

But his eyes remained concentrated on the road. 'I have to. I need to see it.'

He held the steering wheel with a grim determination, tapping it impatiently whenever we reached another obstacle, and there was no shortage of those this morning. We crossed the bridge at the bottom of the town at high speed, giving me just enough time to snatch a brief glimpse of the river below. It was fuller than I had ever seen it, rusty brown water gushing frighteningly high.

With its cream leather seats, digital dashboard and satnav, the Lexus had all the expensive extras that the Mini lacked, but I'd never have been able to negotiate its bulk. I couldn't even see the end of the bonnet. Derek, on the other hand, drove as if he knew the car well, and far faster than he should have, considering the weather and the fact that he didn't know the roads. People with big cars tend to do that, I've noticed, behave as if they're invincible. If you're closer to the road or in a smaller car, you're more aware of your own vulnerability.

But I clung to the seat and kept my mouth shut as we headed along the Ballyliffin road. Derek's breathing was shallow, and I didn't want to distract him any more than necessary. The man's brother had just been murdered; it was time to make allowances.

Instead I gazed out the window. We passed an old farmhouse, a long way in from the shore, once pretty, now sadly ruined with its chimney fallen in, and the golf links on our right, its clubhouse silhouetted against the threatening sky. It hadn't been visible the night before but now I could see that the greens were sodden, some sections completely submerged. There wasn't a single golfer out, which was unusual for a Saturday afternoon. Glashedy Island brooded darkly in the bay, surveying the carnage on the mainland.

After about fifteen minutes with no conversation other than my issuing of directions, Derek seemed to relax a little; his arms became less taut and his hands loosened on the wheel. When we came to the fork after Clonmany that Molloy and I had reached the night before, I found myself instructing him to go right – force of habit, I suppose. The Urris Hills loomed purple and imposing on our left as we passed the sign for the Glenevin Waterfall.

Derek slowed down a little. 'So that's where that is.'

I regarded him curiously.

'Bob and Amanda went there for a stroll on Thursday morning,' he said. 'She said it was lovely. She was always trying to get Bob to take a bit of exercise.'

'They were here on Thursday morning?' I asked. I'd assumed the cycling crowd had just arrived when I'd landed back in town on Thursday afternoon.

He nodded. 'They stayed in some hotel in Derry on Wednesday night. Bob had some meetings, he said.'

'So, you didn't travel with them?' I remembered Bob beeping the horn at Derek from the Lexus.

He shook his head. 'I came up with the other cyclists in the minibuses, along with the truck with the bikes. I joined Bob and Amanda, just after I met you.'

We passed the Rusty Nail pub and the road ribboned on ahead, through the valley, with rocky hills on either side. The lower fields were like lakes and most of the sheep had been taken in but, despite the grey day, Dunaff was visible in the distance.

'It really is rather beautiful here.' Derek gave me an apologetic look. 'Sorry for the wretched place comment earlier.'

'I'm sure I'd feel the same in your shoes.'

Since he appeared calmer, I ventured the question that had been on my mind since we'd set off. 'Why *do* you want to see where it happened?'

He slapped the steering wheel and I jumped. 'I want to know what the hell he was doing out here. You met my brother. He wasn't an outdoors sort of a man. Amanda said she had to twist his arm to get him to go for a stroll on Thursday, otherwise he'd have spent the day in the pub.'

'I see.'

He went on, 'The last place I'd have thought he would die was on a mountain road. Bob was far more likely to die face-down in a plate of steak and chips with a good Châteauneuf-du-Pape in his crystal wine glass.'

Despite the context I smiled. Derek smiled back, and it broke the tension. Still, the image seemed rather distasteful for a man in charge of a charity and it was hard not to be reminded of what Jude had said in Phyllis's flat.

'This is Bob's car, isn't it?' I asked, my hand on the cream leather seat.

Derek nodded. 'I don't have mine with me, and Amanda said it would be okay to take it.'

'And it was parked outside the guesthouse all night?'

Derek shrugged. 'I think so.'

'There was no car at Mamore Gap last night.' Other than Maeve's jeep, I thought, but I didn't say that. 'So, it doesn't seem like he drove himself here. Who do you think did?'

Derek shook his head sadly. 'I have no idea.'

I paused. 'Did you see or hear anything last night at the guest-house? Bob leaving? Someone collecting him maybe?'

He frowned as if to consider this although Molloy must have already asked him. 'We all came back from the pub together. Amanda and myself went inside and both went to bed, I assume. I certainly did. Bob stayed outside for a bit, but I'm pretty sure I heard him come in.'

'Why would he do that? Stay outside after everyone else came in?'

Derek gave me an oddly sheepish look. 'He wanted to have

a cigarette. He couldn't seem to give them up, but he'd kept his smoking secret. He was on the board of a cancer charity for a while. Not great for the CEO to be seen smoking.'

'No, I can see that.'

His eyes narrowed. 'So, you think someone drove him out there and killed him? Is that what the guards think?'

I shrugged, uncomfortably. 'I'm sorry. I don't know. I have no idea what happened either, other than what the guards have released. I'm just thinking aloud.'

There was silence between us for a few minutes again as the road began to rise, and we drove steeply uphill. The powerful car coped with it effortlessly, and I was grateful that Derek had finally tapered his speed. Dunaff Head and Lenan were to the right and the hills of Claggan were ahead, shades of brown and green; pear, olive and rust, the grass looking almost burnt even though it was soaking wet.

Suddenly, Derek stopped the car, giving me a start, and causing the seatbelt to tighten around me. He turned to look at me. 'Fucking weird though, isn't it? I mean a snakebite. In Ireland.'

'Yes, it is weird.' I noticed my voice quivered a little. Derek's erratic driving was making me very uneasy.

'Do they know if that's what killed him?'

I shook my head. 'I think they have to wait for the post-mortem.'

He looked ahead. 'That's what the sergeant said. But then when they released that statement about keeping an eye out for a snake, I didn't know what to think . . .'

'I don't think you're alone there.' I looked across at him and saw that his hand was shaking on the wheel. 'I don't suppose you knew anyone who might have wanted to hurt him?'

He gave me a strange look. 'You mean someone with a penchant for poisonous snakes? No, I don't.'

He moved the car forward again and we both fell silent while he negotiated a particularly severe hairpin bend. The view was dramatic – land jutting out into the sea, the treeless hills with their heather and jagged rocks on all sides. Even with the clouds you could see all the way to Lenan Head.

He sighed. 'It's pretty spectacular up here all right. Galway has some incredible spots, but this is special.'

'Where in Galway are you from?' I asked, relieved at the change of subject.

He replied dismissively, 'Oh, we grew up in the city, I'm afraid. Nowhere like this.'

We turned towards Mamore, passing the *You are entering Amazing Grace Country* sign.

I looked over at Derek with a half-smile. 'Did you know you weren't taking the "Amazing Grace" route, by the way? It's along Lough Swilly, and you were going down by the Foyle. Wrong side of the peninsula.'

Derek nodded, raising his eyes to heaven. 'That didn't matter to Bob, small print as far as he was concerned. Once we were in the general vicinity, he was happy to use the connection. The charity he founded is the Jameson Grace Charity and the care homes are the Jameson Grace Homes. He had a thing about that hymn.'

'Oh?'

'Bob always felt that the first part of his life had been about making money. Then he spent some time in Nigeria and claimed he had this Road-to-Damascus moment which made him decide to spend the rest of his life helping people. Like John Newton.' Derek shot me a wry look. 'Guess we know what hymn will be played at his funeral.'

'I guess.'

He let out a sigh. 'Bob may have liked the good things in life, got a taste for it during the early part of his life, I suppose. But in his later life he did a lot of good, raised a lot of money for a lot of charities.'

'What did he do before?'

'He worked for an investment bank.'

'Right.' I placed my hand on the cream leather seat.

There must have been some judgement in my tone because Derek defended him. 'He didn't just set up the Grace charity, you know, he worked for other charities before that. There are hospitals that wouldn't be able to stay open if it wasn't for the money that Bob raised, machines that have saved lives that couldn't have been bought.'

I nodded mutely. Derek Jameson wasn't in the mood to consider any criticism of his dead brother, and that was understandable. He'd only just learned of his death. But certain facts remained. Bob had been keeping secrets from his wife, Jude Burns didn't like him and at least one person had wanted him dead.

We passed white stones on either side of the road bearing the words *Magic Road*. Molloy and I had missed them the night before coming from the other direction, although they wouldn't have been visible at night anyway.

Derek asked me about them, and I explained the optical illusion for which the road was famous. It was said that if you stopped your car at the white stone, and released the handbrake, your car would appear to be rolling uphill. I'd never tried it – it had always seemed rather eerie to me. But as I related it to Derek, I managed to get, if not a smile, a brief lightening of expression for my trouble.

'I wonder if it would work with a bike.'

111

'I don't know.'

'It looks like a good tough cycle route,' he said. 'Maybe we should have planned to come through here after all.' Then his face fell again as if he'd briefly forgotten why we were here.

Five minutes later, we drove between the heather- and rock-covered banks and the grotto appeared on our right.

'It's just here,' I said quietly. 'Pull in here on the left, there's a parking area.'

A wave of tiredness washed over me and I had a flashback to the night before, imagining the fear Maeve must have felt, here on her own late at night. It occurred to me that I should give her a call and see how she was doing. Once I was out of this car and back in my own space, I'd do it.

In the meantime, I looked over at Derek whose eyes were spilling tears.

Chapter Eleven

A strange sheen glinted off the soaking heather. The light was eerie, almost falsely bright as if someone had turned on a fluorescent lamp whose beam was directly on us, while black and purple clouds surrounded. The rocks glittered with the wet and on the road, I saw the fallen stones and soil that Molloy had mentioned. Maeve was lucky they hadn't fallen on her windscreen too; some looked sharp enough to do some serious damage. Although lucky was probably stretching it.

The light darkened suddenly when we got out of the car, as if that same someone had turned off the electrics. It started to drizzle and we pulled up our hoods. I walked up the saturated road to where Maeve's jeep had been when we'd arrived last night. Derek followed me without a word. Everything had been removed now, the cordon, Maeve's jeep, the tarpaulin. You'd never have known that anything untoward had happened. I supposed there would be little to be gained by marking off the bog in torrential rain. At least Molloy had been able to carry out a short search while it was relatively dry this morning.

Our gaze was drawn upwards, to the sheep on the slopes, their wool sopping, their blue and red markings the only bit of bright colour around. The hill was a burned-looking yellowy grey, patched with grey shale as if from a quarry of cut stone. Whatever evidence the rain hadn't washed away the sheep would soon trample, I thought.

Derek stood in the middle of the road, with his hands on his hips, adopting the same posture I'd seen outside Phyllis's shop. I wondered what it was he suffered from? It was the left leg that seemed to give him bother.

'So this is it,' he said. 'This was where it happened. You're sure?'

I nodded and looked at the ground where I'd seen the tarp the night before. 'I was here,' I said quietly.

He turned, his head snapping round in my direction. 'You were here? But I thought the vet found him.'

'She did but I was here shortly afterwards. She's my friend – the vet. She called me.'

I hoped he'd leave it at that. I didn't want to have to field questions about my relationship with the police. And he did. He fell silent again, the wind and rain battering at his hood. Then without warning, he marched over to the edge of the road, where the land rose sharply, dotted with clumps of heather and glistening rocks, standing almost exactly on the spot where the body had been lying under the tarp. But I chose not to tell him that.

Instead I pointed to the bank. 'I think his body came from up there. The rain must have dislodged him and washed him down the hill.'

Derek sucked air through his teeth and winced, as if he was struggling to keep his emotions in check.

'He'd been dead a little while when he fell, I think,' I added gently. I wasn't sure if this would be any comfort, but part of me wanted to exonerate Maeve from any suspicion.

Derek looked up to where I'd indicated, hands shielding his

eyes. Without a word, he set off to climb the hill, his back rigid, legs striding on ahead, seemingly ignoring any pain. After a brief hesitation, I followed, screwing up my face to head into the rain. The ground was slippery and water-logged and there were muddy sections, which were deeper than anticipated. But the mud was a better option than the rocks. The rocks were treacherous; more than once I came close to falling and sliding back down to the road. But I climbed after him, eventually resorting to hands and knees. The man was fit. I was quickly panting and out of breath.

'What are you looking for?' I called.

But he didn't answer me, just kept moving ahead, eventually doing what I did and using his hands to grab onto rocks to steady himself and haul himself up, glancing at the ground every so often. Finally, he reached a large even patch where the view was clear, and he stopped. I joined him a few seconds later and watched as he stood gazing down towards the sea, his hands on either side of his head. I noticed for the first time the muscles on his shoulders and back, filling his *Trans-Pyrenees Challenge 2015* jacket.

Lenan Head was in the distance with houses dotted along the shore, but everything was cloaked in a grey mist and the turbulent sky looked ominous. What was he feeling? I wondered. Grief? Survivor's guilt? You'd imagine survivor's guilt must be severe with twins. A combination of the two?

I stood beside him, the rain battering against my face. Though it wasn't heavy, at least nothing compared to what we had been experiencing, the wind up here made it worse than it was.

'What the hell happened to him?' Derek said finally, his eyes glistening, shaking his head in confusion.

'I don't know,' I said helplessly.

'And the way he died.' He looked down. 'It's macabre. It's almost like black magic or something – voodoo.'

'Yes,' I said quietly, surprised that now he was here, in the spot where his brother had died, he was prepared to acknowledge that someone must have wanted to hurt him. I supposed he didn't have much choice.

'What the hell had you got yourself involved in, Bob?' he said, almost under his breath.

'Do you think that's what happened?' I asked curiously.

He looked over at me as if he'd briefly forgotten I was there. 'What do you mean?'

'That he might have become involved with the wrong people?' Then: 'Sorry. It sounded like that's what you meant.'

Derek shook his head. His eyes were narrowed against the wind and rain and it was hard to see his expression under the hood. 'I don't know. He knew a lot of people, so maybe he made a few enemies. But what normal person would do something like this? Kill him somewhere like this?' He let his arms hang helplessly by his sides. 'God knows when he might have been found.'

We looked around us. The nearest house was at the bottom of the hill, probably only a few miles away, but I knew what he meant; this place did seem so much wilder than that. And Bob's body hadn't been visible. At least not until the weather dislodged it from wherever it had lain.

'I expect there would have been a search when he didn't come back to the guesthouse,' I said.

'Yes, but even then, who the hell would have known to look *here*?' He looked around at the desolate, sodden ground, heather and rocks and waterlogged mud, the grey sea visible in the distance.

For the first time, it occurred to me that maybe that was the killer's intention, that Bob Jameson's body should not be found for some time.

116

Derek kept staring at the ground; his hiking boots were soaked. 'And I suppose the rain has washed away any evidence.'

'I expect so.' I didn't mention Bob's shoe. 'The guards were up here searching but they had very little backup, no Technical Bureau. I guess they can't block off the whole area. Apart from anything else they wouldn't be able to keep the sheep out.'

Derek strode about in circles as if trying to work something out, while I stood watching him impotently. Suddenly he squatted down on his hunkers. He'd spotted something.

I walked over. 'What is it?'

He picked it up and showed it to me and his voice quivered. 'It's his watch. Bob's watch. I'd know it anywhere. Clasp is broken.'

It was a large silver watch with a black leather strap. Scratched and worn, it struck me as a surprising watch for a man who liked expensive things in life.

Derek rubbed his hand against his nose. 'So, they weren't out to rob him anyway.'

I wanted to tell him to pick it up with a tissue, not to get his prints on it, but I was too late and with the rain it was probably pointless. Molloy and McFadden must have missed it, I thought. Easy enough considering how waterlogged the ground was. They'd have to drain the whole area to search it properly.

With a jolt it occurred to me that the snake could still lurking here. If snakes lurked. Mountain Rescue had been on the alert while they were searching, but people had been warned to stay out of this area just in case. The prospect made me a little nervous; I wasn't great with snakes. I said as much to Derek in a stumble of words and he nodded.

'We'll go.' He took out a handkerchief, wrapped the watch in it and shoved them both into the pocket of his jacket. 'I'll give this to the guards.'

As we drove back down the hill in the Lexus, the rain became heavier. But passing the sign for the waterfall, Derek looked at me. 'Would you mind?'

I shook my head. It was still bucketing down but if this was one of the last places his brother had been happy, then who was I to deprive him of seeing it? 'Of course not. Although I expect we may not be able to get too far up the path.'

I was right. There was a sign in the car park indicating that the footpath was closed due to flood damage and it wasn't difficult to see, even from where we were, that the river was overflowing and dangerous. The path was completely blocked off.

Derek seemed disappointed. 'Amanda said it was really pretty,' he said. 'That it had been romantic.'

I did wonder, if Bob and Amanda had enjoyed such a romantic stroll on Thursday morning, then what had caused them to have that row on Thursday night? I was tempted to ask Derek about it, but the look on his face as he gazed at the gushing river beyond the sign stopped me.

He sighed, hands in the pockets of his jacket. 'I'm glad they had that, at least.'

There was something about the way he said it that made me suspect he wasn't just thinking about Bob and Amanda.

I hesitated before speaking. 'It must be hard not to be able to talk to your wife at times like this. I mean I know you *can* talk to her, but . . .' I stumbled, feeling sure I was saying the wrong thing, or saying it badly.

But his face when he turned to me was soft. 'No, you're right. I do miss that.' He looked down. 'To tell the truth I've been feeling guilty.'

'Why?'

'I've developed some feelings for someone else and I'm not sure if it's right.' He looked up at me and smiled sadly. 'I feel as if I'm being unfaithful even thinking about it.'

When we stopped at the Garda Station at Glendara so Derek could drop in his brother's watch, I stayed in the car. I didn't feel like explaining why I'd been with him at Mamore Gap. I'd done nothing wrong in simply doing a grieving man a favour, but I wasn't sure Molloy would see it that way. He might see it as my usual interfering, even in his present more amenable frame of mind.

While I waited, I watched a man with a brush sweep water from his front garden onto the street. I didn't think I'd ever seen a more pointless exercise: the more he did it, the more it just kept flowing back in around him. But he kept at it, doggedly swishing away. I found it almost mesmerising to watch.

Eventually Derek emerged from the station and sat in the driver's seat without a word. There was something decidedly weary about him, though he seemed tense too. His back was rigid.

'Are you okay?' I asked. I imagined how alone he must be feeling. He hadn't said anything more about what he'd mentioned at the waterfall, but I hoped for his sake he managed to find some happiness.

He sighed. 'Just feeling a bit helpless, I suppose. And sad.' He spotted the man with the brush, arched an eyebrow and I wondered if he was thinking what I had been. 'The guard in there – not the sergeant, the other one, McFadden, is that his name?'

I nodded.

'He tells me the town is completely cut off now.'

'Yes, there are a number of bridges down and most of the access roads are impassable.'

He looked over at me. 'I wonder if there's something I can do to help. I'm an engineer. Maybe I could be of some use.'

'Maybe. Although I think the county council have it in hand.'

His brow furrowed as if he was trying to work something out, and I wondered what he was thinking. It struck me that Derek was one of those people who found it difficult to relax, who needed to keep moving for his peace of mind. Even more so today than usual, I suspected. I glanced at his taut frame and I wondered if he'd used sport to cope with his wife's diagnosis.

'Anyway,' he sighed. 'For the moment I'd better get back to Amanda. I've been gone long enough.'

He started the car and drove us back up to the guesthouse. Before he went back in, he thanked me for my help, and as I climbed back into the Mini, I watched him walk up the path and into the house, round-shouldered and defeated, his gait slow and laboured, his limp more obvious than it had been at the Gap.

By the time I'd reversed the car, I realised that I didn't feel like going back to my cottage. All that awaited me there was unpacking and laundry, plus, waves of tiredness were washing over me again. Derek Jameson might be craving something to keep him busy but the climb up the bank at Mamore had taken the last bit of energy I had. I needed a coffee before I drove any further, even the few miles back to Malin.

I crossed the river again, where the rushing water was even higher than earlier. In fact, it was higher than I had ever seen it, hardly surprising with the unrelenting rainfall. In the town square the large banner for the charity cycle swung from one of the telephone poles, bedraggled and torn.

I parked in front of the bank and headed towards the Oak, stopping in the doorway to admire McFadden's poster. He'd chosen an image of a cobra, but the words were pure McFadden.

DANGER! If you see a snake do not approach. Do not try and catch it and do not shout at it! It may be harmless, but it may also be poisonous and deadly. Last encountered Mamore Gap. Might be hiding in greenery or undergrowth. Please warn children accordingly and phone Glendara Garda Station at the number below if there are any sightings.

Despite myself I smiled. I opened the door to a pub that was full, not heaving as it had been the night before but still very busy. At the bar, Tony came over, mopping his brow.

'Glad to see you're still open,' I said.

'Aye,' he gave me a wry look. 'And we will be until we run out of milk. I got a bit of a fright last night, thought we might have some flooding ourselves, but it looks as if we're on high enough ground not to be in any danger.' He leaned forward, his elbows on the bar. 'I heard about poor Phyllis.'

'Yes, it's awful. There'll be a lot of damage, but at least she saved her books.'

Tony nodded sagely. 'Well that's all that'll matter to Phyllis. Once her books and her dog are safe, she'll be happy enough. What can I get you?'

'Coffee, please. Maybe a cappuccino if you still have some milk? Double-shot. I'm having waves of jet lag.'

He grinned. 'Oh aye – it's worse coming this way, isn't it?' He paused to think. 'God, is it only Thursday you got back? It seems like weeks.'

It sounded mildly insulting but I knew what he meant. While he turned to the coffee machine I looked around for a seat but there wasn't a single spare table.

'It looks as if you're providing a valuable service.'

He nodded as he steamed the milk. 'I think we might be the only place open. Lots of people have just shut their doors and shored up with sandbags. The fire station have them for anyone that needs them. Some businesses have workers who couldn't get in or were afraid they wouldn't get home if they did.' He turned. 'You know they're looking for accommodation for those who can't get back to their homes tonight? It's to get worse apparently.'

'I heard. It's hard to imagine it any worse.'

My phone beeped in my pocket and I took it out to look. Leah, who'd been lucky enough to get back to Buncrana before the flooding started, had sent me a link to a Facebook post. It was a video taken on a mobile phone. I opened it. The video showed a pedestrian gate at the front of a house where water levels had reached the ground-floor windows. Brown water flowed through the gate carrying branches, weeds and other rubbish. Suddenly, there was a loud bang and the gate came loose. It detached itself and went floating down the road. The force of the flood had blown the gate off its hinges.

'Jesus,' I said aloud, causing Tony to turn. I showed him my phone.

He shook his head in disbelief. 'Where's that?'

I looked. 'Burnfoot, I think.'

'I told you, it's worse it's getting,' he said darkly. 'We'll be going around the square in boats, before we're finished.'

At which point it occurred to me that I'd forgotten yet again to check the leak in the office. I'd need to go down as soon as I'd had my coffee. There was a tap on my shoulder and I turned to see Maeve, looking wrecked, dressed in a navy boiler suit.

'Are you still working?' I asked. 'I was just going to call you and see how you are.'

'Ach, I'm all right.' She smiled. 'No choice but to keep working, unfortunately. One of the vets can't get here from Derry so I'm on constant call.'

She ordered a coffee from Tony to take away and we stood to one side to wait for our drinks.

'So how are you, really, after last night?' I asked, lowering my voice. 'You must be still pretty shaken.'

'Too busy to think about it, to be honest. Whenever I do think about it, I try to put it out of my mind.'

'You know there was a snakebite? That's why Harry was examining his hand so closely.'

She nodded. 'Aye, I heard. Bloody strange. A snake around here? Someone must have been keeping it as a pet. God knows what species it was. There's a massive trade in exotic animals now, it's awful. A load of Komodo dragons was seized at an airport recently . . .'

'Maybe the snake wasn't kept as a pet.' Maybe it was brought up here for one purpose?' I was thinking of what Derek had said about black magic.

She raised her eyebrows. 'To kill your man? Ach, surely there are easier ways to kill someone. You'd have to source the snake, take care of it, feed it, house it, keep it somewhere safe and secure. Transport it, all the time keeping it alive and well and away from people.'

'How would you transport it?'

She shrugged and gave it some thought. 'I supposed it would be simple enough really, a large box with a blanket or lukewarm hot water bottle and breathing holes would do it. Although if you were dealing with a poisonous snake, then you'd need to know how to handle it,' she added. 'Was it poisonous?'

'They don't know,' I admitted.

'So, they have no idea if the man's death had anything to do with the bite?'

I shook my head. Tony handed me my coffee over the bar, I thanked him, and when I turned back Maeve was still thinking about the snake.

'You can't exactly programme a snake to do what you want, either,' she said. 'Most of them aren't aggressive, unless they feel threatened.'

'And if it was threatened?'

'If it was scared it would probably lash out all right.' She narrowed her eyes. 'Why? Is that what happened?'

I shook my head again. I had no idea.

'Anyway,' she said, grabbing her own coffee when Tony called her over. 'Does Molloy have any notion *who* could have done it?'

'Not yet, I don't think.'

'I suppose the lads are on their own, if no one is able to get in or out at the moment.'

I nodded. 'The Fire Service are helping with the flood. But, as far as the death is concerned, they're on their own.'

She took a sip of her drink, thoughtfully. 'Had he ever been in Inishowen before, do you know? The dead man? Any connections here?'

'I don't know to be honest.' It hadn't occurred to me to ask Mary this. I wondered if he'd ever visited her here. From what she'd said, it seemed unlikely.

'If not, I suppose the obvious suspects must be those who knew him. The people who were part of the cycle.' Maeve spoke in a low voice. There were a few of them in the pub.

Then almost on cue, the door opened, and Jude Burns came in with two young women, one with a toddler on her hip. They shook out two large golfing umbrellas and placed them in the bucket left by the door for just that purpose.

I hadn't seen the daughters clearly until now. One was blonde, and I recognised her as the cyclist I'd seen the first day calling for the spider tie that had almost hit me. The other had wild brown hair sticking up in all directions, reminiscent of a young Helena Bonham Carter.

'Jesus, that's some hairdo,' Maeve remarked as she took another sip of her coffee.

We watched as the two women grabbed the one table that had just come free. It was just to the right of the fire, prime position on a day like today. Jude said something to them and approached the counter.

'I'd better run, I'll see you later,' Maeve said hurriedly, nodding a hello at him on her way out.

Jude greeted me with a smile and placed his huge hands on the bar. 'We've just been down at the Garda Station giving statements. Not that we could tell them very much.'

'I'm sure you did your best.'

'We tried.' He went on, 'Unfortunately, we still can't leave. The cycle isn't going ahead, of course – it wouldn't have anyway with the weather, but now we can't get home because of the roads.'

I looked around me at the crowded pub. 'You're not alone there. At least you have beds – there are some here who might be sleeping on floors, people who can't get back to Derry or Buncrana.'

Jude nodded slowly. 'True. I need to stop feeling sorry for myself. I'm sure it's a right pain in the arse having us here, taking up beds. People will be glad to see the back of us.'

I disagreed. 'I think people just feel bad for you, bad that what happened, happened here.'

He clicked his teeth and looked away. 'Could have been anywhere.'

I said nothing, surprised again by his almost complete callous lack of interest, in the murder of someone he knew. I didn't particularly know Jude but it did seem at odds with the rest of his personality.

He noticed my response and shrugged. 'I know it sounds cold. But the truth is that Bob Jameson made enemies. The guards will have their work cut out trying to work out what happened to him.'

He was right about that. 'Looks like it. Not many people are likely to have seen something at Mamore on a dirty night like that.'

'Mamore?' he echoed. 'That's the name of the place he was found?'

I nodded. 'Mamore Gap. It's a fairly spectacular spot.'

He breathed in. 'Not really the attention your lovely peninsula needs. Sorry we brought it on you.'

'It's hardly *your* fault,' I said, although even as I uttered the words, I was aware of Jude's frosty exchange with the dead man in almost the exact same spot where we were standing now, and his words in Phyllis's flat and just now. Why did he hate him so much?

There was a pause, as if Jude was aware of that himself. And for a second I wondered if he was going to tell me. Then he seemed to refocus, nodding in the direction of the table where his two daughters were sitting.

'Look, why don't you join us? It looks as if we've taken the only spare table. Come over and meet my daughters and my grandson.'

The toddler was playing with two teaspoons, bashing them together and chuckling, and I was still holding a relatively untouched cappuccino.

So, after Jude had ordered, I followed him over.

Chapter Twelve

By the time we arrived at the table, the toddler's mother had extracted the teaspoons from his sticky hands and given him a napkin. She'd fashioned it into a snake, and the little boy was pushing it around the table making hissing noises. It seemed a little macabre in the circumstances, until it occurred to me that maybe this was her way of warning him to stay away from the snake if he came across it.

The mother was the sister with the madly tossed hair. The other daughter was the blonde, bleached and cropped. Both were slim and carefully made up, in contrast to the ruddy rain-beaten faces around them. The two large golfing umbrellas must have given them far more protection than mine had done. I still hadn't collected it from Stoop's or the bank, or wherever I'd left it.

Jude did the introductions. 'This is Lissa,' he said, indicating the mother of the baby. 'And this is Sue. And this little monster is Peadar.'

They looked up at me and smiled. Sue shunted in and Lissa moved from her seat, so they were on the inside bench with Peadar on his aunt's knee, while their father and I sat facing them. Tony's turf fire heated my face, maybe a little too much, but I didn't care. The whole world felt damp now, so I was grateful for anything that provided a bit of dry warmth.

'Ben's one of the local solicitors,' Jude said as he distributed the coffees. He'd ordered orange juice and toast, which Tony had said he'd bring over in a bit.

There was something pointed about the way he mentioned my profession that made me a little uncomfortable, and my suspicion was confirmed when he followed up with, 'She might be able to give you some advice.'

This was more than just a friendly invitation to coffee.

But Lissa didn't take the prompt. She took her cup from her father and began playing with her hair, twisting and separating the strands with her fingers. It occurred to me that Stan would wince at the damage she was doing. The toddler began tearing the tissue snake apart, as if mimicking his mother.

'Where do you live?' I asked, taking a sip of my drink.

Jude replied for her. 'Lissa and I live in Sligo. Sue lives in Galway now.'

'Would you not be better going to a solicitor closer to home?' I said. 'I know plenty of good solicitors in Sligo.'

Lissa glanced from her sister to her father. 'I can't go to anyone in Sligo,' she said finally.

'Her ex is too well known,' Jude added, his voice lowered. 'She won't get unbiased advice.'

I looked at him doubtfully. The idea that having *less* information might make me a better option for advice made me even more uneasy. I regularly encountered clients who wanted me to hear only their version of the truth and I always tried to find a way around it. If I suspected I wasn't hearing the full story, I asked Leah for background information or looked up whatever I could myself. I was always interested in what people weren't prepared to tell me themselves.

'That seems unlikely,' I said with a smile as I took a sip of my coffee. 'Sligo is a big town.'

'*Would* you have some time?' Lissa leaned forward, biting her lip. 'I know it's a weekend, but really, I'd be very grateful.'

'There's something worrying her,' her father said. 'You might be able to put her mind at rest. I'd be grateful too.'

I thought about how ready Jude had been to help Phyllis move her books, and I sighed and gave in. 'Okay. We can go down to the office after we've finished these if you like. I have to check in anyway.' I smiled. 'There was a leak yesterday and I can't imagine it's got any better overnight.'

Jude looked relieved. Minutes later Tony arrived over to the table with orange juice, toast and homemade gooseberry jam, just as the toddler grabbed a small perfume bottle from one of the women's bags and started to bang it on the table. Sue snatched it away from him and put it back, and it was only at that point that I registered that Jude's other daughter hadn't reacted at all to the conversation we'd had. She'd continued playing with her nephew, without saying a word, as if the whole thing had nothing to do with her.

Twenty minutes later I turned the key in the office with a certain amount of trepidation and Lissa in my wake, having left her son with her sister and father in the Oak. My trepidation was twofold. Firstly, would I be able to help Lissa with whatever was troubling her? And secondly, what would be waiting for me in the bathroom? I'd left the leak considerably longer than I'd intended and while the office was on higher ground than Phyllis's bookshop, it was marginally lower than the Oak.

There was no water coming out to greet me, at least. I directed Lissa to the waiting room and made a beeline straight for the bathroom where I was relieved to find that other than an over-flowing basin, the leak wasn't any worse than it had been the day before. So, I emptied the basin, put it back under the leak and went back out to join my new and reluctantly acquired client. She was sitting where I'd left her, smoothing her hair nervously.

'All good,' I said cheerfully. 'The roof isn't going to cave in just yet. We can stay here in the waiting room if you like,' I added. 'Bit less formal.'

Lissa nodded. She seemed even less self-assured out of the protection of her father, if that were possible.

'Fancy another coffee? Or tea?' I offered. 'I think we have some milk.'

She gave a tight shake of her head, so I took the chair opposite and clasped my hands together. 'So, how can I help you?'

She hesitated again, her gaze not fully meeting mine, so I spoke again. 'Okay, firstly, I should ask you, have you taken advice already? Because if you've already got a solicitor at home I can't . . .'

She cut across me and said, 'I don't. Dad was right. There's no one I can go to there.'

'Right, okay.' I stood up, grabbed an attendance pad and a pen from the reception desk and sat back down. 'Firstly, what's your full name? Are you Burns?'

'No. I took my husband's name – it's Bennett.'

I wrote it down. 'Okay. Go ahead. Tell me how I can help you.'

'It's about my husband, Chris.'

I looked up. 'Your dad mentioned something about him. This would be Peadar's dad?'

She nodded and looked down while I began to take a note. Then she sucked in her breath. 'I think Chris is trying to kill me.'

I stopped writing and looked up. Lissa pressed her hand to her forehead, eyes glittering. Either she was telling the truth, or she truly believed that she was telling the truth.

'Dad doesn't know,' she said. 'And he can't know. He'd kill Chris himself if he knew. And I might be wrong.'

I put the pen and pad down on the seat beside me. 'Do *you* think you're wrong?'

She shook her head, tears blurring her eyes. 'No. But before I'd have even finished telling him, Dad would be locked up for assault or murder. He wouldn't care about the consequences. He hates Chris already and that's only because he thinks he left because of the baby's diagnosis of childhood leukaemia.'

I leaned forward, my elbows on my knees. 'Is that *not* what happened?'

She closed her eyes briefly. 'No. I left *him*. Because I was scared of him. Scared for both of us.'

I sat back. 'I think you need to tell me everything from the beginning.'

'Okay.' Lissa took a deep shuddering breath. 'When I met Chris, I thought he was perfect. He was handsome and kind.' She smiled weakly. 'Really fit too. We got married quickly and I had Peadar. He gave us the best of everything, we wanted for nothing – he treated me like a princess.' She swallowed.

'Go on.'

'But then I started to wonder where all the money was coming from. He worked as a lorry driver – there was no way he'd have been able to afford the things he was giving us, the holidays he was taking us on – on the wages he was making. My dad's an accountant and he was never able to afford the things that Chris was. So, one day I challenged him. We were having a row. We'd been talking about possible bone marrow transplants for Peadar and I didn't think he was listening to me.' She paused.

'What happened?'

'He hit me,' she said flatly. 'Just once, but hard. No questions asked. Nearly broke my jaw. Didn't do the classic apology afterwards, saying he regretted it and begging me to forgive him. There was none of that. He just pretended it never happened.' Her eyes welled and she rubbed her sleeve against her nose.

I placed my hand on her arm. 'And you didn't tell anyone? A friend maybe? Not even your sister?'

She shook her head. 'I couldn't. I just stayed in, hid away until the bruising cleared. Pretended I'd gone to a spa.' She gave a thin smile. 'Chris was always sending me to places like that. Sue said I was lucky to have a man who spoiled me.'

'But you stayed with him?'

She nodded. 'Stupid maybe, but I did. I was distracted by Peadar's treatment and thought that was more important. Things just went back to the way they were, as if the punch truly had never happened.'

'As long as you didn't challenge him.'

'Yes. But after a while I began to think that maybe he was involved with something illegal. Drugs maybe.' She gave me a shrewd look. 'Not taking them, he wasn't stupid enough for that – he's a keep-fit freak, always in the gym, did the Iron Man Challenge and everything. But I thought maybe that was where the money was coming from. Maybe he got involved with steroids or something?'

I waited.

'I overheard one of the guys he worked with saying that Chris could get hold of anything you wanted – if you had the cash. That he was like a crooked Amazon.com. And I realised he was smuggling stuff.' She began playing with her sleeve. 'His job helped. He travelled all over the country in that lorry. He could be delivering anything. I think he made contacts and realised he could make a lot of money.'

'So what did you do?'

'I watched him, started spying on him. Taking down dates and places and details of where he was travelling to, in my phone. Took photographs of his phone and the numbers he was calling, numbers that called him.' She looked down at her hands and I saw that they were red and raw. 'Thought that might be my way out. If he thought I knew something and could prove it, he might let me go. That once I kept my mouth shut, he would leave me alone.'

My eyes widened. This was very naive. The most dangerous time for a woman in a domestic abuse situation is once she has made the decision to leave – most murders by partners or ex-partners take place at this time. And though I had no idea what Chris was like physically, he'd participated in an Iron Man Challenge and Lissa was fragile and delicate looking; she would break like a twig.

'You were brave,' I said. 'That sounds very risky.'

Her eyes glistened again, the mascara starting to run. 'Brave and stupid, as I found out. I was listening to him on the phone one day and I heard him say, "It would be worth serving a fucking life sentence for."' She looked up. 'People get life sentences for murder, don't they?'

I nodded.

'The day after that he found my phone and looked through it. He saw what I'd been doing. He smashed it on the Aga, and it cracked.' Her voice shook. 'I thought he was coming for me, that he was going to hit me again. Peadar was in the playpen and I was terrified he'd hurt him too.' She balled her hands into fists.

My heart pounded, imagining what it must have been like.

'But just as that happened my father appeared at the door. I got to it before Chris could and I let him in. My father is a much bigger man than Chris, so once he was in the house Chris didn't challenge him.' Her eyes were wet. 'I didn't tell Dad what was happening. I just left with him that day and I haven't gone back. I was afraid that if I stayed, I wouldn't get another chance.'

'Probably a wise thing to do. And your father?'

She looked down. 'I told him that Chris couldn't cope with the diagnosis and I was better off on my own with my family to support me. That's why Dad thinks that Chris was leaving me and not the other way around.'

I sat back, trying to take all this in. 'When did all of this happen?'

'A few weeks ago. My sister Sue had decided to do the cycle and Dad had decided to get involved with it too, so I said I'd come along as support. I thought it would be a good way to get out of town for a while. Plus I didn't want to stay in Dad's house on my own with Peadar. I was afraid Chris would come after me.'

'And have you seen or heard from Chris since?'

Lissa's jaw tightened and a shadow crossed over her face. 'That's the thing. He hasn't even sent me a text since that night, which isn't like him. Dad's disgusted that he hasn't wanted to see Peadar. I was relieved. But . . .' She started pulling at her hair again, ripping one strand from the other.

I leaned forward. 'But?'

She looked up at me, her eyes filled with fear. 'I'd swear to God I saw him up here, this weekend.'

'Here? In Glendara?'

She nodded. 'Last night, outside the guesthouse. I thought that he'd followed me here.'

The guesthouse that Bob Jameson was staying in before he was killed, I thought. The guesthouse he was taken from to his death. Was it possible there was a connection?

Lissa ran her hand through her hair. 'Oh, I don't know, maybe I was imagining it. I'm so nervous now and it was dark and raining. Maybe I'm being paranoid. Maybe he didn't even mean it when he threatened me.'

And with that, I saw in Lissa what I so often did, an abused person desperate to believe the person they love didn't mean to hurt them, in the face of all the evidence to the contrary.

'But he's already shown you what he is capable of,' I said quietly. 'He hit you.'

'But I don't know if he seriously meant he was going to kill me. He was just mad at what I'd been doing.' Lissa's eyes were wide and pleading.

I said nothing. I wanted her to reach where she needed to on her own. And she did.

Seconds later she admitted, 'But the truth is I'd been afraid of him for a while. He was changing.'

'Go on.'

'His parents both died within about six months of each other. There was some family stuff that went on for him around that time, a problem with a will, I think, and it hardened him. Money seemed to become more important to him than anything else. And then Peadar got sick, and he hit me. After that he seemed to just retreat into himself. He just stopped talking to me. It was as if *he* was disappointed in *me*.'

'Did you tell anyone that you saw him here, or thought you saw him?'

She shook her head.

'What about your sister? Couldn't you tell her about all of this?'

Lissa looked down. 'Sue is going through a rough patch – she's had some news she's been struggling with. I don't think she could cope with anything else at the moment. She and Chris used to get on, but now he hates her for some reason.' She trailed off. 'I can't tell her.'

My tone was firm. 'You need to go to the guards, Lissa. Trust your instincts. If your life is being threatened, you need to tell them. You have no choice.'

Her eyes widened and she looked suddenly panicked. 'I can't – I'm afraid he'll do something to the baby. I just need to talk to him. Persuade him that I'm not going to do anything, that I don't have the numbers or any of the information any more – they were all on the phone he destroyed. That all I want is to be left alone.' The words came out all in a rush.

But I stated vehemently, 'From everything you've told me, that just doesn't seem safe.'

'I can do it. I just need to do it without my father finding out.'

'But Lissa, that just doesn't make sense. You said it yourself. It's a question of your own safety and the safety of your baby. The guards are here to protect you.'

She looked at me askance. 'Two guards in a town that's completely cut off, who are already trying to investigate a murder? And find a missing snake?' A wry smile hinted at a lighter side to her personality that must have been there before all this happened. 'With the best will in the world, how on earth are they going to protect me?'

I hated to admit it but, damn it, the woman had a point.

'There are orders we can apply for in court . . .' I began but I trailed off. I was floundering. I knew it and so did Lissa. She'd be long gone by the time I'd applied for any Protection Order.

She stood up, ready to go. 'Thank you for the chat. I appreciate it.'

'Won't you at least alert the guards?' I pleaded.

She pulled her bag onto her shoulder. 'Let me have a think about it. Look, it's helped just to talk to someone about it. How much do I owe you?'

I waved my hand dismissively. 'That's all right.'

She seemed surprised, but she couldn't know how hard it was not to recall my sister in situations like this. Faye had been killed by a man who, despite an educated and privileged background, was not dissimilar to this Chris.

Lissa closed the door behind her leaving me feeling more than a little helpless. I made myself a tea using the last of the milk and sat in Leah's seat at reception to drink it, while I tried to gather my thoughts. I glanced at the window. It had started to rain again.

Should I speak to Molloy about Lissa? I wondered. It was different to the situation with Mary in that Lissa had specifically asked me not to, so I'd be betraying her trust if I did. But what if she was in danger? I had a copy of the *Guide to Good Professional Conduct for Solicitors* upstairs in my office.

Relieved to find that Marina had tidied up – I guessed that's how she'd spent the day before while I was busy seeing clients – I found the *Guide* easily enough and flicked through to the section on solicitor–client confidentiality. Exceptions could be made where someone's life was in danger, *where there appeared to be a serious risk to the well-being of the client or a third party.* According to the *Guide*, the solicitor was required to judge *whether the threat was sufficiently serious to justify a breach of the duty of confidentiality.*

Which made me feel better about telling Molloy about my chat with Mary. The difficulty with Jude Burns's daughter was that she was right: Molloy and McFadden were stretched to their limits in trying to cope with the double crises they had on their plates. How much protection could they give a woman in danger with a flood and a murder on their hands?

I put the *Guide* on my desk and crossed to the window to look out onto the street. It was only drizzling now, far lighter than it had been, but it hadn't stopped for any decent period in two days. The rain had wreaked havoc, the town was in chaos and I was of no help to anyone. Despite Molloy, for the first time, saying he could actually do with my assistance.

I rubbed my sleeve against the glass and my eyes came to rest on two people across the street, standing in the alley between the flower shop and the chipper, both of which were closed now, with sandbags piled against their doors. I was grateful anew for the step up into our office. They talked intensely for a few minutes and then they hugged, parted and left to walk in opposite directions. I was taken aback to see it was Derek Jameson and Sue Burns, Lissa's sister. What was going on there? I wondered. They'd been friendly that first day when I watched them checking their bikes, but who knew they were that close?

I waited until they were both out of view, then I went back down to reception and stared at the computer. There was always the net. Maybe I could do a little digging. See what I could find out about Bob Jameson, for a start – his background, family, friends, the sort of man he was. Because I was certainly getting two very different impressions. I could see, also, if I could find any connection between Jameson and Lissa's husband Chris. Chris had been seen outside a guesthouse from which a man had been taken and killed. Could it really be a coincidence?

I sat at Leah's desk and turned on the computer, noticing as I did so some notes that Marina had left to go with dictation she'd set. I wondered fleetingly if she was still around. With so many roads impassable it was possible she hadn't managed to leave, unless she'd gone immediately after I'd seen her at the house. Might I have a house guest for a few more days or would she stay with Harry?

I pushed the notes to one side and opened Google, thinking that I'd start with the article Molloy had shown me on his phone. When I typed in Bob's name, several obituaries appeared – it seemed that each of the weekend papers had done one. It amazed me how quickly they appeared, though I knew there were pre-prepared ones if you were a certain age. I caught Bob's age as fifty-five, still a bit young for his death to have been expected.

The piece Molloy had shown me was a news report with nothing I didn't already know, but there was a link now to the same paper's obituary, so I clicked on that and settled down to read about the dead man's life.

Bob Jameson had grown up in Galway and attended a boys' school there, before studying history of art at Trinity College Dublin, followed by a master's in Oxford. That explained the slightly plummy accent. I remembered that he'd met Mary when he was in Trinity. After college he'd worked for Oak Knap Investment Bank in London for several years before returning to Dublin to work full time in the charities sector after a stint with an Irish overseas development organisation in Nigeria. He'd been head-hunted for the Nigerian charity after a chance meeting at a charity event he'd run in London while still working as a banker. He'd developed a bit of a talent for this side-line apparently. Art auctions, charity balls, races – it seemed that Bob Jameson was the man to go to if you wanted to raise a large amount of cash. He had endless charm and the ability to persuade the most unlikely people to donate, to prick their consciences. His contacts with the very wealthy through his day job at the bank had helped.

When he'd returned to Ireland from Nigeria, he'd worked for several different charities and served on the board of a number of hospitals – St Mary's in Cork and St Finbarr's Psychiatric Hospital in Galway were named – until eventually he'd committed himself to a charity he had founded himself, the Jameson Grace Charity for Alzheimer's and dementia. As CEO he'd raised millions to build two separate Jameson Grace care homes in Sligo and Galway, and Dublin was next on the agenda. He was particularly noted for a highly publicised wills campaign to persuade people to include the Grace charity in their wills. Apparently Irish people, though generally a charitable bunch, weren't so great when it came to bequests, so Bob had set about trying to change that.

I leaned back in the chair, rubbed my neck and stretched my arms over my head. I remembered that campaign, the stack of leaflets that arrived by post that we were asked to put in our waiting room. I'd thought about it at the time and chosen not to do it. I felt it was people's own decision who they left their money to. I asked testators if they wanted a charitable bequest when taking instructions and regarded that as enough. I wasn't sure about pushing them towards one particular charity by leaving the leaflets in the waiting room.

Returning to the obituary, I read that, in 2011, it was discovered that the salary Jameson had been taking from his charity vastly exceeded that which had been sanctioned by the board. This wasn't unheard of – there'd been a few scandals of this sort of late – but I did wonder if this was what Jude had meant when he said that for Bob, charity began at home. The obituary said that the Charities Commissioner had investigated but that it was quickly rectified. Two years later, Bob Jameson was given an award for his work with the Jameson Grace Charity.

The piece finished by saying that Bob Jameson enjoyed sailing and rugby, and was a regular at any rugby matches where Ireland or Connaught were playing – the picture at the top of the obituary showed him cheering Ireland at a Six Nations match. It said that Bob was survived by his wife Amanda, two children Oisín and Finn, and his brother Derek.

I sat back, chewing on a pen I'd picked up. The overall impression was that the excessive salary had been a blip, that in any event he'd done so much good that he was worth it. Which was pretty much the message I'd got from Derek earlier. But was it true? Jude Burns certainly felt differently. I flicked through the other obituaries, but they all had pretty much the same information.

I looked for Lissa Bennett's husband Chris. But there was nothing. Not even a Facebook page.

Before I turned off the computer, I had a quick look at the main news sites since I hadn't been able to get hold of a newspaper, and found that Glendara and Inishowen were dominating the national news. I suppose I shouldn't have been surprised; a town cut off by floods was news enough but throw in a mysterious death and a snake and we'd have journalists invading the town if they could get here. That was one advantage of being cut off, I supposed.

People had uploaded photographs and videos and the papers had included some of them in their articles. The clip Leah had sent me of the gate being blown off was there, along with an image of a massive sinkhole into which a tractor had fallen, and another of what looked like a small grove of trees growing out of the middle of the road, but was in fact a collapsed bridge. I shuddered. These were live updates of what was happening just outside my door.

Before I left, I did one last check on the bathroom, emptying the basin again and placing it back under the leak.

Chapter Thirteen

I left the office and walked up towards the square, trying my best to stay dry, with the intention of calling into Stoop's for my umbrella, if that was where I'd left it in my jet-lagged fuzz. Hunched down with my collar up, I collided with Phyllis who was hurrying around the corner, sloshing through the puddles, caring considerably less about staying dry than I was, though still wearing her bucket hat. It was only when we disentangled ourselves that I saw that Liam was with her and they both looked worried.

'Is everything all right?' I hoped the water hadn't risen any higher in her shop.

The bookseller was breathless. 'The river's burst its banks. They're evacuating the houses like they did in Buncrana. Have you time to come and help?'

'Of course. Will I bring the car?'

Liam nodded. 'Aye, do. I know it's only a wee thing, but it might be useful to cart stuff up. The Beacon Hall has been opened up for people who can't get home, so we're moving everyone in there. There's heat and light at least. For the moment.'

As I hurried off to the car he called after me, 'Just don't go too close to the river or you'll get stuck. Park on past the supermarket. We'll see you down there.'

I ran to the car and drove down the hill. It didn't take long to see what was happening; as Phyllis said, the river had completely burst its banks. The road was submerged on both sides and the bridge emerged from the flood as if from some large lake. The supermarket car park was awash; kerb stones, forced up as if by an earthquake, floated in the murky brown water, and trolleys bobbed about like pleasure boats.

I did as Liam had suggested and parked on higher ground, at what I regarded was a safe distance, and I stuffed my trousers into my boots before getting out of the car: they were wet anyway but I could do without them flapping around my ankles.

And I joined the group heading towards the flood. A pretty terrace of houses faced the river; it was somewhere I'd always thought would be a lovely place to live, but now they were in trouble. The residents had tried to protect themselves; there were sandbags everywhere, but when the river had burst its banks they hadn't made a damn bit of difference. Their front gardens were under at least a metre of water, pouring through the letterboxes in some.

In a field to the left, white spots bobbed about like fairy lights at a garden party. I found myself rooted to the spot, trying to work out what they were, until Liam appeared beside me. 'They're cars from the garage.'

I turned. 'What?'

'Cars. They're floating in that field. The lights go on when the alarms go off.'

'You're kidding. Are they okay like that?'

He shook his head. 'There's a real danger they'll end up down the river but there's not much we can do about it. For the moment this is more important.'

He nudged me towards the terrace, and I went with him. Seconds later Phyllis appeared.

It was a shocking sight; filthy water poured freely into kitchens, sitting rooms and garages while people were helped through their windows, laden down with bags and clothes and books, pillows and pictures and pets. Members of the Fire Service carried older people in their arms and on their shoulders, and a man with a tractor and trailer gave people lifts through the water. In places where people attempted to wade, the water was up to their thighs. Children were carried too; some cried with fear, others laughed with excitement, completely different responses to the same predicament. I saw dogs and cats and guinea pigs, and two goldfish in a tank which floated upright through the chaos.

I threw myself into the mix, helping wherever I could, carrying children and bags and one very unhappy marmalade cat. The sensation was like wading through treacle, the brown flood water with its myriad loot so much heavier than the sea. At times, it was like being in a surrealist painting. Random items of kitchenware bobbed past, a bread bin, a sock, a shoe, a bowl with cereal floating out of it, an electric lamp. I saw a passport and I grabbed it; someone would be glad of that later, I thought. I saw McFadden helping Stan out of a window and remembered that he'd bought one of these houses last year after his flat had been burned down with the pub. The poor man wasn't having much luck with places to live.

When everyone was safely out, I began giving lifts to the Beacon Hall in the Mini, packing people's belongings in as best I could. At one drop-off I caught sight of Jude Burns carrying a multitude of bags, trailed by a family with two kids; four drenched people, pushing hair away from their eyes, muddy and fed-up.

On my last trip up, I helped carry some bags myself into the main auditorium and saw that there were blow-up mattresses arranged in lines on the floor.

'Hardware shop,' Phyllis said as she appeared at my shoulder, her arms full of duvets and pillows. 'They donated a load of camping stuff. Very generous of them.'

'Just as well we have this place,' I said. 'At least there's plenty of floor space and a big kitchen.' The town had done a big job on the hall last winter and now it was warm, dry and insulated. It was good timing.

'And showers and toilets.' Phyllis put her bundle down with a heavy sigh. 'The important thing is that everyone is safe.'

I looked around me. People were beginning to get settled and the kitchen was full of people making tea. Things seemed calmer.

Until a loud panicked voice sounded in the doorway. 'Where's Pat Doherty? My dad.' A large woman with reddish hair and freckles appeared, her face flushed and anxious. 'Where's my dad? He can't walk properly. Did you get him out?'

'He's fine,' McFadden called over from where he was helping Stan with his belongings. 'He wasn't there. He'd gone to mass.'

The woman patted her chest in relief and slumped down into the nearest seat.

I turned my attention back to Phyllis. 'Is there anything else we need?'

'Bedding,' she said without hesitation. 'Can you get out to Malin and pick some up from home? I'll get some from the flat, but I know I haven't enough. How is the road out that way?'

McFadden was still nearby and within earshot. 'It's okay so far, but if you get out you mightn't get back, or you might get trapped here for the night. The Malin bridge should be fine but there's flooding at McSheffrey's. It's tidal but you never know . . .'

'Right, I'll go while I can.' I remembered what it had been like earlier on.

I made my way out to the car, where the light was strange and dark; rain was coming again within the next few minutes. Where the hell was it all coming from? I wondered. More to the point, when was it going to stop? I shuddered, with a sudden sense there was something otherworldly about what was happening, a harsh reminder of the belittling power of nature.

Tony from the Oak appeared, carrying a large cardboard box, as I opened the car door. 'I hear Stan's flooded,' he said anxiously.

I nodded towards the hall. 'He was, but he's okay. He's in there.'

'Good.' He looked relieved. 'He can stay with us. I'm going to do food for people down here tonight. I'll do a big pot of something with rice.'

'That's great. It looked as if the supermarket was flooded too so . . .'

He nodded. 'I have plenty of tins. Should only be for a night or two, hopefully just tonight.'

Before I could get into the Mini, a large black car drove in through the gates of the hall, causing us both to look up. It was the Lexus I'd been a passenger in earlier on. Though Derek had offered his services, I hadn't really taken him seriously, so I was surprised to see both him and Bob's wife emerge from the car.

Derek did the introductions and I had my first glimpse of Amanda Jameson close-up. She was a little younger than Bob, I thought. She was blonde and attractive and carefully made up, but there were tired lines around her eyes and her skin was slack. She was wearing a pink waterproof jacket, black trousers and runners.

I offered my condolences and she accepted them graciously. When I asked if she was sure she wanted to help, she smiled weakly. It was only hours since they'd had the news about Bob's death.

'What else are we going to do?' She shook her head. Her voice was soft. 'We're going stir crazy up there in that B & B just waiting for them to release Bob's body. And anyway, it's what Bob would have wanted; his whole life was about helping people.'

Did I imagine a snort? Jude was nearby carrying something high above his head. If I imagined it, then Derek did too. He glared at the larger man's back, put his arm around his sister-in-law, and they went into the hall, accompanied by Tony who said if they were sure, he'd find something for them to do.

The Mini started first time, but I drove to Malin as slowly as I could, constantly afraid of flooding the engine. About a mile out of Glendara I met a familiar car. It was the car of Maeve's husband, which she'd been driving since her jeep had been impounded. We pulled in alongside each other and spoke through the windows. Maeve was soaking, hair in wet tendrils around glowing cheeks.

I grinned. 'I know everyone's a bit damp at this stage, but you look as if you've been for a swim.'

She made a face. 'Don't. I've been helping to fish sheep out of a sheugh.'

'The joys of being a vet in wet weather.'

'But,' she said with wide eyes, 'you'll never guess where I'm off to now. There's been a sighting of the snake and I've been asked to go and have a look.'

'You're kidding.' I pulled at the handbrake. 'Where?'

'The golf club, would you believe? Greenkeeper found it, probably crying into his hands with the awful state of the greens. Somewhere on the sixteenth hole. I didn't realise it could have travelled that far since last night, but apparently some snakes can travel up to three to five miles an hour.'

'Wow. What will you do if you find it?'

'Be very careful,' she said with a wry look. 'We've no idea

what species it is or if it's dangerous or not. The greenkeeper tried to get a picture but no luck.'

'Yikes.'

She nodded towards a sack on the passenger seat. 'Hopefully we'll be able to catch it. Then we'll keep it in the clinic until someone who knows what they're doing arrives.'

I put the Mini back in gear. 'I'll let you go, so. Good luck!'

I drove on, crossing the old bridge into Malin, where the green was almost completely submerged. Guinness greeted me at the back door and I let him out. He darted out between my legs likes a bullet from a gun but returned within minutes.

How much time do I have? I wondered. Not much, unless I wanted to take the risk of not being able to get back to Glendara. But I was parched, so I put on the kettle and made a cup of tea, which I drank while moving from room to room. Marina's door was open; a glance inside confirmed that it was empty. I was glad to see that, like the office, she'd left it surprisingly clean and tidy.

In my own bedroom I changed out of my damp clothes, found some thick socks and wellies to go with my clean gear (I'd be able to give Phyllis back her massive pink spares) and a proper waterproof jacket. Then I grabbed as many blankets and sheets as I could from the hot press, and a sleeping bag which I pulled from the top of the wardrobe. I stuffed them all into a huge laundry bag. Then I raced out the door, leaving Guinness inside with food and water and a sandbox. He looked most unhappy at this arrangement but not at all keen to stay outside, so he hadn't much choice. I gave him a quick head rub; God knows when I'd see him again. I had a feeling I'd end up staying in town overnight. As an afterthought, I ran back inside and grabbed a toothbrush.

The roads were worse on the way back in, if that were possible. But I made it back to the hall to find Phyllis making hot tea and handing around her homemade biscuits. Tony had provided brown bread sandwiches and soup, which was being heated in a big cauldron on the two-ringed cooker in the hall kitchen. The smell of the soup reminded me that I hadn't eaten since breakfast, so when Phyllis asked me if I was hungry, I gratefully accepted some food and she and I sat in the foyer for a break and a chat.

'What a weekend to arrive back,' she said, taking a bite from a salmon sandwich.

'I know. Bit of a contrast to Florida.'

My phone buzzed and I took it from the pocket of my jeans. It was a text from Maeve, with a picture of the sack I'd seen in her car, but this time it had something in it. Something long and slithery. I passed it to Phyllis.

She pushed her glasses onto the bridge of her nose and frowned. 'What am I looking at?'

'It's from Maeve. She's caught the snake,' I said. 'They found him on the golf course.'

Her expression cleared. 'Oh, that's a relief. I hope he goes to a good home.' She handed me back my phone. 'If I'd been any-where near that man, I'd have bitten him too.'

'What did you say?' Neither of us had noticed Amanda behind us, carrying a pot of tea, but the soft voice I'd heard earlier now had a definite edge.

Phyllis flushed, clearly mortified. 'Oh God. I'm so sorry. I didn't mean that . . .'

But Amanda didn't even look at her; her gaze was fixed on my phone.

'They've caught the snake,' I said gently as I showed her the picture.

She put the teapot down and took the phone from my hand.

Her eyes welled. She didn't comment, just gave me back the phone, picked up the pot and walked off. Phyllis was still pink.

'Why did you say that?' I asked in a whisper.

She held her brow in disbelief. 'Ach, that was awful. I'll have to apologise to her properly. I didn't know she was here. I went off to get blankets too and I'd only just come back when you arrived.'

'Did you know Bob?' I didn't think anyone in town knew him apart from Mary. And then I remembered that Phyllis and Mary were old friends.

She shook her head. 'Not really, but I know how he treated Mary.'

I leaned in. 'Go on.'

She lowered her voice; she wasn't going to make the same mistake again. 'Mary could have had anyone she wanted, but she put her life on hold for that man. More than once, I tried to persuade her to travel with me; she'd have loved it. But she always wanted to be here. Where he could find her if he needed her.'

'Did he visit her here?'

'Never set foot in the county till this weekend as far as I know. But Mary, she kept thinking . . .' Phyllis paused and then she gave a shrug. 'Oh, I don't know what she was thinking, but she was wrong anyhow. He never gave her anything but grief.'

'Did she think he was going to leave his wife?'

Phyllis shrugged again.

I lowered my voice even further. 'Mary was a bit vague about their relationship. At first, I thought their romantic relationship was in the past and they were just friends, but then . . .'

Phyllis let out a sigh. 'Maybe that's the way it was from his perspective.' She gave me a crooked look. 'What do they call it – friends with benefits? But it certainly wasn't what Mary thought. And he sure as hell did nothing to discourage her.'

I thought about this for a minute. 'I presume that's why the charity-cycle crowd were staying with her? Her connection with Bob?'

Phyllis frowned. 'I presume so. I didn't know until Thursday that Bob was involved at all. Mary didn't mention him, just said she had a crowd of cyclists staying with her.' Phyllis stood up and gathered up her cup and plate. 'Anyway, I think we might have done all we can here. People seem to be settled.'

Liam appeared in the doorway of the kitchen while we were washing our dishes. 'There's to be an emergency town meeting,' he announced. 'To organise people and see what needs to be done.'

Phyllis turned from the sink. 'When?'

'In an hour, upstairs, in the band room.'

Phyllis looked at her watch. 'Okay, I've time to get back up to the shop and check on Fred.'

'I'll give you a lift,' I said. I needed to empty that basin again.

Chapter Fourteen

'Oh God. It's still coming down.' Phyllis yanked her bucket hat onto her head. 'As if it hasn't done enough damage.'

We made our way across the lake that had formed in front of the main door, to the car, only too glad of our wellies. Although drumming on the roof of the hall while we'd been having our chat had left us in no doubt that the rain had started again, it was still startling to witness the torrent of water flowing down the hill. Each time I emerged from a building now, the landscape had changed, the floods making everything unrecognisable and threatening.

As we drove to the square, we passed Harry's car, on its way back down towards the hall.

Phyllis clocked it and gave me a sneaky glance. 'I think McFadden called him to come down and check people out. No bad thing. Just as well we have a doctor in the town.'

I changed into second gear as I went up the hill. It was always an experience having Phyllis in the Mini; tall as well as broad, the top of her head brushed against the roof of the car and I usually spent my time pushing her voluminous skirts off the gears, which I did now.

'How long has he been seeing Marina?' I asked.

Phyllis smiled. 'Does it bother you?'

'Not in the slightest. I just wondered, that's all.'

'Not long I don't think, a few weeks, a month? It's moved pretty quickly though, from what I've observed.'

Phyllis spent much of her day glancing up from whatever book she was reading, pushing her glasses down her nose and peering out at the town through the bookshop window. And her shop was across the road from Harry's surgery.

'Oh really?' I was curious, despite myself.

'Let's put it this way – I'm not sure how many nights she's spent curled up with Guinness in your cottage during the past few weeks.' Phyllis winked.

'I'm happy for him,' I said. 'And her.'

'And . . .' Phyllis left a dramatic pause. 'You know what I'm going to ask.'

I did.

She crossed her arms. 'What's going on with you and the sergeant?'

And there it was, the question I'd been trying to answer for myself the past six months. I pulled into the square, parked and put my head on the steering wheel. 'Oh Phyllis, I don't know.'

She placed her hand gently on my shoulder. 'Go on. Tell me. You know I won't tell anyone else.'

I smiled. The odd thing was, I did know that. Despite Phyllis being a desperate gossip, and a close observer of people, everything she passed on was out of genuine concern. She hated injustice and if keeping a secret involved facilitating that injustice, she was happy to be known as the blabbermouth who couldn't keep her mouth shut. But if you told her something in confidence, she was utterly trustworthy.

I took a deep breath, looking straight ahead as the rain streamed down the windscreen. A white mark, which had remained there throughout the heavy blasts, was still there, illustrating the stubborn staying power of a bird dropping.

'He asked me to marry him.'

'What?' Phyllis's voice rose several octaves. I was surprised people outside on the street couldn't hear her. 'Molloy?' She sat back, looking pleased. 'Well, I didn't think he had it in him.'

'I haven't said yes.'

She raised her eyebrows. 'Have you not? And why's that now?'

I shook my head. 'I don't know. It was an odd proposal.'

Phyllis cut across me. 'I'm not sure what you expected – he *is* odd, Molloy. Mightily attractive but decidedly odd . . .'

I looked across at her, amused. 'Really? Mightily attractive?'

'Of course.' She gave me a nudge. 'And don't change the subject. What are you going to do?'

'I truly don't know. We weren't even together when he asked me. We'd broken up when he was in Cork and then he reappeared at Leah's wedding when there were those murders last summer.' I looked across at her. 'He just came out with it. I don't know if he asked because I was seeing Harry, or what. I just didn't see it coming. Even if we'd still been together it would have been unexpected. I didn't know how to react.'

Phyllis grinned. 'So is that why you ran away to America?'

'Maybe.' I nodded. 'Something like that – I had pretty much decided to go anyway. I needed a change of scene. But I did go a little early.'

She clicked her teeth. 'Poor Molloy.'

Suddenly I felt sheepish. I'd never really thought about Molloy's feelings. He was so damn stoic a lot of the time that it was sometimes easy to forget he was capable of having them.

'The thing is, I don't know if he meant it. It was almost as if

154

he regretted it as soon as he'd said it, as if he'd surprised himself as much as me. His face sort of froze.'

Phyllis's mouth curled into a smile. 'And what did yours do?'

'I suppose mine froze too.'

Phyllis looked at me, her eyes full of mischief. 'Maybe his freezing was a response to yours freezing. Maybe yours froze first.'

I met her gaze and we both burst out laughing.

'But I don't know what he expected,' I protested when we'd pulled ourselves together. 'We'd been apart for months. I'd been seeing Harry, not that that was going to continue.'

'So, what exactly did you say?' She examined my face. 'I mean, I presume you actually said something. You didn't just grab your passport and do a runner.'

Which reminded me, I thought, I'd better not forget to hand in that passport I'd found floating in the river. I could feel it still in my pocket. I told Phyllis and asked her to remind me.

'I will, but don't change the subject,' she said again sternly. 'What did you say?'

'I told him I'd need a bit of time and he said that was fine. He seemed almost relieved . . .'

'And neither of you have mentioned it since?'

'Exactly.'

'But you were together last night, weren't you? Or did I imagine seeing you getting into his car when you left the pub?' She gave me a shrewd look.

Typical Phyllis, I thought, she'd been watching us from her flat. I reddened. 'Yes. It just seemed the natural thing to do.'

'Well, doesn't that tell you anything? I agree he's a wee bit impenetrable, Molloy. And that can't be easy but . . .'

There was a knock on the window of the Mini and I jumped. I think we both did, immersed as we were in our counselling session. I wound down the window and Liam peered in, umbrella over his head.

'That meeting's been postponed for an hour. It's at five now.'

We climbed out of the car and made our way across the square with Liam. Phyllis gave my arm a little squeeze as we walked along, a silent acknowledgement of what we'd been discussing.

Liam and I left the bookseller at her flooded shop, watching as she opened the door and stood for a few seconds on the threshold as if to steady herself, before embarking determinedly across the shop floor, like a huge cruise ship, wading through the brown water. Fred looked mournfully down at her from the top step.

'Are you okay?' I called after her. She'd left the door open.

She waved without turning around. 'Not a bother. Don't worry about me. Once my books are safe, I'm happy. Close the door for me, will you?'

We closed the door. The shop already smelled dank.

'Poor Phyllis,' Liam said sadly.

'I know.'

'Any idea who that is?' he asked suddenly. His gaze had switched to his estate agents' office across the square.

I looked. A man was examining the listings in the window, a young guy of about thirty, unshaven, wearing a green Barbour jacket and carrying an umbrella. I shook my head. He didn't look familiar, but then I didn't have a very clear view.

'Well, rain or no rain, if he's in the market for something, I'd better go and see what he wants!' Liam said. 'I'll see you at the meeting.'

As Liam crossed the street, the man turned and I caught a glimpse of his face, confirming what I'd thought – he was a stranger. It was only when I reached the corner on my way to my own office that it occurred to me that he could be Lissa's husband.

He was about the right age and there weren't many new people in town that I hadn't seen, since no one could get in or out. I glanced back at Liam chatting to him, and he seemed affable enough. But I knew from bitter experience that affability was no bar to violence.

Lissa had given me her mobile number so I texted her and asked her to send me a picture of her husband, repeating my advice that she should really report the whole thing to the guards. I felt another twinge of worry about her. Even if there was little that they could do to protect her, I'd feel better if someone else knew. But she didn't reply.

When I turned the corner, Molloy was pacing up and down on the footpath outside my office, on the phone. He wasn't waiting for me, since he couldn't have expected me to be there on a Saturday, but he glanced up, met my eyes with his tired grey ones, and raised his hand.

'Time for a quick coffee?' I mouthed.

He nodded, stood behind me as I put the key in the lock and opened the door, and followed me in, continuing with his conversation. I caught snatches of it as I went to the kitchen to fill the kettle and to the bathroom to empty the basin. Most of it seemed to be about weather, accessibility, the roads and when they might be clear.

When I emerged from the kitchen, he signed off, put the phone on the counter and breathed out. 'An army crew will be able to build a temporary bridge at Quigley's Point but not until the floods abate, so it looks as if it's just McFadden and myself for the foreseeable.'

'Cripes.' I paused. 'Although I hear Maeve caught the snake.'

He nodded, taking his hat off and placing it on the reception desk. It was saturated. 'At least that's one less thing to worry about. I need to have a chat to Maeve as a matter of fact. She was to let me know what species it is. See if it gives us any more clues as to how Jameson died.'

'They're not normally aggressive, are they?' I asked, remembering what Maeve had said.

He shook his head. 'I'm no expert but not unless they're trapped or cornered, I don't think. But then again maybe it depends on the species?'

I leaned one elbow on the reception desk. 'So why was Bob Jameson bitten, then?'

'I have no idea. What are you thinking?'

'I'm wondering if the snake was set on him?' This was something I'd been wondering about. 'Jameson wasn't exactly fit but surely he'd have been able to move away in time, unless he stepped on it or something. I mean, how did he end up being bitten on the hand?'

Molloy was silent for a second.

'Well?' There was something he wasn't telling me.

'He was tied up,' he said eventually. 'We found a rope and there were marks on his wrists and ankles.'

I realised that must have been what was in the other evidence bag he'd handed to McFadden. One for the shoe, one for the rope. Something didn't add up though.

'He wasn't tied up when he was found, though, was he? When he fell on Maeve's jeep.'

'No. He must have managed to untie himself either before or after he was bitten but subsequently collapsed and died. And then his body was washed down the hill.'

I digested this for a second before I spoke again. 'Which solves how he got down the hill. But he must have walked up there himself presumably? It would have been nigh impossible to carry him up that bank if he was unconscious or helpless. He was a big man.' I remembered climbing up there on my hands and knees with Derek and I hadn't been carrying anything, let alone trying to drag an unconscious man.

'Agreed. He must have gone up there, willingly or otherwise, with whoever it was who killed him, and then got overpowered or knocked out. At which point he was tied up.'

I sucked air in through my teeth. As ways to die go, it was a pretty unpleasant one.

'Although we'll know more when the post-mortem is done,' he added.

'But where on earth *did* the snake come from?' I asked.

'Maybe someone was keeping it as a pet?'

'Who would keep a snake as a pet?'

Molloy shook his head wearily. 'You'd be surprised. The weather's been mild, so we could assume it just escaped from wherever it was being kept . . .'

' . . . If it hadn't bitten a man who was tied up at the time.' I finished his sentence for him.

'Exactly.'

I scratched my chin. 'Seems such a strange way to kill someone though, doesn't it? I mean someone must have gone to an awful lot of trouble.'

Molloy nodded. 'Assuming it was the snakebite that killed him. We still don't know that. Also, a very hands-off way of killing someone. Little physical contact. Leaving a snake to do the dirty work, so you could almost convince yourself you hadn't played a part in it.'

I hadn't thought about it that way. It had seemed more personal to me, but maybe Molloy was right. Something else struck me. 'Do you think it could have been a message?'

Molloy looked at me with interest. 'A message to whom? Not to Jameson himself. He's dead.'

'His wife? His brother? Someone connected with him? Someone connected with the charity? Everyone who was here for this cycle is connected in some way with the Jameson Grace Charity.'

'I'm having some background checks done on our Bob Jameson and his charity.' Molloy nodded at his phone on the reception desk, which had been beeping and lighting up since he'd put it there. 'And it looks as though he wasn't as squeaky clean as he made out.'

'Really? I saw that he got into trouble at some stage for taking too high a salary – he had to pay it back but there weren't any other consequences, I don't think.'

'Only the tip of the iceberg apparently. He seems to have made a lot of enemies behind the scenes. A few things just waiting to bite him in the arse.'

I grinned. 'Unfortunate choice of words.'

'What? Oh yes.' Molloy copped it but didn't smile. He looked as if he didn't have the energy.

I heard the kettle click off and I went into the kitchen to make the coffee. I shouted at him over the partition. 'What kind of things?'

Molloy followed me in and leaned against the wall with his arms crossed. 'It's bound to come out now that he's not here to defend himself and get injunctions or what not. But there have been several complaints which have brought the Jameson Grace Charity to the attention of the Regulator. There's an investigation ongoing which has only just started digging.'

'What kind of complaints?' I chucked some coffee into two mugs. I noticed they were chipped – I needed to get a few more.

'Complaints about the care homes, about the treatment of the residents there, along with broader issues to do with the charity and the misapplication of assets. It's all a bit of a mess, from what I can gather.'

I poured water into two mugs.

'Jameson left debts in places where he'd put on events,' he continued. 'Events where it was announced afterwards that a huge amount of money was raised. More damagingly, there were discrepancies between the money raised and what ended up in the hands of the charity itself. Questions that Bob Jameson would soon have had to answer.'

I looked up. 'Even though it's Bob's charity – he set it up?'

'He may have been the chief executive, but charities are audited. They have to pass muster with the Charities Regulator and make annual returns. The Jameson Grace charity had shown up some serious issues. Not least of which – he'd been raising money to build another Jameson Grace Home and a big chunk of it has gone missing.' He looked at me. 'There was a very big sword hanging over Bob Jameson's head before he died. The full story just hadn't got out yet, but it was about to break.'

'So that's why people were still raising money for him. They didn't know.'

'Possibly.'

'Do you think that's why he was killed? Something to do with money?' I handed Molloy one of the mugs. 'Sorry, no milk.'

'Thanks.' He shook his head. 'God knows. Although I'm not sure what would be gained by killing him. Surely it would be better to just take him to court?'

'You'd think.' I paused. 'What about his family? Do they benefit from his death?'

'If he was the one who siphoned off the money, he certainly

hid it well. He had all the trappings of wealth but everything he had was mortgaged to the hilt.'

I took a sip of my coffee, locking eyes with his tired grey ones. Despite everything he was doing to protect the town from the flood, the guards' priority being to preserve life, he was still working away at trying to find out what had happened to the dead man. No wonder he looked exhausted.

'It's funny. The only person who's said anything negative about him, at all, is Jude Burns.'

'The huge motorcycle guy? The paramedic?'

I nodded. 'From what I can tell, he couldn't stand Bob Jameson. He said something like "with Bob Jameson, charity began at home" but he wouldn't say what he meant by it.'

'But yet he was helping to raise money for Jameson's charity?' Molloy said.

I shrugged. 'I know. He said his mother had Alzheimer's. I wondered if she was in one of the Jameson Grace care homes.'

'Maybe he was one of the people who made a complaint?'

'Maybe.' I waited. 'So, if Bob Jameson embezzled money, where did it go? Where did he put it?'

'Good question.' Molloy raised his mug to his mouth.

The mug was one Phyllis had brought back from holidays a few years back. It had a picture of a spider monkey and the words *Greetings from Mexico!* on it.

'I wonder where the snake is from?' I asked. 'Its natural habitat, I mean?'

Molloy's gaze followed mine and he looked at the mug in his hand. Then he looked at me. 'I don't know. As I said, I'll have to check with Maeve. I've just had a missed call from her as a matter of fact. Why?'

'I wonder if the snake might have been from Nigeria?'

'Nigeria?'

'I've been looking at Bob Jameson's obituaries and he did some work in Nigeria. Lived there for a few years doing charity work. Lots of snakes in Nigeria.'

Molloy raised his eyebrows. 'Mmm. That's worth checking out, I suppose. Maybe there's a connection, revenge from something he did back then.'

I took a sip of my coffee, feeling quite pleased with myself. Molloy smiled, making me flush, and I was transported back to the conversation I'd had with Phyllis in the car. She was right: one of us was as bad as the other.

He drained his coffee and looked at his watch. 'Anyway, it's nearly five – are you coming to this meeting?'

Chapter Fifteen

We left the office, Molloy and I, intending to walk down together. But Jude Burns was waiting for me when we came out, standing on the opposite side of the street under one of those huge golfing umbrellas of his. He looked apologetic as he crossed to meet us.

'Sorry, I saw you go in with . . .' He nodded at Molloy, clearly unsure of his name. 'I didn't want to disturb you, so I thought I'd lie in wait.' He smiled sheepishly, an expression that seemed ill-suited to a biker of his dimensions. 'Can I have a quick word?'

Behind the smile he looked worried. 'Sure,' I said, glancing at Molloy. 'I have to get to this meeting, though, so I haven't got long.'

Molloy headed off, phone to his ear again, and I turned the key again to go back into the office. Jude shook the umbrella out and folded it, leaning it neatly against the door jamb.

'Is everything okay?' I asked.

He followed me into the reception area. 'Not really.' He paused. 'I wondered what Lissa had told you.'

I gave him a narrow look. 'You know I can't tell you. You're an accountant, so you know about confidentiality. It's up to her to tell you if she wants to.'

He looked down, one hand on the reception desk as if he

needed it to balance him. 'Ah, I know. Just thought it was worth a shot. I'm worried about her. I think there's more to this break-up with Chris than she's letting on.'

'Why do you say that?' I asked carefully.

He looked troubled. 'She's scared. There's something making her nervous, jumpy. She's always been a little fragile, Lissa.' He looked away as if immersed in his own thoughts. 'Sue's a different kettle of fish. Took off to London on her own when she was still a teenager, not a bother on her.'

'They seem close, though.'

He met my gaze again and nodded. 'They are, though Sue's younger by a few years. The confidence of the second kid.' He smiled briefly, then said simply, 'I don't know what to do.'

I stood beside him and we both turned in, elbows on the reception desk, like an altar. I had the feeling that there was something he wasn't telling me either.

'Have you tried to talk to her?' I asked.

He shook his head. 'I hoped she'd tell me herself without my pushing.'

'And why do you think it is that she hasn't confided fully in you?'

He turned to me with a guilty smile. 'Because I tend to be a bit over-protective where my girls are concerned.'

'So, she might be afraid of how you'll react?'

'Possibly.' He frowned and corrected himself. 'Probably. I've always felt they only have me to take care of them and so . . .' He shrugged helplessly.

I hesitated, choosing my words with care. Lissa may not be willing to tell the guards, but I knew how relieved I'd be if I wasn't the only person who knew that her life had been threatened. I *wanted* her to confide in her father.

'Maybe if you spoke to her and made it clear that you won't overreact? That you'll respect her wishes, just be there to support her however she needs you? Would that be worth a try?'

He opened his mouth again to speak, then stopped and smiled. 'Okay.'

'Good.' I paused. 'Do you mind my asking? You haven't mentioned their mother.'

His smile faded and he looked away. 'No, well, she's been gone a long time.' His voice faltered and I didn't push it.

'Well, they're lucky to have you in their corner.'

'I don't know about that. Their grandmother, my mother who I mentioned had Alzheimer's?'

I nodded.

'She was the one who took care of them. She lived with us for years, brought them up really. They were certainly lucky to have her. Maybe I'm more trouble than I'm worth.'

'Was she in one of the Jameson Grace Homes by the way? Your mother?'

He frowned. 'Why?'

'I just wondered. Since you were raising money for them.'

'She was.' There was a pause and he didn't seem willing to elaborate. After a few seconds, he straightened himself to his full height and shook my hand. 'Anyway, thanks for this. I'll take your advice. I will try and talk to Lissa again, calmly.'

'Glad to hear it.' I glanced at my watch. 'Now I really do have to get down to this meeting.'

He nodded. 'I'm going too so I'll walk you down. It looks as if we'll be here until tomorrow at the earliest, so I might as well try and be of some use.'

So, I left the office for the second time, in different company, trotting a little to try to keep up with Jude's lolloping walk.

We walked down past the graveyard, eerie in the fading light, gravestones emerging from a muddy lake like a scene from *Poltergeist*. It had stopped raining again, though who knows for how long. The times that it was dry, I found myself looking at the sky to see where the next rainclouds were forming.

'You're going to have a hell of a clean-up job when the floods subside,' Jude remarked, golfing umbrella swinging redundantly by his side.

I agreed. 'The community is good, though – they'll pull together and help each other out.'

'So I've seen.'

At the bottom of the hill, the floodlit hall was in sight; a troupe of people heading in and out with blankets and trays of food.

'The main problem will be insurance, I expect,' I said. 'We might have a few battles on our hands in the next few weeks.'

He smiled. 'No better woman for it, I suspect.'

'I hope you're right.'

I looked across at his face and realised I'd warmed to this gentle giant, but he was still the only person who had openly indicated his dislike of the murdered man. We were nearly at the hall. It was now or never if I wanted to ask him anything more. I might not get the opportunity again.

So, I just came out with it. 'How well did you know Bob Jameson?'

He stopped walking. 'Why?'

This seemed to be his standard response to any question to do with Jameson or his charity. Why was he deflecting so much?

'It's just, you seemed to have rather strong feelings about him.'

He looked at me crookedly. 'I might not have liked him very much, but I didn't set a snake on him, if that's what you're thinking.'

'I wasn't thinking that. But I did wonder why exactly you disliked him so much.'

He looked down. His expression had changed, as it always did whenever the dead man's name was mentioned. 'We knew each other when we were kids.'

'I noticed him calling you Julian in the pub,' I said.

Jude nodded with a scowl. 'That's my full name. Bob knew I hated it.'

I had a flashback to my own teenaged years. I knew what childhood grievances could do to a relationship. Plus, I'd seen what had happened to Stan and Tony who, despite being half-brothers, had very different childhoods. It had taken a lot of give and take from both to reach the point they were at now.

I glanced up to see Derek carrying a bag of bedding on his shoulder into the hall. He waved with his free hand and Jude returned the greeting. So, his antagonism didn't extend to Bob's twin, I thought.

'I was friends with both Bob and Derek,' Jude said, as if reading my mind. 'You couldn't be friends with one and not the other, they came as a package. The twins didn't have a great home life, but Derek was a nice guy. Bob was a bully in school, and he was a bully as an adult.' He shook his head. 'I know you're not supposed to speak ill of the dead but there really is no other way of putting it.'

'How so?'

'Derek was frightened of all sorts of things when he was a kid: heights, the dark, spiders, dogs.' He smiled. 'When he came over to our house, we used to have to lock poor Lolly up in the shed. She was only a tiny thing, a little terrier, but Derek was terrified of her.' He sighed. 'There were so many things Derek was terrified of, and Bob took advantage of that.'

I narrowed my eyes. 'How?'

He clicked his teeth. 'Ah, he'd put a spider in his brother's schoolbag, lock him in a room and turn off the lights, that kind of thing. All harmless enough pranks, but cruel to someone with those kinds of fears. He liked seeing Derek scared. Their father was a bully too. They were both afraid of him, but Bob got the brunt of it. It was as if he needed someone to bully in turn, to be bigger than.'

'Even if that somebody was his twin?' I said.

'Even though it was his twin,' Jude agreed. 'Derek managed to get rid of most of his fears eventually and, as they grew older, they began to play tricks on *each other*. But while Derek's tricks were funny, Bob's were mean.' He rubbed his neck. 'Bob's tricks were always mean. I think they still did it; played tricks on one another, a bit of one-upmanship. Bit childish but there you go, maybe that's twins for you.' He gave a half-smile.

'So what did you mean by the "charity begins at home" comment?'

He raised his eyebrows. 'About Bob, you mean?'

I nodded.

He straightened his shoulders and inhaled. 'Bob was a greedy bastard. When they were kids, you'd give them both a present; you know how twins always get the same things?' He paused. 'Well, Bob would break his, and then take Derek's for himself or give it away to some girl he wanted to impress, so Derek was stuck with the broken one.' He looked away. 'He wasn't much different as an adult.'

'But you're raising money for his charity? You and your daughters?' I was baffled, particularly in the context of what Molloy had just told me in the office.

Jude looked down at the umbrella he was holding and started to stab the ground with the metal point. Four taps, like the pint and the tea. 'As you guessed, my mother was in one of his care homes. The one in Sligo. She died there. I couldn't afford the fees and Bob gave me a massive discount. Whatever difficulty I had with Bob Jameson, he provided my mother with somewhere to live when she was really ill. If she hadn't gone there, she'd have had to go to Dublin and the girls wouldn't have been able to visit her.'

'I see. So, he did have some good qualities.'

'Not many, but I suppose I was grateful to him for that.' He sighed. 'Sue wanted to do the cycle when she spotted something about it online. Pay something back.'

'And that's why you volunteered to come along? Because Sue was involved?'

'It was when I found out that *he* was coming too that I decided to come. Not quite as philanthropic as I appear, eh?' He held his hands up in surrender. 'I didn't trust him, and so I felt better being part of it. Plus, I'm a trained paramedic so at least I could be of some use.'

As much as I liked Jude, something didn't add up. He hadn't really answered my question. I still didn't know exactly why he hated Bob Jameson so much.

He laughed as if noting my confusion, but he'd misinterpreted it. 'You think I'm a helicopter parent, don't you? Minding my daughters as if they were little girls.'

I gave it one more shot. 'I'm just trying to figure out what exactly you thought Bob would do, if you weren't here?'

But Jude shrugged and didn't answer, as if he'd already said too much. He lifted the umbrella and began striding again towards the hall, leaving me no choice but to trot after him, and once we'd reached the gates, my chance was gone. He held open the huge door and while we climbed the stairs to where the meeting was to be held, I resolved to push him again whenever I got the opportunity. There was something he wasn't saying.

Halfway up the stairs we began to hear voices. And at the top, we found the door to the band room was open and the room was packed, with not a spare seat to be found. The meeting was already in session, with lots of people speaking at the same time while the chairman of the town council tried to make himself heard over the din.

Jude and I slid in along the rear wall and found a spot to stand. From what I could gather, and it wasn't easy to distinguish one voice from another, there were concerns about rising water levels, property damage, old people, insurance, animals, roads, bridges, food supplies, medical supplies and possible power outages. All perfectly legitimate concerns; the problem being that each person believed their concern should take priority.

Finally, Molloy managed to call order, and the chairman of the town council took the floor. Short and balding with a combover and a significant paunch. which his pink shirt did not entirely cover, I was familiar with the man from photo calls and exhibition openings, posed pictures in the local paper when he was usually adorned with a chain of office. He'd wisely chosen to leave the jewellery at home on this occasion.

He cleared his throat. 'Now ladies and gentlemen, we have an agenda – so if we just stick to that we should cover everything, and everyone will be happy.' He rifled through his notes and began. 'Item one . . .'

Maeve appeared beside me. I hadn't even heard her come in.

'Everything all right?' I whispered.

'Did you get my pic?'

I nodded. 'Is he alive? The snake, I mean?'

'You didn't get the second one I sent you?'

I shook my head and she took her phone from her pocket, tapped it and passed it to me. The screen showed a photograph of an olive-green snake, about a metre long with black markings and a yellow collar.

'He's safe in the clinic, the wee skitter, as happy as Larry. Totally unconcerned about all the trouble he's caused.'

I handed her back the phone.

'Dozing happily in a tightly sealed tank to prevent any more escape attempts,' she added.

'Glad to hear it.' I paused, then whispered again. 'What species is he?'

She grinned. 'Nothing too exotic. A British grass snake — totally harmless.'

'You're kidding? After all that.' So, the Nigerian connection was a non-runner, I thought.

'He may have inflicted the bite but he's not our killer.'

'Did you tell Molloy?'

She nodded and was about to say something else until someone shushed us. She made a face and put the phone back in her pocket.

I looked around me at the rows of heads in front. Mary from the B & B was sitting in the same row as Phyllis and Liam, Tony and Stan were in the row behind, and the back row appeared to be occupied entirely by the newcomers in town; I spotted Derek and Amanda, and Jude's two daughters and grandson among them, although the two families were separated by three or four seats. Derek was wearing a purple T-shirt with the words *Sligo Ironman Challenge 2019* across the shoulders, and it made me think about the conversation I'd just had with Jude. I wondered if Derek's childhood with a bullying father and brother had made him determined to be physically strong and fit as an adult.

When Jude spotted his daughters, he gave me a nod and went up to join them, leaving me with Maeve. Sue looked up at her father and moved Peadar onto her knee to make room for him. The toddler often ended up on his aunt's knee rather than his mother's, I noticed.

The councillor finally finished his speech with a reminder that sandbags could be collected from the fire station. Then he stepped aside and Molloy stood up to address the crowd.

'Good evening, everyone. As you all know we have an additional crisis aside from the floods. A man died here last night under very strange circumstances. A visitor to our town.' He gave an almost imperceptible nod to Derek and Amanda whom he had spotted in the last row and they bowed their heads. 'As most of you also know, he was also bitten by a snake, though I must add that *no* link has been established between the bite and the man's death. And the good news is that the snake has now been captured and, importantly, we have confirmed that it is a harmless grass snake.'

There was a general hum around the room as people absorbed this latest development. Maeve gave me a wink.

'Can we eat him, if we run out of meat?' shouted some wag from the corner.

Molloy ignored him and continued. 'The fact remains that we are treating this man's death as suspicious. We are investigating it as best we can, under very difficult circumstances. Clearly we don't have the back-up and expertise we would usually have in a case like this because of the difficulty in accessing our town, so we ask all of you to pass on all and any information that you think might be useful in bringing the perpetrator or perpetrators to justice.' He paused, phrasing his next few sentences carefully. 'Also, I'd like you all to be vigilant, to exercise caution and concern for your own safety, and for your friends and neighbours. I do not wish to cause unnecessary alarm, but the reality is that since the town is cut off, the perpetrator is likely to be still among us.'

There was a collective shiver as people looked at each other. Did I imagine it or was there a special look of suspicion reserved for the outsiders?

'The last thing I will say is that clearly in all the circumstances, Garda McFadden and I are under considerable pressure on a number of different fronts and while we would appreciate any assistance that might be forthcoming, we would also appreciate people not adding to our workload by taking unnecessary journeys or getting themselves into difficulty unnecessarily. That's all for now. Take care of each other.'

Before he had a chance to stand aside, loud footsteps sounded on the stairs. Everyone turned towards the door as Hal McKinney the undertaker almost fell through it, breathing heavily and loudly. He waved urgently at Molloy, about to take his leave from the top of the room.

Molloy looked down at him. 'What's wrong, Hal . . .?'

The undertaker finally caught his breath. 'It's McSheffrey's Bridge. It's cracked. There's a big gaping hole where the road used to be.' The man's eyes were wide with shock. 'It just gave way.'

Maeve paled visibly beside me – a bit of a surprise considering she'd just captured a snake. 'I've just come that way, fifteen minutes ago.' She looked at me. 'The road to Malin is cut off. You're stranded.'

I frowned. 'I can go home by Culdaff, though, can't I?'

She shook her head. 'That road's flooded too. It has been since early this morning. Someone waved me back and I had to do a U-turn and go by Malin. That'll ebb away at some stage, but it hasn't yet.' Her eyes narrowed. 'Actually, I've just realised I'm not going to be able to get back to Moville now either. There's a tree down on the other road. We're both stranded.'

My shoulders slumped. 'Our little enclave is getting smaller and smaller. It's just the town now.'

A strange silence fell over the room as if everyone else was absorbing the implications of the latest development too. On Sue's knee, Peadar dropped his toy onto the floor and started wailing as if he'd picked up on the atmosphere in the room. But his cries broke the silence and a hum of conversation started again.

Then Hal spoke again, from the door, as if he'd recovered himself. 'I have a spare room I can offer to anyone who is stranded.'

Someone else stood up. 'I have two – the lads are away to Dublin, so I have plenty of spare room. I could even put someone on the couch if they're stuck. It folds out.'

Another voice came from the front of the room. 'I've a wee spare room too, with two single beds. And I've a granny flat.'

Voices started to emerge from all around the room, with people speaking at once. Before things got out of hand the councillor called for order again and placed his sheaf of notes purposefully on the table in front of him.

'Okay,' he called. 'Can you all come up to me, one by one? I'm going to put together a list of people who need accommodation and those who can offer it. And we'll match people up.'

He clicked his pen officiously. I got the impression that he was glad of a reason to use it, that at least he knew what he was doing if he was writing something down. People started to shuffle to the top of the room, reminding me of a queue for holy communion at a funeral.

Maeve gave me a crooked look. 'Should we join the queue for accommodation, do you think?'

'I've a couch in the office,' I said doubtfully. It was a two-seater – it might accommodate me at five foot and a bit, but I wasn't so sure about Maeve.

Molloy appeared at my shoulder and I turned. 'Have you a sec?' He corralled me over to the side of the room and spoke in a low voice. 'You won't be able to get back.'

'I know.'

Surreptitiously he slipped me a key. 'Stay with me.'

'Okay.' It sounds ridiculous, but I felt the oddest flutter in the pit of my stomach. 'Thanks.'

I'd never spent a night in Molloy's house. While we were trying to keep our relationship under wraps it seemed too public for me to stay overnight in the sergeant's house, just behind the Garda Station. Even now it would be quite the declaration for my rather recognisable car to be seen there, first thing in the morning. The pair of us seemed to have slipped into something even less clear than before, if that were even possible, but somehow, I didn't care and hadn't since I'd got back. Maybe Phyllis was right, and I'd been overthinking things all along.

I was about to ask Molloy if Maeve could stay too, when she appeared at my shoulder again.

'I'm staying with Phyllis. I presume you're . . .' She looked in Molloy's direction, but he was already engaged elsewhere. A woman in a bright red coat had pulled him to one side.

I nodded. 'Are you sure she'll have room for you with all the books? She's moved everything from the shop up to her flat, you know.'

'She says she does.' She grinned. 'I'll have no shortage of bedtime reading material anyway. Look I'd better go and ring home, let them know and see if they're all right.'

I watched her walk away, unsure what to do next. A gloom

had fallen over the room, darkening skies visible through the windows, turning from pale grey to charcoal. I looked at my watch – it was half six but seemed later. Molloy gave me a nod as he left with the woman in the red coat – some new crisis, I assumed – and it occurred to me that I should probably ring my parents and let them know I was all right. They were bound to be worried if they'd heard about what was happening here.

My thoughts were interrupted by raised voices across the room, and I looked over, taken aback to see Jude's daughter Sue having an argument with Amanda, Bob Jameson's widow. She was pulling on the sleeve of Amanda's coat as if trying to force the older woman to talk to her, but Amanda didn't want to engage. It seemed a strangely aggressive attack on a recently bereaved middle-aged woman. Jude, who'd been speaking to Phyllis, strode over to intervene. He whispered something to his daughter, gave her a warning look, and she withdrew, re-joining her sister and nephew.

I cast my eye around the room and saw that Mary, who was now with Phyllis, had been watching what was going on too. Phyllis put her hand on Mary's shoulder as if to comfort her.

I went over to join them. But as I approached, Phyllis cleared her throat as if changing the subject and when she spoke her voice was unnaturally loud. 'We were just wondering if we should pool food and all eat here together in the hall? What do you think?'

Phyllis was a terrible dissembler, but I said nothing. 'Maybe.'

Her suggestion brought back flashbacks of the previous summer and a storm that had left Molloy and I stranded overnight on an island. This was becoming a bit of a habit, I thought, although I'd never been stranded with the whole town before.

'I was going to suggest it to "himself".' Phyllis glanced at the councillor, still taking names, beginning to become a bit flustered, his sheets of paper looking a little less neat. 'Although maybe I'd better leave him alone for a bit – he looks as if he can only manage one thing at a time.'

'I'm not sure,' Mary said, biting her lip. 'I should probably take care of my guests first.' She glanced over at Amanda and Derek, seated now on two chairs side by side, staring straight ahead and not speaking, each clearly immersed in their own thoughts. 'Although I have plenty of food so anyone who wants is welcome to come up and eat with me. My rooms are full, but I could easily fit a few more around the tables.'

Phyllis touched her on the shoulder again and said, 'That's kind of you, Mary. I'll pass that around.' She sighed. 'Maybe you're right – it would be too complicated. Maybe it's better that people help each other on a piecemeal basis.'

She smiled at her own pun, but her eyes flickered in concern at her friend. Mary looked haunted, I thought, with dark shadows beneath her eyes. She seemed to have aged about five years in the past twenty-four hours.

Without warning the lights went out and we were plunged into darkness. There was a shout from the front of the room, a voice I recognised as Derek's.

'Where's the fuse box? I'm an engineer.'

Liam's mobile phone illuminated his face and washed it in a blue hue. 'It's at the bottom of the stairs.' He shuffled in the darkness. 'I'll show you.'

Other phones started to appear around the room too, some using flashlight apps, which were surprisingly effective. We'd be in serious trouble if the mobile phones stopped working too, I thought. No one had even suggested looking for candles. Liam and Derek brushed past us and for the next few minutes we could hear their voices downstairs. Eventually the lights came back on, provoking a hum of relieved chatter.

Derek reappeared in the doorway, sounding authoritative. 'Just a tripped switch this time, but I think we should be getting candles and torches together in case there's a proper power outage.' He even looked a little better than he had earlier, I thought. Finding something useful to do had helped him.

'Handy to have an engineer around the place,' someone remarked.

'For a tripped switch?' someone else said with a laugh.

Derek's face flushed a dark red. It was the same voice as the snake-meat comment, I thought. Whoever it was, they were hushed quickly. Derek opened his mouth to speak again, then appeared to change his mind, and returned to his seat.

Shortly afterwards people began to file out of the room to head back to their houses, the B & B or their nests downstairs, a gloomy silence to their movements. Maeve, Phyllis, Liam and I looked at one another.

'What now?' Phyllis asked.

'Sit it out?' Liam said. 'Everyone seems safe for the moment. The only thing we can do is wait till morning and hope it stops raining and the floods subside. Then we'll have work to do.' He smiled. 'Pub? Fetch candles and torches and meet in the pub?'

'We *have* been told to stay dry and warm and out of the way,' Phyllis said brightly.

'I can't,' Maeve said. 'I've had a few calls and I'm going to have to try my best to see who I can get to.'

'Need any help?' Liam asked.

Maeve shook her head, suppressing a smile. Trying and failing, I suspected, to picture Liam with a sheep in his arms. 'No – I should be fine. The farmers will all have help organised. Thanks anyway, Liam.' Her smile faded. 'Just as long as I don't come across anything like I did last night.'

'Keep your phone charged,' Liam warned, causing the rest of us to check ours, of course.

Mine was at 25 per cent. I'd forgotten to bring my charger from home, but I had a spare in the office I could collect. In the meantime, the Oak pub with its roaring fire was a far more attractive option than going back to the sergeant's house on my own.

Chapter Sixteen

It was still dry when we emerged from the hall, and it was so good to be able to breathe in some fresh air without battling the wind and the rain. It felt oddly calm, making it hard to imagine that we were cut off from the rest of the world. Until, that was, you came across a stretch of water you couldn't cross, or saw a floating oil tank, or an abandoned car, or a doorway plugged with sandbags. With the daylight almost gone, the town looked strange and unfamiliar, reminding me of J. G. Ballard's novel *The Drowned World*, about a post-apocalyptic, flooded London. I almost expected to see huge swamp-like plants and boats navigating their way through the square.

All of which meant that it was a relief to walk into the unchanged surroundings of the Oak. Tony had lit a very welcoming fire and we made our way to the table closest to it, Phyllis and I collapsing into the battered old couch while Liam went up to order drinks.

'So,' Phyllis said, pulling off her hat and placing it on the table. 'My shop is closed and so is your office . . .'

'It would be anyway since it's the weekend,' I added.

'And there's nothing we can do for the moment while the Fire Service and the county council have everything in hand . . .'

I knew what was coming next.

'So, I think we should find something useful to fill in our time.' Phyllis rubbed her hands together. 'Let's see if we can figure out what happened to the late Bob Jameson.'

And there it was. There was a twinkle in the bookseller's eye that I knew of old. I also knew that any protest would be futile.

'Let's start with the last time we saw him alive,' she said. 'Here in the pub, snogging his wife. What time did he leave here? And who saw him leave?'

'I didn't,' I replied. 'He was still here when I left.'

'Same here,' Phyllis said, momentarily disappointed.

'Are you chatting about our snakebite victim?' Liam asked, having arrived back with a tray of hot drinks and a pint of Coke. 'Tony says he's rapidly running out of milk, by the way. We'll all be on the espressos tomorrow.'

'Actually,' I said, 'Molloy said it was a harmless grass snake, so it looks as if it wasn't the snakebite that killed him. Unless there's another one lurking around somewhere.'

Phyllis grabbed her hot chocolate. 'Or he was allergic, or something.'

'I saw him leave,' Liam said, sinking into a low armchair. 'He left the same time as I did.'

'Was the wife with him?' Phyllis asked.

Liam bowed his head in acknowledgement. 'She was, and the brother.'

'Twin,' I added.

Phyllis turned to me. 'Oh, are they twins? Mary never mentioned that. They don't look very alike.'

Liam gave her a quizzical look. 'Mary?'

'Mary and Bob Jameson were old sweethearts,' Phyllis said, taking a sip of her chocolate. 'About six million years ago.'

Liam raised his eyebrows over his Coke. I assumed he too found it hard to imagine Mary as part of a couple. 'But they were still in touch?' he asked.

Phyllis nodded. She avoided Liam's eye, some attempt to be discreet for Mary's sake, I assumed.

But Liam wasn't letting go. 'Hang on a second,' he said, placing his glass back on the table. 'Were they still . . .?'

'Possibly,' I said. 'They certainly kept their relationship a secret. Anyway,' I said, to change the subject, 'it was Derek himself told me they were twins, but I agree, they didn't look alike. I think they had very different lifestyles.'

'But this was his first visit to Inishowen?' Liam asked.

'First and last,' Phyllis said ominously.

'What did you see when you saw them leave?' I asked Liam.

He shrugged. 'Ach, not very much. All three of them got into a taxi, to go back up to Mary's, I presume. They could have walked but of course it was lashing.'

'How did they seem?' Phyllis asked intently. I wondered if she was getting her teeth into this for Mary's benefit or out of simple curiosity.

'What do you mean?' Liam asked.

'Bob and the wife,' she said irritably. 'And the brother, I suppose. Were they getting on or arguing? Having a laugh or what?'

Liam spread his hands. 'I don't know, do I? They seemed all right. Too busy trying not to get drenched, I'd guess. I was having the same problem myself – trying to put up my umbrella and getting whacked in the face with it.'

'So, they got back to the B & B anyway,' Phyllis said thoughtfully, taking another sip of her drink. 'I presume Molloy or McFadden will have spoken to the taxi driver to confirm that.'

'I spoke to him this morning as a matter of fact,' I said and they both turned to me. 'It was Jack from Glendara Taxis – he gave me a lift in from Malin. All he said was that he thought Bob Jameson was a heart attack waiting to happen. That was before the news came out about the snakebite and everyone thought that's what had killed him.'

'He was an unhealthy-looking man all right,' Phyllis said grimly. 'But I suppose we won't know anything till the post-mortem. So what about when they got back to the guesthouse, I wonder?'

'Derek said he and Amanda went straight to bed,' I said.

Liam's eyes narrowed in amusement.

'Separately,' I added quickly. 'Bob stayed outside for a cigarette. Derek says he thinks he heard him come in, but he can't swear to it.'

'A cigarette?' Phyllis said, her brow furrowed. 'Wasn't he head of a cancer charity at some stage?'

'That's why he kept it a secret, apparently, but he just couldn't give them up.'

The bookseller made a harrumphing noise. 'Seems like that man was full of secrets.'

Liam frowned. 'But it was pelting. Would he really stay outside in that weather even if he was desperate for a fag?'

'Actually, I'm pretty sure I noticed a shed,' I said. 'Maybe he had his cigarette in there?'

'Maybe.' Phyllis sat back with satisfaction. 'And maybe someone was waiting for him there and nabbed him.'

'Or persuaded him to go with them,' Liam suggested. 'He was a big man, he'd be hard to transport if he was unconscious.'

This tallied with what Molloy had said, that Bob Jameson went willingly with whoever it was that had killed him.

'I'll ask Mary about the shed,' Phyllis said, eagerly taking out her mobile phone. And before we could stop her, she had dialled the number and was walking away from the table. Liam took another slug of his pint.

I sat back for a few seconds, the firelight warming my face. I watched Phyllis pace up and down the pub muttering into her phone and Liam contemplating things through the prism of his glass, and I was fascinated by their curiosity, their eagerness to investigate what had happened to this stranger in their town.

'So, who was your prospective customer?' I asked.

Liam frowned, mystified.

'The man looking in your window earlier,' I clarified, remembering suddenly that Lissa hadn't replied to my text. I'd never received the photograph of her husband that I'd asked for.

'Oh him.' Liam shook his head. 'He wasn't a prospective customer. Said he was just curious what the prices were like up here. He seemed a bit lost, to be honest, as if he was killing time.' He trailed off; something had caught his eye at the bar. 'There he is now, as a matter of fact. He's just come in.'

I looked up. The same man in the Barbour jacket was ordering a drink. Before I could say anything, Phyllis returned to the table and sank down with a sigh.

'Mary said there's a turf shed at the side of the house, where she parks her car. She doesn't allow smoking in the house, so she knows it's where some of her guests go to have a fag.'

Phyllis took a deep breath and patted her chest 'She said she knew Bob was a smoker, had been since college, but whether he came in last night or not, she couldn't tell me. Said she goes to bed at half nine because she has to be up at six to do the breakfasts.' She smiled. 'I think she sleeps like a baby with all that sea swimming she does. Plus she said she'd had a broken night the night before.'

The row, I thought to myself, the row between Bob and Amanda had woken her the night before. 'So she heard nothing?'

'She did say she heard the front door slam sometime before twelve. But she couldn't tell who it was or how many there were. She said she went straight back to sleep.' Phyllis looked at Liam. 'That could have been Derek and Amanda, I suppose, couldn't it?'

Liam's brow furrowed for a second and then cleared. 'Aye. That would be about right, time wise. I think it was about half eleven when they got into the taxi.'

'Right,' I said. 'So, Bob could have met someone outside the B & B, who took him up to Mamore Gap.'

I glanced over at where the man in the Barbour jacket had taken a seat on one of the bar stools. Was he Lissa's husband? Had she seen him outside the B & B last night? Could he really have had something to do with Bob Jameson's death? And if so, why? What was the connection between them?

'That's much more likely than having him hauled from his bed,' Liam said. 'His wife would have known if that had happened.'

'Unless she was involved,' Phyllis said darkly.

I nodded. Liam was right. 'Bob Jameson was fully dressed when he was found so he hadn't gone to bed.' I didn't mention the one shoe. 'And you're right, Liam – he was a big man – so it seems likely that he went willingly with whoever it was. It must have been someone he knew.'

I glanced up at the bar again. The man in the Barbour jacket was of much slighter build than Bob Jameson. I couldn't imagine how he would have been able to overpower him.

'And the wife never noticed him missing?' Liam said. 'All night?'

'She fell asleep, waiting for him to come back in and then was worried when she woke up early in the morning and found he wasn't there. Wears earplugs apparently.'

'Phyllis is right – it could have been the wife or the brother who took him away,' Liam said. 'He'd have gone willingly with either of them.'

'Okay, but even if one or both had a motive, on what premise did they get him to go with them?' Phyllis said, closing one eye to think. 'They'd hardly have suggested a walk at that time of night in the lashing rain, would they? In fact, whoever it was, what ruse did they use to get him to go with them?'

'Blackmail?' I suggested.

'Bribery?' Liam said.

We sat there, the three of us, stumped, sipping at our drinks.

'Did Mary say she heard a car?' I asked eventually. 'Or just people coming in?'

Phyllis shook her head. 'All she heard was the front door.'

I wondered if this was what Phyllis and Mary had been talking about in the Beacon Hall too; had Phyllis been quizzing Mary, or was Mary asking her friend if she could figure anything out?

'Is there anyone who lives close to Mary who might have been looking out the window and seen anything?' I asked.

But I knew the answer before Liam and Phyllis shook their heads. Part of the attraction of Mary's was that it was out on its own, on the brow of a hill with spectacular views of the surrounding countryside. We were all clutching at straws, and we knew it.

Suddenly the pub door opened, and Derek and Amanda came in. There was a hush, the usual response to the recently bereaved. They walked straight up to the bar, avoiding any eye contact. But they were unlucky in having to wait for a few minutes while Tony served Barbour-jacket man at the end of the bar so they stood there looking a bit lost. When Amanda pressed her hand to her forehead, looking distressed, Phyllis stood up and made her way over to them.

I was surprised. I'd have thought the bookseller was the last person Bob's widow would want to see after the remark about her dead husband. And I was even more surprised when, after exchanging a few words with them, Phyllis returned to our table to say, 'Shove up. They're coming to join us.'

Liam stood up and shook hands, offering condolences. They both looked awful, Amanda, in particular. Her eyes had a glassy quality that I hadn't noticed before. She'd changed clothes since we'd seen her at the hall: she was wearing a glittery top over her black trousers as if she was dressed up to go out. It seemed a little off, but I suppose the pub was a better option than sitting in the B & B all evening.

'Can't be easy being stuck somewhere you don't know at a time like this,' Liam said, once they were settled in their seats.

Amanda muttered, 'No, it isn't.'

Tony appeared with their drinks, nodding as he set them down. 'On the house.' He smiled as he handed Derek his bottle of non-alcoholic beer. 'You and the sergeant are the only ones who drink those.'

Once they'd thanked him and Tony had returned to the bar, it quickly became clear exactly why our companions had chosen to put Phyllis's comment aside and join us at our table. They couldn't stand to be in one another's company, and we provided dilution. Neither Derek nor Amanda addressed a single comment to one another, nor looked in one another's direction the whole time they were with us. Derek, in particular, seemed taciturn and tense.

I wondered what had happened. Derek had been comforting

Amanda at the B & B this morning, although I realised now that I only had his word for that. The memory of the two of them sitting wordlessly beside each other in the hall came back to me, along with Amanda's uncomfortable scene with Jude's daughter Sue. And then there was Derek's considerably more comfortable encounter with Sue that I'd witnessed from the office window. What was that all about? With a jolt I remembered something he'd said a few days ago, at the waterfall, when we'd been on our way back from Mamore. About developing feelings for someone else. Could that someone else be Sue? There was quite the age gap between them.

I was mulling this over when I noticed that while Liam and Phyllis had managed to get Derek to chat, Amanda was staring bleakly at the wall. I was beside her, so she fell to me.

'I really am so sorry about Bob,' I said, feeling somehow that I needed to say it again. 'I met him briefly here in the pub last night. Such an awful, awful thing to happen.'

'It's absolutely unbearable.' She cast a cold eye in Phyllis's direction, so maybe she hadn't forgiven her after all. She'd had work done on her face, I saw now; the giveaway swelling above her mouth was more obvious when she frowned. 'I don't know what I'd have done if that doctor hadn't given me something.'

So that explained the glassy eyes, I thought. What had Harry given her? I wondered.

'Must have come as such a shock.'

A tear snaked down her cheek, and she took a tissue from her bag and rubbed her nose. 'I can't imagine how someone could do something so terrible.'

'You've no idea who might have wanted to . . .' I began tentatively. God, I just couldn't help myself, could I?

But she shut me down immediately, her voice flat. 'There

was no one. Everyone loved Bob. Bob was hugely respected and admired for all of the hard work he'd done for so many causes over the years.'

It was the same mantra I'd heard from Derek, almost word for word. I took a sip of my now cold tea and changed the subject. 'Do you work for the charity too?' I found myself using the tone in which I'd ask a child what they wanted to be when they grew up. I wasn't sure why.

But it worked. Her expression softened and she seemed pleased. 'I'm an interior designer.'

It occurred to me that maybe it wasn't something she was asked very often; she was a woman who'd lived in the shadow of her husband. 'What kind of work do you do?'

'Anything I'm asked, to be honest. I did our home.' She paused, and her eyes welled up again. She dabbed at them with the tissue. 'I enjoyed doing it so much that I started doing it for our friends. Bob even arranged to have my services raffled in some of the charity auctions he's done, so that's kept me busy . . .'

She trailed off and I was distracted by Derek getting up from his seat. He brushed by us with an urgency that was verging on rude, and Phyllis and Liam looked up too, frowning, as if he'd left in the middle of a conversation. I had a feeling I'd overheard Liam talking up the golf club. I watched him stride across the floor to the bathrooms at the back of the pub and with an effort I returned to my chat with Amanda.

'You must have spent a lot of your time going to balls and charity functions.'

She nodded. 'Bob loved them; but then he was the life and soul of the party, me not so much. I'm more of an introvert really, but he coaxed me out of my shell.' She smiled sadly. 'Made me travel.'

'I saw that he worked in Nigeria. Were you with him?'

She touched her collar bone; the skin there was pink and blotchy as if she'd been rubbing it. She did that now, scratching at a raw patch just above her neckline as if she wasn't even aware she was doing it. 'Yes, we lived there for three years. We were very happy there. We adopted two children.'

And with that I adjusted my mental image of their family. Oisín and Finn were not typically African names.

She gazed at the wall again. 'Two lovely boys. I wouldn't have wanted a girl. Girls can be such bitches.'

The language seemed at odds with her appearance, and the venom in her voice made me flinch. But she didn't seem to notice.

Instead her eyes filled. 'It's so hard being trapped here, not being able to give them a hug. I've spoken to them on the phone, but it nearly makes it worse.'

'I can only imagine.'

She twisted a silver cross on a chain around her neck. 'At least they have each other. They were siblings when we adopted them so they're very close – always have been.'

'Like Bob and Derek,' I said with a half-smile.

But she didn't respond. Instead she lowered her eyes and took a sip of her coffee.

Phyllis and Liam were deep in chat, so I took my chance. I reached out for her and lowered my voice. 'What do you think might have happened to Bob, Amanda?'

She shook her head, but I persevered. 'I'm sure you're right about him being liked and respected, but the fact remains, someone did wish him harm. Don't you want to know who that was?'

She covered her mouth with her hand as if afraid of what she might say, then she turned away. 'There's always someone out there capable of killing any one of us.'

Chapter Seventeen

At that moment, Phyllis asked Amanda something which prevented me from asking her anything else, which was probably just as well. Then Liam clambered to his feet, kicking one corner of the table and almost causing a glass to fall – he'd found himself in the low armchair, very comfortable but a devil to get out of. And he followed Derek to the bathroom.

While they were gone the chat inevitably turned to the weather. According to those who called to the table to commiserate with the bereaved visitors, there was an expectation that the worst was over, and that the water would abate overnight. In the morning bridges would be repaired and the clean-up would begin, and things could finally start to get back to normal. I hoped they were right. But in the meantime, we had tonight to get through. After a valiant effort from Phyllis, Amanda fell silent again and I left her to her thoughts. I suspected it was partly my fault.

'Anyone hungry?' Phyllis asked, as Derek and Liam finally returned to the table.

'We'd better get back to the B & B. I think Mary is preparing something for us there,' Derek said, looking at his watch. He seemed reluctant to leave, maybe not relishing the prospect of being alone again with his sister-in-law. But Amanda stood up obediently, and without meeting his eye allowed him to help her with her coat.

'I'd better get back too,' Liam said. 'The wife will be wondering if I've floated off . . .'

He stopped suddenly, glancing shamefacedly at Bob's widow, but she didn't seem to have noticed. There really was something childlike about her. Maybe it was the sedative Harry had given her.

'Fancy coming back to mine?' Phyllis asked me with a gentle nudge. 'I haven't a lot in, but I made tomato soup yesterday, which should still be all right, there's some bread that we can toast and there are tins. I can easily throw something together.'

'Are you sure?' I asked. The only other option was to get chips and take them back to the stationhouse alone, which wasn't particularly appealing. Then I remembered the chipper was closed.

'Of course,' she said. 'I'll have to prepare something for the poor vet when she gets back anyway, and I could do with the company.'

'That would be great, Phyllis, thank you.'

'And,' she lowered her voice mischievously, 'you can text the sergeant if you like. I'm sure he hasn't eaten either.'

The four of us made our way outside in a huddle. It was eight o'clock and night had fallen while we'd been in the pub, but unusually for a Saturday night in Glendara, there were hardly any cars about; people obviously heeding the warning to stay put until the floods had abated. It meant that the acoustics were strange; footsteps issued cavernous echoes amid dripping gutters and the swish of ground water. It reminded me of Venice off-season.

After saying goodbye Derek and Amanda set off walking towards the hall as they'd left the Lexus there. As soon as they were out of earshot Liam whispered furiously.

'Jesus Christ! I just walked in on Derek in the jacks with his hands around that guy's throat.'

Phyllis whirled around. 'Who? What guy?'

Liam glanced at me. 'Your man who was up at the bar, who was looking in my window earlier. The fella in the Barbour jacket.' He rubbed his neck anxiously. 'Derek had him up against the wall. I thought he was going to hit him. He *was* going to hit him,' he corrected himself, 'if I hadn't walked in and stopped him.'

'Why?' I said.

'I have no idea. But I'll tell you one thing.' He looked at Derek's departing figure. There was a gap of at least five full feet between himself and Amanda on the footpath. 'That man has got a wile temper on him.'

He walked back to his car, still shaking his head, while Phyllis and I set off towards her shop, splashing and squelching down the hill.

'I wonder what that was about?' Phyllis said. 'Do they know each other, or did he just lose it with some random stranger?'

I was asking myself the same question with some supplementary ones thrown in. But before I could give it any proper thought, something occurred to me and I stopped to take out my phone. 'You go on, Phyllis. I need to ring Charlie, my neighbour, and get him to check on Guinness.'

'And Molloy,' she said. 'Ring Molloy.'

I smiled. 'Okay, okay. I'll follow you down.'

The phone's screen showed 5 per cent, so there should be a call or two left in it and if not, I could get the charger from the office. I dialled the number, but before Charlie could even pick up, there was a shout from down the street. Phyllis was bellowing at the top of her lungs, 'Help! Come quickly.'

I ran down the hill as fast as I could, and came to a halt at a figure slumped in the doorway of the bookie's office. It was a woman, chin on her chest, eyes closed as if she had passed out. She was sitting in about four inches of water that had gathered there and Phyllis was kneeling beside her. She lifted the woman's chin and my heart sank. It was Jude's daughter, Lissa. Her face was grey, her mouth blue, but it looked as if she was still alive, if only just.

'What's happened to her?' I asked. 'Has someone . . .'

Phyllis spoke urgently. 'I think she's taken something,' she said, hand on Lissa's forehead and listening for her breath. She was totally unresponsive. The bookseller pushed at my shoulder. 'Go. I'll stay here with her while you run and fetch Harry.'

Harry's surgery was just across the street and, though it would be closed now, he lived in the flat above it. I ran splashing through the water, breathless by the time I rang the doorbell, relieved to see that there was a light on upstairs. I pressed the bell and rapped furiously on the door, disconcerted when a female figure appeared through the glass.

Marina.

She opened the door.

'Oh,' I said, taken aback. 'I thought you'd gone.'

Not only had I thought she'd gone but she hadn't appeared for any of the rescue jobs earlier on, although most of the town had got involved. And she hadn't been at the town meeting, which even the visitors had attended.

She shook her head, looking embarrassed, as if she could tell what I'd been thinking. 'I left it too late to go. Are you looking for Harry?'

'Yes.' I nodded, pulling myself together, remembering the emergency at hand. 'Someone's collapsed.' I waved towards the

195

other side of the street. 'Over there outside the bookies. Where is Harry?'

'I'm not sure, but I'll ring him,' she said, pulling her phone from the back pocket of her jeans.

Harry answered straight away. Marina explained what had happened calmly in plain concise language (it appeared she was better in court than on paper) and hung up.

'He'll be five minutes. He's just down at the hall giving blood pressure medication to someone who didn't manage to get theirs out of their house.'

Twenty minutes later, the harsh light of the hospital corridor hurt my eyes as Phyllis and I sat staring wordlessly at the examination room door, waiting for it to open. I'd called Mary at the B & B and left a message for Jude to come to the hospital as soon as possible. I'd also texted Molloy.

As I sat there looking around me, at the sterile green and grey walls, I was sharply aware that we were in the same hospital as Bob Jameson's body, lying in a freezer downstairs still awaiting a post-mortem. I'd seen the sign for the morgue on the way in when we'd followed the gurney into the little community hospital, and it had given me a shiver.

I hoped to God that Lissa wasn't about to join him. She hadn't yet regained consciousness. Phyllis and I had watched helplessly while Harry had given her oxygen and adrenaline and arranged for the ambulance to take her in. I was feeling huge pangs of guilt. Lissa Bennett had come to me for help and I had done nothing, just let the whole thing sit while I hoped she would confide in her father or the guards. I'd been feeling guilty about breaking Mary's confidence and so I'd kept Lissa's. It looked as if I'd kept the wrong secret.

I shifted around on the hard plastic seat trying and failing to get comfortable, so I stood up to pace up and down the corridor. What the hell had happened to her since she'd spoken to me? She hadn't replied to my text, although that of itself didn't mean anything. Was it possible her husband had something to do with this? Was Barbour-jacket man her husband? And if so, why had Derek attacked him?

Suddenly the outer door burst open and Jude and his other daughter Sue came running in. Sue had Lissa's toddler in her arms as usual. Their eyes were wide and panicked.

'What happened?' Jude demanded, his face taut. 'Where is she?'

I tried to explain as best I could, while Phyllis intervened with calming words, her hand on Jude's arm. His face fell when I told him what had happened, but along with the shock there was recognition, I was sure of it.

The door to Lissa's hospital room opened and Harry and a nurse came out. Harry said something to the nurse and she headed off down the corridor, while he came over to our little group.

'How is she?' Jude asked. 'Will she be okay?'

Harry looked questioningly at him.

'I'm her father.'

'Okay,' Harry said calmly. 'Well, she's asleep but she's stable. She's on a drip.' He paused as if to let Jude take it in. 'She's taken some sort of a depressant, a sedative.'

Jude's eyes first welled in relief, then he looked at the floor, deflated, shoulders slumped. Was it possible this was not the first time this had happened?

'We think it may be a new drug called GHB,' Harry said. 'She regained consciousness for a few minutes, and she said G. I think to help us.'

'What's GHB?' Jude asked.

I'd heard of it, having read something about it in one of the US newspapers, but didn't know much about it.

'It a new club drug, easy to make, difficult to trace. Very popular at the moment. It's a party drug; it's been replacing ecstasy. We've been seeing it up here a bit – not very regularly but a bit. It's very dangerous, very easy to overdose. Has your daughter taken drugs before?' Harry asked gently.

Jude looked down. 'She had some problems when she was younger, but that was years ago. She's been fine for a long time.' He glanced at Sue who nodded.

This was something Lissa had chosen to omit when she had been asking my advice. What else has she not told me? I wondered.

'Okay,' Harry said. 'It's hard to know exactly what happened. But she may not have been experienced with this drug. We think she may have taken it with alcohol, not normally done, hugely dangerous. It's also hard to gauge the dosage if you're not used to it. The truth is, we're not sure.'

Jude frowned, confused. 'Where did she get hold of it?'

The doctor shook his head. Not one he could answer.

'So she'll definitely be okay?' Jude asked again anxiously.

Harry nodded. 'I think so. We have her on IV fluids, and we're monitoring her vital signs. She should recover fully, but she needs rest to wait for the drugs to work their way out of her system.'

'That's fine. We can stay here as long as she needs.'

'Okay. But,' Harry cautioned, 'the psychological side of things will need to be dealt with if she's been clean for a long time.' He gave a weak smile. 'I'm afraid I neither have the time nor the resources to deal with that now. We can only deal with her physical health.'

'I understand. Thank you, doctor.' Jude pumped Harry's hand. 'We're very, very grateful.'

The doctor nodded in acknowledgement and walked back out through the swinging door to deal with the next crisis. He looked nearly as exhausted as Molloy. No sooner had the thought crossed my mind when Molloy himself walked in, looking awful. This crisis was taking a toll on all the people who had important jobs to do. What was I saying? It was taking its toll on everyone.

'What's happened?' Molloy addressed his question to me but this time it was Jude who did the explanations.

He thanked Molloy for his concern but made it clear that this was a family matter and not one with which the guards needed to concern themselves. They had enough to do, he said, he didn't want to take up their time unnecessarily. I said nothing. The fact that Jude seemed to accept without question that his daughter's overdose was self-inflicted meant that he didn't yet know what had been going on between Lissa and her husband.

'I'd like to speak to her myself, if that's okay. Can I see her?' Molloy asked.

'She's asleep, I think,' Jude said. 'They have her on a drip.'

'Okay, I'll come back later. I won't stay long but I do need to speak to her.'

Jude nodded. 'I understand.'

He agreed to call Molloy when Lissa was up to talking, then headed into the hospital room himself while Sue sat down beside Phyllis with the toddler on her knee. Yet again, Sue had said nothing throughout, her attention concentrated on her little nephew.

After Molloy left, I stood there for a few seconds watching the toddler play with a toy car while trying to corral my thoughts. Then I realised I had no choice. I had to tell Molloy about Lissa's husband. She'd told me this morning that her life was in danger and this evening she'd nearly died. That was a coincidence I couldn't ignore. If I'd told someone earlier maybe this wouldn't have happened.

I was about to find myself breaking solicitor–client confidentiality again, twice in twenty-four hours, something I always tried to avoid. But Lissa was in a small community hospital struggling on a skeleton staff. Barbour-jacket man or not, if her husband wanted to do her harm, he could easily get into this hospital to finish the job and I wouldn't be able to live with myself if that happened.

I followed Molloy out through the double doors and called after him. He turned and raised his eyebrows and, in a low voice, I told him as quickly as I could about Lissa's visit to the office.

'Right,' Molloy said, his hand on his chin. 'And her father doesn't know? He seemed very keen to get rid of me.'

'I'm pretty sure he doesn't know. She said she hadn't told him because she was afraid of what he might do.'

He nodded. 'The doc tells me it's impossible to tell if the drugs were self-administered or not. GHB comes in a spray and you add it to a drink. It leaves the system within hours so it's impossible to test for, but it seems likely that's what it is.'

So, he'd spoken to Harry before he'd come in, I thought. He must have met him outside the door. I noticed he hadn't chosen to mention that to Jude.

'So, someone else could have added it to her drink?'

'Yes,' he said.

When I returned Jude was still in with Lissa, and Sue and Phyllis were on the floor with Peadar, playing with his car. Phyllis clambered to her feet with a groan when she saw me and sat back down with a sigh. She had an odd expression on her face when I sat beside her.

'What's up?' I asked.

'Huh?' She looked at me confused. 'Oh, nothing.' With an effort, she smiled. 'A bit dizzy, just. It's a while since I've been crawling around on a floor after a wee one.'

Her eyes flickered towards Sue, who was smiling at something her nephew had done, then she widened her eyes and got to her feet. 'Shall we go and leave this family in peace?'

Chapter Eighteen

Wading across Phyllis's shop floor was a thoroughly bizarre experience. A place that had been so familiar to me was now alien and strange; I couldn't imagine what it must have been like for Phyllis. I caught that dank smell from earlier, and water lapped against the walls and stairs as if in some maritime cave. Even if you kept your eyes above flood level, the bookcases were empty and warped and bowed with the wet, as if they might collapse at any minute. The bookseller would have to invest in a completely new fitout. I hoped she was well insured.

But when we climbed the stairs to her flat things became even stranger. Phyllis had done some rearranging since I'd been up here with Jude earlier on. The winding stairs led directly into the small hallway, which was dark and lined with books, two layers of them, making for a very narrow passageway indeed.

A yawning Fred padded towards us and Phyllis bent over to scratch the dog's ears. 'I need to get you out for some exercise pet, don't I? You haven't been out since this morning.'

She moved slowly through the hall trying not to dislodge any of the stacks, not easy for a woman of her dimensions. The doorway to the sitting room opened a few feet at most, just enough for us to squeeze through, and Phyllis felt her way through the opening, moving sideways like a crab, pulling her bag in after her.

I followed her in, and Phyllis flicked on the lights. Here too bookshelves lined the walls from floor to ceiling, but their over-flow was on chairs, on windowsills, on coffee tables, on the carpet also. Books of all kinds – new and second-hand, hardback and antiquarian, orange Penguin paperbacks, Crime Club classics, all subjects and all genres, fiction and non-fiction, poetry and prose – covered every available surface. They were stacked on the floor and piled on the furniture. This room was even more cave-like than downstairs.

'Cripes,' I said. It was almost impossible to move.

'Hmm.' Phyllis looked around her. 'You might be right. I moved some books from the spare room earlier, in case I needed to give someone a bed. And you haven't seen the attic. I moved some up there after you left.'

I tried to imagine Phyllis climbing up into her attic and failed.

Always ready to have a laugh at her own expense, she caught my expression. 'Just as well I have a sturdy ladder.' Her eyes nar-rowed in amusement. 'Anyway, I think we might have to make ourselves comfortable in the kitchen for this evening.'

We reversed back out of the sitting room and made our way towards the small kitchen, past another half-wall of books. It occurred to me that Phyllis might have been a little over ambi-tious with her invitation to Maeve even if she had cleared space in the spare bedroom. But she assured me that there was room enough for someone to stay there.

With difficulty (especially for Phyllis herself) we made it into the kitchen. Once there we could move around, since it was the one room in the flat where there were no stored books, although there were cookery books, and many of them, brought back from

Phyllis's eclectic travels around the world and neatly arranged in a bookcase above the cupboards. Food, books and travel were Phyllis's three loves. And Fred, of course, who had overtaken all three in recent years. He came in to join us, carefully manoeuvring his way around, his tail low, having learned to be careful from hanging out with Phyllis in the bookshop all day.

I perched on a stool while Phyllis got cracking on some food, pouring each of us a glass of crisp white wine from the fridge before she did anything else. 'I think we've earned one, don't you?'

I clinked her glass with mine. 'Absolutely.' The wine was delicious. Phyllis never failed to deliver on the food and wine front.

She leaned her bosom on the table as she took a good sip. 'That poor girl.'

'I know.'

'I got a wile fright when I saw her lying there in the doorway of the bookies. I thought it was another death. It's good that she has a sister to take care of the little one.' She frowned. 'What was her name again? The sister?'

'Sue.'

'Sue,' she said quietly. Her brow furrowed, in an expression like the one she'd had earlier at the hospital, as if she was trying to work something out.

'What is it?'

Phyllis shook her head and took another sip. 'Just something I found a wee bit odd. I can't shake the feeling that it was a bit off.'

'Go on,' I urged.

'Sue got really upset, suddenly, when you went off to talk to Molloy.' There was a brief pause as she glanced up at me over her glass. 'I presume that's where you went?'

I nodded. 'What's so odd about her getting upset? She'd just found out that her sister had nearly died.'

Phyllis's gaze flickered past me to the cookery books, as if trying to recall exactly. 'That's the thing. I'm pretty sure it wasn't her sister she was upset about. We talked about her and she was fine, if worried. Perfectly normal. But when I mentioned Bob Jameson, that we were extra jumpy this weekend with what had happened to him, and that we'd got a terrible fright when we'd seen her sister, her eyes welled up.'

'Really? Are you sure?'

Her eyes locked on mine. 'Certain. She started to cry, couldn't seem to stop herself. It was almost as if she had been holding it in and what had happened to her sister allowed her to show it. It seemed so strange when her father clearly couldn't abide the man.'

'Was she sad about his death?' I asked, realising that I'd barely heard Sue utter two words since I'd met her. I didn't know her at all. Whatever Phyllis had been able to find out was a hell of a lot more than I had.

The bookseller shook her head. 'I don't know. It wasn't clear and I didn't ask her. But she definitely didn't want me to see; she hugged the wee fella to hide her tears and pretended she was fine. But the mention of his name certainly triggered something. I didn't know she knew him, did you?' Phyllis frowned. 'I mean, I knew that Jude knew and disliked him, but I didn't realise there was any other connection between the two families.'

'Neither did I,' I said, deep in thought, while picturing again the moment I'd witnessed between Sue and Derek, Bob's brother.

I sighed. The whole thing was becoming very entangled. For the moment I decided to enjoy my wine and put all thoughts of the Jamesons and the Burns aside for a few hours.

While Phyllis went to root in her cupboards, I finally called Charlie about Guinness and he said he'd be happy to take him in. Amazingly my phone still had a charge, although it died the second Charlie rang off. And fifteen minutes later I was sitting in front of a bowl of homemade tomato soup, toasted olive bread, tea and wine. Fred was at my feet. I'd taken my boots off and he seemed content to rest his head on my socked feet.

Despite Phyllis nagging me to text him, Molloy had told me at the hospital that he had no idea what time he would be back, so I was in no hurry to get back to his place. Plus, I could walk there so I could have a second glass of wine. Which Phyllis poured me after a brief enquiring look. I breathed out. It felt as if today needed to end and then all could go back to normal. The right people would arrive to help with the death, we could start the big clean up and the right people would arrive to help with that too. We'd all had enough.

Finally and reluctantly I forced myself to leave at about ten o'clock. I'd have loved to spend longer with Phyllis in her cosy kitchen with Fred at my feet, but with my phone dead I felt uneasy, so I needed to collect my charger from the office on the way to Molloy's.

As I was pulling on my wellies, the door sounded downstairs. Phyllis had left it unlocked so she didn't have to wade down to let Maeve in. And within a minute, the vet herself appeared, looking hungry and exhausted and in need of a hot shower and a glass of wine. I left Phyllis to provide those and I pulled on my coat again to head off alone to Molloy's stationhouse.

The town was eerie, the streetlights reflected in the black water like a Van Gogh painting, and though I was alone on the footpath, I found myself hurrying along, sharply aware of the recent spike in violent incidents.

I reached the office with a degree of relief and went in, the door sticking a little as I opened and closed it behind me; it must have expanded in the wet. I hoped now that the rain had stopped that it would revert to its normal size in a day or two, although if an expanded door and small leak was the extent of the flood damage I'd suffered, I would consider myself as having got off lightly.

Once inside I switched on the light and hunted about for my phone charger. It wasn't in the usual socket at reception, so I ran upstairs to my office to see if I'd left it there, turning on the light by the door and scanning my eyes around the room, relieved to spot it on the floor by the standard lamp. I crossed the room, picked it up and shoved it in the pocket of my coat, switching off the light again. But when I went back downstairs, I felt a sudden shiver. I knew I must be imagining it, but I began to feel that I was not alone. What was wrong with me? I'd never felt jumpy in the office before – it was my space. Had someone been in there? The only people who had keys were Leah and Marina, which caused me to have a sudden thought – had Marina given back her key? Unease crept across my scalp.

My mobile was completely dead and suddenly I didn't want to leave the office alone without a working phone, so I plugged it in and waited for the beep to show the connection was back. Time slowed to nothing while I waited so I checked the bathroom again. The ceiling was still dripping although not so badly – the basin was half full so I picked it up and turned to empty it into the handbasin.

A noise outside made me stop pouring for a second. A thunk, like something falling. It was coming from the little yard out the back where we kept the bin and the oil tank. I stopped breathing and listened. Had I imagined it? I started pouring again, my ears straining to hear. But there was nothing. I placed the empty basin back under the drip, turned off the light and stood there quietly.

I realised how pointless this was; if there was someone out there, they had already seen the light on, but I didn't want them to see my face. I pushed aside the little curtain at the window over the handbasin and peered out. But there was nothing I could see. The lights from the town dimly illuminated the yard, enough for me to see the oil tank but nothing else.

Damn it. I was on my own and I sure as hell wasn't going out into that tiny yard to tackle whatever or whoever was out there. And I wasn't going to bother Molloy or McFadden with what would probably turn out to be a fallen bag of recycling either. Whatever it was could wait till the morning along with everything else.

I went back to reception. By now the phone was charged up to 5 per cent, enough to keep me going till I reached the station-house. Before I left, I checked the waiting room. Of course, there was nothing and I told myself off for being silly. I probably just needed a good night's sleep. Jet lag again.

Before I reached the front door, my phone buzzed in my hand and I jumped. It was a text from Molloy. He said he'd be later than he thought – in fact, he might not get back at all tonight. The floods were worse in some areas than others and he and McFadden were helping people move their belongings into accommodation that had been offered. I texted back, offering to go and help (although I wouldn't have been able to drive after the wine), but he said they had enough helping hands, he just felt he should be there. Then my phone died again. I grabbed the charger and left the office, glad to be back out on the street again. The contact with Molloy had stilled my breathing and made me feel more normal.

The street was deserted as I walked the rest of the way down the hill. The sergeant's house was behind the Garda Station, dark and unattended, temporarily redundant now that the Beacon Hall had become the emergency accommodation centre and McFadden was off somewhere with Molloy. I hoped the station would become a hub of activity again in the morning if back-up finally arrived.

There was a laneway leading to the sergeant's house, which went along the side of the station. It was unlit and dripping, but I took it, emerging at an ordinary, unassuming, three-bedroom detached house. It was intended to accommodate the local sergeant and his family, but Molloy had lived here alone, on and off, for the past ten years. I reached the door with relief, took the key from my pocket and let myself in.

In the hallway I felt around for a light switch, found one and made my way into the living room. Molloy had been back for the six months or so since Glendara's Garda Station had reopened, but you'd never know it. There was no trace of him or his personality. The room held a sofa, two armchairs, some books on the shelves and an ancient television that I wondered if he ever watched. As I made my way back out into the hall, I wondered how much time he spent here. In the kitchen a mug and a plate lay on the draining board, washed but not dried or put away.

As I stood there listening to the hum of the fridge, I was tempted to snoop but I knew I'd find nothing – Molloy was always so hidden. It bothered me, the fact that he gave nothing away. But when I'd said as much to Maeve once, she'd just laughed. Then her smile had faded, and she reminded me that I myself wasn't the most open of books; I'd taken years to tell her about my sister's violent death and I used my own second name and my mother's maiden name. She added that she completely understood why I'd made those choices but that if that wasn't being hidden, then she didn't know what was. She'd given me a half smile and a wink and said, 'I think you're perfect for each other.'

I put the kettle on and found some teabags. I stuck one in the mug Molloy had rinsed and I looked around me while I waited for the water to boil. It made sense now why Molloy hadn't encouraged me to come here. My own cottage was much more welcoming. This was a depressing sort of a house – a temporary place, not a home. The kettle boiled and I made some tea and took it upstairs with me.

There were three bedrooms off the small landing but two had nothing but a bed, a chair and a built-in wardrobe. The third was clearly where Molloy himself slept although he did little else by the looks of things. A neatly made double bed, a built-in wardrobe and a chest of drawers was all there were in the room. There wasn't even a bedside locker; a pile of books sat on the floor by the bed.

I went to the chest and opened the top drawer. There were two stacks of freshly laundered T-shirts, one of white and one black. I took a white one out; it smelled of Molloy, or whatever washing powder he used, clean and fresh. I'd remembered to bring a toothbrush, but I had no clean clothes with me, so, I took off what I was wearing, and put it on. Before I climbed into bed, I looked through his books. The top one was Roy Foster's *Modern Ireland 1600–1972*, not something I was tempted to dive into tonight, and the rest were also history or biography. Nothing appealed. But I knew I wouldn't be able to sleep yet, so I plugged my phone into the socket by the bed and with a mug of tea in my hand I prepared to do some more sleuthing online. This would be my bedtime reading tonight.

I wanted to find out more about Bob Jameson and his life, more than I had already. His brother and wife had been less than forthcoming, but there had been chinks of light during other conversations, narrow gaps which, if I prised them open, might reveal something more.

It was possible there was some information online about the charity he had set up. Even if the salary issue had been resolved, and there were no conclusions yet in relation to the other alleged irregularities, surely there would be some mention of them somewhere? It was the kind of scandalous wrongdoing that made journalists salivate, the hypocrisy drawing readers in.

I did a search for Bob Jameson just as I'd done before, this time scrolling past all the obituaries I'd looked at already. Images of Bob and Amanda emerged, at charity functions and black-tie affairs; he usually laughing while she sometimes looked a bit lost. Then I came across a full-page feature for the *Irish Independent* from December just gone, with the headline *The Amazing Grace Story; what a hymn meant for one charity boss*. I settled down to read it, taking a sip of my tea.

I'd hoped I might find something more revealing than in the obituaries, but the article was one of those fawning *Hello!*-type pieces praising the man's achievements and his happy family life. Bob spoke about running an orphanage in Nigeria as being a sort of penance for his time in London. When he'd seen the poverty that existed in Nigeria, he'd regretted everything he'd done when working in big business. He'd felt guilty but when he'd heard the story of the 'Amazing Grace' hymn, he'd accepted that a person could completely shed their earlier life and be reborn. Nigeria had been Bob Jameson's storm, his Road-to-Damascus moment, that Derek had told me about on the way to Mamore. There was a photograph too; a posed family portrait in front of a huge Christmas tree with presents underneath, Bob and Amanda with their two kids, smiling young black men. The piece mentioned one as playing hurling and the other was study-ing Irish at University College Galway.

But it did make me wonder if something had happened in London. I'd been interested in Bob Jameson's charity but maybe the key to his death lay with his past life instead. I checked his obituary again for the name of the investment bank he'd worked for; Oak Knap Investment Bank, then did a search for it. There were lots of business pieces, which I skipped, but when I came across a *Daily Mail* article I sat back. The headline was so lurid that I flinched – *British Bank in Floors of Whores scandal!* Bingo! There it was.

According to the piece, the bank for which Bob Jameson had worked owned apartment buildings that were used for prostitu-tion. There was even mention of Bob himself; he was on a list of people who were on the board, all of whom denied knowledge of what was going on, claiming it was simply a property investment. There was a reference at the end of the piece to the bank's other investments, a multimillion-pound property portfolio, which included apartments bocks where tenants were left without heat-ing or functioning fire alarms, and care homes which made vast profits despite their residents being neglected and underfed.

I absorbed all of this and then climbed out of bed, found a pad of Post-its in my bag and wrote down the name of the bank. Then I got back in and took another sip of my tea. I was beginning to get a more coherent picture of the dead man; Bob Jameson involved in less than savoury activities in the past, now a reformed individual. But was it true?

I returned to finish reading the family feature, interested to see if there was anything there about Amanda, but she was little more than a shadowy presence in the piece, a Melania to his Donald. I stopped dead at a reference to his twin. Although Derek wasn't named, Bob mentioned that his brother had suffered an accident when they were kids, and that once he regained consciousness Bob had sat with him in hospital for months. I wondered if the accident was the cause of Derek's limp. It was an experience that had made them even closer, Bob said, but it also made him appreciate proper nursing care and how important hospital funding was. Which set up the carefully prepared pitch for funding for the Jameson Grace Homes that followed.

I finished my tea and stretched down to put the cup onto the floor, reflecting on what a useful piece of furniture a bedside table was, then scrolled down to the comments section at the end of the piece. There was a surprising number of them, but one caught my eye. It was a reaction to what Bob had said about rebirth, and the connection to the 'Amazing Grace' hymn.

Rebirth, renewal my arse – shedding his skin like a snake, more like. When a snake sheds its skin, it is still a snake underneath, just like Bob Jameson!

The tone of the article was nauseating enough to provoke that kind of a response. But the word snake stood out as if it were in flashing green lights. I looked to see who had posted it, but it was anonymous. Then I wondered if it had been posted before or after Bob Jameson was killed. When I checked it was January, only weeks after the piece had come out, so before.

I breathed out. Even if the snakebite hadn't been the cause of death – and that hadn't been established yet, only that the snake wasn't venomous – the snake's presence still bothered me. It had to have some significance. A search on Wikipedia revealed that, *Historically, serpents and snakes represent fertility or a creative life force. As snakes shed their skin through sloughing, they are symbols of rebirth, transformation, immortality, and healing.*

Was whoever killed him making a point about Bob Jameson's

'rebirth'? I took a screen shot of the comment on my phone to show Molloy. Scrolling through the rest of the comments, there was no further mention of a snake but none of them was any better. Amanda was off the mark if she was labouring under the illusion that her husband had been universally liked.

I felt my eyes closing, so I put the phone to one side and turned off the light. Ten minutes later I realised I'd forgotten to brush my teeth, so I went to the bathroom where Molloy's old-fashioned razor and shaving brush gave me a flutter, probably because it was the only thing in the house that revealed anything vaguely personal about him.

My heart sank when I heard rain on the roof again, but at some point in the middle of the night the man himself came in, climbed into bed and put his arms around me.

Chapter Nineteen

I woke at eight, alone and momentarily disorientated, hardly surprising considering this was the fourth bed in six days I'd woken
in. Once I'd figured out where I was, I stretched luxuriously and
listened out for the inevitable rain. But there was none. I could
even hear some birdsong, the first I'd heard since I'd returned to
Inishowen, although I never heard too much birdsong outside my
own window in Malin with Guinness prowling about. I hoped
he was okay. Charlie had said he'd take him into his house and
if there was one thing Guinness enjoyed doing, it was torturing
Charlie's poor, sweet-natured old corgi, Ash.

Thinking of prowlers reminded me of my unease in the office
the night before. Had someone been there out in the yard? I'd
call in later, in the daylight, to check. I wouldn't mention it to
Molloy, I decided. He had enough on his plate. Had I dreamed
his return in the middle of the night or had he come back and left
again? How long had I been back in Inishowen? Three nights? It
felt like so much longer. In many ways it felt as if I hadn't been
away at all.

Eyes open properly now, I spotted an old-fashioned clock radio
that I hadn't noticed the night before and I turned it on, managing to catch the tail end of the news and weather. Amazingly,

there was no more rain forecast for a few days. Did this mean that the worst was over?

I hauled myself out of bed and to a hot shower. When I came back into the bedroom, I didn't feel like putting on the same clothes I'd worn the night before, so I found a pair of boxers of Molloy's and another clean T-shirt and I put them both on. I heard the front door slam, then Molloy's footsteps on the stairs. He came into the room just as I was doing up my jeans. I looked up and he smiled wearily.

'What?' he said.

'What do you mean, what?' I asked.

'You look guilty.'

'Well, you look wrecked,' I retorted.

His eyes closed, and he sank down onto the bed. 'I *am* wrecked. But it looks as if we're on the home straight. As far as the weather is concerned anyway.'

'So I hear. The forecast after the news was good. And I see it isn't raining.'

'Nope – it hasn't for about six hours and the floods are already starting to abate, thank the Lord. The bridges are still down, of course, so the town is still cut off but at least the repair crews can finally get to us. And the pathologist is coming in by helicopter this morning, so we should have a post-mortem on Jameson later today. Finally.'

'Oh, that's good.'

He ran his hands through his hair. 'Do you fancy some breakfast? I have rolls. They mightn't be too fresh, but we can stick them in the oven. And there's coffee.'

'Great.'

'Follow me down when you're ready.' He left the room.

I finished dressing and grabbed the Post-it pad and my phone and charger and put them in my bag, before I went downstairs.

There was a smell in the kitchen like fresh baking and Molloy had made a pot of coffee, which meant the room had taken on a completely different feel to the night before. There was even some weak sunlight streaming in the window, casting a line across the table.

While we got the food ready, I told Molloy what I'd found online the night before and about the comments, in particular, posted by the anonymous snake troll.

His eyes narrowed. 'Once you lift up the rock, there seems to have been a queue of people wishing Bob Jameson ill.'

'Not that you'd know by listening to his wife or brother,' I replied, putting some plates on the table. 'They seem to think he was a saint.' It was only when I said that aloud that I realised how odd that was, particularly when it came to Derek, in the context of what Jude had told me about their childhood.

Molloy took some mugs out of a cupboard above his head and put them on the draining board. 'There's no denying that someone, or more than one person, wanted to kill him in as unpleasant a way as possible. *Someone* went to some trouble to get hold of that snake, get it up here and out to Mamore. It may have been harmless, but the fact remains Bob Jameson was bitten and grass snakes are generally not aggressive unless handled or stepped on. So what the hell happened?'

'And why all the way out at Mamore?'

'Exactly.'

'Less chance of him being saved,' I suggested. 'Take him to a remote spot to kill him?'

'Possibly. Anywhere less remote and they'd have been seen.'

'Even out there, if Maeve had seen a vehicle, she'd have stopped to see if anyone was in trouble. Especially on a night like that.'

Molloy nodded, pouring out coffee. 'Hopefully the post-mortem will tell us more. At least we'll know how he actually died.'

I took the mugs to the table and fetched some milk from the fridge while Molloy examined the rolls as he took them out of the oven. 'God, I think these are going to be a bit chewy.'

'What about the rope?' I asked.

He tipped the rolls onto a plate and put the plate on the table. 'Brand new, the kind you could get in any hardware shop. He was overpowered, tied up, then bitten, then died.'

I gave him a quizzical look. 'But the bite definitely didn't kill him.'

'No, unless there was an allergy or something. Subject to the post-mortem confirming that, of course.'

I got some knives out of a cutlery drawer and stood there absorbing the image. 'I wonder if he was conscious when he was bitten? If he knew what was happening to him? Would he have been frightened?' It was hard to imagine the confident, cocky individual I'd met, tied up and fearful.

'He wasn't tied up when we found him, so he was conscious at some stage.' Molloy shrugged. 'And if he'd spent time in Africa, he'd have known the implications of being bitten by a snake. He wouldn't necessarily have known it was harmless.' He took the knives from me and put them on the table; I wasn't moving quickly enough.

I shivered. I had no problem with any kind of creepy crawly and I was rather fond of rodents, but I had an irrational fear of snakes that I wished I could shake off. I wouldn't have liked to have been in Bob Jameson's shoes.

Molloy rooted out some jam and butter and finally we sat down to eat. He smiled. 'Well, isn't this a domestic little scene?'

I looked up, butter knife suspended in mid-air. There was something in his tone that made me suspect he was going to address the elephant in the room. But did I even want him to?

He gave me a wry look. 'Did you think I was never going to mention it again?'

'I . . .'

'Did you *hope* I was never going to mention it again?'

I shook my head. 'No. I . . .' I seemed to be failing to complete a sentence. Just as well I wasn't in court.

'Come on, Ben. I asked you to marry me and you ran away to America for six months. It's hardly the response a young man setting his cap at a lady is after.' He raised his mug in a toast.

I looked down at my chewy toasted roll. Then I realised he was laughing. I wasn't sure how to react.

He took a sip of his coffee. 'It's fine. It was a spur of the moment thing on my part too. I surprised myself when I said it.'

'Did you?' I knew it was ridiculous of me to feel hurt, but I did.

He quickly reached out for my hand. 'I wasn't surprised about how I felt about you. But I was surprised by *that*. I mean, we weren't even together.'

'I had noticed that.'

'You were with that doctor.'

I avoided his gaze, concentrating again on my buttering. 'I wasn't really "with" him.'

He raised his eyebrows. 'No? It seemed as if you were. Anyway, it was a bit impulsive. Not really the kind of thing I do.'

I looked up and my eyes met his. 'Is that why you asked me? Because you thought I was with someone else?'

'No,' he said slowly. 'At least, not entirely. I may have been afraid of losing you, but I also knew I'd let you down and you had good reason not to trust me, with everything that had happened. I wanted you to know that you could trust me and that I wasn't going anywhere and . . .' He faltered and shook his head. 'Oh, I don't know. I thought it might have been something that you wanted. I cocked up, though, didn't I? It wasn't what you wanted at all.'

'Not then, no.' I paused. 'Or now, I don't think. Do *you* want to get married?'

He didn't reply.

'*Do you?* Come on, you were the one that asked.'

'Okay then. No, I suppose I don't.'

We looked at each other for a few seconds. Did Molloy not want to be with me? If there was one thing I had realised while I was in the States, it was that I wanted to be with him. What if he didn't feel the same way?

'So, what are we going to do now?' I asked, an uncomfortable pinch in my stomach.

Molloy took a deep breath. 'Okay, here goes. Cards on the table. I don't want to get married, but I do want us to be together, properly and publicly.'

'You mean go on dates, have dinner – that kind of thing?' I suddenly had this irresistible urge to laugh. It seemed we were more similar than I thought. Maybe Maeve was right.

He smiled. 'That kind of thing. If that's not too normal for you?'

I breathed out. 'No, I think I'd like a bit of normal for a while.'

Relief flooded his face. 'I'm glad.'

'Me too.' I felt an odd lump in my throat.

He put his hand on mine. 'Unfortunately, we have some way to go before we find calm water again, if you'll pardon the pun. I have to leave again now. There's an army crew coming to put up a temporary bridge at Glentogher so we can reopen the road to Derry, and the pathologist needs to be picked up from Ballyliffin. Although I'll get McFadden to do that.'

'Ballyliffin?'

'The hotel has a helicopter pad.'

'How long is that going to take? Before the roads reopen, I mean.'

He stood up and took his mug and plate to the sink where he rinsed them, his morning routine apparently. 'It'll take most of the day, I suspect, to get a temporary bridge constructed. It's very impressive how quickly they can do it, though. Hopefully you should be able to get back home by tonight. We should have one of the roads to Malin open too.'

'That would be good.'

He turned, grabbed his hat, and kissed me on the cheek. It seemed an oddly formal thing to do until he whispered into my ear, 'You're wearing my boxers, aren't you?'

A smile spread across my face.

When the door had slammed behind him, I poured myself another coffee. For the first time in a long time I felt content. I'd got whatever it was out of my system during my stint in the States and we could now settle down to having a normal existence. It would be good to get to know Molloy properly. I hadn't realised I'd wanted it so much. I wondered what people would think, then realised that we'd probably discover that we were the town's worst kept secret – and there were a few of those.

And then there were my parents. What would they think of Molloy if they met him? I remembered suddenly that I'd meant to ring them the night before. I took my phone out of my bag and dialled their landline now. No luck. I tried their mobiles, but I got voicemail on both, so I left a message on both.

My phone beeped in my hand as I put it back on the table, with a text from Maeve. Tony had opened the Oak, not something he usually did on Sunday mornings, but he was making an exception today. Maeve and Phyllis were heading there in half an hour and wondered if I wanted to join them. I texted back a yes. Then I looked at my watch again. I had half an hour to kill.

I drummed my fingers on the table, then poured myself the dregs of the coffee pot. I wondered how Lissa was doing this morning. If what Harry had said was true, she should be on the road to recovery. But had the drugs really been self-administered? I remembered what Phyllis had said about Sue. Lissa's younger sister was a bit of an enigma.

I picked up my phone again, opened Facebook and searched for both Burns sisters. I'd set up a page for myself a while back and though I never posted anything, it was useful for keeping up with community events. It had also proved to be quite fertile when I'd wanted to find out about people: people were surprisingly lax about what they posted online. I, on the other hand, was a lurker.

Lissa did not appear to have an account but Sue's page was open access. Her profile said that she was a nurse. I wondered if that was why she was always with Peadar, concerned for his health and vigilant about it. But when I checked the hospital where she worked, I saw that it was a psychiatric hospital; St Finbarr's in Galway.

As expected, there were lots of pictures of her nephew. She clearly doted on him, although I knew that already from having seen them together. There were also pictures from nights out, it seemed that Sue was quite the party girl, particularly recently. Some pictures had the words GNO below. Girls night out, I presumed. Disappointingly there were none with Lissa; I'd thought it might be a way to see what her husband Chris looked like. Sue's most recent post was a link to a donation page for the cycle.

I looked again at her profile. St Finbarr's, the hospital where she worked, was familiar. I was sure I'd come across it in the past few days. A few taps were enough to confirm that it was one of the hospitals where Bob had served on the board. A coincidence? Probably not if what Phyllis had said about her reaction to the mention of Bob's death was true.

I breathed in the fresh air, gratefully, when I left the house, the clear sky a bonus I hadn't been expecting. But the ground was very wet, still inches of water in parts, so I chose my footing carefully. I wondered about the chances of getting some exercise. I hadn't seen the beach since I'd got back. I wouldn't be able to get to Lagg until the road to Malin had been repaired but it was possible that I could get out to the Isle of Doagh.

Still considering this, I ran into McFadden when I emerged from the alleyway to the sergeant's house. He was opening the Garda Station.

'Morning.' He grinned knowingly at me. 'Couldn't get back to Malin then?'

'Nope.' I pretended I didn't notice his innuendo-laden tone. If the chat I'd just had with Molloy was anything to go by, our relationship wouldn't be a secret for long, if it ever had been.

McFadden looked marginally less exhausted than Molloy. When I said as much he nodded wearily. 'Aye, I got to my bed for a few hours at least. Hopefully we're over the worst.'

'Any news on the roads reopening?'

'Later today some should be passable. You should be able to get home anyway.' He looked up at the sky. 'Assuming it holds off like the forecast promises. We don't need any more fucking rain for at least a month.'

On that frank pronouncement, I left him to open up, and walked on towards the Oak to meet Phyllis and Maeve. Before I reached the square, thundering footsteps behind me made me jump and I stepped to one side. When I turned, Sue Burns was bearing down on me, jogging along the Malin Road in her cycling gear.

'Morning,' I called brightly.

She stopped. 'Morning.' She gave me a rather distant smile and I suspected she wasn't entirely sure who I was. She'd been ready to run by me until I spoke.

I was a little shamefaced at having stalked her on Facebook fifteen minutes earlier, but it was the first time I'd seen her alone, without nephew, father or sister in tow. The first opportunity I'd had for a one-to-one chat. 'It must be good to be able to get out for a run without getting soaked.'

She managed a half-smile. 'I'm pretty desperate for a bit of exercise to be honest. My bike is still up at Malin Head with all the others.' She crossed her arms protectively across her chest as if she was cold, although it was mild enough this morning.

'How is your sister doing today?'

'Oh, she's good,' she said. 'A lot better, actually. Dad's taken Peadar up to see her. It was good that you found her.'

So, she did know who I was after all, I thought. 'I'm glad to hear that,' I said. 'You must have got a terrible fright, all of you.'

'Yes. We're glad she's going to be okay.' She moved to head on, to get back to her run.

But I wasn't ready to let her go yet. 'It's been a rough weekend, what with what happened to Bob.'

Reluctantly she stopped again and shook her head. I felt like Columbo with his 'one more thing' question. 'Oh, I didn't really know him. But yes, that was awful too.'

'Didn't you?' I threw in the only link I could be sure of. 'You work in St Finbarr's Hospital, don't you? Bob was there too, at some stage, wasn't he?'

Not surprisingly, she looked startled, but she recovered quickly. 'There are a lot of employees there. It's a big place. I wouldn't have had anything to do with the board.'

But she knew he'd been on the board, I thought. How many nurses know the board members of the hospitals they work for?

She placed her hands on her hips and her eyes locked on mine. They were a deep blue. 'Can I go now?' she said smartly. 'Or do you have something else you want to ask me?'

Chapter Twenty

While Sue made her escape my phone rang in my pocket. It was my mother. Relieved, I answered it. 'Hi, Mum.'

But she was in a hurry too, I could tell. It seemed everyone wanted to get away from me this morning. 'Hi, we got your message. Glad to hear you're all right and things are getting back to normal up there. We're just on our way out to church, so I'll speak to you later.'

'Okay . . .' I heard a voice in the background call her name. I was pretty sure it was Stuart.

'Okay, bye then.' And she cut me off.

I looked down at the screen, more than a little confused. My parents had never been huge churchgoers but since my sister's death they hadn't darkened the door. I couldn't decide if this latest development was a good or a bad thing.

But as I made my way back up the street, I could see that they weren't alone. Glendara was a hive of activity, with the church bells pealing out for Sunday morning mass and crowds trooping up the path through the graveyard, deriving comfort from some return to routine, I assumed. I spotted Amanda Jameson among them, fully made up and dressed in a coat and scarf. For the first time it occurred to me that she'd packed quite the wardrobe for a few days watching a charity cycle. I'd seen a few changes of outfit already. This morning she was alone, with no brother-in-law to support her, but her head was held high. Amanda was another woman I struggled to make out – one minute she was vulnerable and scared, the next unexpectedly confrontational. It was impossible to tell whether she meant anything she said.

As I pushed open the pub door, I calculated that I'd spent more time in the Oak in the past forty-eight hours than I ever had over a weekend. The pub was busy again, the smell of coffee and turf fire hitting me as soon as I walked in. Maeve and Phyllis were at the bar ordering drinks.

Tony greeted me with a cheerful smile, tea towel tossed over his shoulder. 'We have milk!' he announced. 'The supermarket found some plant milks that they didn't know they had when they were clearing the shelves. We're going hipster!'

'In that case I'll have a hipster latte,' I responded with a smile.

'The pathologist is here,' Phyllis said, when Tony had turned back towards the steamer.

'How do you know?' I asked. This was certainly a new day; two major pieces of news, straight off.

'She wanted to see the snake,' Maeve said. 'She's been down at the clinic already this morning, brought a reptile expert with her.'

'No post-mortem results yet?'

'No. I don't think she'd tell me anything anyway, but I think she's only doing it now.'

We took our coffees to the window. It was too tempting not to. The sun was streaming in, making the place brighter than it had been in days.

'I'm going to try and go for a walk somewhere today, since I have to go back to work tomorrow,' I said, taking a sip of my coffee. 'On the shore if I can. I'm getting a bit cabin feverish.'

'How was your night in the sergeant's house?' Phyllis grinned mischievously. 'Was that cabin feverish?'

I ignored her with a half-smile. 'How's the road out to the Isle of Doagh?'

'I'd say you could get to Pollan beach out by the Castles,' Maeve said. 'It's tidal.'

'Anyone want to come?' I looked from one to the other.

Maeve shook her head. More work I assumed.

'I will,' Phyllis said. 'Fred hasn't had a decent walk in days, and it looks as if I'll be spending the next while trying to get the shop sorted. He'd love a decent run out, stretch the old legs.'

'Phyllis was telling me about that poor girl last night,' Maeve said. 'I hope she's okay.'

'I think she'll be fine. I just ran into her sister.'

'What was the name of that drug again?' Phyllis asked. 'G something . . .'

'GHB,' I said. 'It's a new drug apparently . . .'

But Maeve had stopped with her mug halfway to her mouth. 'My God, G?' She put the mug back down. 'One of my clients' kids died from that. It's awful. It's liquid ecstasy. Used to be a date-rape drug.'

'Date-rape drug?' Phyllis was appalled.

Maeve nodded. 'And now, weirdly, it's really popular with young women. No calories, no hangover, it's like liquid confidence, it seems. It makes you happy, you think nothing's wrong, even if you're upset about something. You can even exercise on it.' She gave a sigh. 'But there's a shocking rate of overdose. You can go into a coma really easily . . .'

As she spoke, something was bothering me, something in the far reaches of my brain that I couldn't quite get hold of. Something Molloy had said about how the drug was administered. Sprayed into a drink, he'd said. I had a memory of a child playing with a perfume bottle before it was snatched away from him. I tried to place it. And then suddenly I had it. It was Peadar. He'd been playing with a spray perfume bottle he must have taken from his mother or his aunt's bag. Sue had been very quick to grab it back from him.

Phyllis was speaking. 'That's what happened to Lissa. Isn't it, Ben?'

But I was still thinking things through. That entry on Sue's Facebook page; GNO didn't mean Girls Night Out, it meant night out on G. But why had Sue been taking the drug? She was a nurse, for God's sake. Then I remembered Lissa had mentioned her sister had been going through a rough time. Was Sue the one who had given her sister the drug?

Before I could get any further, the coffee machine, the music and the lights all went off at the same time. There was a loud expletive from Tony at the bar, followed by 'Oh, for Christ's sake. That's all we need.'

He called Stan to take over while he headed down the back of the pub and out the back door, then reappeared within a few minutes with the announcement that water had got into the fuse box.

He looked exasperated. 'Just when we thought we were out of the woods.' He raised his voice. 'Look, I'll have to close. I'm sorry, folks. It's not safe. We should be open again in the morning.' He ushered us all out the door, muttering, 'That'll teach me to open on a Sunday.'

Outside, Maeve set off, saying she was going to try to get home for the first time in a day and a half, and Phyllis looked at me. 'We might as well go for that walk now, don't you think? We might not get the chance later.'

I nodded. 'You get Fred and I'll get the car.'

On my way to the Mini, I called into one of the smaller food shops for a bottle of water. I was thirsty after all that coffee and knew the salty air at the shore would make it even worse. The shop was buzzing, though the shelves were virtually empty. Plenty of water though; I guessed it was counterintuitive to stockpile water with so much rain about. I wondered what state our poor supermarket was in.

I was queueing at the till to pay when I realised that the toned shoulders of the T-shirt-clad woman in front were Mary's. Her basket was overfull – she'd obviously been stocking up on whatever groceries were left. I felt a wave of sympathy for her, having to grieve in secret while keeping her hostess face on.

I touched her arm and she turned. When she saw me, her eyes glistened, and I thought she was going to cry. 'Oh Mary, I'm sorry. I didn't mean to upset you. Are you okay?'

She looked haunted, shadows beneath her eyes, but still so very striking. I wondered how on earth she could have put her life on hold for so long, for a man who was married to someone else? If that was what she had done.

'I'm fine,' she said brightly. 'Delighted it's stopped raining. Hoping to get out for a swim later.'

'Can I help carry anything? You look laden down.' And not just physically, I thought.

And with that her mask slipped and she dropped her voice to a whisper. 'We've had a huge row. It's been awful.'

'You mean Amanda?' I whispered.

She nodded. We made our way over to the magazine display shelves, the only part of the shop that was deserted, because there was nothing there.

'What happened?' I asked.

'She found me cleaning their room,' Mary said. 'I've been trying to hold it together, I really have. But I found tickets.'

'Tickets?'

'From a travel agent in Derry. They were leaving, the two of them.' She corrected herself. 'The four of them. There were tickets for the children too.'

I stopped dead. 'Where were they going?' It occurred to me that a search of the dead man's belongings was one of the first things Molloy would have organised if he'd had the manpower, if he hadn't been battling a flood at the same time.

'Cape Town. South Africa.' Mary gave me a wry look. 'Today. They were one-way tickets.'

'You're kidding. So it wasn't a holiday.'

She shook her head. 'Amanda came in and found me looking at them. I hadn't been snooping, I swear. They were under some coats that I was hanging up. But she completely lost it with me. Said she knew about me and Bob, that I was his slut. That I shouldn't think I was the only slut he'd had. Called me all sorts of names.'

'Oh Mary.' So Bob *was* planning on doing a runner, I thought. The 'meetings' that Derek had referred to in Derry on Wednesday were about planning his getaway. Before the guillotine fell.

'How did she know about you and Bob? It wasn't Molloy, was it?' Molloy had said he'd be discreet, but it may not have been that simple.

'I think it must have been Derek.' She looked down. 'I knew him when Bob and I were together years ago, when they were both in Trinity.' She gave a half-smile. 'The twins. Long before he met Amanda.' She took a deep breath. 'Bob must have told him we were still in touch. I shouldn't be surprised. Those two told each other everything.'

Which might explain why Amanda and Derek hadn't been speaking the night before, I thought. But why would Derek have told her? What possible motive would he have had now, when she was grieving?

But before I could ask anything else, Mary pushed a tear out of her eye, straightened her back and pulled herself together. 'I have to go. I have to get back to make lunch.' She squeezed my hand. 'Thank you for the chat.' And she walked back to the till, elegant and poised.

On my way back to the car I checked something on my phone, and it was exactly as I suspected. Ireland had no extradition warrant with South Africa.

Phyllis was waiting for me with Fred at her heels and the dog sat happily in the back, head peering between the two seats, tongue lolling out of the side of his mouth, as I drove along the Ballyliffin road.

'I ran into Mary in the shop,' I said as I passed the turn-off for the mountain road. There was a barrier at the junction with a sign saying *Road closed due to Flooding*. 'She was really upset.'

Phyllis put her hand to her throat and looked across at me. 'Oh, poor Mary. I keep meaning to call up to her. Although it's very awkward with those people still staying with her.'

'She said Amanda knows about herself and Bob.'

Phyllis breathed in sharply. 'Oh God, that won't make things any easier for either of them. I didn't exactly warm to the wife, but she *was* his wife and she *has* got two children with him. She hasn't had it easy either.'

I slowed down at a large area of water on my side of the road, stopped and waited for the cars on the other side to pass.

'What do you know about the relationship between Mary and Bob?' I asked.

Phyllis rubbed her sleeve against the window. The car was beginning to steam up with two people and a dog breathing in the same space. 'She never came out and said that she was having an affair with him. But she wouldn't, would she? I mean, people don't.'

'But was she?' I felt as if I was cross examining in court. Trying to get to a particularly slippery truth.

Phyllis looked at me with a half-smile. 'Oh, I think so, aye.'

'So she did meet him then? It wasn't just emails and text messages?' The way ahead was clear so I pulled out to overtake.

'Oh, she met him all right. Not consistently over the thirty years or whatever it was. I think years would go by when she didn't see him. He worked abroad quite a bit.'

'London and Nigeria?'

Phyllis nodded. 'I think there were periods when they weren't even in touch, not just the times when he was out of the country.' She sighed deeply. 'And then he would reappear in her life and the whole thing would start again. I don't know if it was at his instigation or hers. But she would seem very happy for a while and then sad again. As if her hopes had been raised and then dashed. I don't know if they would break contact at her instigation or his. I suspect his.'

'Did she talk to you about it?'

Phyllis shook her head. 'Ach, not really. She's quite guarded, Mary.' She smiled. 'For the most part I think she's very self-sufficient. Pretty content. Loves Inishowen. You'd be hard pressed to get her to leave it. You know she swims miles every day?'

'Yes.'

'But whatever it was about him, she loved Bob Jameson. Gave her heart to him when she was young and never got it back. But she only ever had part of him.'

'So it seems.'

'If I dared to suggest that she break contact with him and cut him out of her life she'd shut me down and not talk to me for ages. So, I just stopped doing that.'

'And recently? Has there been more contact between them than usual?'

She shook her head. 'I don't know. I only realised he was part of the cycle when I heard his name this weekend. I'd never met him, and Mary didn't tell me he was coming. Maybe she was afraid of how I'd react.' She smiled. 'Afraid I'd have a go at him. Which I very well might have done if I'd got the chance, but he was never without the wife.'

My mind had snagged on something Phyllis had said earlier and I returned to it now. 'You said Amanda didn't have it easy either. What did you mean by that?'

Phyllis gazed out the window again. 'Oh, she's had her issues, I think.'

'What do you mean?'

'Mary told me she had difficulty having children. I think that's why they adopted their two Nigerian kids. It caused her to have a breakdown. She's had mental health issues all her life I think, even spent time in a psychiatric hospital relatively recently. Mary never said so, but I suspect that was one of the reasons Bob gave for staying with her.'

I wondered fleetingly if the hospital could have been St Finbarr's in Galway. Where Sue Burns worked and where Bob had been on the board.

Phyllis interrupted my thoughts to point out a whitewashed, half-derelict farmhouse. It was the same one I'd noticed on the way out to Mamore with Derek. She rubbed at the window again. 'That's where Mary grew up.'

'She lived there with her parents?' I asked.

Phyllis nodded. 'Unusual at the time to be an only child. I think she wished for a big family, with lots of brothers and sisters.'

'I can imagine.' The house was in a beautiful setting, but it must have been a lonely enough place to grow up. It was out on its own with a long straight laneway leading down to it.

A few minutes later, I took the turn-off to the Isle of Doagh and headed for Pollan Bay beach. We parked at the Castles where there were a few cars already. We climbed out of the car to a brittle blue sky and a strong wind that I hoped would help dry out the land. Fred took off immediately like a bullet across the wet sand, tail flying.

'Poor dog, he's dying for a bit of fresh air,' Phyllis said, taking his lead from the dashboard and wrapping it around her wrist. In her other hand was a bone-shaped container of plastic bags. 'He's been cooped up for days. All he's had is a quick poo walk in the evening. Mind you, that's all any of us have had.' She grinned. 'Oh sorry,' she said abruptly, stepping aside to let a man brush past.

It was Barbour jacket man, the man I suspected was Lissa's husband Chris. He glared at Phyllis who glared back at him. The bookseller was never one to take rudeness lying down.

'You're welcome, you rude skitter,' she called after him.

He strode off and we watched him climb into his car.

'I'm not surprised Derek Jameson had him by the throat,' she muttered. 'That's the man from the pub, isn't it?'

I nodded.

'Who the hell is he anyway?'

I sighed. 'I wish I knew.'

I glanced back at his car as we made our way over the stones and down onto the sand. *Was* he Lissa's husband? He was about the right age and there was something surly and unpleasant about him, but I couldn't be remotely sure.

Phyllis was still thinking about Mary. She kicked at the seaweed as we walked along the shore. 'It's not easy loving someone who belongs to someone else, you know.'

Phyllis was clearly biased because Mary was her friend, but I suspected Amanda's allies would feel differently. It made me wonder for the first time about Phyllis's own romantic past.

Fred came rushing back and she threw a stick for him. 'It's all about marriage here. No matter how liberal we pretend we are.'

'Maybe,' I smiled. I wondered what Phyllis would think of my chat with Molloy this morning. I'd tell her when I got the chance.

But, now, she was in full flow. 'There was a couple in Glendara, a wile nice couple, but they split up. It happens, nothing wrong with that.' Phyllis waved her hand dismissively. 'It wasn't anyone's fault. They both moved on. She had a new partner, he moved to Buncrana and had a new baby, with a much younger woman, of course.' She grinned at that.

'Go on.'

'Then, very suddenly, the wife died, heart attack or something, I can't remember rightly. It was very sad. And at the corp-house, he's there, the ex-husband, in prime position beside the coffin. That's fine, a bit odd he's beside the coffin, but maybe you'd expect him to be since they have kids together. But at the funeral, there he is again, the ex-husband, sitting at the top of the church, front row, the chief mourner.'

I looked at her. 'Really?'

She brushed away a lock of hair in the wind. 'Pretending everything was just as it was, as if they'd never split up.'

'Even though everyone knew they weren't together?'

She nodded. 'Even though everyone knew they hadn't been together *for years*, that they both had new relationships. God knows where her new partner was, or his – down the back with the gravediggers probably.'

'That is strange all right.' Although now that I thought about it, I remembered seeing a death notice for a man I knew. Though his marriage had broken up long before, his wife was mentioned while his new partner wasn't. 'But that's not the case here,' I said. 'Bob and his wife were still together.'

Phyllis shrugged. 'I know.' Fred returned with the stick and she threw it again, gazing after him as he rocketed towards the shoreline.

'What's that?' she asked suddenly.

I looked. There was something lying on the sand, close to the water, a box of some description. It looked as if it had washed up with the tide.

'Why do people drop litter in such a beautiful place?' Phyllis sighed. 'Let's take it away.'

We walked towards it. It was a big plastic storage box with a blue lid, of the kind you'd get in Tesco to store books or toys. It was lying on its side. When we reached it, Phyllis clamped her hands onto her knees and peered down. 'There's a blanket in it.'

I looked. She was right.

She frowned. 'That's strange.'

'What?'

She pointed. 'Look, there are lots of little holes in the lid. They've been made with a screwdriver or something, they're like breathing holes . . .' She trailed off and looked up at me, her eyes wide.

And with that, Maeve's words echoed in my ears: *simple enough really, a large box with a blanket or lukewarm hot water bottle and breathing holes would do it.*

It was a relief to park in front of my cottage in Malin. I'd been back so briefly that the past twenty-four hours away had seemed way longer than they should have done.

Phyllis and I had driven back into Glendara with the plastic box in the boot. It was a tight squeeze, but I wanted to keep it away from a dishevelled and sand-covered Fred. My mind was racing – was this what the snake had been transported in? Had the man I thought was Lissa's husband tried to dispose of it by chucking it into the sea? Lissa had said that her husband was a lorry driver: *Chris could get hold of anything.*

At the station, McFadden had taken the box with little comment. I expected nothing very much would surprise him after this weekend. I told him about the man we'd seen before we found the box and he said he'd ask Molloy to give me a call. I also told him what Mary had told me about the airline tickets.

Charlie came to his door with Guinness in his arms, looking mightily relieved to hand him back. Like most cats Guinness doesn't like the wet, but he's also a tom, so being confined to barracks with a corgi he regarded as an inferior might not have suited him as much as I'd thought.

'Thanks, Charlie,' I said, taking the protesting cat from him. 'I hope he wasn't too much bother.'

I took Charlie's non-committal response to mean that he had been quite a bit of bother. He grunted. 'I hear the roads have reopened.'

'One of them anyway. I came around by Culdaff. Hopefully we're on our way back to normal,' I said.

'Aye.' He looked out at the still completely submerged green. 'It's been a bit wet all right.'

I put Guinness onto the ground, and he followed me down Charlie's path and back up our own, lifting and shaking his paws whenever he had to step into a puddle. On the doorstep, he wrapped himself repeatedly around my legs, nearly tripping me up as I turned the key in the lock. I bent down and rubbed his head. I was pleased to see him too.

But a shower, I thought. I must have a shower. And some food.

Chapter Twenty-One

I dumped my keys in the kitchen, turned on the heat and headed upstairs, grateful for the fact that I had an electric shower. I spent a good ten minutes in there, reasoning that water wasn't exactly at a premium now, though I was sure the boffins would correct me on that. I washed the sand from my hair and tried to sort through my thoughts, forcing myself to think, not about what had happened over the past few days, but the week ahead. Tomorrow, being Monday, I'd be back at the office, and, as I'd remarked to Jude, I suspected there'd be many fractious people having rows with their insurance companies over flood claims.

But as I stepped out of the shower, dried myself and put on some clean clothes, I found my thoughts inevitably returned to the events of the weekend. Molloy hadn't called me back about the man at the beach and I was worried about Lissa. I also wanted to ask her about Sue. I decided that once I'd eaten, I would go and see her at the hospital. I glanced at the pile of dirty clothes I'd left on the chair, including Molloy's boxers, and remembered I had to give him back his key. Maybe I could kill two birds.

A cup of tea and some tinned soup later and I was driving

239

back the way I'd come. It was amazing how quickly the floods were abating now that it had finally stopped raining. On my way back through Culdaff, I noticed that there were a few cars about, people venturing out for a Sunday evening drink now that the weather was better.

There were several people standing in the doorway of the Bunagee Arms as I drove by. I was surprised to see Marina among them, chatting to a man. With the difficulty in getting about, it surprised me that she had come here for a drink rather than staying in Glendara. I tried to catch a glimpse of who she was with, thinking I'd be surprised if Harry would have had time for a drink, even now.

Then the man turned, and I saw his face. It was Barbour-jacket man, the man from the beach and the pub and Liam's window. Hairs rose on the back of my neck. I seemed to be seeing him everywhere now.

I pulled in about twenty metres past the pub and took a surreptitious picture on my phone from across the road. My mouth was dry, but I didn't think they saw me – they were too engrossed in their conversation. The man was having a cigarette and Marina was berating him about something, her face flushed an angry red – she looked to be almost weeping. I watched for a few minutes until they went back into the pub. The show was over, but at least now I had my picture.

I continued to Glendara, my stomach tightly knotted, feeling oddly betrayed. Marina had been working for me, running my practice, living in my house and going out with my ex-boyfriend. So what was she doing with this man?

One question came tumbling after the other. Was he Lissa's husband? A violent man who had threatened her life. Had he brought the snake here? Was he involved in Bob Jameson's death?

Was that why Derek had attacked him in the Oak? I stopped myself — with all those questions, my mind was running away with me.

I drove through Glendara, where the surface water was starting to drain away too, and out towards the hospital. I checked at reception to make sure that Lissa was still there and I found her room easily enough, hesitating for a moment before knocking. A voice answered and I opened the door.

The first thing I noticed was that she was no longer on a drip, a good sign I presumed, and although I hadn't seen her after she'd been admitted, she looked a hell of a lot better than she had on the footpath outside the bookies. Her hair was screwed up on top of her head in a weird topknot and she was scrubbed free of make-up, making her look younger or slightly older, I couldn't make up my mind. Different anyway, more vulnerable. Stray strands of lank hair hung alongside slightly protruding ears I hadn't noticed before.

She was on her own and she did not look happy to see me. I asked her how she was, and she shrugged, wordlessly. I wondered if it was possible that she had done this to herself after all. Since she wasn't in the mood for small talk, I showed her the picture of the man that I'd taken in the doorway of the Bunagee Arms and asked him if it was Chris, her husband.

'No, that's not him,' she muttered disinterestedly. But she had turned her head away, and I knew she hadn't even looked.

Irritated, I moved the screen, so it was directly in her vision. 'Look properly, Lissa. You must know that I thought that Chris had hurt you, after what you told me in the office.'

She spun her head around to face me. 'You told the guard what I said to you, didn't you?' she said accusingly. 'Dad said he wanted to speak to me.'

241

So Lissa Bennett was not taking my sharing of her secrets as well as Mary had done.

She glared at me. 'I thought solicitors weren't allowed to betray client confidences.'

Ironically, I probably had a better case for breaching confidentiality in Lissa's case because her life had been directly at risk. Subsequent events had shown that, whether self-inflicted or not. 'I thought you were in danger, Lissa. You may still be. You needed to be protected.'

'You still shouldn't have told him.'

'There *are* circumstances in which it is acceptable to breach client confidentiality. One of those is where there is a serious risk to the wellbeing of the client or a third party.'

When she met my gaze, still furious, I shook my head incredulously. I waved at the bed. 'Look at you. What if I didn't say anything and someone came back to finish the job? I'd have been responsible.'

She looked at me for a further second and then looked away, her anger abated, or exhausted by the effort it took to be angry. 'No one did this. I took it myself, the G. It makes me happy, stops me thinking about bad things. I'd do it again.'

'Where did you get it?'

She looked away again, and I snapped, 'You might have died, for God's sake. Left Peadar without a mother.'

She started pulling at her hair again and I noticed now that all the endings were split. 'He has Sue. She's better with him than I am anyway. He'd be better off with her.'

I raised my voice. 'You don't believe that! In the office you told me that you were scared for Peadar. Everything you've done has been about protecting him. Plus, I know you got the G from Sue.'

She looked down at her hand which now held a clump of hair. There was silence for a few seconds before she looked up, her eyes welling with tears. 'She didn't give it to me. I took it. She didn't know. I just needed to feel not scared for a while. I wanted to be like her. Brave.'

'I understand,' I said more quietly.

Her eyes darted everywhere. 'But Sue's able to handle it. I'm too stupid . . . I couldn't even do that right.'

'Why would Sue take it?' I asked. 'When we spoke at the office you said she was going through a hard time.'

But Lissa remained silent. As far as she was concerned, I'd blabbed her secrets to the guards, so she wasn't about to share someone else's, and I couldn't really blame her. So, I played my last card. She still refused to look at the picture, so I asked, 'Do you know a Marina Connor from Sligo?'

Her head whipped up to face me, unable to hide her shock. 'Why?'

'She's here, in Glendara. She's been my locum solicitor for six months. You could just as easily have found yourself asking her for advice as me.' I derived some grim satisfaction out of telling her that.

Her face clouded. 'I'd never have asked *her* for advice. Not in a million years.'

I leaned in. 'Why, Lissa? What do you have against her?'

Her face soured. 'She's Chris's sister.'

My throat tightened. No wonder she didn't trust me. 'So that's why you said you couldn't get independent advice in Sligo.'

'They all know each other, there. If I went to any of the solicitors in Sligo, they'd tell her if I asked for advice.'

'I doubt that's true.'

'You told, didn't you?' she snapped.

There wasn't much I could say to that. She looked away and I took a half-step closer. 'Look, you don't have to agree with what I did, but will you look at this picture for me, please? Just take a quick glance.'

Begrudgingly she took the phone from me. And this time she didn't even need to reply, her expression was everything. Her breath quickened and she pulled back, her face frozen in fear.

The door was pushed open and Molloy appeared. I took the phone back, as if I'd been caught doing something I shouldn't. Maybe I had been.

'Is everything all right?' he asked.

Lissa looked at the wall, unhappily. 'I need to sleep,' she said, truculent again. 'The nurses said I have to sleep.'

But Molloy was unruffled. 'I just need to take a quick statement. I'll only take up a few minutes of your time,' he said calmly.

'I'll wait for you outside,' I said and I left the room.

The sickly hospital smell in the corridor did nothing to decrease my unease. Molloy appeared within a few minutes and I told him what I'd discovered. He leaned against the wall, hands behind his back, looking as if the wall was the only thing keeping him upright right now.

'That's all very well but she won't make a statement,' he said.

'About Chris threatening her?'

'About anything. If it weren't for you, I wouldn't even look for one. She'd just be another addict who fell off the wagon.'

'You got my message earlier?' I asked. 'About the beach?'

He nodded. 'We'll have that box tested and we'll pick your man up if we can find him.'

'He's not exactly hiding himself away.'

'Did you give McFadden a description?'

'I have a picture.' I smiled. 'I'll text it to you.'

Molloy gave me one of his looks, but he didn't ask.

I sighed. 'And now it turns out that he's my locum's brother.'

Molloy shook his head. 'It does seem as if they're all very closely connected to Bob Jameson.' A nurse walked by and we moved into a darkened corridor off the main one. Molloy counted the cast of characters off on his fingers. 'Amanda is his wife, Derek his brother.'

'Twin,' I added.

'Twin,' he said. 'Even closer. Mary was his ex,' he continued.

'Not so ex, if what Phyllis says is anything to go by.'

He raised his eyebrows at that and tapped another finger. 'Jude knew him at school and has hated him ever since.'

'He told you that?' I asked.

Molloy nodded. 'Oh yes, he was quite upfront about his dislike. Plus, his daughter Sue nursed Jameson's wife in a psychiatric hospital.'

I looked at him with interest. 'How do you know that?'

'Amanda told us. Why?'

'Because Bob was on the board of that same hospital at some stage. When did she tell you that?' I was curious. It seemed like such an odd thing to come out with.

'Saturday morning. Just after Jameson's body was found. She was in a terrible state, screaming and crying. She asked for a sedative, said Sue might have something.'

'Why would a nurse have a sedative with her?' I wasn't ready to tell Molloy about my suspicions about Sue and the GHB.

'That wasn't terribly clear. Although she was hysterical, a bit all over the place. She changed her mind and asked us to call the doctor. I think Harry gave her something to calm her down.' He sighed. 'So, we have Amanda, Derek, Jude and Sue. And now maybe your locum and her brother. I suppose it's not surprising that those involved in the cycle were connected, but it does make trying to work out what happened to him more difficult. Lissa seems to be the only one without any direct connection to Bob Jameson.'

'But she's married to Chris,' I said.

'Then there are all the other people who wished him ill online,' Molloy added. 'The comment about the snake shedding its skin.' He stared at the floor tiles as if something might be revealed in their cracks.

'Was there anything in the post-mortem?' I asked finally.

Molloy nodded. 'Yes. There was.' He took a deep breath. 'Bob Jameson died of a heart attack, would you believe?'

My eyes widened. 'You're kidding. So, he wasn't murdered?'

He shook his head wearily. 'God knows. But someone brought him up to Mamore Gap, tied him up and left him there. And brought a snake up there to keep him company. The pathologist is waiting on blood tests to see if he was drugged with anything.'

Outside I climbed into the Mini and Molloy went to his car. He drove out ahead of me, looking tired and downcast in the glare of my headlights.

Chapter Twenty-Two

Monday morning came far too quickly for someone with delayed jet lag. Having fallen asleep almost as soon as my head hit the pillow at eleven o'clock, I spent the hours between 3 and 6 a.m. wide awake and staring at the ceiling, looking at the various puzzles that had presented themselves over the past few days from every possible angle.

I kept thinking about Molloy's remark about Bob Jameson's connections to the people we'd met, and I thought about how difficult it was to get anyone to speak about the dead man truthfully. Not quite a conspiracy of silence but close.

Sometime after six I fell into a deep sleep only to be hauled out of delicious unconsciousness by a cruel alarm clock at eight o'clock. And now I had a headache, that dull ache that comes from a broken night's sleep. Coffee was a necessity if I was to stay awake at the office, but the full pot I consumed didn't help the headache much. And, opening one cupboard after another confirmed what I suspected; I had no food, other than cat food, which I faithfully dished out with water much to Guinness's obvious disgust.

'I know you prefer milk but I'm all out,' I said to him as he looked up at me expectantly. 'Anyway, water's better for you.'

He remained unmoved. I was back in the cat's bad books again. I sighed, took a couple of paracetamols, and headed into the office without breakfast.

Once in Glendara, I realised there was no way I could work a full morning on a pot of coffee, so I decided to see if the supermarket had any of those pastries that they make up with frozen dough, assuming they had reopened after the weekend. I could handle a pain-au-chocolat, I thought, driving around the square. When I passed the bank, I remembered that I needed to take Marina off as a signatory on the office cheque book. With some of the less savoury relatives she appeared to have, I decided I'd better do that sooner rather than later. So, I pulled in. The bank's main door was open for the first time since Friday.

I was surprised to hear crying coming from inside: despite what you might think, not a particularly common occurrence on a Monday morning. And this wasn't weeping, these were angry tears, more of a temper tantrum than upset.

The voice sounded familiar and, when I went inside, the blonde head was instantly recognisable even from the back. Amanda Jameson was standing in front of the only counter that was open, having a complete meltdown and screeching at the poor bank clerk. Connie, who had changed my dollars for me on Friday, was one of three people at work in the bank this morning, along with a security guard and a thin man with acne whose sole job seemed to be to encourage people away from the counter and towards one of three machines. He was hovering behind Amanda, wringing his hands, while the customers at the machines tried their best not to stare.

But it was impossible not to overhear; Amanda's usual tone might be whispery but she had a voice that carried when she wanted it to. We all heard that she had 'tried to conduct her business using a machine but the machine had refused to cooperate'. Having lost her temper with the machine and then the acne-faced young man, she had joined the queue for the counter, where she was now berating Connie.

'There's nothing I can do, Mrs Jameson. I'm sorry. If the account is frozen, it's frozen,' the bank clerk said firmly.

'And what exactly do you expect me to do for money?' Amanda's voice reached an even higher pitch if that were possible. 'What do you expect *my boys* to do for money?' Her hands were splayed on the counter and she was leaning into Connie's face. A queue had already begun to form behind her.

Connie looked helplessly at Amanda, then glanced briefly over her shoulder and caught my eye. She didn't try to convey anything, but I could see she was struggling, and though the whole thing was decidedly none of my business, I tapped Amanda on the shoulder. 'Can I help?'

She whirled around, and her eyes widened in satisfaction. 'Just the person. A solicitor. You'll be able to tell this *girl* they can't do this.'

Connie looked at me pleadingly.

'Why don't you come with me and explain to me what has happened?' I said calmly to Amanda. 'And we'll see if there's anything I can do to help.'

'But . . .'

I lowered my voice. 'You don't want the whole bank knowing your business, now do you? Maybe you could come and have a private chat with me and then we can come back if there's something that needs to be cleared up. Would that make sense?'

Amanda looked around her as if noticing for the first time the other customers in the bank. I wondered how often she did her own banking. But I was surprised when she agreed to come with me, and without protest, as if relieved to hand the reins over to someone else.

Connie gave me a grateful smile and handed Amanda back her documents. I was turning to go when she stopped me. 'Oh, hang on, there's something here for you.' She handed me the red umbrella. 'You left this behind you last week.'

'Thanks, Connie,' I said, making a mental note to ring her later about Marina. I still hadn't done my own banking.

Amanda walked beside me listlessly and wordlessly as if she'd exhausted all her energy. When we got into the office, I made her a cup of black coffee and left her sitting in the waiting room while I turned on heating, computers and lights.

Leah wasn't in yet, which surprised me. Connie's presence in the bank had indicated that the roads were okay out her direction. Then my phone buzzed with a text.

Feeling a bit rough this morning. Is it okay if I'm a bit late? Sorry, I know it's your first morning back. L

Of course, I texted back. *Take your time.*

I put the phone down and checked the drip in the bathroom to give Amanda a few more seconds to pull herself together. Then I remembered suddenly that I'd intended to check the yard the day before after my strange feeling on Saturday night. So I opened the back door and stepped out briefly but could find nothing out of the ordinary.

I was glad to see she had calmed down considerably when I returned.

'Feeling any better?' I asked as I sat down beside her.

She was draining her mug of coffee. 'A bit. Thanks,' she said, handing me the empty mug as if I was her butler.

'That's okay.' I put it on the floor and sat beside her. 'Do you want to tell me what the problem is? You don't have to, of course

– I'm sure you'll have your own solicitors dealing with Bob's probate in due course.'

She stared at the floor.

'Maybe it would be a good idea to ring them,' I suggested. 'See if they can help.'

She shook her head. 'There's nothing that can be done. Everything's frozen. It's been frozen for a while. I just thought that girl in the bank . . . in a small country bank.' She shrugged and looked away.

'You mean, you knew everything was frozen?'

She nodded.

'Before Bob even died?'

'Yes.' She looked down at her hands: the nails, though painted, were bitten to the quick. 'We have nothing. Or at least nothing we can get our hands on. There's a court order freezing all the accounts. The only thing we have is the house and that's mortgaged to the hilt.' She played with her wedding ring, twisting it around her finger. 'I thought that young one in the bank might have heard of Bob's death and might . . .'

'Be inexperienced enough to let you have some money?'

No matter how stuck Amanda was, trying to get a bank clerk to make a mistake so she could access money to which she wasn't entitled said something about her that I didn't like. But it did seem odd to me that their personal accounts had been frozen, no matter what was happening with the charity.

'Bank workers don't have that kind of power any more, you know. Everything's centralised.'

She nodded. 'I know. I just thought . . .' She shook her head. 'The boys have been ringing looking for money, bottomless pits the pair of them. Bob used to give them cash, he always had a stash of cash.' Her eyes welled with a kind of desperation. 'I can't access a cent. Can't even pay *that woman* for our accommodation.'

'What about Derek?' I suggested.

She shook her head and looked away.

'They were brothers,' I prompted gently. 'Surely, he would help if you asked him.'

If I'd thought the scene at the bank was as fiery as Amanda Jameson could get, I was wrong. Her face flooded with anger. 'We wouldn't even be in this mess if it wasn't for Derek. Derek was the one who reported the charity to the Regulator. He's the reason the accounts are frozen. He's the reason that I can't feed my kids.'

This seemed a bit of an exaggeration considering the ages of the 'kids', but I was still surprised. 'Really? Derek?'

'Oh, it was anonymous, but we knew it was him.' She looked at the ceiling as if trying to keep the tears from overflowing from her eyes and tumbling down her cheeks. This was the first true grief I'd seen from her and it was about money.

'Did Bob know?'

'Of course, he did,' she snapped. 'And after everything Bob did for him. Derek wouldn't be alive if it weren't for Bob.'

I remembered the feature in the paper. 'Are you talking about Derek's accident?'

She looked up. 'Derek jumped off a roof when they were kids and he ended up in hospital. Bob stayed by his bedside every day for months. And that was just the start. Bob spent his life trying to help Derek, without a word of thanks.'

She muttered something under her breath. I thought she said 'runt'. It was what Bob had called Derek that night in the Oak. At the time I'd thought the term was affectionate, but it didn't sound that way when Amanda used it.

Her voice went up a notch. 'And then he reports him? How dare he?'

'But I thought there were several complaints, a number of allegations being investigated.'

She reared up. 'Where did you hear that?'

This time I didn't respond. I had no idea if it was public knowledge or not.

She clicked her teeth. 'Bob knew nothing about any of it, but he was still the one getting the blame. Not that Derek cared about that.'

'Bob knew nothing about what?' I asked.

'It was all a misunderstanding. It would have been sorted out. Bob would have been able to sort it out.'

I thought about the four airline tickets Mary had found in their room. Bob had no intention of 'sorting' anything out. Had he been killed to stop him leaving?

I tried another tack. 'So, you were angry with Bob, then?'

Her eyes flashed. 'He should have cut Derek out, brother or no brother. But oh no, he insisted on continuing as if nothing had happened. Thought they could make it up. Bob was too loyal. He even let Derek be event coordinator for the cycle.'

I wondered about the row in the B & B, if it had been about Derek. But Amanda denied it even happened. She said that it was the second time she'd had to deny it, that the guard had asked her about it too. She said she'd never thrown anything at him in her life, she'd never thrown anything at anyone.

But I'd seen for myself that Amanda was capable of just the kind of meltdown that Mary had described. Before I could ask her anything else, she stood up.

'I need to go. Thank you for the coffee.' And with that she flounced out of the waiting room and was gone.

253

I picked up her mug, spying that there were documents on the carpet too. They must have fallen down the back of Amanda's chair. I picked them up; they were bank documents. I knew I shouldn't have, but I snuck a look. She'd filled out a withdrawal slip for five hundred euro for the Jameson Grace Charity account. Amanda Jameson had been trying to take money from the charity's account, an account that was definitely frozen.

The door opened again. I quickly folded the forms and shoved them into my pocket, but I was relieved to see that it was Leah.

'Well, she was in a hurry!'

'You met Mrs Jameson then?'

Leah nodded, glancing back at the door. 'She nearly knocked me over on the footpath, pregnant or not.' She paused; eyebrows raised. 'Hang on, is that the widow of the man who . . .?'

'The very one.'

'I thought I recognised the name.' She dumped her bag on the reception desk. 'Oh well. I'll forgive her a bit of brusqueness so.'

'I don't think she likes women very much,' I said.

'What was she doing here?' Leah looked concerned. 'You're not acting for her, are you?'

I shook my head. 'She was a bit upset at the bank, so I took her in here to calm her down.'

Leah took a deep breath; she seemed a bit breathless herself. 'You okay?' I asked.

She nodded, tapping her chest. 'Par for the course.' She narrowed her eyes. 'You know that man was in here last week? That woman's husband.'

My head snapped up. 'Bob Jameson – the man who was killed? Here in the office?'

'Yes. I'd swear it was him. Big man with grey hair. I saw his picture in the paper.'

'What was he in here for?'

She shrugged. 'He just called in on spec, I think. Don't think I even caught his name at the time. Marina met him in the doorway. And I don't know what it was about, but he spent about half an hour in your office with her.'

'Jesus.' I felt like I had to sit down. Surely this was something Marina should have mentioned. We'd had coffee together the morning after his body had been found, for God's sake.

'When was this?' Forty questions formed in my head but that was the first one that came out.

Leah paused to think. 'Thursday lunchtime?' She opened the appointments book to check and shook her head. 'No appointment, although Marina should have put him in the other book. I'm sure it's not there though. She always forgot.' She took out the other book, the one where we listed people who just called in without appointments, opened it and shook her head again. 'Nope.'

I remembered something. Thursday was the day I'd arrived back. 'You closed early that day, didn't you? I called in at a quarter past five and the place was locked up.'

Leah put her hand to her cheek. 'Oh God, did you? Sorry about that.' She closed her eyes to think. 'Thursday, that's right. I was feeling a bit queasy, so Marina told me to head off about five. I must have just missed you.' She frowned. 'I didn't know she was going to close up though.'

'It doesn't matter.' I waved my hand dismissively. 'But Bob Jameson called in and you've absolutely no idea what it was about?'

'Sorry. I barely spoke to the man. I'd have rung you if I knew anything. I kind of assumed that Marina would tell you if there was anything to tell.'

I crossed my arms and leaned against the desk. Leah was right. She certainly should have.

Leah took off her coat. 'That was mad wasn't it, all the same? A snake, I hear?'

I nodded. 'Well, it was a heart attack that killed him apparently. But yeah, he was bitten by a snake too.'

'Where did the snake come from?'

I told her about finding the box at Pollan Bay and the man with the Barbour jacket. Her eyes widened and she tutted. 'You couldn't make it up.'

'It seems the man is Marina's brother. You didn't meet him, did you?'

She had a think and then shook her head. 'No, I didn't. I don't think she even mentioned she had a brother. She wasn't that chatty about her family at all. I know her parents are dead, that's about it.' She went to hang up her coat.

'So how did you cope with the floods?' I called after her.

She came back smoothing her blouse over her small bump. 'Ach, we were all right. The weather was awful, but we just stayed put for the weekend.' She smiled. 'One of the advantages of living on a hill. We missed all the drama. I hear Glendara was cut off.'

'That's right. You were better off staying away from any drama in your condition. Bedding down on the floor of the Beacon Hall wouldn't have been too much fun for you. How are you feeling?' I noticed she was still a little pale.

'Ach, I'm grand. Was a wee bit dizzy this morning when I woke up, and I didn't want to get into the car until I felt better. Or rather Kevin wouldn't let me get into the car until I felt better. I'm fine now though.' She nodded towards the door to the bathroom. 'I see that leak is still going. Must get that seen to. If it starts to rain again, we might be in trouble . . .'

'Oh yes. It won't be easy to get anyone though. People have far more problems than a little leak in the bathroom.'

'I'll ask Kevin to have a look,' she said as she took her seat at the computer. 'Right. Let's get started.' She logged in and moved some files towards her. 'Bugger, Marina has left me a right load of stuff . . .'

'Actually,' I said, leaning over the reception desk. I still had Amanda's documents burning a hole in my pocket. 'Would you mind looking something up for me before you start anything else?'

She pulled a notepad and pen towards her. 'Sure.'

I rooted for the Post-it pad in my bag, the one I'd had in Molloy's place, and I handed it to her. 'It's a Companies Office search. I want you to find out whatever you can about the Jameson Grace Charity.'

'That's the charity the cycle was for? What do you want to know?'

'Oh, just the basics, who is on the board of directors, if they have charitable status, if they've filed the appropriate returns, that kind of thing. Anything else you can turn up.'

'Okey doke.' She didn't ask any questions. She was used to my oddities at this stage.

I went upstairs. On the landing. I called down, 'Leah?'

'Yeah?'

'Did Marina leave back her key?'

'The key to the office?' There was a pause and the sound of some rummaging about. 'Doesn't look like it. She never gave it to me anyway, and it's not on the hook.'

I wasn't happy about this, but it did give me the excuse I needed to talk to her again. But before I did anything else, I rang Connie at the bank and asked her to prepare the necessary paperwork to remove Marina as signatory, adding that I'd call in to sign it when I got a chance.

Then I worked away for an hour or two, disturbed only by the odd phone call. I was relieved to see my impression had been correct; despite her messy working methods, Marina was a decent solicitor. Her work was good, everything was relatively up to date and, with the morning as quiet as it was, it was easy enough to catch up. I suspected what was going on outside my window was considerably more frantic; the growl of tractors and diggers passing by showed that the clean-up process had begun in earnest.

When I went down for a coffee at eleven Leah told me she'd made lots of appointments for the rest of the week. She also had the results of the searches I'd asked her to do, which she handed over as she sipped her tea.

The first was a Company's Registration Office search with a list of directors. I scanned the page quickly and apart from Bob Jameson, none was familiar, though I was a little surprised his wife wasn't there. Then I saw Leah had handwritten a name at the bottom of the sheet: *Julian Burns*. I had to look at it twice.

'Julian Burns – Jude – is a director of the Jameson Grace Charity?' I read it again, before looking up. This did not tally with anything Jude had said to me. The impression he'd given was that he was only involved in the cycle to keep an eye on his daughters. That he might have any deeper involvement with Bob Jameson's charity simply didn't add up.

Leah frowned. 'Who?' She took the sheet back from me and examined it. 'Oh no. He was the registered accountant for Oak Knap Investment Bank. This is the printout for the bank. They were registered in the UK. That's a UK companies office search.'

Momentarily confused, I checked the Post-it I had given her

again and realised I'd written the name of the bank that Bob Jameson had worked for along with the charity's. Leah had thought I'd wanted her to do searches for both.

She was looking at me now. 'Is that all right? I've given you whatever I could find for the Oak Knap Investment Bank *and* the Jameson Grace Charity. That's what you wanted, isn't it?'

I nodded. 'That's great.'

I hadn't intended Leah to check the bank, but I was glad she had. When I'd been looking at the bank, I'd ignored the business pages but Leah in her usual forensic fashion had checked everything. She'd separated the information she'd dug up into two sections, one for the bank and one for the charity. Without realising it I had started with the bundle for the bank.

'So Jude Burns worked for Oak Knap?' I said.

Leah nodded. 'It was a small investment bank in the UK. It closed its doors some time ago but Julian Burns's name keeps coming up because the bank got into difficulty with some investment properties – there was some hint of the bank laundering corrupt payments. This was before all this due diligence stuff we have now.'

'Okay,' I said slowly.

'It looks as if he took the fall for the bank, as the company's accountant. They seem to have blamed him and denied any knowledge themselves.'

My eyes widened. 'And he just took it?'

She shrugged. 'Looks like it. I think he may even have been struck off. Regained his licence again at some stage but the company got into all kinds of bother. Allegations of involvement in criminal activities. No charges were ever brought, but it looks pretty shady.' She made a face as she pointed to one of the sheets. It was the 'Floors of Whores' piece that I'd found myself.

I flicked through the rest as I drank my coffee. Jude had certainly been disingenuous when he'd said he and Bob had known each other when they were kids. They'd known each other a lot more recently than that, and not just because Jude's mother was in a Jameson Grace Home.

When I finished my drink, I took the sheets and went back upstairs to have a proper look through. There were no more major surprises as far as the bank was concerned but the Jameson Grace Charity was chaotic. They hadn't filed any returns for three years. How could they continue to operate? I wondered. Especially when it came to running the care homes.

I was still scratching my head in disbelief at what they'd managed to get away with, when Leah appeared at my door. 'I think you should come down and hear this.'

Frowning, I followed her back down the stairs. Obeying her instructions, I put the dictation headphones on. They were hot. Marina's soft voice came through.

Firstly, can you do up an attendance, Leah, as follows? Bob Jameson attended at the office on the twenty-third of April to give instructions for a will. Can you do up a draft will as follows? I Bob Jameson of Station Road, Salthill in the county of Galway make this and for my last will and testament, hereby revoking all former wills and other testamentary dispositions at any time heretofore made by me . . .

I pulled the headphones off. 'So, that's why he came in? To make a will?'

It seemed even more odd now that Marina hadn't told me he'd been in. Surely, she would have known I'd discover that she'd dictated his will.

'I wonder what it says,' I said as I moved to put the headphones back on.

But Leah pushed a sheet of will paper towards me. 'Way ahead of you. I know he won't be coming back in to sign it, but I thought you'd want to see it typed up.'

I picked it up. The will began with the standard 'commorientes' clause.

If my wife Amanda survives me by a period of thirty days, I give devise and bequeath the whole of my estate to her. I appoint her my executrix and I direct her to pay all my just debts funeral and testamentary expenses. If my wife does not survive me, the following provisions shall apply . . .

There followed various legacies, which I read through quickly until I came to one that made me catch my breath.

I give devise and bequeath the sum of twenty thousand euros to my daughter Sue Burns.

I sank my elbows back into the counter. Sue Burns was Bob's daughter? What the hell was going on? I read it again and again until Leah's voice broke into my thoughts and I remembered that none of this meant very much to her, having been absent all weekend.

'Lunch,' she said firmly, already putting on her coat. 'Come on. I can't wait for food these days. If I don't eat, I get faint.'

'Okay, okay, I'm coming.' I put down the will, got my coat and we headed out to the Oak.

My head was spinning. One thing was for sure – the Burns family and the Jamesons were a hell of a lot more entangled than either was prepared to admit.

Chapter Twenty-Three

Town was busy again, I was glad to see, with the usual Monday lunchtime bustle. The roads were still wet, but it hadn't rained for almost thirty-six hours, so it seemed we were on the home straight.

Many of the bridges that were down would take time to repair or replace but at least one of the roads to Derry was now passable, which meant that those who had come for the charity cycle could now leave if they wanted to. I assumed Derek and Amanda would be gone as soon as Bob's body was released, and that Jude, Sue and Peadar would leave as soon as Lissa was released from hospital. Two families just waiting on a green light. Two families I'd now discovered were far more connected than I'd previously been led to believe.

My mind was reeling with what I'd just discovered. There was a now a double connection between Jude Burns and the dead man. It put the frosty exchange I'd witnessed between the two men on Friday night into a new context, and also the exchange between Amanda and Sue in the Beacon Hall. And possibly, the row between Amanda and Bob that Mary had overheard and witnessed.

If Sue was Bob Jameson's daughter, then presumably he'd had an affair with Jude's wife, the wife he rarely mentioned. Was she still around? I wondered. Had they divorced? Did Amanda know that Sue was Bob's daughter? If so, how had Bob having a child with someone else affected her when she'd been struggling to conceive? Sue was older than their two adopted children. Was that what had caused her breakdown? Phyllis had implied that Amanda had mental health difficulties when trying to conceive but also more recently. Sue worked in the hospital where Amanda had been a patient and Bob had served on the board. Had the relationship been exposed then? And the six-million-dollar question – *did Jude know?*

I was surprised to see Jude himself with Phyllis in the Oak. They looked cosy at a table by the fire and they didn't notice us come in. As I watched them laugh together, I wondered for the first time if something could happen there. I would have been pleased before, but now I wasn't so sure. It was decidedly possible that Jude had something to do with Bob's death. He'd have had good reason to hate him if he'd had an affair with his wife *and* made him take the fall for the bank. But all of that happened such a long time ago. Why wait so long to take his revenge?

Leah made a beeline for the bar and I went over to Phyllis and Jude, taking note anew of Jude's size; he'd certainly have the physical capability to do away with Bob, maybe even carry or drag him up Mamore Gap . . . although we now knew that the man had died of a heart attack. Also how would he have transported him? I couldn't imagine Bob travelling on the back of Jude's motorbike. Having said that, the girls must have driven here with Peadar. They must have a car.

I processed all of this at high speed as I approached their table. Lord knows what kind of an expression I was wearing. When I got there, they both looked up, and Jude smiled, his usual warm smile. Could I really be looking into the face of a killer?

'Lissa's getting out later today,' he said without any preamble. 'I'm just thanking this lovely woman for helping her, but I should be thanking you too.'

'Not at all. I did very little.' So, they could be leaving town today, I thought. Not much time for a chat.

'Do you want to join us?' Phyllis asked, but her tone wasn't exactly encouraging, and she didn't seem particularly upset when I said no. Now wasn't the time, I thought. I'd collar Jude on his own before he left the pub.

Leah was halfway through a chicken sandwich when I joined her, after I'd given Tony my order at the bar. I looked at her, surprised. 'How did you manage to get served so quickly?'

She grinned and spoke through a mouthful of food. 'I ordered over the phone from the office. I told you I can't last very long these days.' She nodded towards the table I'd just left. 'Who is that with Phyllis?'

'That's Jude. One of the people involved in the cycle. He's a motorcyclist, a paramedic and an accountant.'

Her eyes widened. 'Jude the accountant? The one who got in trouble over the bank?'

I nodded.

She took a sip of her water, eyes still on the bookseller and her new friend. 'They look very close. Is there something going on there?'

'I don't know. But I wouldn't mind having a chat with him on my own. See what he says about what we found out this morning.' I lowered my voice. 'The Sue Burns in Bob Jameson's will is his daughter.'

Leah looked confused, but before I had a chance to explain the door opened and Jack, the taxi driver who had given me a lift on Saturday morning walked in, newspaper rolled up under his arm. He headed straight for the bar and perched on a stool at the far end, flicking out the paper and smoothing it in front of him.

'One sec,' I said to Leah, who looked up in surprise as I got to my feet.

The bathrooms were just behind where Jack was sitting, so I could pretend I was heading there. I said hello as I passed, and he looked up from his paper and sat back on his stool.

'How are ye doing now?'

I crossed my arms. 'Not too bad. Hopefully we're on our way back to normality.'

'Aye. With a bit of luck.' He returned to the racing pages.

I made to walk on and then stopped as if something had just occurred to me. 'Oh, did you get to speak to the sergeant, by the way?'

He turned and frowned, one hand resting on the counter. 'What about?'

I said discreetly, 'About the man who died. Giving him and his wife and brother a lift back that night. There might be nothing, but you might be able to tell him something.'

Jack clicked his teeth. 'Aye. I've been meaning to, but I haven't had a chance. The car gave up the ghost, electrics all went in it on Saturday afternoon on the way to Clonmany and I had to get towed. A wile handling, so it was.' His eyes narrowed. 'But do you know something? There *was* something strange about that. I remembered it after I was talking to you.'

I leaned in, holding my breath. 'Strange about what?'

'About that night. That fare.' He closed over the paper. 'That man came back over to me just as I was turning the car, the man that died.'

'What for?' Jesus, I thought. Had Bob asked this man to drive him somewhere? Had this taxi driver been the person who had driven him up to Mamore, to his death?

But no. 'He wanted a light. He'd noticed the lighter on the dashboard and knew I smoked.' Jack shook his head disgustedly. 'I can't give the feckin' things up.'

'Go on,' I said patiently.

'He said he was the exact same. Couldn't chuck the damn things. So, we had a fag together.' Jack looked guilty. 'I know I shouldn't have but it was pissing down out of the heavens, so I let him sit in the car and we had a wee chat.'

'Can you remember what about?'

He nodded. 'That was the strange thing . . . with what happened afterwards, I mean.' He stopped and looked off into the distance. 'Aye, it was strange.'

Just at that moment, Tony came over with Jack's pot of tea and there was the usual toing and froing with payment and change, and by the time it was all finished I was ready to scream.

When Tony had finally departed, I took a deep breath. 'What was strange, Jack?' I asked.

'Aye, well, that man was bitten by a snake . . . That's right, isn't it?'

I nodded impatiently. This we knew. And yes, we knew this was strange. But it was hardly news at this point. 'Yes?'

Jack took a drink of his tea and put the cup carefully down onto its saucer. 'Well, that man was feckin' terrified of snakes. Scared out of his wits. And he told me that, just hours before he came face to face with one.' He leaned back and crossed his arms. 'Now what are the odds of that?'

'Really?' I tried to imagine how something like that would have come up in conversation at midnight between two strangers having a cigarette in a car. But I didn't need to ask. Now that Jack had decided to speak, he was in full flow.

'Aye. We were talking about films. The kind of chat you have sharing a fag when one of you has had a few pints. He was going on about some charity premiere or some such he'd been to the week before. Some posh do.' He raised his eyes to heaven. 'Full of old big talk, he was, to be honest. But then I said I loved *Indiana Jones and the Temple of Doom*, that I'd watched it seventeen times and he said he couldn't watch it because of the snake pit. That he was absolutely shit-scared of them, he had a snake phobia.'

He shook his head sadly. 'It was stupid chat really, but I thought afterwards, the poor feckin' eejit. It must have been his worst nightmare, being up on that hill with something he had a mortal fear of.'

I tried to take this in. Fear of snakes wasn't unusual, and not exactly a major problem if you lived in Ireland where there were none. But Bob Jameson had lived and worked in Nigeria, so it must have come up at some stage. The man was bitten by a snake before he died and there was even a point at which it was assumed by most people that the snakebite had killed him. Surely somebody should have mentioned that he had a fear of them. Someone who knew him well. Like a wife? Or a childhood friend? I glanced over but Phyllis and Jude had left the pub.

The taxi driver took a deep slug of his tea. 'Do you think I should tell the sergeant?'

I nodded. 'I do. I definitely do.'

Before I could process anything further, Tony handed me my sandwich over the bar. I re-joined Leah and I ate my lunch while I tried to work out what to do next.

When I emerged from the Oak half an hour later, Marina was

coming out of Harry's place across the street. Her gaze dropped when she saw me, wishing to avoid an encounter, but I wasn't going to let that happen. So I told Leah to go on without me.

'Half three,' she called after me as I hurried across to cut Marina off. 'Your first appointment is at half three, remember.'

'I'll remember.' I tried my best to avoid the remaining puddles, calling Marina's name when I reached the other side, slightly breathless.

She looked up and attempted a half-laugh, a pretence that she was happy to see me. 'Don't worry, I'll be leaving later today.' But there was tension in her face.

'Stay as long as you like. But I think you forgot to leave your key to the office.'

Her unease was replaced by relief. 'Oh sorry.' She started to root in her bag.

I took a half-step closer to her and lowered my voice. 'Why didn't you mention that Bob Jameson was in the office?'

She stopped mid-search without looking up.

'Marina?'

She straightened, without meeting my eye. 'I didn't think there was any point. He wanted to make a will. He never signed it, so it's not as if it will have any significance now.'

I touched her shoulder and forced her to look at me. 'What aren't you telling me? Why would a man like that come to you to make a will when he's only in the area for a short time? You'd barely have had time to draft it, let alone have him sign it.'

Her expression darkened, but she didn't reply.

'Come on, Marina. Did you know Bob Jameson?' I asked. 'Before this week?'

She looked down for a few seconds, examining the footpath, making up her mind. Finally, she looked up. 'Yes, I knew him.'

I crossed my arms. 'Go on.'

She let out a deep breath. 'He recognised me on the street, that's why he came into the office. I don't even know if he ever intended on signing that will. You're right – if the cycle had gone ahead, he'd have left town by the time it was ready. I think he just came in to gloat.' Her tone was bitter.

'Gloat about what?'

'To show that he was untouchable. That no matter how much I hated him, he could pay for my time, like a prostitute.'

I put my hands up in protest. 'Okay. I'm not sure I've ever made that comparison between the two professions, but I suppose . . .'

She cut across me. 'Those homes of his, the Jameson Grace Homes. They're nothing but a way to screw the life savings out of people. Once you're in, you're trapped.'

'What do you mean?'

She looked me straight in the eye and for the first time our gazes were level. 'Bob Jameson conned my family out of their life savings. My father was in the early stages of dementia, but we didn't know it yet. Jameson made him give him the deeds to the house. Some "security" if anything happened to him.' She made quotation marks with her fingers. 'My father knew there was something wrong with him and he was frightened. Jameson took advantage of that. He played on his fear.'

I opened my mouth to speak but she got there first. She put her hand up to stop me.

'He convinced Dad that he'd be saving his family a lot of grief if he had a residential home organised for himself, when the time came. And it did. He went into the home, but it left my mother destitute: they threw her out of *her* home.'

I frowned. I was confused. 'But how could that happen?'

She took a deep breath. 'Bob Jameson set up this system almost like a living will. You sign all the documents while you're well, then it's triggered when you're not able to care for yourself. He takes everything. Ostensibly to pay for the home, but that's utter bollocks.'

'What do you mean?' I'd never heard Marina speak like this.

'The Jameson Grace care homes are appalling; the residents aren't fed properly, or washed regularly, or given the proper medical attention. Only the absolute minimum is done for them, despite millions being raised every year to keep them going. It's extortion.'

Marina looked away, her eyes glittering with fury and grief. 'And once you're in, you can't leave, because as far as the state is concerned you have a home, but you have no money left to pay for anywhere else. Everything is gone because Bob fucking Jameson has taken it all.'

I protested in disbelief. 'But your mother? What about the Family Home Protection Act? How could they evict her?'

Marina shook her head in disgust. 'Oh, Jameson was smart. He had her sign a release, a declaration. And she did it. Because she was frightened too; she knew there was something wrong with my father and she was worried about how he was going to be cared for.'

'I see.'

'He, of course, didn't want her to tell anyone. So, when he asked her to sign, told her it was the solution to everything, she did it.' She smiled bitterly. 'She was part of that generation of women who were used to doing what their husbands told them to. Even the good ones.'

'God, that's awful.'

She shrugged. 'So, we had no comeback. My family couldn't

understand why, as a lawyer, I couldn't do anything. I tried my best, but it tore my family apart. It was taking too long. My mother and father both died before anything was sorted.' She looked at her feet. 'It was one of the reasons my marriage broke up. I got a bit obsessed with it.'

'Were you one of the people who lodged a complaint with the Regulator?' I asked.

'Yes. For all the good it did. Nothing happened quickly enough. It destroyed my brother.'

'Chris?'

If she was surprised that I knew his name, she didn't show it. She just nodded. 'He tried his best to get money together for our mother, desperate to raise some cash. Got himself into all kinds of dodgy stuff in the process.' She bit her lip. 'Chris has changed beyond all recognition over this. All he cares about is money. Says he'll never be destitute like our mother. His marriage broke up because of it too. Bob Jameson destroyed two marriages and our entire family.'

It occurred to me that if Chris had hit his wife then he was responsible for destroying his own family, but I didn't say it. There was something I wanted to ask her first.

'Marina, you dictated that will, you know what's in it.' I paused. 'Bob Jameson left a legacy to Sue, Chris's sister-in-law. The will said she was his daughter.'

She met my gaze.

'I know Chris is here, in Inishowen. I've seen him. You can't tell me that's a coincidence.'

Then it hit me. Of course! This was why Marina had tried to keep herself hidden; why she'd left the pub so abruptly that first night, why her mood had changed as soon as she'd walked in and seen them all. It was nothing to do with Phyllis. She must have been trying to avoid the Jamesons and the Burns all week-end, although it didn't seem to bother her brother. Was that what they'd been arguing about?

Her eyes welled and she looked down. 'Chris just told me what happened with Lissa. I'm so ashamed of him. I never thought my own brother would do something like that.'

'What did he tell you?'

She took a deep breath. 'The family were having tests for bone marrow donation in case Peadar needed it and it came out through that . . . that Bob Jameson was Sue's father. I don't know what the circumstances were, but it seems to be true. But when Lissa told Chris, he lashed out. The man he hated most in the world had suddenly become part of his family.'

So Lissa and Sue knew Bob was Sue's father, I thought. Presumably that meant Jude did too.

Marina was still talking, shaking her head with tears running freely down her face. 'It's absolutely no excuse and he regrets it so much. But he's been so screwed up since our parents died. The only thing that gives him any relief is the gym, all that bloody Ironman stuff. And he nurses a pathological hatred for Bob Jameson.'

'Do you think Chris might have had something to do with his death?' I asked. I remembered the conversation that Lissa had overheard, the one that had caused her to think that Chris was trying to kill her. The words 'It would be worth serving a fuck-ing life sentence for.'

She shook her head vehemently. 'No. He's not capable of that. I'm sure of it.'

'But he's capable of hitting his wife because her sister is the daughter of the man he hates?'

She looked away uncomfortably.

'Why didn't you tell me any of this?' I asked. 'Or Molloy? Maybe knowing all of this would help find out who killed him.'

She replied, 'I know it sounds awful, but I just didn't care. I was glad he was dead. I was grateful to whoever did it and I didn't,' she corrected herself, 'don't, particularly want them caught. Whether it was Chris or anyone else.'

She stood her ground and looked at me as if waiting for a reaction or objection on my part, but I didn't have one. Finally, she took something out of her bag and handed it to me. 'Here's your key. Thank you for the job. I enjoyed the work, most of it anyway.'

As I watched her go back into Harry's surgery, I knew that this had been part of the problem. That Marina wasn't the only one who hated Bob Jameson so much that they didn't care whether his killer was caught.

Chapter Twenty-Four

I crossed the square again, mind whirring. So much for Bob Jameson turning over a new leaf in Nigeria. All that 'Amazing Grace', Road-to-Damascus rhetoric was nothing but a scam to create a persona people trusted enough to head up a charity for which people would raise money. I assumed most who were taking part in the cycle had loved ones in the Jameson Grace care homes. And as far as the broader charity was concerned, while dementia might not affect all families, aging certainly did, which meant that Bob Jameson had tapped into a highly lucrative concern, taking advantage of people at a time when they were desperate and vulnerable. I wondered if the online comment about the snake shedding its skin had come from someone whose loved one was in a Jameson Grace Home, who had lost everything in exchange for care that was below par. Or someone who had raised money that had gone directly into Bob Jameson's pocket.

But why the wall of silence about it? In public at least. The snake comment was anonymous. Even Marina had to have her story forced out of her. Were people embarrassed to speak out? To admit they had been conned? Or were they afraid? Trapped? Once they were resident in a Jameson Grace Home there was nowhere for them to go if they'd parted with all their assets.

I'd seen older clients, frightened and abused, often by their own relatives. Sometimes it was pride that prevented them from speaking out and sometimes they were afraid to tell anyone what was happening and too vulnerable to stand up for themselves. Which was why I firmly believed that older people needed advocates.

Bob Jameson had been getting away with it for a long time, but from what Molloy had said, the authorities were finally closing in. Presumably that had been why he was planning to leave. Was the money secreted wherever he was going? Whatever the answers were, the questions certainly broadened the range of suspects for the man's murder. And I needed to speak to Molloy.

I walked quickly past the office, hoping Leah wasn't looking out the window waiting to reel me in. In the Garda Station Molloy and McFadden were both there. McFadden was behind the counter doing some paperwork while Molloy was just finishing a call.

'Okay, thanks,' he said. 'I'll let them know.' He raised his eyebrows when he saw me and, when he put the phone down, he announced, 'The body is being released, so the family can take him home and have a burial at least, or cremation or whatever.'

'And leave, presumably?' I said, leaning my elbows on the counter.

'Well yes, leave Inishowen, not the country. They're still part of a murder investigation.'

I told him everything that Marina had just told me.

'I'll pass all of that on,' he said with a nod. 'The case will end up in the hands of the NBCI now, since we haven't managed to make any progress. Especially since there are suspects from all over the country.' He sighed. 'It looks like we failed on this one.'

'We did kind of have our hands full, Sarge,' McFadden said, without looking up from whatever he was doing.

The phone rang again, and this time it was McFadden who answered it. His brow furrowed as he listened to the caller and then he passed the handset to Molloy. 'It's the hospital. Something's happened. I can't catch what the matron is saying. She sounds in a bit of a panic.'

Molloy frowned as he took the phone. 'Hello?'

I couldn't hear the other side of the conversation, but Molloy's response was immediate and unhesitating. 'I'll be there straight away.' He put the phone down and looked at me. 'Do you want to come? You might be able to help.'

I felt a stab of fear. The hospital. The first thing that occurred to me was Lissa Bennett, that her husband Chris had got to her, finally, and that she was properly hurt. I followed Molloy out of the station and to the squad car with a knot in my chest.

'What's going on?' I asked as we drove through town.

He shook his head. 'I'm not sure. Some kind of a row.'

I was sure the matron had told him more than that, but he didn't seem to want to discuss it. I was just surprised to be asked along.

The wet ground hissed under the tyres as Molloy parked as close as he could to the hospital's main door. There was no sign of anything unusual outside, just a grey sky overhead and a still waterlogged car park, the few patches of grass still sodden.

We ran into reception, at which point Molloy seemed to know where he was going. And I was just about to follow him when the entire Burns family appeared.

I was relieved to see that Lissa was with them, folding up a sheet of paper, having clearly just been discharged. She still looked pale and shaken, but she was alive and conscious and had obviously suffered no further mishaps. Jude and Peadar greeted me with smiles, the daughters without, a neat gender split. It seemed I'd managed to get myself on the wrong side of both Burns women.

'What are you doing here?' Jude asked, his smile turning to concern. 'Is everything all right?'

Before I could reply, loud voices drifted from the corridor Molloy had just taken. Clocking the sign for the first time, I realised it led to the morgue. I ran down it with the sense that Jude was at my heels.

The narrow hallway outside the mortuary was clogged with people: Amanda Jameson, Molloy and Mary plus a hospital porter and Hal the undertaker, who was wringing his hands and looking distinctly agitated. There was an odd smell, which I tried to ignore. Morgue chemicals presumably. Formaldehyde? I felt a shiver.

I presumed Bob's body remained behind the double doors where Amanda was standing, arms crossed, feet splayed like a bouncer; her stance rather at odds with the Chanel-style navy suit that she was wearing. Another new outfit.

'This stupid woman won't get out of our way,' she said imperiously. 'Get rid of her please, Sergeant.' She seemed awfully close to clicking her fingers at Molloy.

Mary, standing a few feet away, was in tears, big, wet tears rolling down her beautiful face.

Molloy raised his hands. 'Can someone please tell me what's going on here? Slowly and calmly. I've only just been informed that Mr Jameson's remains are being released. So, what exactly is the problem?'

'He should be buried here, in Inishowen,' Mary said quietly. 'This is where he died. He belongs here.' She rubbed her sleeve against her cheek.

Amanda's eyes were blazing. 'What are you talking about? Bob was murdered here. He has no relationship with this place. He'd never been here in his life and the first time he comes to this godforsaken place he ends up dead. Why the hell would we leave him here?'

'He'd be with someone who loves him.' Mary looked down. She was swaying and I wondered if she was about to faint. 'You don't love him.'

'I'm his wife. I have children with him. It doesn't matter a damn what I think of him.' Amanda shook her head in disgust. 'He had tons of tarts. Don't delude yourself you were special . . .'

Hal and the poor morgue assistant stared at the floor, clearly mortified.

Molloy turned to me. 'Ben, can you help us here? Who has custody of a body in circumstances like these?'

Molloy knew the answer to this, he was just seeking confirmation, so I gave it. It was clearly why I'd been invited along. 'The personal representative. So, either the executor if the deceased has made a will, or the administrator if they haven't. The personal representative has custody of the body until burial or cremation.'

'There is no will,' Amanda said firmly. Her jaw was set.

I looked at Molloy. 'Mr Jameson's wife would be his personal representative if he hadn't made a will.'

Mary's legs buckled, and she slid down the wall and put her head in her hands. Hal and the porter went back into the morgue. Hal must have been asked to transfer the body back to Galway or wherever Bob Jameson was to be buried.

Footsteps sounded and Derek Jameson appeared, looking startled. He glanced warily from one face to the other. 'What's going on?'

'She's finally lost it,' Amanda said, pointing to the slumped and weeping Mary.

'Mary?' Derek said gently as he leaned over her.

She looked up at him. 'Can I at least see him?' When there

was no response from him, a semblance of hope appeared in her eyes. 'Could we at least have the funeral here? He can be buried or cremated wherever you want. Just something, please.'

'You're completely deranged,' Amanda spat. 'Do you know that? Deranged.'

And with that, Mary rose to her feet. Anger seemed to give her energy, though her voice was calm. 'You didn't care about him. All you cared about was money, a big house and a big car and fancy things.'

Amanda's features rearranged themselves into a smile. 'That was all he cared about either, you fool.'

There was a shocked silence. The last taboo, speaking ill of the dead. Mary shook her head and turned to Derek, a pleading look in her eyes.

He spoke softly to her. 'Bob has to go back to his children, to his home. That must happen, Mary. You understand that, don't you?'

All hope leached from her face and she started to cry quietly as if she'd lost him all over again.

Amanda's smile had faded. 'Why are you being nice to *her*?'

But Derek ignored her and took Mary gently away by the hand. 'Come on, let me call someone for you.'

'Phyllis,' I suggested. 'Call Phyllis.'

He nodded and they left. And then there was just Amanda, Molloy and me, standing in a white corridor with a buzzing light, watching them both walk out of view.

Amanda's voice cut through the silence. 'Moves fast for a man with only one leg, doesn't he?'

Chapter Twenty-Five

'Thank you for that,' Molloy said as we hurried out of the hospital. I think we both wanted to get away from Amanda Jameson as quickly as possible. 'Turns out there are times when it's handy to have a solicitor around.'

'That's okay,' I said distractedly.

I was thinking about clothes. Specifically, the suit that Amanda was wearing. I'd remarked on it before, the number and range of clothes that she'd packed for a weekend watching a charity cycle. I now knew that this was because her intention had been to leave permanently with Bob and the boys from Derry and that she'd packed accordingly. But someone else had packed more than he needed. Derek. When Amanda had made the crack about Derek's leg, I'd looked at his feet and had a flashback to the hiking boots he'd worn that day we'd gone out to Mamore. It hadn't hit me at the time, but why would you need to bring boots on a cycle? Surely you wouldn't pack anything you didn't absolutely need. And hiking boots were heavy items.

Molloy's voice broke into my thoughts. He was also thinking about Derek. 'So, Derek Jameson has only one leg. Was that something you knew?'

Before I could respond my phone buzzed with a text from

Leah. *Where are you?* and I checked the time. It was quarter past three and I still hadn't come back after lunch. It was no wonder she was chasing me.

Molloy said he'd drop me back at the office.

There was no sign of the Burns family when we left the hospital. I didn't know what the sisters' car looked like but there was no sign of Jude's bike either. Jude Burns had lied, if not actively, then certainly by omission. But had I lost my chance to find out what they knew?

We were waiting to pull out onto the main road when Molloy suddenly exhaled, leaning forward over the steering wheel to get a better look. 'That's quite a sight!'

I looked up. Whizzing by us, at quite the pace, were at least fifty bikes, the cyclists dressed in bright shades of Lycra. Many of them were smiling, finally inhaling some fresh air. Molloy wound down his window so we could hear the hum of the spokes and I found myself smiling too. There was something uplifting about such a kaleidoscope of colour after the grey days just past.

We waited until they had all gone, the big truck which had carried the bikes bringing up the rear along with two minibuses and a motorbike. I checked the rider, but I was sure it wasn't Jude. I presumed it was the second paramedic, who must have been staying in Malin Head.

I supposed it was a good thing that they'd decided to do all or some of the cycle after all. If the Jameson charity was being investigated properly, then hopefully any money raised would go to the right source, maybe even to improve conditions in the homes. As I watched them depart, leaving Inishowen for good, something snagged at my thoughts, but it would have to wait. I was needed at the office.

As expected, the afternoon's appointments were mostly issues with insurance claims arising out of the floods. I listened carefully to each story and took detailed instructions from each client, but my mind kept drifting back to that corridor outside the mortuary and the expression on Mary's face when she realised that Bob's remains would be going with his family. Though she must have expected it, it was the embodiment of absolute grief on her face that I couldn't forget. There were many people who disliked Bob Jameson, but Mary had loved him. Having observed Amanda at close range, I suspected that other than Derek, she might very well have been alone in that. I hoped Derek had done what I'd suggested and called Phyllis.

By half past five I'd made up my mind to see for myself how Mary was doing. But when I got into the car, I found myself turning towards Mamore rather than the B & B. Maybe it was a touch of cabin fever again or maybe it was because I hoped the drive would help me to clear my head before I spoke to her, but I found myself driving the whole way out to the Gap.

It was a far more pleasant drive than it had been on the previous two occasions. The fields were recovering, and the sheep and cattle were back grazing again. I even saw some figures on the golf course. Passing Mary's old family farmhouse, I remembered the story Phyllis had told me about the separated couple, the funeral and the pretence. As I'd remarked at the time, Mary's situation was different in that Bob was still with Amanda, but I still felt for her, being excluded from his death as she had been from his life. I wondered if there was any truth to what Amanda had said, that Mary was just one of Bob's many 'tarts'. If Sue was Bob's daughter, then surely that had been another affair. But maybe Amanda was just lashing out because she was hurting herself? I tried to feel sorry for Bob's widow, but she was difficult to warm to, despite what she had clearly suffered.

I reached Mamore, so different now on the clear day, and I pulled in at the grotto. I left the car and climbed to the spot where Derek and I had gone the day after Bob had died, to the area which I'd thought must be close to where his body had lain. I stood there with my hands on my hips and breathed in. The air was sweet and fresh, and the view was stunning, the sea blue in the distance, the Hills of Urris purple and green.

As I looked towards the right, I wondered if I could see Mary's parents' old house. But, of course, it was too far, it was way the other side of Clonmany and Ballyliffin. It made me think again about the ugly scene at the hospital and Derek's kindness in the middle of all the pain. His kindness to Mary rather than Amanda.

But those boots, I just couldn't get them out of my head. The plan was that they would only be in Inishowen the night before the cycle, so he wouldn't have had time to go for a hike, unless he planned to do it later along the route, which seemed unlikely – it was a demanding cycle. We knew that Bob must have come to Mamore willingly, with someone he knew. Was it Derek who had taken Bob up here? Amanda had said Bob wanted to make up with his twin, to fix things between them. Was that why Bob had come with him? And if Derek was an amputee, then presumably his footwear was important – he needed to be prepared for whatever activity he intended undertaking.

Jude had painted a picture of two unhappy boys, both bullied by their father, one also bullied by the other. It was hard to believe the frightened child with his myriad fears whom Jude had described, was the same Derek Jameson I'd met this weekend; a man who, despite his disability, exuded strength. And then there was Bob's one and only fear, his fear of snakes. Which no one who knew him had chosen to mention, despite the strange circumstances of his death. The two had to be connected.

Then I remembered Jude's allusion to the tricks the twins played on each other when they were kids. That they still played on each other as adults. *But while Derek's tricks were funny, Bob's were mean . . . I think they still did it; played tricks on one another, a bit of one-upmanship. Bit childish but there you go, maybe that's twins for you.*

I took my phone out and for the first time I did a search for Derek Jameson instead of Bob, annoyed it hadn't occurred to me before. In many ways Derek had existed in his twin's shadow. I found a piece in an online cycling magazine with the headline *Amputee completes Alps cycle in record time*, and I remembered the inscription I'd noticed on Derek's jacket.

The piece was accompanied by a photograph of a smiling and triumphant Derek and included a short interview.

I was an odd kid. The runt, even though there were only two of us. I was frightened of everything. But after my accident I made the decision never to fear anything again . . .

There it was again – 'the runt'. Amanda disliked Derek and didn't trust him. But Bob did. He continued to trust his brother, despite everything, despite Derek's reporting of his charity to the Regulator. Mary had said Bob told Derek everything. Had he told him of his plans to leave?

Bob had allowed Derek to be the event coordinator for the cycle. McFadden said that Mary knew someone involved in the cycle, which was how she'd got the booking. I'd assumed that person was Bob, but if she was supposed to keep her relationship with Bob a secret, it couldn't have been him. Was Derek the one who'd arranged the accommodation? To ensure all the players were staying in the one place? Had Derek set all of this up, just to kill his brother?

I felt my neck prickle. It seemed to fit. But why? Why would Derek Jameson kill his twin? Anger at Bob's dishonesty? At his corrupt behaviour? Revenge for something that had happened when they were children? Revenge was a dish best served cold but forty-odd years was practically frozen solid. And it seemed that Bob was the leopard who never changed his spots. He had been consistently dishonest all his life. Had something happened lately between them? Something that tipped the balance? The final straw?

I tried to focus on the view, to clear my head and see if anything slipped into place without being forced. Something was moving in the distance, something tiny, like a fly moving up a wall. It took me a few minutes to realise it wasn't a car but a cyclist. I took out my phone, turned on the camera, and zoomed in, enlarging the view. It was Derek, negotiating one of the hairpin bends. Not wearing a helmet. He must have taken his bike from the truck as it travelled through Glendara. I watched him for a minute, my mind replaying the conversations I'd had with him over the past few days.

What possible motive could he have had for killing his twin? Derek's wife had dementia; she was in residential care. I presumed it was one of the Jameson Grace Homes. Was it something to do with that? Had he found out about the conditions in the homes? I tried to imagine how it would feel to discover that your brother was responsible for ill-treating someone you loved. Derek seemed kind. I pictured his expression again when he'd spoken to Mary in the hospital. He had spoken so gently to her. And then suddenly it hit me.

I remembered what Derek had said that day at the waterfall, about having feelings for someone else, someone other than his wife. He'd said he felt guilty about it. I'd thought at first it was Sue, after I'd witnessed their encounter in the alley. But he was just making an effort with her, as her uncle.

Could it have been Mary he'd been talking about? His brother's lover? Mary had said she'd had offers but no one compared to Bob. Was it possible Derek had been one of those offers? Bob had never been to Inishowen before but what if Derek had? Had Derek decided to kill Bob here, on purpose? Where he could comfort Mary afterwards and pick up the pieces?

I looked down again at Derek and watched him tackling a serious climb. Amanda was right about one thing. It was difficult to believe he had only one leg. I called the Garda Station.

Twenty minutes later I drove up the steep hill behind Molloy's car. Derek's orange cycling jersey was just ahead, disappearing and reappearing as he rounded one of the hairpin bends. A minute later and he was visible again, pushing with huge determination up an almost impossible gradient. He must have heard us behind him – Molloy was beeping at him to pull in – but still he kept going. There was no way he could outrun two cars, but he wasn't going to stop until he absolutely had to. It was impossible not to admire the man's grit.

On a short straight stretch, Molloy overtook him and parked crossways across the road, cutting him off. Finally, Derek came to a stop and he stood, one leg on either side of the bike.

I pulled in behind and he smiled when he saw me, sweat dripping down his face. 'I was right. It is a great place for a cycle.'

'Mr Jameson,' Molloy started.

'Sergeant.' Derek nodded in acknowledgement; hands taut on the handlebars.

'May I have a word with you?'

'Of course.' Derek dropped the bike, placing it carefully onto the grass verge. Then he straightened and positioned himself in that strange stance I'd witnessed the first day outside Phyllis's bookshop. I now knew the reason behind it.

'I rang Phyllis as you suggested,' he said to me. 'Poor Mary, loyal to the end. My brother wouldn't appreciate that, of course. Bob would have left her without a backward glance.'

'You knew he was leaving?' Molloy asked.

'Not where, he wouldn't tell me that. Somewhere that doesn't have an extradition agreement with Ireland would be my guess,' Derek said with a smile. He winced suddenly as if he was in pain and he sat down onto the closest rock using his hand to steady himself as he lowered himself down. 'Look, I'll make things easy for you. As I'm sure you've guessed, I killed my brother.'

And there it was.

'Why?' Molloy asked.

'You know, I've been thinking about that since it happened, and I think I've been meaning to do it for years. Possibly since we came out of the womb.' He gave another half-smile. 'Him first, of course. Our mother said I was half-starved in there because Bob took everything. Sign of things to come.'

Molloy crossed his arms impatiently, but Derek wasn't going to be rushed.

'Freud would say it's self-loathing since twins are a mirror of each other. But I'd rather not think that, if you don't mind.' He paused. 'Plus, though I may have wanted to kill him, I didn't actually *intend* to. Bob's death was an unintended consequence of my actions.'

'What happened, Mr Jameson?' Molloy had had enough of Derek's philosophising.

Derek took off his cycling gloves, folded them and placed them on his knee. 'My brother was about to get away with it. *Again.* Teflon Bob Jameson never had to deal with the consequences of his actions, he just sailed through life, creaming off the top. I wanted to teach him a lesson, get him to change his mind about leaving, give back the money he'd taken. Maybe have a real Road-to-Damascus moment, who knows?' He looked away. 'Turned out that was too much to ask, of course.'

He took a deep breath. 'I planned to take him to a remote location and scare him with a snake. Sounds juvenile but it was the only thing he was remotely scared of. Apart from our father, of course, who, thankfully, is long dead. I did some work for the county council some time ago, on the roads. So, I knew this spot.' He glanced at me with an apologetic smile. 'I'm sorry, I lied about it being my first time in Inishowen.'

I remembered his expression when I'd mentioned that the county council had the flood damage in hand. He must have suddenly been concerned that he'd encounter someone he knew.

Molloy's patience was really wearing thin. 'Go on.'

'I wasn't sure when they were leaving but I knew it must be soon. He'd have to be gone before the whole truth came out. I originally intended doing it on Thursday night, which was the only night we'd be here. But the weather made me put it off and then I couldn't get him on his own. The pair of them spent the whole bloody night fighting, as usual.'

'Amanda and Bob?' I asked.

He nodded. 'I even had to separate them. I presume it was about money, or Sue, that's what they usually rowed about.'

The row Mary had witnessed, I thought.

'But then I had another chance on Friday when we had to stay an extra night because of the flood.' He smiled. 'It was almost as if fate was telling me to get on with it. There was a break in the rain for a few hours after we came back from the pub. It was perfect. Bob was outside smoking. I'd seen him with the taxi driver, but he'd gone. Amanda had gone to bed. I persuaded him to go for a drive. We played pranks on one another, Bob and me. Bob knew it must be a prank, but he was cocky; there's no way he'd have welshed out of it.'

Derek lifted one of his cycling gloves and started to hit his knee with it. 'I like to think that Bob had a conscience, that on some level he felt he owed me some sort of goodbye. But I suspect he just didn't want to risk waking Amanda up and have her make a fuss. So he came quietly.'

Derek leaned forward and straightened one leg, rubbing at his thigh. 'I knew Bob would insist on driving, even though he'd been drinking. He was just that kind of a dick, wouldn't let himself be driven. When we got here, we climbed up onto the hill. I taunted him, *if the runt with one leg can do it.* He was unfit, and pretty drunk, so he was gasping for air when he got to the top, easy to unbalance. I hadn't been drinking, though he thought I had.'

'Non-alcoholic beer.'

He nodded. 'I haven't drunk alcohol in five years, but Bob's never even noticed. I knocked him over, overpowered him and I tied him up. Would you believe he was laughing? Still thought it was a prank. That was one good thing about Bob – he could take a joke.'

'Until . . .' Molloy prompted.

'Until I left to go back to the car. He shouted after me, he was afraid I was leaving him. So when I came back he was pleased. Until he saw what I had in the sack.'

'The snake,' Molloy said.

Derek nodded, running his hand through his hair. 'He was terrified. Helpless and terrified. Bob liked power, and he liked using it over people, in the guise of charm. So, I liked seeing him powerless. Plus, I'd lost my leg through fear. I was using Bob's greatest fear against him and liked the symmetry of it. Maybe it's the engineer in me.'

'What did you do?'

'I showed him the snake. I kept it in the sack, but he knew it was there. I tried to appeal to his conscience, talked to him about the people who would suffer if he didn't replace the money he'd taken. Tried to persuade him that he could come back from this, change his ways.' He gave a wry look. 'Even used his "Amazing Grace" story: *anyone can find redemption, it's never too late.* I couldn't believe I was doing it.'

He sighed. 'But it didn't achieve anything. He just kept shaking his head. And then he just passed out. I don't know if it was the booze or the fear.'

'Passed out or died?' Molloy demanded.

'Passed out,' Derek said. 'I know when someone is dead, and Bob wasn't dead when I left him. I decided to leave him there overnight, with the snake for company. I thought it might help him come to his senses.'

'Did you untie him before you left?' Molloy asked.

He shook his head. 'He must have untied himself. I intended coming back for him the next day, truly I did. But I must have underestimated how unfit he was.' He looked down. 'The bastard had a heart attack.'

I was surprised to see Derek's eyes glisten, just as they had that day when we'd come up here together.

He breathed in. 'When I heard what people were saying, that a snakebite had killed him, I thought at first the snake hadn't been as harmless as I thought. I challenged the person who'd got it for me, and I wasn't happy.'

The row with Chris in the pub, I thought. Chris had supplied a snake that was supposed to be harmless, but Derek was afraid he'd produced a venomous one instead. He must have known how much Chris hated Bob.

'You may not believe me, but I didn't intend to kill him. At least not consciously. I just wanted him to answer for his actions, for once in his life.' He met Molloy's gaze. 'Guess that makes me guilty of manslaughter.'

'Your leg, Mr Jameson. How did that happen?'

Derek raised his hand to shield his eyes against the light. Actual sun was breaking through the clouds. 'When I was fourteen, I landed on a nail when Bob pushed me off a roof. He persuaded me not to tell anyone, said it would get better on its own and that we'd get in trouble if I told.' He shook his head. 'What he meant was, *he'd* get into trouble. So, I kept it to myself until it had gone so far that I ended up getting sepsis and losing part of my leg.

'He never even said sorry. Instead he turned it to his advantage. He mentioned my accident in every interview he did. *My poor brother, I took care of him.* He got so much mileage out of it that you'd think he'd planned it. Same with our mother's dementia.' He looked up. 'And Jude, you know about Jude?'

'Sue?' I said.

He nodded. 'Playing the big fella as if it was perfectly normal to have a kid with another woman. He knew years ago apparently, but it came out only recently.' His tone was incredulous. 'Introduced her to Amanda, knowing that she was tied to him financially and would have to just tolerate it. Jude just had to put up with it, too, for the good of his daughter.' He clicked his fingers. 'Again, no consequences for Bob.'

Derek closed one eye as if he had a headache and massaged his temple with his fingers. 'And now he was going to do a runner with millions. Those homes were going to be investigated but Bob wouldn't be here. He'd be gone. Ordinary people would be punished, and Bob would escape scot-free as usual.

'I knew that my wife wasn't being cared for when she was

in one of Bob's homes, but at least I was able to move her.' He smiled sadly. 'Everything we have will go to taking care of her now. Others aren't so lucky.'

I remembered what he had said about his wife being in a place where she was happy. I'd assumed it was one of Bob's homes but clearly it wasn't.

'And the money?' Molloy asked.

Derek bowed his head. 'This will come as a huge disappointment to Amanda, but I have absolutely no idea what happened to it. I thought Bob would tell me if I left him to stew overnight, but the old bastard died instead.' He looked up. 'I'm afraid I led Amanda to believe that I knew. It helped to keep her quiet.'

Molloy and I watched McFadden drive Derek Jameson away in the squad car, his bike strapped to the roof.

Molloy shook his head. 'He's protecting someone. Someone untied Bob and it wasn't Bob himself.'

'Why are you so sure?' I asked.

'Derek Jameson is an engineer. He's perfectly capable of tying a knot that couldn't be untied by a drunk man in the pitch dark. Plus, someone let that snake out of the sack. And we never found a sack; the snake was transported to Donegal in a box and we found the box.'

I digested this. 'I suppose there's nothing left for him now so he's free to take the blame for Bob's death.' I paused. 'There's something I should tell you.'

'Go on.'

'I came up here with him, that time he found Bob's watch. He asked me to show him the way. It seemed a little odd at the time, why he would want to come here.'

'Do you think he was looking for the rope?' Molloy asked. 'Trying to work out how Bob got free?'

'I don't know.' Had I been wrong about Derek Jameson's motivation for killing Bob? He hadn't mentioned Mary. So had it really been just an accident? A prank gone wrong?

Molloy's voice cut into my thoughts. 'I need to go and speak to Jude Burns before he leaves.'

'You're going to the B & B?'

He nodded.

'I'll come with you.'

Chapter Twenty-Six

I drove back to Glendara, over the newly accessible bridge, through the town and up to Mary's B & B with Molloy just ahead. Jude's motorbike was still parked at the entrance to the shed, but Bob's big black Lexus was gone. Had Amanda left already? I wondered. There were a couple of other cars there: I saw Molloy look oddly at them as we passed.

The front door was ajar, so Molloy and I went in without knocking. We stood in the hall for a second. There were noises coming from upstairs, people calling out to each other from one room to another, packing up by the sound of things. Seconds later, Jude himself came down the stairs carrying two bags.

Molloy looked up. 'Good. You're still here.'

'I think we're the last. We were waiting for Peadar to wake up from his nap. Is everything okay?' Jude asked, brow furrowed.

His daughters appeared behind him, Sue with Peadar in her arms as usual and Lissa dragging a wheelie case behind her, thunk-thunk-thunk down the stairs. They arrived at the bottom in a clump, dumping their bags at their feet.

'May I have a word with you?' Molloy asked. 'It won't take long.'

'Sure.' Jude glanced uneasily at his daughters. 'Alone?'

Molloy said, 'It's probably better if you're all here.'

'Okay.'

'I'd like you to tell me again about your relationship with the dead man. We've discovered some connections between you that we previously weren't aware of.'

Jude sighed, resting one arm on the banister. 'I thought that might happen, as soon as you had a chance to look properly. Are you sure you want to hear it? It's a long bloody saga, to be frank. Whatever you've found out is probably true.'

'Start at the beginning,' Molloy said firmly.

Jude took a deep breath. 'I knew Bob Jameson well, better than I admitted.' He glanced at me. 'Better than I wished. But it was true what I said: I knew the twins at school; Bob and Derek, the loud one and the quiet one, the big personality and the studious one. The bully and the bullied. I was there for Derek's accident.' He paused. 'Do you really want me to go back this far?'

Molloy nodded.

'Okay. Bob taunting Derek as usual, daring us all to climb onto the roof of their turf shed, knowing Derek was terrified of heights and that we'd all get into trouble for it. Bob always had to push things to their limit.' He closed his eyes for a second. 'Derek did it although he was absolutely shit scared and Bob taunted him until he fell off the roof in terror. Landed on his feet and seemed all right, at least he pretended he was.'

He shook his head. 'I'm not sure how, but the result was that a few weeks later, Derek got sepsis and had to have his leg amputated from below the knee. He was fourteen. That wasn't the way Bob spun it, of course. He made it look as though he was the hero who sat beside his brother's hospital bed for months, never admitting that he was the one who had caused the accident in the first place.'

He rubbed his neck. 'Because I was there, and I knew the truth, Bob tried to keep on the right side of me ever since. Bastard.'

He shot an apologetic look at his daughters who were both now sitting on the stairs. Peadar was between them, fast asleep again, leaning against his mother.

'Why didn't Derek say what had really happened?' Molloy asked.

Jude shrugged. 'Fear? He was terrified of his father. They both were. You couldn't tell what that man's reaction would be. He'd have turned on Bob or Derek – one of them would have got it in the neck. And their mother wasn't well. Bob said at some stage that she had early onset dementia, but I don't know if that was ever diagnosed.'

'Was that why Bob decided to set up the charity that he did?' he asked.

Jude snorted. 'That's what he said. But then Bob could always spin a tale, turn circumstances to his own advantage. After the accident, the twins decided to stick together, and not mention the roof they shouldn't have been climbing on. And they've done that ever since. I was the only other person who knew.'

'You knew Bob Jameson as an adult too,' Molloy said. 'Tell me about the bank.'

Jude looked down at the carpet for a few seconds. His daughters were watching him like hawks, I noticed. I wondered how much of this they knew, Sue particularly.

He straightened himself, steeling himself for the next part of the story. 'A few years after I qualified, I took a job in London. Bob got me a job with the investment bank he was with. Say what you like about Bob Jameson, but he was always successful, knew how to press the flesh and charm people. He was on the board of that bank. He was still trying to keep me onside. I don't know why. Maybe because the old bastard of a father of theirs was still alive.'

His gaze flickered past Molloy to the wall behind. 'It was a mistake taking that job. Possibly the worst mistake I ever made after saying hello to the twins on the first day of school. Bob could never keep his worse nature in check.'

'Go on,' Molloy said.

'Bob wanted a fall guy. That's all I was to him. A stooge. He got me in deep, made me risk my professional reputation and then used me as a scapegoat when the bank got into trouble. Criminal proceedings were threatened against the bank and the board and they used the old line – it's all the accountant's fault.'

'And was it?' Molloy asked.

Jude met his gaze again. 'In a way. In that I allowed myself to be bullied by Bob, do whatever he told me to do. At that stage things had taken a downturn in the City.' He looked at his daughters and grandson again. 'We were living the high life, big house, high mortgage in a very expensive city. I had two daughters so I couldn't afford to lose my job.'

He shot a glance at Sue, the meaning of which was impossible to miss. He was looking for permission.

'Tell him,' she said.

He sighed. 'I agreed to take the fall for Bob in return for him keeping a secret.'

'Go on.'

'Michelle, my wife, and Bob had an affair. It was short lived, and she regretted it, but Sue is Bob's biological daughter. I found out when she was two. Bob guessed or he knew, I don't know. He couldn't have kids with Amanda, so he wanted to have a relationship with Sue. But I refused. He said he'd take it to court, force a DNA test. But I couldn't bear that; Lissa and Sue were sisters and I never wanted Sue to know she wasn't mine. So, we made a deal.'

'You took the fall for the bank in return for his backing off?'

He nodded. 'Yes. The reality was that I had been involved, had turned a blind eye to certain things. So I felt I deserved to be punished, And I got away lightly. The bank got away lightly. No criminal proceedings against me, just my membership of the Institute of Chartered Accountants revoked. That's when I trained as a paramedic. Although I have my membership back now.'

His eyes glistened suddenly, and they flickered towards Sue and Lissa. 'You see, nothing that happened to me could have been as bad as losing Michelle. When she told me, we had a huge row and she left.' He rubbed at his eyes. 'I like to think she'd have come back, but she didn't get the chance. Her car went into a truck on the M11 that same day and she died instantly. Which was another reason why I couldn't just hand Sue over to Bob Jameson. I had to keep my girls together.'

There was silence for a few seconds, with nothing but the tick of Mary's old grandfather clock. I tried to imagine Jude's grief at that time. What it must have been like to find out about something like that, then lose his wife so tragically before they had a chance to deal with it. It was no wonder he refused to lose Sue.

'So, when did you find out about this?' Molloy asked Sue.

She looked down, and I realised how fragile she looked now too. Her eyes were hollow. She had her hand on her nephew's head and it hit me why they were so close. How insecure she must have felt about family when she found out Jude wasn't her father, how anxious she must have been to keep them all close.

'Only recently. When they were doing tests for Peadar's bone marrow. Dad had kept it from us.'

'And just to clarify, Mr Burns, you've always known?' Molloy asked.

He nodded. 'Since Sue was two, when Michelle told me. Their affair was long over, but I think it was becoming clear at that time that Amanda couldn't have kids and so Bob was forcing the issue. For a man who always got what he wanted, it was the one thing he couldn't have.'

His expression soured. 'Of course, as the years went on, he couldn't keep to the deal. Bob's word was never worth anything. He kept trying to interfere in Sue's life, trying to help. Got her a job in St Finbarr's where she found herself nursing Bob's wife, of all things. It was as if he wanted them to meet. He found a place for my mother in one of his nursing homes.' He shook his head. 'He was a devious bastard. I didn't trust him as far as I could spit him.'

'Did Amanda know Bob was Sue's father?' Molloy asked.

'Not until very recently.' He glanced at Sue. 'She knows now.'

'I told her,' Sue said, looking down.

Jude slapped his hand on the banister. 'So that's my relationship with Bob Jameson. But I didn't have anything to do with his death, if that's what you're thinking. I was here all night, on Friday night. Peadar wasn't sleeping and he came into Grandad's bed.' He glanced down at his grandson who was certainly sleeping now.

Molloy was silent for a second, as if considering something before he spoke again. 'We've arrested Derek Jameson. He's admitted to being responsible for his brother's death.'

Jude looked down. 'I see.'

'You had no idea?'

'No.'

'Did you know that Bob Jameson had a fear of snakes?' Molloy asked.

Jude looked up and for the first time his mouth curled up into a smile. 'No, I did not. But thank you for that.'

I recalled what Derek had said about liking seeing his brother powerless.

Jude paused. 'Is that all, Sergeant?'

Molloy nodded. 'For the moment. We have your contact details if we need to speak to you again.'

Jude and his daughters walked to the door with their bags. At the door he said something to Lissa and Sue, and they went outside while he returned to Molloy.

'Sergeant.' He lowered his voice. 'Since it's cards on the table time I should tell you Lissa has admitted it was Sue's GHB that she took. Sue had some difficulties after she found out that Bob was her father. We kept it to ourselves because she's a nurse. But now you know the context.'

Molloy shook his head, unhappily. 'You really should have provided us with all this information before now, Mr Burns. It could have helped us find some answers.'

Jude's eyes hardened. 'I'm afraid, Sergeant, while I may not have killed Bob Jameson, the only thing I'm sorry for is that I wasn't the one who did. If it was Derek, I'm grateful to him.'

Molloy opened his mouth to speak but Jude got there first.

'The girls don't know because it would upset them, but that nursing home my mother was in was appalling. Luckily, she wasn't there very long. I was about to move her when she had a stroke and she died instantly. So, you see I've allowed Bob Jameson to ruin every corner of my family's life. I am ashamed of that. I am ashamed that I never properly stood up to him but, most of all, I regret that I wasn't the one to kill him.'

He held Molloy's gaze for a few seconds. Then, he turned and walked back. Through the open door, I saw him take his grandson from his daughter, the daughter he had brought up as his own.

Molloy hesitated for a second and then followed him, with a warning back at me. 'There's something else I want to ask him. Wait for me.'

Molloy was gone for longer than I expected. So I waited for a while and then made my way back down the hall to the kitchen. Mary was there alone, sitting at the same worktop with a cup of tea in front of her. She looked beaten and exhausted; her eyes red-rimmed. I wondered how much good Phyllis had done.

When she looked up at me, her eyes were full. 'I made a fool of myself at the hospital, didn't I?'

I shook my head. 'No, of course not . . .'

'I just wanted a wee bit of acknowledgement, you know? Recognition of my role in his life. So it wouldn't all have been such a waste.'

'I know.'

'But that isn't going to happen, is it?' Tears blurred her eyes.

I sat down beside her. 'Probably not, no. It's just the way it is.'

She ran her finger around the rim of her cup. 'I've never been able to talk to anyone about Bob. Not even Phyllis. If I mentioned him, she just got annoyed, wanted to defend me. Tell me I deserved better.' She closed her eyes briefly. 'I didn't need her to defend me. I knew he loved me.'

I reached out to touch her hand. 'Why don't you tell me about your relationship? As if I'm hearing about it for the first time.'

She smiled, as if she knew I was just trying to be kind, but she went along with it. 'Bob was fun, he could always make me laugh. He changed as he got older, but he never stopped being

301

able to make me laugh.' She reached inside her shirt and lifted out a silver chain. 'He bought me a ring. I've never taken it off.'

It was the chain I'd noticed her playing with when she'd come into the office that first day. There was a ring on it, a solitaire, with a precious stone like an engagement ring. Green, like her eyes.

'It's pretty,' I said, although it was impossible now not to wonder where the money to pay for it had come from.

'He said some day I'd be able to wear it on my hand, but that never happened.' She tucked the chain back in. 'I've often thought that it was my own fault that he never left her.'

'Why was that?'

'I was like a second wife to him, the one he told all his problems to. I don't think he could have stayed married to her if he hadn't had me.'

'It must have been hard for you, the times when he wasn't in Ireland.'

She took a deep breath. 'I saw him while he was in London. We planned to be together when he came back. I'd even told my parents about him. They said they'd move out of the farm. They were getting too old to stay there anyway and they wanted to move into town. They'd have been able to have a carer for my mother and I could have helped.' She paused. 'We would have been living there, Bob and I, looking out over Trawbreaga Bay.'

I was pretty sure Bob had been married while he was making plans to live with Mary in Inishowen – Mary had said that he'd married Amanda a year after they split up and I'd seen pictures online of them at charity balls in London. He was also having a short-lived affair with Jude Burns's wife. But I said nothing. Leah had been right about one thing. There was a haunting sadness in Mary's smile.

Molloy appeared in the doorway. Mary saw him but didn't react, just a little nod of acknowledgement.

She squeezed her eyes shut. 'But then he went to Nigeria. My parents both died while he was out there. He never met them, he wasn't at their funerals. All the milestones of my life. I was there whenever he needed me but . . .'

I finished the sentence. 'He wasn't there for you.'

She brushed a tear away. 'Each time something significant happened, I thought he'd be there, that something would change. But it never did. I'd get a phone call or a letter, or more recently a text. But never him.' She looked down. 'Never him.'

I realised that Nigeria must have been a turning point for Mary. When Bob had come back with two adopted children, he'd been more bound to Amanda than ever.

She hugged herself and rocked a little to and fro. 'Oh, it was awful when he was in Africa. I remember thinking, what if something happened to him there? And no one knew that I was the most important person in his life?' There was a plea for understanding in her eyes. 'Who would tell me? I wouldn't even figure. *I might not even know.*' She sighed. 'After he came back, we'd meet, and it was lovely. But he never came here. I always had to go to him.'

'And now he was going away again?' I said quietly.

Mary looked up. 'I know what you're thinking, but it wasn't intentional.'

I stiffened. Was this what I had been afraid of? Was this why Bob had died? I felt Molloy shift his position behind me too.

'What do you mean, Mary?' I asked. 'What wasn't intentional?'

Her eyes drifted to somewhere over my shoulder. 'Afterwards, yes, I thought it was good that he'd died in Inishowen, close to me. That, at least, I knew. I didn't have to hear about it later. But

I thought it would be different, that I'd be able to hold onto him for a bit longer.' She looked down at her cup again. 'But it didn't work out that way.'

I tried to keep the panic out of my voice. 'Are you saying you had something to do with Bob's death, Mary?'

Finally, she looked at me. 'Aye. I did.' Her eyes flickered to Molloy.

I reached out my hand to her. 'Tell me what happened, Mary.'

She pressed her fingers against her eyelids and took a deep breath. 'I saw him leave with Derek. I didn't trust Derek.'

'Why didn't you trust Derek?'

She shook her head as if she didn't want to say.

'Derek was here before, in Inishowen, wasn't he?' I said. 'Working. He told us.'

She nodded slowly. 'He stayed here.' She swallowed. 'Derek told me things about Bob. He said that I didn't know what Bob was really like, that he'd hidden a lot of his life from me. He tried to turn me against him. Said that he had feelings for me himself, that he always had.'

At that point Molloy came into the room properly and leaned against one of the chrome cabinets. 'What happened that night, Mary?'

She looked up at him. 'I couldn't sleep. I hadn't been able to sleep since they'd been here. I tried to be professional about it, but it was painful cooking and cleaning for Bob and his wife, sleeping down the hall from them. And Derek kept trying to get me on his own. It was awful.'

'That's why you wanted them to leave?' I said.

She nodded. 'Oh God, how I wished they had, now. If they'd all left when they were supposed to, none of this would have happened. When I saw Bob and Derek drive away that night, I started to worry. It was dark and wet, where on earth could they be going? So, I followed them. When we got to the crossroads after Clonmany I knew where they were going. Derek had been to Mamore when he was working here and he'd talked about the magic road. I wondered if he wanted to show it to Bob, use it to play a trick on him somehow.'

'Go on.'

'When I got there, they were on the hill. I could see torch-light. So I waited around one of the bends until the car was gone, then I drove up. I had my own torch in the car. When I got out I could hear shouting. Bob was still there. When I climbed the hill I found him tied up and terrified. He told me there was a snake in a sack beside him.'

Her eyes glistened. 'I untied his hands but, while I was doing it, he just kept getting angrier and angrier. He told me he was leaving for good.' She shook her head. 'I'd waited for him all my life and now he was leaving, again. The last time he'd adopted two children, this time I'd never see him again. I told him how hurt I was, and he just laughed.' Her voice cracked and she paused, as if appalled by what she was about to say next. 'He said that I could have Derek.'

She looked up to stop the tears spilling. 'I'd loved Bob Jameson for nearly thirty-five years. I'd been there when he needed me, every single time. In all that time I'd never slept with another man, never even kissed one, even in the times when we weren't in touch. And now he thought . . .'

I reached over and touched her arm. She swallowed and brushed tears onto the chrome. 'He implied that it was all arranged between the two of them, that he was just fine with it. That Derek was a better fit for me anyway, as if he could just pass me on like a gift.'

'Go on, Mary,' Molloy prompted quietly. 'What happened?'

'I just lost it. I opened the sack and took the snake out with my bare hands. I didn't care if it was poisonous or not at that point. If it bit me, it bit me. I didn't care. Bob's feet were still tied. I was so angry that I threw the snake in his face.

'The snake bit him on the hand and slithered off. Bob froze. Neither of us knew if the snake was venomous or not. Then Bob clutched his arm, and I realised he was having a heart attack.' Her voice shuddered. 'I untied him and tried to revive him.' She bit her lip. 'I tried my best to remember my nursing training, but I knew he was dead.

'Then it started to rain. I panicked and I ran. For some reason I took the sack, I don't know why.' Her eyes moved to Molloy again. 'I tried to save him. I didn't like leaving him out there, but I knew he'd be found. I'd have gone back to get him if he hadn't.'

'And you didn't tell anyone what happened?' Molloy asked.

Mary shook her head. She paused and looked up. 'You know they went for a walk to the waterfall?'

'Glenevin?' I remembered stopping off there with Derek.

'*My* waterfall. I'd told him about it, but he went there with her.' She touched the chain around her neck again. 'I wanted him to see what he'd missed out on, all these years. Where he'd have lived with me. But the first time he saw it was with his wife.'

I realised that Bob didn't have the emotional intelligence to know how important that place was to her, to keep just one thing for her. Perhaps that's what ended up being his downfall, his inability to rate other people's feelings.

Mary's voice was flat. 'It's all been such a waste.'

'But what about here?' I said, looking around at the huge kitchen. 'What about your business? Surely, you're proud of this.'

She looked at me in surprise. 'This place? I hate this place.

This was somewhere I built when I heard Bob had adopted his boys, when I knew we wouldn't be having a family of our own. I'd have sold it in a heartbeat if Bob had ever . . .' She shook her head in disbelief. 'I waited over thirty years for him to visit and the first time he comes, he brings his wife. It would be funny if it wasn't so pathetic.'

I looked at her sad eyes, the grief for a man she loved, just as real and raw as if he'd died in an accident that she'd had nothing to do with. Like Derek, she had nothing left, nothing that mattered.

After a rather shocked McFadden had handcuffed Mary and driven her away, Molloy and I went back into the kitchen. Molloy picked up something from the stool on which Mary had been sitting and showed it to me. It was a newspaper cutting of the family feature on the Jamesons from the *Irish Independent*. I remembered Stoop saying that Mary never missed her *Indo*. I wondered if it had been the last straw for her.

I handed it back to him. 'What did you want to speak to Jude about?' I asked.

'I wanted to ask him if he'd heard anything on Friday night. He said no, but if his bike was parked where it is today . . .' He trailed off.

I looked at him quizzically. And then it hit me. Jude's motorbike was parked in front of the shed in which another car was parked, a car that could only be Mary's. Jude's motorbike had been blocking Mary in, all weekend.

'He'd have had to move it to let Mary out,' I said.

'Exactly.'

'He knew.'

Molloy nodded. 'He knew.'

Chapter Twenty-Seven

Saturday night, the following weekend

I knocked on the door, shading my eyes against the sun, a bottle of wine in my hand. We'd had relentless blue skies since the weekend before, and people were already beginning to complain about the dryness and the heat.

Molloy opened it with a smile. 'Why didn't you use your key?'

I handed him the bottle and stepped into the hall. 'I thought we were dating!'

I followed him through the house, past tantalising cooking smells in the kitchen, and out into a backyard I didn't even know existed. I was amazed to see that he'd put out some chairs and a small table, on which he'd laid a wine cooler with an open bottle of wine and cereal bowls with olives and crisps.

I looked up at him with an urge to laugh, the same urge I'd felt when we'd discussed 'the proposal that never was'.

'So, we're really doing this then?' I asked.

He poured me a glass of chilled white wine and handed it over. 'Looks like it.'

I reached into the pocket of my jeans and handed him a key, his key.

'Keep it,' he said, as he clinked my glass and we sat, on the rather bockety kitchen chairs. He sighed and took a sip of his wine. 'Two full days off.'

'Garda Station empty again?' I asked.

'They're both on remand, in Dublin. Looks as if there'll be no trial, pleas to manslaughter for both, I'm told. I hope that remains the case.'

'They didn't try too hard to escape discovery, either of them, did they?' I said, taking a sip from my own glass. It was dry and fresh. Molloy's taste in snacks might not be too sophisticated but he knew his wines.

He shook his head. 'No, although it wasn't as if anyone was helping us to catch them either. Not even the wife, although it's clear she knew Derek, at least, had something to do with it. He was keeping her quiet pretending he knew where the money was hidden.'

'Was Bob just going to take off with the money, then? With her and the kids?' I asked.

'Looks like it.' He handed me the bowl of olives and I took one. 'We still have no idea where he stashed it, although the wizards will be going through all the financials so we'll see what we can turn up.'

I popped the olive in my mouth. 'So, they're both pleading guilty. It's sad really. Neither of them has anything very much to come home to.'

'No,' he said thoughtfully. 'Both their lives were dominated by Bob Jameson. Mary was clearly distraught at what happened. But with Derek, it's strange, you'd think he'd have some regrets, having caused the death of his own twin. But he seemed very calm, still seems to be from what I've heard.' He smiled. 'He's teaching fitness classes in Cloverhill.'

Cloverhill was the remand prison in Dublin.

'A bit of a cold fish,' I said, picking out another olive. I was hungry. I wondered what Molloy was cooking.

'Possibly not always that way,' Molloy said, taking another sip of his wine. 'The Sligo Gardai have arrested Chris Bennett, by the way. He's admitted supplying the snake to Derek. That's why he was outside the B & B on Friday night.'

I nodded. So, he wasn't trying to hurt Lissa any further. It didn't change what he had done to her already, but I was relieved about that, at least.

'Derek and Chris met doing Ironman competitions.' Molloy smiled mischievously. 'I hadn't told you before, but Chris brought the snake up on Thursday and stored it in the yard in your office, and then camped on your couch for the rest of the weekend when he got trapped because of the floods.'

'I knew it!' I said. 'I knew I'd heard something when I was in there on Saturday night. That's why I found the office locked on Thursday. He'd arrived with his buddy in a box.'

'Now in the hands of a reptile specialist, you'll be glad to hear,' Molloy added. 'None the worse for his ordeal.'

'Good.' I might be uneasy around snakes, but it didn't stop me wanting a good home for it. 'Will Chris be charged with anything?'

'We'll have to wait for the DPP on that. He says that the arrangement was that in return for supplying the snake, Derek would try and get some of Chris's family's money back from Bob. I don't know how realistic a possibility that was.'

'I hope Jude's daughters will be okay,' I said. 'Although with Jude to keep an eye on them, I think they will be.' I smiled. 'I think we might be seeing Jude again. Phyllis has stayed in touch with him.'

'Good for her.' Molloy stood up. 'I'd better go and check on this food.'

While he disappeared inside, I took yet another olive. They weren't bad. My phone rang in my bag and I took it out. It was an unknown number, a Dublin number. I answered it.

'Hello?'

A hesitant female voice said, 'Hello, is that Miss O'Keeffe? Your parents live in Chapelizod?'

My throat tightened. I felt a flicker of fear. 'Yes.'

The voice sounded relieved. 'My name is Pat. I live in the house opposite your parents, same estate. I'm sorry, I haven't met you, we haven't been here very long. And I don't want to come across like a nosy neighbour . . .'

I cut across her. 'Go on.' My heart was thumping.

'It's just, some people have moved in with your parents. There was a young man there for a while and he seemed all right, but there are at least four others there now and to be honest I don't know where they're all fitting. Your parents' house is the same size as ours.' I heard her take a deep breath. 'I've called over and your mum and dad say they're fine, but it just seems a bit odd.'

I swallowed. My mouth was very dry. 'No, you did the right thing. How did you get my number, by the way?'

The voice sounded sheepish. 'I'm afraid I told your mother that we were heading to Donegal on holidays and thinking of visiting Inishowen, and I asked her for it. I hope I've done the right thing. They're not young and, well, I was worried.'

'You did the right thing,' I repeated. 'Thank you very much, Pat.'

Stomach churning, I rang my parents. Voicemail on all three numbers.

Fear clutched at my chest as I ran into the kitchen. Molloy read my expression immediately. He held my hands as I told him what had happened, the words tumbling over one another as they fell from my mouth.

'I'm going down there, straight away,' I said. 'I have to.'

'I'll come with you. I'll drive. I've only had half a glass.'

I gave him a relieved hug: it seemed 'normal' coupledom would have to wait. Or maybe this was what passed as 'normal coupledom' for us.

Acknowledgements

Inishowen experienced real and serious flooding in August 2017. The suggestion to use the heavy rain as a backdrop for this book came from Inishowen teenager Bláithín Gillen. I was hesitant at first but when I spoke to people about their experiences, I changed my mind. I try my best to portray Inishowen in all its drama and beauty, and the floods were a major incident at the time.

Much is fictionalised here for plot purposes (McSheffrey's Bridge did not crack!) but if you wish to know more about what really happened, there are plenty of articles online. All the national and local newspapers covered it at the time.

I'm hugely grateful for the continuing help and support I've received from people in Inishowen and, in particular, I want to thank Fidelma Tony, Joe Butler, Róisín Doherty and Lily McGonagle for their help with this book. And of course, Bláithín for the initial idea!

Thank you to my young nephew Christopher for supplying the victim's name and the murder method. I really hope he doesn't know someone called Bob Jameson. Thank you also to William and Ethel Telford for sharing their experience of charity cycles, Simon Mills for the medical detail, Úna Ní Dhubhghaill for information on the charities sector, Neil Hegarty for the book's title, Neville McCormick, Mark Tottenham, Emma and Ronan, Derek and Claire (from Sicily), Mick, and my brother Owen.

All errors are of course my own and, on that note, if I've forgotten someone, I apologise!

Thank you to all at the Tyrone Guthrie Centre at Annaghmakerrig. Thank you to my publishers Constable/Little, Brown and Hachette Ireland and to my brilliant agent Kerry Glencorse of Susanna Lea Associates. Love and thanks to my family, and to Geoff, my grown-up family.